PANAMA RED

The Ninth

Kelly Turnbull Novel

PANAMA RED

By

Kurt Schlichter

Paperback Edition ISBN: 979-8-9985943-7-3
Panama Red - Kurt Schlichter - Paperback - 120225 - Complete - v54

For Irina

ACKNOWLEDGEMENTS

After nine years and nine novels, there are a lot of people to thank for helping me get to this point in this best-selling series. Right up front, I want to thank each and every reader for gobbling them up almost as soon as they launch. Nothing is more gratifying than hearing how much you enjoyed the books.

I want to thank Irina Moises, my wife and my writing partner, whether or not her name is on the book. She is a huge part of the series, and I think you will really enjoy the book we wrote together, *Lost Angeles: Silver Bullets on the Sunset Strip*. It's not Kelly Turnbull, but you'll have fun with Eddie Loud and Trixie Gamble!

Over the years, I have gotten a ton of support for the *People's Republic* and other books from old friends and new. I live in terror that I will inadvertently leave out someone who has helped me through this nearly decade-law process and supported my books, so consider this a *partial* list: Larry O'Connor, Drew Matich, @GMFWashington, Jim Hanson, Samantha Nerove, Dr. Seb Gorka, Tom Sauer, Matthew Betley, Glenn Reynolds, Colonel (R) Bill Wenger, Cam Edwards, Tony Kinnett, Joe Piscopo, Joe Sibilia, Jesse Kelly, Storm Paglia, Dana and Chris Loesch, Jim Pikl, Chris Stigall, Derek Hunter, Buck Sexton, Will Cain, Patrick Hatten, Captain John Konrad, the *Ruthless* gang, Pat & Robert, Hugh Hewitt, and Duane Patterson. We cannot forget ace copy editor Adam Kissel. Many other folks have helped me as well. If I left a name out, it's my fault.

The unique vibe of the books is due in large part to my artist, the great Sean "Salty Hollywood" Salter. Check out his *Silence Dogood* series of graphic novels. He is currently hard at work on the upcoming Kelly Turnbull graphic novel *Blue Flame*. It's going to be awesome.

Thank you to everyone who got *The Attack, American Apocalypse: The Second American Civil War*, and *Lost Angeles: Silver Bullets on the Sunset Strip*. As always, I appreciate my *Townhall* supporters, Twitter followers and subscribers, and Locals followers.

Of course, Andrew Breitbart is directly responsible for this. He was a visionary who told conservatives that if you don't like pop culture as it stands, go make your own. Well, here you go, Andrew!

AUTHOR'S NOTE

So, nine years later, here is the ninth Kelly Turnbull novel. I wrote *People's Republic* back in 2016 because I was bored with the predictable, tiresome, man-action pap out there, plus I wanted to do what the legendary Andrew Breitbart told us we must do to win – jump into the culture and make our own stuff instead of waiting for Hollywood and the rest of the pop culture industry to do it for us.

Hundreds of thousands of copies later, here we are.

We have not gone Hollywood yet. There have been folks sniffing around the intellectual property because, frankly, it's awesome – funny, fun, action-packed, and anti-woke. But there are a few problems for someone wanting to make movies out of these books. The first is that they are a huge middle finger to the kind of neurotic SSRI addicts who gate-keep the industry. The second is that doing it justice means spending tens of millions of dollars on production and distribution; I won't sell to someone who won't do it right.

And this brings us to the third problem – me. Kelly Turnbull must remain Kelly Turnbull, not some neutered femboy who shares his feelings openly and without restraint. Until someone is willing to meet my conditions, you can watch Kelly's adventures in the theater of your mind.

But, we are going graphic – Kelly Turnbull will be out in graphic novel form with a brand-new adventure. I've seen the preliminary work, and it's fantastic. Look for *Blue Flame* in 2026.

Now, where does *Panama Red* fit in the canon? Obviously, some of my predictions have proven true while others have not – hello, President Trump 1.0 and 2.0. Don't sweat it; the books still work, and hopefully this one will, too.

Now, I have jumped around chronologically with the series, mostly because I felt like it and wanted to write the stories I wanted without being bound to put them out in chronological sequence. But there *is* a chronological sequence. If you are interested in it, it goes like this:

Crisis (2020)
The Split (2021)
Indian Country (2017)
➜ *Panama Red* (2025)
People's Republic (2016)
Wildfire (2018)
Collapse (2019)
Inferno (2022)
Overlord (2023)

There are the three books about when America splits apart, and five where it moves toward a rough reunification. *Panama Red* is right in the middle, almost a standalone in the sense that it's not building toward a bigger outcome. It exists solely to be fun. I hope that it is!

KAS, November 2025

And Moses stretched out his hand over the sea; and when the morning appeared, the sea returned to its full depth, while the Egyptians were fleeing into it. So the Lord overthrew the Egyptians in the midst of the sea. Then the waters returned and covered the chariots, the horsemen, and all the army of Pharaoh that came into the sea after them. Not so much as one of them remained.

Exodus 14:27-28

PANAMA RED

PART I

1.

"*Erin go* sit your ass back down," Kelly Turnbull told the indignant Irishman who had just stepped up to him. "*Erin go bragh*" roughly translates as "Ireland forever." Turnbull was not Irish and was irritated to be in Dublin when he could be back in Texas. But duty called – again – in the form of Clay Deeds. "Beware of intelligence chiefs bearing missions," his handler had reminded Turnbull at the beginning of the phone call. A HALO jump where he landed in muddy peat, followed by a chilly hike into Dublin, and here he was, in a pub, dealing with yet another idiot.

The story of his life.

The Irishman was in his thirties, large but not solid– one of those guys used to intimidating smaller men with his bulk and blarney. A trio of his lads stood behind him, waiting to see how this went as Turnbull sat on a worn stool at the bar, back to the wall, facing the front door. He liked to see his opponents coming, and he had been watching the grumbling mick eyeballing the pair of Americans for a half-hour.

"Your friend here ordered a black and tan," the unfriendly son of St. Patrick sputtered, nodding toward Casey Warner, who sat on the next stool over. "That's *offensive*."

Turnbull liked the Irish better when they didn't whine about their feels like pre-Split college students. He himself had ordered a straight Guinness, which he now sipped, his eyes locked on those of his interlocutor. It was as if drinking pumpernickel disguised as beer, thick and bitter, like Kelly himself.

A black and tan today was Guinness mixed with Harp. The black and tans over a century before were Brit paramilitaries who had ungently suppressed the Irish.

"So, too soon?" Turnbull asked innocently.

The Irishman's eyes bulged. Casey, whose thoughtless order to the barkeep had provided a pretext for hassling the yanks for these regulars of The Towering Cock– the pub's sign out front, with its elongated rooster, was a favorite selfie stop for tourists – spoke up.

"No offense," Casey said, smiling under a pair of black, square Army-issue birth control glasses that made him look like one of those awful liberal women who used to destroy beloved brands back before the United States split in two. "How about I buy you lads a drink?"

"Shut your mouth, you little poof. I'm talking to your bodyguard here."

Casey cocked his head. Turnbull sighed.

"Before you go on and end up sorry," Turnbull said. "I suggest you Red-Google Sergeant Major Mike Vining. Looks can be deceiving. I'm not protecting my friend from you. I'm protecting *you* from *him*."

"Thanks, Kelly," Casey said, honored. He looked at the Irishman and explained: "Mike Vining is kind of a meme."

"Stop talking," Kelly said.

"Oh, you think you're doing some protecting?" the Irishman demanded, the point sailing gently over his head. Too much beer and too many people buying his tough guy pose over the years had made him overconfident. He leaned forward and whispered.

"This is an IRA bar, my friend."

"So, I can get some retirement planning help along with a buzz?" Turnbull answered in hushed tones.

"You think you're clever, yank?"

Turnbull was done, especially with the Irish. The last time he had dealt with a bunch of Fenians, they had sucked him into a machine gun-fueled war on the streets of Boston. This current mission called for discretion. A brawl would be indiscreet.

"No, I think I'm bored. Go back to your table, read some poetry, play a fiddle, do a jig, but get out of my face. Do it now."

The Irishman sensed, even through the fog bank of pride and Jameson's, that he should comply, but his boyos were right there watching. He puffed up his chest and opened his coat.

"You know what this is, yank?"

Tucked in his waist was what looked like a small .25 caliber semiautomatic, maybe a Beretta or a Star. Turnbull glanced at it without reacting.

"It's a gun," the Irishman explained.

Turnbull shook his head.

"That's not a gun," he said. Then, his left hand shot out, pulling the Irishman close as Turnbull's right hand drew his hulking black .45 Wilson Combat CQB Elite 1911 and shoved the yawning chasm that was its muzzle into his foe's abdomen.

"*This* is a gun," he said. With his thumb, he pulled back the hammer. "And it's pointed at your liver, which is especially important to you as an Irishman."

The Irishman's eyes were fixed downward on the massive pistol pressing into his soft underbelly.

"Now, go back to your table and sit down," Turnbull instructed, adding, "I *mean* it."

The Irishman nodded. Turnbull relieved him of his Saturday night special before letting him go. The lads followed him back to their seats.

"Smooth," Casey said. He slid his Walther PDP pistol back into his belt. If it had gone south, he would have dropped the two closest henchmen.

Turnbull confirmed that pressing the barrel into the Irishman's gut had not taken it out of battery then holstered the .45.

"A black and tan in a Dublin bar... what's your malfunction?"

"I thought they'd be over it," Casey protested.

"They're Irish. They're never over anything."

"So, where's our boy?" Casey asked.

"Supposed to be coming any time now."

Casey nodded, then turned to the sullen barkeep.

"Guinness, please." The pub owner scowled and pulled up a glass to draw a pint. Casey turned back to his partner.

"Kelly, you got any idea how to pull this off?"

Turnbull shook his head.

"Not a one." He sipped some more of the black, bitter brew. The barkeep drew a fresh draft, swept some excess foam off the glass, and dropped it in front of Casey, who licked his lips as he examined the pint.

"I guess this is just a black, then."

"Just drink it," Turnbull said, his weary eyes on the front door.

"I'd post a selfie with this pour, but, you know, OPSEC."

"Are you still X-ing?" Turnbull asked, annoyed. He found the idea of social media tiresome.

"It's Twitter again this week," Casey replied. "Elon switches back and forth a lot. But I have hundreds of thousands of followers as @FullAutoGalt. I'm an influencer, Kelly."

"You're influencing me to slap you upside the head."

"Well, I never post on missions. Plus, The Towering Cock's wi-fi sucks."

Turnbull checked his watch. It was five past 8:00 p.m. Their boy was late. He took a sip from his pint and glanced up at the television. It was showing soccer highlights. Out on the pitch was a guy in a wheelchair, a fat dude riding a Rascal scooter, and several players were furries.

"The match between the Irish People's team and the People's Republic of North America team ended in a glorious draw today! This equity match drew an overflow crowd of supporters!" The announcer was a transvestite. The camera, either by oversight or sabotage, scanned the nearly empty stands. Turnbull noted that the People's Republic had apparently changed its flag once again, putting the light purple stripe symbolizing "minor attracted persons" even higher than it had been on the last iteration. The brown stripe had been downgraded; apparently, Latinx folx had been uppity and were being penalized within the hierarchy of identities.

There was a commotion at the front of the pub, with several folks entering and patrons suddenly whispering and standing. It was not hostile; Turnbull did not sense danger, though his hand hovered over the grip of his .45 anyway.

"He's walking over," someone said.

"Is it really him?" asked a lass who was probably named Maureen.

"What is this, the Second Coming?" asked Casey.

"You mean Bono?" Turnbull asked, aware that the Irish had largely cast off Christianity in favor of globalist pap.

"Bono skipped out to Miami because of the taxes, and U2 is playing state fairs," Casey said. "No, it's got to be our boy."

Two bruisers entered and looked around. Turnbull assessed them as fighters, probably mixed martial arts guys, not just untrained local toughs like the one he had just sent packing. No bulges, though – if they were armed, their guns were in their back waistbands. Of course, a citizen being armed was highly illegal, and it would give the local cops the excuse they needed to throw away the key.

Then Rory O'Riordan entered. He was shorter than one might expect, standing at about 5'9" and carrying 190 pounds of pure muscle. They called him "The Lethal Leprechaun," or did before he started getting popular and the promoters ditched the moronic moniker as he fought his way to the world championship of brawling.

They might soon be calling him "Mr. Taoiseach" – pronounced "tea-shuck." That was the title of the chief executive of the Republic of Ireland.

Turnbull was no fashionista – the last time he bought a suit was an experience more painful than any firefight he had ever been in – but even he could see that O'Riordan's clothes were tailor-made and probably worth more than the new United States government paid Turnbull a year. The Irish celebrity's wristwatch drew gasps from the adoring crowd that formed around him – Turnbull did not recognize the brand, but it was a customized Audemars Piguet Royal Oak Offshore Grande Complication that cost more than the Hill Country ranch Turnbull dreamed of buying someday. A lot more.

He wore a button that read "Campaign for the Irish." It was green, orange, and white with a clover motif.

A couple more slabs of corned beef, also wearing buttons, followed the local hero inside; one dull-looking fellow stayed by the door. That was good. They were at least marginally professional, though Turnbull noted that none of them had picked up on the pair of salty yanks over at the bar watching their principal with great interest.

Instead, the guards were scanning for close threats as their boss greeted the patrons. He seemed to know most of their names, though he was introduced to a few of them. Turnbull had been around politicians before – he had done personal security for ambassadors, secretaries, and even Vice-President Grenell in sketchy overseas places – but this O'Riordan had the touch. Most pols were stiffs, barely keeping up a façade of interest as they had to meet n' greet endless numbers of people and listen to their tiresome chatter.

Not O'Riordan, though. No, this guy seemed interested in everyone he spoke to, and if he wasn't, he faked it better than any politician Turnbull had ever seen, except maybe Bill Clinton. He knew the ex-president from before the Split, when Turnbull once had to pull him out of a hot tub in Dubai along with a couple of topless KLM stewardesses who happened to both be named Heidi to foil an al-Qaeda kidnapping attempt. Clinton could make you feel like you were the only person in his world when he talked to you; O'Riordan had that gift, too.

Maybe this retired wrestler *could* win the upcoming election. No wonder the Irish establishment was scared. But when people get scared, they get desperate. That was why Clay Deeds sent him and Casey to The Towering Cock.

"They haven't made us yet," Casey said, taking another sip. It left a little foam moustache on his upper lip.

"Wipe your face," Turnbull snarled, his eyes still on the commotion. The guards were watchful but not rough, letting familiar locals get close to the candidate.

"If someone wanted to smoke him...," Casey began.

"Yeah," Turnbull said.

Casey did not have to suggest they stay and wait for O'Riordan to come to them; that was obvious. Approaching the candidate would alert those big dudes, and they would vector in. It could get out of control quick, especially if they saw the Americans were strapped. No, better to let O'Riordan do his thing. The Towering Cock was not a huge establishment. He would find them.

He did, a few minutes later. Some chatty ginger was bending his ear, and O'Riordan's eyes wandered, meeting Turnbull's and locking on. No fear, Turnbull noted. The guy really was hard.

Turnbull nodded slightly, and O'Riordan replied with his own subtle bob. The ginger who had been going on kept talking, oblivious. O'Riordan smiled broadly, clasped the man's shoulder, then moved on toward the back where the Americans waited.

His guards fell in with him as he approached. Turnbull had a moment to take another gulp and put down his pint. O'Riordan stepped up to them and looked them over, as did his primary guard.

"Rory, they're strapped," the guard said evenly. No panic, just the fact. If Turnbull had been inclined to reach for his Wilson Combat .45, the man would have been all over him.

"Are they now, Bran?" O'Riordan replied, then addressed the Americans. "You know, guns are outlawed here in Ireland. And in your People's Republic."

"Not in the United States," Turnbull said. "Back home, guns are mandatory."

O'Riordan guffawed. Bran was stone-faced.

"So, you two are here to protect me?"

"That's right," Turnbull said.

"And you think I need your protection?"

"I don't think. I follow orders. And my orders are that no one kills you before the election."

"So, it's in the new USA's interest that I be the Taoiseach?"

"Above my pay grade. I'm just supposed to make sure you don't get waxed. And we have intel that the People's Republic may be trying to make that happen."

"I heard the rumor. A hit team from your blue states is supposed to be here in Ireland. We're looking into it. But it could be true. If they do me, the people in power benefit, as long as the corrupt establishment keeps its hands clean."

"Deniability," Casey said.

"So, the blues are sending a whole hit team and the reds are sending just the two of you?"

"Yeah, it seems like overkill," Turnbull conceded. "After all, there's only one of you to protect."

O'Riordan chuckled, while Bran remained silent.

"I've got security. Bran here has been with me since we were brawling on the streets in Finglas back in the day. I know my boys and trust them. What do you bring to the table?"

"Guns," Turnbull said. "Lots of guns."

"If you or your boys get caught packing heat, the government will have the Garda hook you up and lock you away," explained Casey. "That's the excuse they're looking for to take you out of the picture. But we aren't your boys."

"I like your glasses," O'Riordan said. "A man with the courage to wear those things in public is a man I'd like on my side in a fight. So, you propose to provide me with deniability?"

"That's right," Turnbull said. "We'll be with you, but not *with* you."

"I handle close security," Bran declared.

"You have that covered pretty well," Turnbull stated. "But the threat we are tracking isn't drunks who want to take a shot at the title or some nut with a kitchen knife. If they really are here and they come at you, they'll come heavy. That's the threat we'll handle."

"With a couple of pistols?" O'Riordan asked.

"Do I look like the kind of guy who plans on getting into a gunfight with a pistol?" Turnbull asked. "We brought our gear. If it goes off, you hit the deck and let your boys get you out of the kill zone."

"We'll deal with the blues if and when they make a move," Casey said. "Unless we find them first."

"What will you do if you find them before they move on me?" O'Riordan asked, genuinely curious.

Turnbull smiled thinly.

"That's our business," he said. "See, now you have your own deniability."

"All right," O'Riordan said. "You do what you do, and I'll keep doing what I do. What I do is talk to the Irish people. My consultants tell me we're faring all right, if the powers that be actually count the votes fair and square."

Turnbull shrugged – ballot box stuffing was not his problem. His problem was ensuring this character made it to election day intact.

O'Riordan's eyes flicked upwards, and he grunted. Turnbull's eyes followed the TV screen. There was a tremendously obese woman, Polynesian and wearing a grass skirt, standing out on the rugged Irish coast, staring at them from the screen. She said something in her native tongue. A subtitle popped up: "I am Irish."

"See, this is the problem," the budding politician said, shaking his head. "This is why I am running."

The next one was some sort of Eskimo. He had a harpoon and was in downtown Dublin standing in front of a statue of former Taoiseach and Hitler fanboy, President Eamon De Valera. The subtitle was once again "I am Irish."

"How about the bloody Irish be Irish?" the fighter demanded.

Around them, the patrons muttered their approval.

"See, this is my campaign," O'Riordan said to Turnbull, but really to the audience of drinkers and drunks. "The parties, Fianna Fáil, Fine Gael, they're the same. All the same. Irishmen, real Irishmen, are about the most contrary bastards on the planet. They're stubborn and they love to fight, or did love to fight until the feminists and the communists took over and cut most of their nuts off. The real Irish had to be replaced. Both parties conspired to import half the damn Third World. One out of four Irishmen wasn't even born in Ireland! Me? I'm the alternative, the Irish alternative!"

He had clearly given this speech a few hundred times before. Turnbull listened, emotionless. Not his war, not his fight. Up on the television screen, a four-foot-tall Bushman wearing a loincloth in a field of clover, was speaking in his southern African desert click language: "I am Irish."

"No, you're bloody not!" O'Riordan shouted at the screen. The pub dwellers nearby began to cheer.

"Better cool it down, Rory," Bran warned his boss. "There's probably a grass or two in here waiting for you to break the PIH." He was referring to the Prohibition of Incitement to Hatred Act 1989, which basically outlawed saying anything the government didn't like.

"This is Ireland," O'Riordan spat, disgusted. "There's always a grass." Informers had been the curse of Emerald Isle rebels and dissidents since Cromwell.

"So, we're good?" Turnbull asked him.

"Yeah, sure. You do what you do, just maintain that distance."

"Deniability," Casey said.

"Deniability," O'Riordan reiterated.

Turnbull finished his pint.

Turnbull and Casey took a room in a two-star hotel off the beaten path on the north side of town, where O'Riordan's base of support lay. They had walked the quarter mile there from The Towering Cock according to Bran's directions – the chief bodyguard had called ahead to get things ready. They had seen a lot of native Irish out, most smoking, many half or more in the bag. And they saw a few of what O'Riordan had taken a great deal of heat for calling "invaders," the Third World importees the establishment was bringing over as fast as it could.

A half-dozen Middle Easterners lounging outside a late-night kebab shop – Turnbull assessed them as Afghans – gave the Americans the stink eye. Turnbull gave it right back. Maybe somewhere in their collective ethnic memory, they recognized an American who was not to be messed with, an American who had sent a fair number of their brothers off to meet their reward of six dozen virgins. They resumed their conversation, and Casey and Turnbull continued on their way.

The hotel's proprietor was a friend of the candidate – O'Riordan had a lot of friends – and he seemed very comfortable with having two dangerous-looking strangers stay in a room at the end of the hall for cash without asking any questions. The lodgings were serviceable, with a pair of single beds that seemed to have been designed for hobbits. Turnbull glanced out the window – there was an empty street lined with other two and three-story buildings, and they were on the second floor, so if they had to jump, it was doable.

Turnbull pulled the blinds, cutting off the view of the street. The windows faced east, so the sun would come pouring in at dawn. Casey bolted the door – it was a heavy bolt – and Turnbull removed the contents of one of their duffels, laying them out on the bed.

They had a pair of Sig Sauer MCX Rattlers in .300 Blackout, with suppressors, Steiner DBAL A3-Red lasers, and Aimpoint Micro T-2 optics. They were short assault weapons, about 16" (not counting the suppressors) when you collapsed the stocks. They were as concealable as you could be in an urban environment.

They had also brought an accurized HK417 that fired a 7.62×51mm cartridge for longer range firepower. It was broken down to fit in the duffel, and Casey set about reassembling it, adding the scope and the suppressor. There were mags of ammo for both types of weapons.

"You know, Kelly, if we're trying to be discreet, I'm not sure we can go with these."

"We'll figure it out."

Turnbull reached down into the duffel and took out the secure satphone. There was a number preprogrammed into it. He punched it.

Clay Deeds picked up before the second ring. Turnbull put it on speaker so he would not have to repeat the conversation. He preferred not to have to talk.

"Did you make contact?" Deeds asked.

"We did," Kelly said. "He's cooperating."

"Good. That was not assured. His psych profile is long and colorful, but I think the technical term for him is 'crazy.' Too many punches to the brainpan."

"He seemed okay to me," Kelly replied.

"That's not exactly evidence to the contrary," Deeds said. "Look, the election is in 48 hours. His consultants think they have the countryside wrapped up, so he's staying in Dublin and campaigning there until the vote. Looks like he's ahead. If they take him out, they have to rerun the election, and no one else can generate the numbers he can. We need him to win, Kelly. The US is running short of friends. And the People's Republic likes it that way."

"What do you have on the opposition?"

Deeds paused. A pause was never good.

"We think Circe is running the op."

"Circe? You're kidding. She's here?"

"That's what we think. She's got a team. They are in-country, but we have zero intel on who they are, only that they are there."

"We've been looking for Circe for a while. She's good. Very good," Turnbull said.

"Assuming she's a she. Circe might be a man pretending to be a woman. All we really know is that she is a People's Republic operative with a big body count."

"Circe is kind of like Voldemort," Casey added. "A mysterious, deadly villain. Instead of no one speaking her real name, no one knows who she really is."

Turnbull glared at his partner, then turned back to the satphone.

"Still no photo or any new info on her?" he asked Deeds.

"Nothing yet. But if you can ID her, that's a win right there, Kelly," Deeds said. "If you can kill her, that's even better."

"Everyone you've sent to kill her is dead," Turnbull replied.

"That's why I sent you and Ron Weasley."

"Hey!" objected Casey.

"I don't know who that is," Turnbull said.

"Harry Potter's lame buddy," Casey said petulantly. Turnbull tried to ignore him, but he went on. "Although in the new book, *Harry Potter and The Man Who Claimed He Menstruated*, he does help Harry kill Voldemorta. See, Voldemort comes back and he's a tranny."

"Just stop," Turnbull demanded, though he was vaguely aware that J.K. Rowling was currently a political refugee living in Boca. He turned his attention back to Deeds.

"Do you have anything on their location? If we can find them before they move, we can take out the threat and get out of this country. It's damp, and everyone from here has freckles."

"We're doing what we can. In the meantime, just make sure no one offs O'Riordan."

"Now that Circe is on the board, that's easier said than done."

They finished with the long weapons and stowed them under the bed, out of sight to a casual visitor. The proprietor sent up some sandwiches – tasteless, mushy ones. The British influence over its former colony persisted.

At 1:13 a.m., there was a knock. Turnbull and Casey had slept in their clothes, sans shoes. Both bolted upright, their respective pistols off their nightstands and aimed at the entrance. Turnbull nodded at his partner and slid out of bed to take up a position by the door. Casey's pistol was locked onto it. The room was dark; there was a thin line of light under the door from the hallway sconces.

"Yeah?" Turnbull asked, still taking aim.

"It's me," said someone from the other side. "Bran."

Turnbull kept covering the entryway while Casey rolled onto the floor and brought up one of the Rattlers. It was already locked and loaded.

With his left hand, Turnbull yanked back the bolt and then turned the knob. He pulled the door open slowly, the barrel of his Wilson Combat greeting their visitor. Turnbull assessed him quickly – no weapon, just a manila envelope in his hand.

"I'm alone," Bran said. He had probably looked into the maw of a handgun before because it didn't seem to bother him.

Turnbull glanced past him, and the hallway was clear. He pulled the door fully open, and the Irishman came inside. The only light came in through the blinds from a streetlamp outside; Turnbull did not bother to flip the switch on the overhead light. He closed the door behind the visitor.

Bran's eyes went to the assault rifle Casey was pointing at him. That did impress him.

"You brought the heavy artillery," he said. "You'll need it."

Turnbull let his gun fall to his side, though it could be back on target in a flash.

"What do you got?"

"We have a lot of friends in the government," Bran said. "They have to keep a low profile, but they are everywhere, and they talk to us. We put out the word to people who might be in a position to help, and we got some information."

Bran paused. Turnbull waited. Bran continued.

"Two days ago, six men came in from Mogadishu on People's Republic passports."

"Which Mogadishu?"

"The one in America. The one that got renamed."

"Minneapolis," Casey said. "It used to be called Minneapolis."

"Six guys, so what? What caught your source's attention?" Turnbull asked.

"They looked Somalian. And spoke it. But there are not a lot of Somalis out there named Smith. And fewer have a fast pass entry in the system."

"Pre-cleared to enter Ireland?"

"Yeah. When you're pre-cleared, you're supposed to be waved right through, no questions asked. No luggage checks, either. It's usually for politicians or rich guys or celebrities, that lot. But other times, it's not clear why. You're not supposed to ask. The fast pass was purged, by the way. It's no longer in the system."

"I'm guessing your source was in the border guards at the airport."

"Probably a good guess. It's called the Garda National Immigration Bureau, or GNIB. But there's more. We know where they went."

"Where?" asked Turnbull.

"I have the address, but it's in invader territory, a migrant neighborhood where these jokers won't stand out. They took a taxi van. The driver remembered because they spent the whole time chattering in, I guess, Somalian."

"Makes sense," Casey said. "The government lets them in, then it's hands off and they are on their own."

"Deniability," Bran said. He handed over the manila envelope to Turnbull, who opened it and squinted in the dim light. It contained six GNIB printouts, with names and photos taken at the airport border control checkpoint. None had a Somalian name. There was a Smith, a Roberts, and so on.

"Recognize any of them?" Casey asked.

"Nope," Turnbull said. "They look like Somalians."

"The address is in there, too," Bran said.

"Did your source notice a female with them?"

"Nope."

"How about traveling alone?"

Bran guffawed.

"A lot of women travel alone to Ireland, tourists, on business, or looking for love. You got anything more specific?"

"I'm not even sure I'm looking for an actual woman."

"I feel that, boyo. Can't be too careful," Bran said ruefully.

Turnbull let that slide past.

"We'll take care of this," he said.

"When?" asked Bran. "Tomorrow afternoon is the election eve rally at Irishtown Stadium. We're looking at tens of thousands of people showing up."

"Deniability," Turnbull replied.

"I still can't get used to this wrong-side driving," Casey said. Turnbull shifted uncomfortably in the passenger seat of the elderly Toyota Corolla that Bran had supplied to them, navigating off of his burner phone. It was about 3:00 a.m., and there were few migrants on the streets.

"Don't get stopped by the Garda," Bran had cautioned them. Turnbull did not need to ask if their ride was hot. He did run through the scenarios if the Irish police pulled them over in a stolen car carrying automatic weapons. All of his courses of action ended with the Garda officers ended.

"Just drive like a normal person," he told Casey. "Don't get popped. We'll end up inside." He pointed to the imposing Mountjoy Prison. "And you're too pretty for prison."

Casey continued driving. A few minutes later, he asked his navigator for an update.

"We should be there, or nearly there. How far?"

"End of the block," Turnbull replied, looking up from the screen. It was an ugly street in an ugly quadrant of town, full of dingy buildings erected for efficiency a half-century ago and left to decay. Several cars were parked along the curb, one with its driver's-side window bashed out.

"Nice neighborhood," Casey observed.

"Slow up here," Turnbull said.

It was a two-story building with a single naked bulb out front casting a yellow glow. There were no lights in any of the windows. The first floor was some kind of shop that had signage in a Middle Eastern language. The windows were all barred. Other than the public entrance to the shop, there was one other door, with a metal frame over the wood face. That was annoying.

"Go around."

Casey complied, maneuvering the Corolla past and then right onto a side street, then into the alley that ran behind the building. There were two doors, one with the same script on it as the shop, and it was probably its back door. The second door was by a dumpster and had to be from the rooms upstairs. There were lights in a couple of the windows. They drove back around front.

"Park," Turnbull ordered. Casey did so outside the front door.

"Plan?" Casey asked.

"Through the door, upstairs, kill everybody, go home," Turnbull said.

"See, what I love is your detailed, in-depth planning."

"Stop talking. Let's go." Turnbull opened the door and slipped out with his Rattler. The silencer added several inches to the weapon. He tested the designator. The laser worked.

They got to the door, and Turnbull covered the street as Casey knelt with the tools he had pulled from his pocket, his Rattler hanging by a strap. Turnbull scanned up and down the road and across the face of the buildings as Casey worked the lock. He hoped Casey could pull it off; a dynamic breach would be loud and very, very indiscreet.

"Got it," Casey said. He stood, slipped his tools back into his pants, took up his weapon with his right hand, and put his left on the doorknob.

Turnbull faced the door, Rattler up, and nodded. He hoped there was no bolt on the other side.

Casey turned and pulled. The door came open with a creak, and Turnbull rushed inside, red laser dancing on the walls and the stairs in front of him that went up to the second floor. Casey came in behind, shutting the door. It was dark with only a few slivers of light cutting in from outside through filthy windows.

Turnbull began climbing the stairs, the red dot on the door at the top across the small landing. Casey followed, gun forward, offset from his partner to avoid fratricide. There was no need to watch their rear since the front door was shut.

Turnbull took each step quickly but methodically, aiming for a smooth and stealthy approach. He was halfway up the steps when the door at the head of the stairwell opened and light flooded through.

A thin man stepped into the opening, saying something in an alien language. His tone was business-like, but not frightened. Turnbull assessed he was waiting for somebody or somebodies. He was definitely not expecting Turnbull.

Somali? Maybe, but that AK-19 assault rifle – an updated Russian export model AK-47-frame weapon – indicated he was no friendly. Turnbull's red designator was on his solar plexus when Turnbull fired.

It was a four-round burst, with three slamming into his upper torso and the last going through his mouth and splattering red goo on the wall directly behind him. The man got out a grunt as he fell backwards, crashing in a heap as Turnbull crested the stairs. The door opened into the middle of a hall running in two directions. There was no time to dither.

In a split second, Turnbull assessed the man as both Somalian and dead. But just to be sure, he popped a single round into the corpse's brainpan. That made the wall even messier.

"Going left!" Turnbull shouted as he swung around the entryway. The hall extended a few feet to an open space that served as a living room. There were moldering chairs and a sofa, along with a linoleum-topped table that the occupants were using as a workstation. There was a disassembled AK-19 on it, with some rags and a gun oil can, and a wrapped bundle of green plant material.

Turnbull recognized it as khat, a leaf that provides a mild high when chewed. It was popular in Africa, Yemen, and now in Minnesota as well.

Several prayer rugs were spread out on the dirty floor. Across the living room, on the wall facing Turnbull, was a fading poster of the Cranberries, a band he loathed. There was a hallway at the far right of the wall, and it was dark. Turnbull made for it.

Casey had taken off to clear to the right side of the flat, so Turnbull was alone. His laser designator probed for targets down the hall as he advanced. There was noise, like someone scrambling. It was not Casey; it was up ahead. Then someone shouted what sounded like a question, even though it was in a tongue Turnbull did not savvy. Like someone shouting to a buddy, asking, "What the hell is going on?"

Turnbull accelerated, figuring he had ten seconds before the second man repeated himself, this time with lead.

The man was nowhere near that patient.

The wall ahead of him exploded outward with rounds, with the Cranberries poster shredded and plaster flying about the living room. The shooter was not using a suppressor. It was loud, and he was probably deaf inside the room on the other side of the wall. Of course, now the whole neighborhood knew something was up.

Instantly, Turnbull had dropped to the filthy floor between prayer rugs as the rounds cut across the room over top of him. They might be a threat to Casey, but Turnbull had no time to think about that. He looked at where the rounds were coming from on the wall – they were about at shoulder height on a shorter man – and did some calculations on the fly, then let a burst of .300 rounds from his Rattler fly through the wall. It was suppressed, but that does not mean silenced. It was still loud, just not deafening. He let off a burst of five, then another, then another, and then did a combat reload to continue with a fresh mag.

No more shooting from the other side of the wall.

Turnbull got to his feet and moved fast toward the hallway. As he got closer, he spotted the open door to the room on the other side of the wall and sprayed ahead of him, through the doorway and the surrounding hallway wall. Crossing the threshold, he saw a shape on the floor, not moving, and he paused to hit the light switch.

The man on the floor was another Somali, his AK-19 on the floor a few feet away. He grimaced at the sudden light, which was odd since he should have been grimacing from the several bullet holes in his legs and gut.

"You speak English?" Turnbull asked, the red dot from his laser on the man's forehead. There was blood and greenish, khat-streaked saliva dribbling from the corners of his mouth.

The man replied with something in a language Turnbull did not speak, yet the meaning was perfectly clear. Turnbull avenged what he correctly assumed was a grievous insult to his mother with a round through the man's skull.

"Clear!" Casey yelled. His footsteps were getting louder.

"Clear! Check the rest of the floor!" Turnbull shouted – there were other rooms down the hallway, though if no one had come out of them shooting by now, they were probably empty. He knelt down to search the man. Just a cell phone; no papers, money, or pocket litter.

"Clear!" Casey shouted again after finishing the rest of the apartment. He came back into the room.

"Just these two," he said.

"There were supposed to be six."

"I counted seven beds."

"Circe?"

"Wait," Casey said. He went back out into the hall, ducked into the bathroom, and came back with a package.

"What?" Turnbull asked. Casey tossed it to him.

The package featured a man in a ballerina's tutu. It looked like Tim Walz. It might have been Tim Walz.

"Vag-I-Can tampons?" Turnbull read. The package further read: "Because everyBODY has a right to feminine protection, with or without a vagina."

"It's a People's Republic brand," Casey continued. Turnbull did not ask him how he knew.

So, Circe had been there. But where was she now, and where were the other four members of her team?

They walked back into the living room.

"Let's toss this dump for anything else useful," Turnbull directed. "But we need to be quick. Somebody will have called the Garda by now."

"I haven't seen any electronics, besides that phone. Not much else, except some clothes and that broke weapon in the living room. Is that khat? Figures."

"Let's gather the clothes up anyway," Turnbull said. "Maybe there's DNA or something. And take the firing pin."

The phone rang.

Casey and Turnbull looked at the cell phone in Turnbull's hand. "UNKNOWN CALLER." It rang again.

"Well?" asked Casey.

Turnbull shrugged, hit the green button, and put it to his ear.

"Joe's mortuary. You bag 'em, we slab 'em," he said, channeling his twelve-year-old self.

From the other end of the line came a torrent of Somali profanity. Turnbull held it away from his ear until it died down. Then he spoke.

"Get your boss."

More Somali, then silence for a moment. A woman's voice came over the line.

"Who are you?" she asked, throaty, a hint of Spanish. Probably identified as Latinx or Latinx-adjacent. But it did sound like a girl.

"I'm the guy who just smoked your buddies. I assume I'm talking to Circe."

"You're a fascist agent," she replied, a bit surprised.

"Sexist, too, but not so much I won't smoke you when I get the chance."

"You won't, Nazi. This is your last mission." Circe hung up.

"That bitch," Turnbull thought, and then it dawned on him, and he turned to Casey.

"Run!"

He bolted toward the door and went down the steps three at a time, then out the door. Casey was right behind him.

In a flash, Casey was in the driver's seat, and the car was rolling as Turnbull pulled his passenger side door shut. They got about twenty yards before the second-floor suite detonated in an orange fireball. Bits of flaming debris rained over them and across the asphalt.

"Discreet," observed Casey.

"Yeah," Turnbull said. The phone rang. Turnbull took a moment to answer it.

"Missed me, Circe," he said.

"Is that what you racists call me?"

"Yeah, but we were under the impression you were some kind of master terrorist, and you seem to actually be kind of a hack."

"I won't miss next time. See you soon."

"Not if I see you first," Turnbull said and hung up.

"The man hanging up is a power move," Casey told him. "Do you follow Fort Worth Playboy? Undisputed master of The Game. Also, when you text a chick, no punctuation, capitalization, or emojis. They show weakness."

"Just get us back to the hotel," Turnbull said, shutting his eyes.

The pair cleaned their weapons and reloaded mags, then crashed in their beds. Turnbull awoke at 6:23 a.m. to the sound of glass breaking. He grabbed his .45, and then the window pane shattered again, with the blinds kicking.

"What the hell?" began Casey.

"Down!" Turnbull said, rolling onto the floor. More glass, more ruffled blinds, and then two geysers of down puffed into the air from his pillows.

The bullets were coming from somewhere across the road, but they were suppressed. The only noise was the breaking glass, the ripped blinds, and whatever they hit inside. A pile of papers on the bureau exploded as the wood underneath splintered. Another round zipped over Turnbull's head. He grabbed his Rattler.

"Damn, Kelly!" Casey exclaimed, holding his HK417.

Turnbull low-crawled to the window. The light fixture on the ceiling took a hit, and glass fragments showered him. He reached for the blinds, which were twisted and shredded. Sunlight was pouring through. A section of glass that had survived thus far shattered.

Carefully, he rose up and tried to look out, then fell back down.

"Sun's to their rear, damn it. Can't see anything."

"Think they'll assault us?"

"I would," Turnbull replied. A couple more bullets sped into the room.

At that moment, there was a pounding at their door, a door which already had four or five bullet holes in it.

"What the bloody hell are ye doin'?" the innkeeper shouted.

"Get out of here, you idiot! They're shooting at us!" Turnbull shouted. They could hear the sound of the innkeeper scampering away, and more rounds entered the room uninvited.

"We need to be elsewhere, Kelly!"

"Go!" Turnbull said.

Casey made for the door, standing up long enough to pull the bolt and open it with the knob. A round put a hole in the wood not six inches from his head.

Casey pulled the door open and went out into the hall with his HK417. Turnbull waited for a moment until the silent gunfire slowed for a moment – a mag change? – and sprinted out behind his partner.

They ran along the hallway and down the stairs to the first floor. The innkeeper was there on the landline, screaming in incomprehensible Irish-English.

"Put it down!" Turnbull yelled.

The Irishman kept shouting into the phone.

Using his carbine for emphasis, Turnbull repeated himself. The Irishman shut up and hung up.

Casey was back a few feet from the windows, scanning the windows and rooftops of the buildings across the way with the scope on his rifle. Turnbull assessed the situation and figured that if the PR hit team came to finish the job, the optimal place to ambush them was at the front door. The lobby desk seemed heavy; it was the best cover he would have. He set himself, ready to provide the assault team with a big, ugly surprise.

"I got nothing," Casey said, still scanning for targets. "Sun's in my eyes."

They could still hear the impact of bullets in the room upstairs; this went on for another minute or so. Then silence.

"If they're coming, they're coming now," Turnbull said. He was ready for them.

But they did not come.

O'Riordan showed up about an hour later.

"Looks like hell, and that's only from the outside," he said as he came into the lobby. The proprietor gave him some tea.

"Bran, take care of Seamus here," he ordered. Bran proceeded to pull out a roll of bills and start peeling them off to pay for the damage.

Turnbull had his Rattler hanging around his neck.

"No Garda," Turnbull observed.

"They got a report of some rowdy youths breaking windows. Pretty low on their priority list, since someone blew up a building in Mountjoy this morning. Know anything about that?"

"What's a building?"

O'Riordan guffawed, smiling.

"Well, I got my deniability, but you can't deny that you let some of them slip through."

"They weren't all home," Turnbull explained. "The guys who were home won't be a problem. But I'm wondering how they knew we were staying here."

O'Riordan stopped smiling.

"Me too. Damn grasses. The Irish have never been able to keep a secret. That's our weakness."

"I thought it was whisky."

"No, that's our strength. In any case, I'm putting Bran on the case to find the informer."

"It had to be a government informer. But why wouldn't the Garda just arrest us themselves?" Turnbull wondered.

"You think the government wants to risk having to explain a dozen dead policemen trying to take you psychotics into custody? Nah, let the foreigners do the dirty work."

"A lot of deniability going around."

"Yeah, a lot of it. Okay, I have to go run for Taoiseach now, so you lads try not to kill anyone or blow anything up or get into any more gunfights. I'm going to have Bran, and only Bran, take you to another place before he goes grass hunting."

"That way, if word gets out, we know who the informer is," Casey said.

"No," O'Riordan said. "I'm not that clever. I just trust Bran with my life. And nobody else."

Bran took them to a farm outside of town after performing some effective counter-surveillance maneuvers in his car. The only way they could have been followed is with a GPS tracker, and Bran assured them he had swept his car that morning.

The farm was rustic, which was a kind way of calling it primitive. There was a room in the barn that had clearly been used for at least a couple of centuries to hide folks the authorities were looking for. The farmer himself took no interest in them, speaking to Bran in Gaelic and then pointing to the barn. However, a cow did find Casey fascinating.

"Your game seems to be working," Turnbull said.

"Not my type," Casey demurred. Bran came over.

"You'll be safe here until I come get you."

"Thanks," Turnbull replied. "Now, you may need this, if you want it." He held out the .25-caliber semiautomatic he had taken off the bully. Bran looked at it for a moment and took it, slipping it into his jeans pocket.

Bran left them at about seven and returned at about ten. In the meantime, they got some sleep. Bran had told them the farmer's son would keep watch, and it was an uneventful few hours.

"Where are we headed?" Turnbull asked. He had his Rattler under his coat, as did Casey, but their other gear was in the trunk.

"Irishtown Stadium," Bran replied. "That's where Rory is speaking this afternoon. Figured you would want to scout it. I got you security passes so you can go anywhere. But we have a stop first."

"What for?"

"I found the grass."

Their stop was at a chemical warehouse down near the docks. Turnbull, as was his habit, kept track of the route in case he had to exfiltrate. They pulled into a nearly empty parking lot even though every other business around was filling up with workers.

"The employees have the day off," Bran said, answering the question before Turnbull asked it.

The Shane Chemical Supply Co. looked exactly like one would expect from the name. There were pallets of 55-gallon drums containing various chemicals, many of which had labels warning of acid or flammability hazards. And in the center of the open cement floor was a guy tied to an office chair.

He looked uncomfortable.

It took Turnbull a minute to place him, as he had been beaten to a pulp. It was the mixed martial arts fighter who had taken his position by the front door of The Towering Cock. This guy was close to O'Riordan, but no longer. O'Riordan was standing there cradling his bruised hand.

It occurred to Turnbull that the interrogation of a guy trained to take a beating by a guy trained to inflict a beating was going to be a long and unpleasant process.

"Hello, yanks," O'Riordan greeted them, mustering up a smile. "This is Toby. Known him, trained with him, for years. Thought he was a mate. Turns out the Garda caught his brother with dirty pictures of little boys. Of course, that's not illegal anymore – will be again when I'm Taoiseach – but they told Toby they would let word out in the neighborhood unless he became their grass."

"I'm sorry, Rory," the prisoner blubbered. His words were slurred from his swollen face and missing teeth.

"You'd be wise to shut up until spoken to, Toby. I haven't had time to train lately with the campaigning and all, and I'm enjoying this, you bastard."

Toby sobbed. Rory continued.

"Seems the Garda introduced him to a lady, and she had questions. He had answers. She called him late last night and he told her where you lads were kipping."

"Kipping?" asked Casey.

"That's 'sleeping' in Ireland. Anyway, thought you might want to have a word with him before we finish up here."

"Rory, please, I had no choice!"

"Shut up, Toby, and answer what you're asked, or it'll go much worse for you, and it's already going to go pretty damn bad."

Turnbull walked over and bent down. The guy's face was punched into pulp. His eyes were wild with pain and fear. Good. Turnbull could use it.

"Tell me about the girl," Turnbull asked flatly.

"I only met her once."

"What did she look like?"

"Uh, not Irish. Black hair. You know, white. Pretty."

"Distinguishing features?"

"What?"

Turnbull sighed.

"Scars, moles, tattoos? Anything like that? A nose ring?"

"I can't remember."

"Think hard."

"I don't remember!"

"Rory?" Turnbull asked, turning to the candidate.

"Don't you want a few swings? He did almost get you and your mate killed."

"Not my style," Turnbull said and pulled out his .45. He leveled it at Toby's face, then lowered it to the prisoner's kneecap.

"I don't have time to screw around with you, Toby. Answer me." Turnbull pulled back the hammer for emphasis.

"No, she was normal! Pretty, but normal!" Toby wailed, then started to cry.

"Anything else that she said or did?"

"A couple of days ago, she asked about Irishtown Stadium, the rally tonight."

"What did you tell her?"

"What I knew, that we would be doing close protection."

"Anything else?"

"No, I swear."

"Fine," Turnbull said. "I'm done. All yours."

"Okay," O'Riordan said. "Bran, do him a favor."

Bran pulled the .25 semiautomatic and had it to Toby's temple before the prisoner could cry out. The sound of the shot was muffled, but still echoed through the warehouse.

Bran admired his work. Toby did not need a follow-up shot.

"Bran was ex-IRA," O'Riordan explained. "Not the communist provo posers. The Real IRA."

"Actually, the True IRA, which became the Irish IRA," Bran corrected him. "Then the Patriotic IRA. And then Rory's Campaign for the Irish."

Turnbull admired Bran's work. He appreciated men who made hard choices and did what needed doing.

"So, you're not playing?" Turnbull asked O'Riordan.

"No, this isn't a game. We either win at the ballot box or we win in the streets. This is life and death."

"As Toby found out," Casey observed.

"I hope he's the last, but he won't be," O'Riordan said. "They won't just give up power. Not to us."

"Unless they kill you," Turnbull said.

"Yeah, unless they kill me. But you'll stop that, won't you, yanks?"

"If we can," Turnbull answered.

"Well, I have a rally to get to. Bran, could you attend to this mess?"

"Sure, Rory," Bran said. He turned toward his men. "Go find me a barrel that says 'Caution: Acid.'"

It was less a rally than a giant party, with the sun still up for an hour and the weather with a touch of chill. Irishmen and Irishwomen – not a lot of gender-ambiguous Irishothers out that afternoon – wandered through the crowded field of Irishtown Stadium. Most held beers. There were kegs along the sides of the gathering at the end of long, thirsty lines. Some of the patrons would get to the front and immediately return to the rear, finishing their brew in the queue to draw another.

Rory O'Riordan was buying drinks for all of Dublin, it seemed; the guy really must be rich, Turnbull thought.

There was plenty of "Campaign for the Irish" signage, as well as dozens of Irish flags – real ones, not the new ones with the diversity stripes – flying around the stadium. A huge banner hung over the stage at the south side of the field: "Rory O'Riordan – Let Ireland Be Irish Again." They were playing recorded rock music over the loudspeakers, serenading the patrons who were waiting for the program to start. Most bands, but not all, would have nothing to do with the insurgent campaign. All the rebels and nonconformist artists, as always, were firmly with the establishment government.

From where he stood on the football pitch, Turnbull could not see Casey. His partner was somewhere on a roof overlooking the stadium, providing overwatch and being a one-man anti-sniper team. The Garda should have been up there. The cops should have been on the ground, too, but they weren't. There was not a single uniformed cop in the place. That was deliberate; the police were only there to protect the masters, not the proles. But there was still security. The occasional out-of-control drunk was handled by the stalking packs of toughs working for Bran, but as for actual professional security, Turnbull was it inside the stadium.

Bon Jovi came over the speaker, but Turnbull couldn't determine which of his songs it was – it had to be one about how he was going to rock no matter who told him he could not rock. Jon Bon Jovi had played with Bruce Springsteen at the post-Split celebrations in Newark, the People's Republic having been forced to take New Jersey pursuant to the Treaty of St. Louis. But the aging singer had long ago disappeared from public view, having been purged for his original overtly cisgender persona despite his attempt at a comeback song, "Gender's Just A Dream."

Whoa, whoa!
What's in my pants is not what it seems!
Whoa, whoa
Gender's just a dream!

From his vantage point on a warehouse rooftop looking west and north, Casey scanned the line of multi-story apartment buildings facing the main stage. He lay under a heap of blankets designed to give him some concealment; if they saw him first, he was cooked, so he put his trust in not being seen. It would be a several-hundred-yard shot if they took one, either from one of the roofs or one of the windows. There were people on some of the roofs, mostly partying, so a sniper would probably stay off those apartment building rooftops. If they were going to take a long-range shot, it would be from a window, probably on the third or higher floor.

They had used snipers before. They almost certainly would again. Casey continued scanning the windows. There were dozens of them.

Back on the grass of the football pitch inside the stadium, Turnbull wore a long coat and tried to hide his arsenal. The .45 was at his belt and, to keep it hidden, the Rattler hung inside his duster, stock compacted, without the suppressor. He figured that if he had to shoot, he wanted the noise. That might keep people from interfering.

It was not a lily white crowd, though the majority of attendees were Hibernian stereotypes who looked like refugees from *The Quiet Man*. A fair number were foreign, and from talking to Bran, it seemed a lot of the earlier immigrants were not too happy about the second-wave migrants who, instead of wanting to assimilate, insisted on bringing the pathologies of their Third World hellholes along with them. That meant Somalis would not necessarily stand out.

The security badge hung down from his neck. Everyone passing him eyed it. Turnbull hated the attention, but it was necessary. He had to be left alone to do what needed doing. But Turnbull was not sure that one guy with a gun in a stadium could do much of anything when his protectee did not seem to care about getting whacked.

He keyed his mic, which was clipped to his collar.

"Casey, what do you got?"

"Just a hundred possible spots for a shooter," came Casey's voice through Turnbull's earpiece. "You can't talk him out of this?"

"You think anyone can talk O'Riordan out of anything?"

"Nope. He's going to be out there, exposed. Probably a six-hundred-yard shot."

Turnbull furrowed his brow.

"You think they could make that?"

"*I* could make it, but I'm trained. So could you, and you're barely trainable. But Kelly, here's the thing, the khat chewing aside, did those guys strike you as trained?"

"Not very," Turnbull said. A couple of Colleens with full beers and some acne walked by, staring at the big man talking to himself.

"No, not very," Casey said. "What are the chances they have trained snipers? I mean, anyone can shoot up a hotel room from across the street."

"They did miss us."

"Yeah, probably fifty rounds and not a hit. These guys are schmucks, Kelly."

"Khat-chomping cannon fodder," Turnbull replied, considering the situation.

"Four men and the girl, Kelly," Casey said.

"Keep looking," Turnbull said, cutting off the radio call.

He made his way toward the main stage. There was a microphone stand in the middle, but no podium and no bullet-resistant glass. It was wide open.

On the floor of the stadium, off to both sides of the stage, were guards, Bran's guys, checking badges to allow access backstage. Turnbull approached and held his up pass. The meathead nodded, and Turnbull walked back and behind the stage. Wires and cords ran everywhere. There were stacks of speakers and some men at a soundboard.

VIPs, including groupies, milled about, drinking and talking – there was a backstage-only row of kegs. Too many people, all drinking too much, assessed Turnbull. He did not like it one bit.

Bran was there, conferring with some of his guys. He saw Turnbull approach and dismissed his men. Turnbull shared his misgivings, punctuating his monologue with the lavish use of profane adjectives and adverbs.

"Well, what do you want me to do, then?" Bran asked. "I'm not the boss. Rory does what Rory wants. Always has."

"We know there are snipers out there, and he's walking onto an open stage. They'll kill him."

"If they can, but Rory's something other guys aren't."

Turnbull waited for Bran to explain, and after realizing Turnbull was not going to ask him, "What?," he explained.

"Rory's lucky. Like he's got a pocket full of four-leaf clovers."

"Lucky? I'm getting really tired of this Irish Spring crap."

"What?"

"It's an old soap. Anyway, my job is to keep him alive."

"Mine too, but apparently that's not his priority."

"You lose him and you lose this country for good."

"Nah, maybe we just have our own new civil war, like the damn Brits. So be it."

"You weren't there," Turnbull said. "I was. You don't want that."

"None of us wanted any of this. But here we are. Look, yank, whatever your name is, if Rory O'Riordan doesn't go out there, everyone is going to think he's afraid, and then he's cooked. It was cowards who got us in this mess, and a coward isn't getting us out. So, there it is."

"Yeah, there it is," replied Turnbull. He knew he was not going to get anywhere arguing with Bran, or even O'Riordan for that matter. The Irish were more stubborn than mules, and he made a note that if he ever got that Texas ranch he was always dreaming about, he would not have any mules, or Irishmen, for that matter.

"Four men, Somali, plus one woman, brunette," Turnbull continued. "The men are not well-trained. I expect any of them who are not sniping will try to get close. If O'Riordan gets shot at, get him off stage. Throw him over your shoulder and carry him off if you have to."

Bran was dubious about forcing O'Riordan to do anything. "We've gone over this, and I've told my men," he said.

"Tell them again. Everyone's getting searched coming in, right?"

"No one gets inside Irishtown Stadium without being searched."

Turnbull nodded, but he was not convinced. The location had been known for at least a week. Someone could have gotten inside after hours and planted weapons. Maybe that was where the rest of the hit team was the prior night.

"Anything else?" Bran asked.

"That luck of the Irish thing," Turnbull said. "Tell O'Riordan to keep doing that."

The rally began. They did have two musicians play live, but neither was technically Irish. Morrissey, who was English but whose parents were Irish, came up and sang "Every Day Is like Sunday," then complained about "the bloody foreigners" and about the lack of vegan snacks in his dressing room. Next, Johnny Rotten of the Sex Pistols, finally out of an English jail for illegal tweeting, came up. His parents were also Irish immigrants. He played "Anarchy in the UK," but substituted "Ireland" for the United Kingdom. Then they did a bizarre duet of "How Soon Is Now?" Left unexplained was how any of this related to the election, but even Turnbull had to admit it kind of rocked.

"I can't believe this concert is being wasted on you," Casey snapped over the air.

"Keep watching," Turnbull commanded as people around him swayed to the distorted guitar stylings.

It was time for a short break to clear the stage. The crowd was in a good place, half-hammered and pleased to have been treated to two alternative music legends. Turnbull positioned himself about thirty feet in front of the stage and patrolled across the crowd back and forth, looking for targets.

None.

He was near the backstage entrance to stage right when he paused to assess the situation. There was about an hour of sunlight left. In the dark, his difficult job would be nearly impossible.

The emcee walked out from the wings across the stage to the mic stand and began warming up the crowd with lots of talk about Ireland for the Irish and taking their country back. It was all arguably illegal under the speech laws, but the government did not dare come in and arrest him. The reaction of the brew-sodden masses would have made the Easter Rebellion look as twee and precious as a Santa Monica gender reveal party.

"And now," the emcee, who apparently played the dad on some Irish sitcom from long ago, began. "Here is the next

Taoiseach of the Republic of Ireland, a patriot, a man of faith, a true Irishman, Rory O'Riordan!"

The crowd erupted, cheering with beer cups held aloft.

O'Riordan came out from stage right, in a dazzling suit, hand aloft in a fist pump. The crowd was chanting now: "Rory, Rory!"

Turnbull knew he should be watching the crowd, but the man was magnetic. Every eye was on him, and he knew what to do with that power.

He got to the mic and took it with one hand, holding the palm of the other one up.

"Thank you, thank you," he said. "But as much as I appreciate it, this is not an MMA championship. This is about our future, whether we remain who we are. So no more 'Rory, Rory, Rory.' It's 'Ireland, Ireland, Ireland'!"

The crowd went insane, screaming and yelling their approval, then quickly disciplining the outcry into a chant of "Ireland, Ireland, Ireland!"

The stadium seemed to shake under the thunderous chant. The government, no doubt, was hearing it, and if it had any sense at all, it would be terrified.

Turnbull's eyes were on O'Riordan, who was beaming back at the crowd, but something was happening on the ground at stage right. Bran was there, conferring with two men who had run up to him. Clearly, they were panicked. Turnbull moved.

"Go, go, go!" Bran told his men as Turnbull reached him. He turned and shouted.

"Two of my boys are down at the stage left entrance to the backstage area. Gunshots."

"No sound," Turnbull said, barely above the chanting. "Silencer. It's happening. They're backstage. You need to get him off stage now, but you can't take him backstage!"

Bran nodded.

"I'll cover front," Turnbull said, moving back into the crowd and keying his mic.

"Casey, it's on!"

"No target yet!"

"You see him, take him!"

"Roger!"

The crowd was heaving and roiling, united as one, and Turnbull was trying to force his way through it toward center stage. O'Riordan was grinning, just letting the moment happen like the master showman he was.

Then he jerked his head and frowned, as if he had noticed something unpleasant. Turnbull heard a crack overhead. A moment later, a speaker behind O'Riordan blew up in a shower of sparks. The crowd was confused; were these pyrotechnics?

Three of Bran's men were bolting across the platform from stage right. The chanting died down. The crowd sensed something was terribly wrong, even if it did not know precisely what.

From his roof, Casey saw the flash in a window in the lower right quadrant of his scope. It was almost imperceptible, like one of those flashes in a field of vision test. He moved the crosshairs just as the room behind the window was illuminated by a second shot.

A man with a rifle. Just a shadow, but enough. Casey exhaled and squeezed. The HK417 was accurized with a special trigger and barrel for long-range shooting. Casey had put hundreds of rounds through it, and they paid off. The top of the sniper's head vanished in a pink puff of mist.

"Got him, Kelly!"

"I need overwatch on the crowd, they're on the ground!" Turnbull shouted. He felt the energy of the audience changing from joy to fear. His right hand found his Wilson under his coat.

The three guards were pulling O'Riordan toward stage right, and he was resisting. No shock. Turnbull kept moving forward, and he heard a scream, a woman's scream, one of primal fear.

Ahead, maybe twenty yards, visible through the thinnest break in the crowd, was a Somali man with an AK-19. He clubbed a woman who was in his way and raised the rifle toward the stage.

The Wilson was up, and Turnbull's left hand clasped onto it. The sight picture was center mass, good enough. Turnbull fired once, then again.

The man staggered, and the Kalashnikov went limp. Not good enough. Turnbull raised the sight a hair and fired the third round of his Mozambique drill. It smashed into the man's face through his left eye, the hollow-point slug blowing out a generous chunk of brain, skull, and blood over the unlucky patrons to the rear. The assassin staggered and dropped.

Turnbull scanned for another target as the crowd began to flee, but he was like a rock in a river. They flowed around him, staying back from the big man with the big gun with the wisp of smoke coming out of the barrel.

A burst of automatic fire – Kalashnikov, which Turnbull would know anywhere – roared in front of him. From the corner of his eye, he saw one of the three guards pulling O'Riordan away stagger and fall face down on the stage.

The target was there, ahead of him, spraying with his rifle, but Turnbull had no shot. Too many innocent civilians. Too much meat in the way. He pressed forward, reaching a clear spot when the man jerked hard, a geyser of blood erupting from his side.

"Got you, you son of a bitch!" Casey yelled over the air.

The shooter was still on his feet, his eyes wild from adrenaline and khat. He started to raise his rifle back to firing position.

Turnbull fired twice, barely clearing a couple of Irishmen who were running past, both still holding their free beers upright and unspilled.

He had to fire low, and the rounds hit the Somali's pelvis, collapsing it. The man dropped, losing his grip on his weapon.

Turnbull pushed forward. The wounded man's bloodshot, unfocused eyes met his.

Turnbull put one in his chest and a second in his forehead. Then he turned back, bolting toward the stage right backstage entrance. As he ran, he did a reload of a fresh mag.

"I don't see the last one or the girl," Casey said.

"They're backstage! I'm heading there." Now Circe's scheme was clear. Plan A: Shoot O'Riordan onstage, either with the sniper or the shooters on the ground.

Plan B: Be backstage waiting for him when his guards dragged him off if Plan A failed.

And it would probably work, Turnbull thought as he pushed through the guards.

"Keep back!" one shouted.

"Here's my ID," Turnbull said, putting the big black Wilson into the man's face. The guard accepted this identification, and Turnbull pushed through into the turmoil.

"Kelly, I have no visibility backstage," Casey shouted.

"Get down here!" Turnbull ordered, pushing a couple of slow-moving micks aside. They fell to the grass by a soundboard in a tangle of arms and legs, all awash with suds and brew. A trio of aging punks passed by him; one was Johnny Rotten, who he overheard observe, "I've played worse gigs."

O'Riordan was ahead of him, screaming at his men to stop pushing. There were several guards around him, as well as Bran.

"You go get Pete off that stage, you see to him!" he ordered, face red with fury. Turnbull appreciated his loyalty to his wounded man, if not the lack of tactical savvy.

"Where the hell were you?" O'Riordan demanded as Turnbull pulled up.

"Killing the sons of bitches who tried to shoot you," Turnbull replied, just as loud and annoyed. "We got three. There's one more and the girl, and they are backstage. You are right where they want you! You need to go now!"

"I've done enough running!" O'Riordan shouted. All around them, terrified civilians were fleeing.

"He's right!" shouted Bran. "You need to go!"

"I'm not going!" O'Riordan insisted, puffing up his chest. Nobody was moving him any further if he chose not to be moved.

Bran's eyes met Turnbull's, who mouthed an obscenity. Turnbull reassessed his weapon choice. The Rattler was still hanging under his coat, but an automatic weapon here was going to probably take out a bunch of civvies, too. He stayed with his Wilson 1911.

They both began scanning the dwindling crowd of roadies, VIPs, and groupies. Turnbull saw nothing but running, panicked people. But Bran saw something else.

"Gun!" he shouted, and Turnbull followed his eyes.

There was a Somali with an AK, maybe twenty feet off. The man was raising it, yelling "Allah Akbar!"

He was not as fast as Turnbull, and there was a momentary break in the stream of terrified civilians. The two hollow-point slugs smashed into his sternum, and the man went down on his back, the rifle dropping into the grass.

Turnbull took aim for the man's head as he lay on the ground, and the blade of the front sight lined up just as what felt like a sledgehammer smashed into his side.

What hit him was the Rattler hanging under his coat; what hit his weapon became clear as he fell. About thirty feet away, her silhouette broken by passing patrons, was a woman with a silenced automatic pistol – Turnbull's mind pegged it as a SIG even as he fell. She had black hair, was pretty, and had a medium build. And then he landed on his side in the grass.

She pivoted and fired three times toward O'Riordan. Turnbull brought up his weapon and took a shot one-handed, a wild shot. A hit? He couldn't see – maybe he winged her, maybe the round went wild. She vanished. One moment she was there, then the next a clump of screaming Irish passed by, and when they cleared. Turnbull's shaky sight picture was empty. She was gone.

He got to his knees. The pain was like an ice pick between his ribs; one or more were most definitely broken. He heard O'Riordan's voice.

"Bran, laddie! Bran!"

The candidate was kneeling next to his friend's body. One look at Bran's face and Turnbull knew; he had seen dying enough to know what it looked like. O'Riordan lifted his head up.

"He pushed me out of the way and took the bullets!" O'Riordan said, his face betraying his struggle to comprehend what had just happened.

Turnbull said nothing. He considered giving chase after Circe, but which way would he go even if he could run? Every breath was a spear to his side; he wasn't running anywhere for a while.

Casey came up, toting his rifle. That had probably been sufficient ID to get backstage, assuming there were still people checking. The stadium was emptying out fast.

"Oh, hell," Casey said as he looked over the scene.

"Circe," Turnbull said.

"Go after her?"

"She's in the wind," Turnbull said. "We'll get her next time."

O'Riordan was weeping, cradling his childhood friend.

"He's dead," the candidate moaned, as if it needed to be said.

"You're not," Turnbull said. "Because of him."

O'Riordan looked up into Turnbull's pitiless eyes.

"Now get on your damn feet and go win this for Bran," the American commanded.

"For Ireland," O'Riordan said, wiping his eyes with the sleeve of his blood-splattered $30,000 suit.

"Hey," someone shouted from a few meters away. "This one's still alive!"

"We were never here," Turnbull said to O'Riordan.

"Deniability," Casey added.

The Irishman nodded.

There was just one thing left to do before they exfiltrated. Turnbull, painfully and with effort, walked over to where a pair of the MMA guards stood over the Somali gunman. He was on his back, somehow still breathing – albeit with difficulty and lots of coughing – despite two deep, red holes in his chest. He was saying something, blood and khat-inflected saliva erupting from his mouth with each syllable. It was in a language Turnbull did not understand. But the man's widening eyes demonstrated that he understood Turnbull's language as the American raised the .45 to the shooter's face and spoke.

"Die."

2.

"Business or pleasure?" the leering man asked her, his breath betraying the several Jack Daniels and Cokes she had watched him toss back.

Medea Ekaterine Villareal turned to the American sitting next to her in the window seat of the Delta 737ER-900 and forced a smile. He was older, probably in his fifties, with a citizenship pin on his jacket's lapel. He was overjoyed when she sat down beside him in seat 4C of first class; it beat spending the flight next to some sweaty whale or another chatty guy like him. The man had made some tentative attempts to talk to her, but she had brushed them off with a smile and buried herself in a woman's novel that fit the role she had adopted: single, late-thirties, attractive but not memorable.

"Pleasure," answered Genevieve Juliet Burnham. That was the name on her documents. If she had answered "business," that would have been an invitation for him to ask what business she was in. Asking a woman about her pleasure was more difficult; maybe he would take the hint and leave her alone. To emphasize her disinterest, she made a show of diving back into her book.

Her book, which she picked up in the Toronto airport bookshop, was titled *When the Smiling Swan Dreams.* It was an utterly frivolous navel-gazing story about a spunky American woman who finds love with a strong, yet gentle, expert on indigenous peoples during a trip to Canada. The story was set in Canada because Europe, a traditional destination for lonely women looking to give love a second chance, was on the edge of civil war. This genre was never set in the new United States of America; red American men typically embraced what was once labeled "toxic masculinity" and refused to share feelings like some men used to before the Split. The story's heroine made a point of not serving in the military, and therefore not being a citizen; she also refused to carry a gun. In the new United States, she was what passed for an edgy rebel.

The novel wasn't illegal propaganda under the new United States Code; this kind of popular entertainment never went over the line into communist subversion like so much entertainment did before the Split. It instead reflected the frustrations of a sliver of the population, most of whom were without the franchise because they had never volunteered to serve and earned the right to be citizens. They had no vote, and thus no say, in their country. They chafed at living in the half of the old United States run by people determined to never again tolerate the trends that had caused the government to break in two.

That audience was why some popular writers in the new United States filled their works with sly digs at their country; too prim, too proper, too brutal, too stifling for gentle free spirits. But America's free spirits rarely emigrated to the People's Republic, where traditional values were rejected rather than enforced and empathy supposedly reigned. *Smiling Swan* was just another bestselling fantasy for that demographic of women who enjoyed the safety and prosperity of the United States but wanted to maintain their distance from what it took to create and maintain it. Once, before the Crisis and the Treaty of St. Louis divided the USA into red and blue, they would have planted signs in their front yards indicating how hate had no home there, how they loved science, and how no human is illegal, then sat back with some mid-priced Chardonnay and enjoyed their smug superiority over the people who made their world possible. Of course, Chardonnay had mostly come from California, and that was now deep in the blue.

This was the role Medea Ekaterine Villareal had assumed, except she was inhabiting the version from the Great White North. It made sense to fly on a Canadian passport – the Canadian government was thoroughly compromised by the intelligence services of both the United States of America and the People's Republic of North America, so valid Canadian identities were easy to obtain. Even better, most countries considered Canucks harmless, so they rarely got a second look at border crossings.

Her seatmate was not discouraged by her performative reading. Maybe he was lonely, maybe it was the booze, but he was not yet ready to give up.

"Lots of fun to be had in Dallas, if you know where to look," he told her. He paused, hoping she would ask him to elaborate.

"Oh," Villareal said, not bothering to lift her head out of the novel. The hero and heroine were about to kiss in a First Peoples' graveyard that they had saved from being ploughed over to build condos. Villareal found the entire book not only an abomination and a potentially criminal celebration of the cisgender/patriarchal paradigm, capitalism (the heroine was a powerful but emotionally unsatisfied lawyer at a huge Atlanta law firm), and white superiority – she assumed everyone involved was white, though that never came up in the text. Back in the People's Republic, it would not have passed the first layer of the literary publishing oversight process.

"I was in Canada on business. Oil," he told her as if invited to. Villareal quelled the frown that almost manifested on her lips; of course, this creature would be complicit in earthmurder. The man continued.

"I hate having to clear customs in Dallas, as if there's anything in Canada worth bringing back. Plus, it's at least fifteen minutes in line to get my gun back from the gun check desk. I carry a Glock."

Of course he did.

"I'm Canadian," Villareal said, hoping that highlighting his faux pas would get him to stop talking.

"Well, you can get a temporary gun while you're in America. It's cheap. You'll want to have a gun."

Villareal could not resist.

"They don't allow guns in Canada or the People's Republic. Is the new United States really so crime-ridden that you need a deadly weapon?"

"As the man said, an armed society is a polite society."

"What man was that?"

"I'm not sure," the passenger replied, looking a bit surprised at the question. "But he said it, and I think it's true. Plus, being armed makes a point. You can't be a citizen if you aren't prepared to fight." He pointed at his citizenship pin. "This means I served. Navy. And now I am a full citizen. I can vote, be elected, that sort of thing."

"I don't like guns," she declared.

"Canadians," the man said, shaking his head. In fact, she had a SIG P229 with several magazines and a suppressor waiting for her in Texas – she was not going to risk carrying it outbound through Canadian customs; U.S. Customs would think her being packed inbound was cool. But she did not need the pistol to stop this dreadful conversation. She figured that she could crush his windpipe with a quick, deadly blow. That would silence him once and for all.

But it proved unnecessary. The bloom was off the rose of the budding romance her seatmate had been hoping for, and the only thing he said to her during the rest of the flight was a gruff "Enjoy Texas" as they deplaned at DFW.

She walked through the terminal. Her right arm hurt, so she shifted her bag to her left hand, the one she was using to tow her carry-on. The stores and restaurants offended her; the people appalled her.

Villareal always felt the exhilarating tension that came with crossing a border under a false name. The U.S. Customs officer took her deep blue passport with the royal coat of arms embossed on the front and scanned it. The name 'Genevieve Juliet Burnham' popped up.

Villareal scrutinized the officer's face for any sign of anything but the vague disinterest he had shown toward the dozens of entrants who preceded her in line. She detected none. If she had, her options would be limited. He had his Glock 47, and she had her bare hands.

"Business or pleasure, Ms. Burnham?" he asked, bored.

"Pleasure," she said.

"Welcome to the United States and to Texas," he said, handing back her passport. She smiled and moved on to the rental car shuttle. All she carried was a knock-off Coach purse and a small Samsonite carry-on which contained absolutely nothing that would have attracted even the slightest interest in the unlikely event Customs had decided to send her for secondary screening.

Villareal rented a Ford Taurus and was able to drive it adequately thanks to the refresher training she had undergone in Minnesota before the mission. It had been a while since she had driven. Even if she had not lived in Mogadishu, she would probably not have received authorization for a private motor vehicle unless it was operationally necessary. Her actual privilege level was only 6, even though she was half-Latinx – her father was a Cuban communist who came to America because he thought it was ridiculous that he should have to endure the deprivations his ideology inflicted upon the Cuban people. He was part of the cadre, after all. A revolutionary deserved some perks; that included a private school for his daughter, Medea. He gave her the middle name "Ekaterine" in honor of Joseph Stalin's first wife, Ekaterine "Kato" Svanidze. Kato died of typhoid and Stalin actually mourned her; not so much his second wife Nadezhda Sergeyevna Alliluyeva. Stalin drove her to shoot herself.

Now, Villareal had to drive south towards San Antonio. It was a five-hour trek down Interstate 35 with the cruise control pegged at 89 to avoid being pulled over. The temperature was in the 90s, so her window was up and the air conditioner was on, though air conditioning was an earthcrime. She drove with her left hand on the wheel – her right arm ached. It had not fully healed.

She passed several military convoys; the fascist regime was always flexing its muscles, flaunting its warmongery. There was also a plethora of private cars, each one murdering just a little bit of the Earth. And the accursed American flags were everywhere, the old Stars and Stripes, but with many fewer stars than when she had been forced to endure it as a child. It occurred to her that she was not sure about the current People's Republic flag; it kept changing as the stripes shifted position to keep up with the latest arrangement of the hierarchy of oppression.

Everything about the United States grated on her, like the fat people. In the People's Republic, the people were mostly thin due to their healthy, calorie-restricted diets. Certainly, one could get a permit to be obese to avoid fat genocide; fatism was nearly as wicked as transphobia. But the food rationing was actually a feature, she told herself, instead of a bug.

She pulled off the freeway to stop at a truck stop near Temple. Her meeting was not for another 30 minutes, and she took the opportunity to refuel. The heat was intense, nothing like back in Mogadishu, where the Minnesota weather was either mild or frigid. It bothered her a bit that she did not have to present a ration card or verify her privilege level. The red's damnable abundance grated on her even though she knew it all came from the unjust toil of marginalized folx. She looked around for some; one black truck driver was standing, smoking and joking with a half-dozen white ones. He had no idea how oppressed he was.

The gas was cheap– a couple of American dollars a gallon. She only needed a few to top off; what cost her under twenty would have cost ten times as much in the People's Republic equivalent, which were commonly called "Baracks" in honor of the picture on the 100 credit bill.

She parked and got out. A man in a cowboy hat and bolo tie – such offensive costumes that mocked the genocide of indigenous persons were banned back home – approached her. He wore a .45 caliber revolver on his hip. In fact, almost everyone was armed.

The cowboy raised his hand, and her breath caught in her throat. But he was only touching the brim of the butchers of indigenous peoples' headgear.

"Afternoon, ma'am," he said with a Texas drawl, then strode past.

The racist bastard assumed her gender. He got it right, though. Her pronouns were officially she/them– but that was not the point. Villareal shivered. She was swimming in a sea of monsters. She always was while on a mission in the red.

Inside the minimart, her eyes were assaulted by the variety and colorful packaging of the snacks and other products; she remembered that from when she was young, before the Split, before the People's Republic brought some order and planning to the economy. Villareal passed by a shelf with several brands of tampons, and briefly considered buying one; maybe they would work better than the PR designs, not being designed to take into account testicles.

No, that was a wrongthought. She was being seduced by materialism. That's what these bastards did – bought you off with cheap and abundant quality goods. Besides, the packages all came with a picture of some smiling, conventionally attractive cisgender bitch.

Villareal was here in red America, but she did not have to be complicit.

The entire store was an abominable waste, a bribe to the people to surrender their class consciousness for baubles and trinkets. Yet, the people were eagerly buying into it. This was especially true of the many oppressed peoples she saw – black, Latinx, even indigenous. They all seemed happy; none of them appeared even the slightest bit aware of the fascist hell they had been consigned to.

And, of course, there was the total erasure of trans and furry folx. There were none to be seen, nor any signs, posters, or billboards commemorating their various days and months of recognition.

She glanced at her Movado, which she picked up in Canada. Fifteen minutes. She looked around. There was a Wendy's right through a passage between the cash registers and the hot dogs rolling under a heat lamp. There was also a coffee station with four or five varieties. None of it was responsible coffee; they shamelessly used the grounds just once.

Villareal seethed. She went into the restroom, dreading it but needing to, and instead of being pleased that it was not a disgusting mess – nothing demonstrates the tragedy of the commons like public restrooms – she was infuriated at its cleanliness and the fact that not only were there ample paper towels and toilet paper rolls but that there were extras piled on the counter and no one was stealing them.

Heading back through the minimart toward the Wendy's, she surveyed the patrons. Some were obviously truckers waiting for the showers. There were several soldiers. A family with three kids– Villareal considered the wife practically a broodmare– was gathered near the souvenir display. All of the adults were armed, of course, even the girls behind the registers. And all were, as the man said, polite.

She went into the restaurant. There was a counter and behind it the kitchen. The menu offered dozens of entree choices, and this always overwhelmed her when she came into a red restaurant. She recalled going to such places as a kid before the Split, nagging her father to take her to McDonald's and getting a lecture about the exploitation of the workers and the Earth for her trouble, but it was worth it to get a Happy Meal.

The sheer number of choices that the menu board presented was not only confusing but insulting; *of course*, the citizens of the People's Republic would never allow this kind of wasteful exercise, but a nagging thought picked at her mind. The People's Republic couldn't do this even if it wished to.

It made her hate the reds even more, something she would have thought impossible.

Villareal was forced to buy a single cheese combo – after all, she had to eat. The girl at the counter broke off her gossip session with her co-worker and met Villareal at the register. She was maybe twenty, wearing a cute .38 snub-nosed in a thigh holster that fell below the hem of her skirt. She seemed perplexed when Villareal tried to hand over the brand-new VISA card she had been issued for this mission. Setting up real credit card accounts took time and effort; that the PR intelligence service went to that length reaffirmed the importance of her task. For a fraction of a moment, Villareal wondered if she had been found out, but then the woman spoke.

"Honey, you can just tap it." She pointed at a device on the counter, and Villareal remembered. Carefully, Villareal laid the card on the device, and the transaction went through.

"Just a few minutes, honey. Name?"

"What?"

"For the order, hon." Being called "honey" and its variations grated; it was sexist even though the worker presented as a shameless ciswoman. She'd be lucky to only get sent for reeducation back in the blue. But Villareal did not break character.

"Genevieve."

"That's a pretty name, hon. With a 'J'?"

"No, a 'G'."

The counter girl smiled and passed her a cup, then pointed helpfully to the soda fountain.

"Right over there, honey."

Villareal took it, walked over, and selected Coke – she wanted to see what red Coca-Cola tasted like. Infuriatingly, it was better – much better – than the blue version.

Villareal stepped over to the wall, with her back to it so she could watch both the minimart entrance and the door to the parking lot. She noted that there were no cameras. There used to be when she was a kid, and there were a lot in the blue, though robberies were less the impetus than detecting subversion. Perhaps there were no cameras because there were no robbers; perhaps the armed citizens would handle the problem without involving the police.

Above her was a video screen, and she watched an advertisement for some kind of vitamin. There were no ads in the blue; you either bought what was available that day or you got nothing. The commercial was followed by a news report on the unrest in Peru. Villareal watched this with great interest. The regime media was calling it a "communist coup," as if that were a bad thing. The Chinese and People's Republic were blamed – given credit – for the chaos.

Villareal smiled. She hoped that the chaos there had not even begun.

Next, there was a report about what they called a "child molester." The red monsters were going to execute the poor minor attracted person that night and broadcast it. It was sickening how they made love a capital crime – in the enlightened People's Republic, children had sexual autonomy.

Next, there was a slick advertisement with an eager announcer shilling the military and the benefits of becoming a fascist stormtrooper: "America needs you in its armed forces! Enlist now and earn all the privileges of a full citizen! Voting! G.I. Bill! Holding office! Preferences for government benefits!" The footage showed young and some older people in uniform, each announcing that they were doing their part. At the end, a web link flashed on-screen and the announcer asked, "Would you like to know more?"

"I'm thinking of doing it," the counter girl told her friend. "Joining up. Being a citizen."

"I don't like taking orders," the other one answered, blind to the irony.

"Well, I don't want to be hawking hamburgers in Temple, Texas, for the rest of my life."

The other one turned to the crew in the back that was preparing Villareal's order.

"Hey, Susie's gonna be a citizen! We're going to have to call her 'ma'am' or something!"

They all laughed, all but Susie.

"Oh, you're saying I can't make it? That's it. I'm signing up tomorrow."

The others found this even more hilarious, and Susie pouted until one of the back-of-the-house guys pushed out a burger and fries. Susie placed them on a tray and handed them over to Villareal. The blue agent accepted it and carried it to a table by the windows with a good line of sight to both entrances.

She waited. He was late. She was annoyed, but she reminded herself that an excessive focus on punctuality was a component of the white supremacy paradigm. Ten minutes late, her contact arrived. He was white.

She had seen his 2016 Camry pull into the lot and park off in the far corner, as instructed. She was more interested in whether anyone else pulled in after him. No one did. She was satisfied he was not tailed. If he had been followed, she could have got up, walked out to her car, and driven away. Her contact would not even have known it was her.

Ellis Meany had tousled dark hair and a thin goatee, as well as black glasses. Over his shoulder was a small, black pack. He wore distressed jeans and a vintage Levi's jacket over a Sonic Youth t-shirt. Villareal had no idea what Sonic Youth was, assuming it was an opposition group of some kind and wondering how he could be so stupid as to tempt fate by wearing it.

He did not openly carry a gun. That made him a greater nonconformist than his concert tee did.

Meany seemed distinctly uncomfortable as he entered the restaurant through the parking lot door, walked inside, and looked around. No one else paid him any attention; he was just a young man who looked like he had come from what was left of the outsider community in Austin. Looking around, he saw Villareal; when she did not look away, as most attractive women did in the rare cases their eyes met his, he walked over to her and sat down on the four-top's bench seat directly across from her.

"I like trains," he said, his voice quivering.

"My favorite thing is pumpkins."

He relaxed just a bit.

"Nice to finally meet you, Hannah," he said. "Ellis Meany, He/them."

"She/them," Villareal replied with a bashful smile. She noted that Susie at the counter had not heard this latest alias.

Meany smiled, a bit too eager. "It's so good to meet and interact like decent humans," he said. "We had a grad student TA who would meet secretly with us to expose the patriarchal paradigm. I have to keep my gender identity a secret. It murders my soul."

"You're very brave to resist like this," Villareal said sweetly.

He puffed up.

"I take huge risks. But why did we have to meet here?" he asked. "We should have met in San Antonio. We could have got to...somewhere nicer."

Villareal ignored his question. But she had an answer – she could easily see if he was followed, and they were far enough away from the objective so as not to draw attention to it if he had been.

"Do you have what we asked for?" she asked.

"Yes, sure," Meany said, handing over the small black pack. She took it and opened the top. It was a SIG Sauer P229 pistol, several loaded magazines, and a suppressor. "Got it at a gun show, so there's no paperwork. Untraceable. Made me sick being there. I hate these people."

She closed the pack and put it to her side.

"Tell me about where my folx are," she asked.

Even as Meany started to speak, she saw a local sheriff's Ford Explorer pull into the lot and park near the restaurant's door. On the side, it read "K9 OFFICER – STAY BACK."

"They are waiting in the building, like they are supposed to be. Twenty of them." Meany pushed a paper across the table with an address in San Antonio. "For your GPS."

"How are they?"

"I assume okay. I hope they're still there. Most don't speak English, and they barely listened to me."

"Did anyone see them, notice them?"

"No. I mean, I'm just saying they don't seem very focused on the struggle. They pray a lot, and chew those leaves."

"Khat. It's part of their culture."

"Oh, I mean, sure, yeah, that's cool then. I'm not disrespecting their culture. They just don't seem interested in, you know, the revolution."

"We appreciate *your* contribution, you and your comrades."

She was talking to Meany, but watching the cop. He got out of the SUV with his dog – she did not know what breed, but it looked fierce. It wore a harness that said "DEPUTY GILLIGAN."

"You know, I was thinking that maybe it's time that I, you know, went north. Defected."

"A cop is coming inside – no, don't look. Just keep talking."

"I – where was I? Oh, yeah. Okay, there's heat here, you know? The feds arrested a couple of folks from another cell last week. My people, well, if they get taken, they will totally spill on me, and you know what they do to spies."

"What do they do to spies?" she asked, her eyes on the cop and the dog he was leading up the opposite aisle to the counter.

"They hang us."

Meany glanced right, and he went even paler.

"He's got a dog," Meany said.

"So?"

"I've, I've got pot," he said plaintively.

"So?" Villareal repeated.

"It's illegal here. The dog might smell it."

"Stay calm," she directed him. The sweetness in her voice was gone.

The officer went to the counter. He was maybe thirty, so Susie was still in play. She seemed happy to see him, and they shot the breeze.

"You guys gotta get me into the blue," Meany said, leaning in. "I can't take it here. You know what it's like to be here and not be a citizen? To be, you know, artistic."

"Are you an artist?"

"I'm a poet," he said proudly. "I was at the University of Texas in Austin until I got kicked out for protesting fascists. Now, I have to work. Look, I want to go someplace where it's not all capitalism and warmongering and racism."

"Keep your voice down."

"I can go to the blue and be a poet, do my art."

"So, you would come to the People's Republic and be assigned as a poet?" Villareal asked politely, stifling a smile. He would be lucky to be assigned as a janitor. What was it with these red defectors – they always assumed when the revolution came, others would do the dirty work and they would sit around smoking pot and doodling their precious etchings.

Parasites, but they had to be cultivated. The People's Republic needed secret allies inside the heart of the red.

The deputy got his double cheeseburger and fries. Susie gave him a coffee she had poured from the machine by the drive-through window and presented it to him triumphantly. He and Gilligan the dog began walking back into the dining area, this time down their aisle.

"He's coming," Meany whispered unnecessarily, and a bit desperately.

Gilligan the dog alerted and then sniffed at Meany. Meany froze; the cop stood there, holding his tray. Villareal sat still; she was not used to dogs, as they were considered bourgeois and frowned upon if allowed to live at all in the blue.

"He likes you," the deputy said.

"Yeah," said Meany, leaning away from the animal.

"Come on, Gilligan," the deputy said. "Let's go. You folks have a nice day."

The pair walked on. Meany shuddered.

"You're fine," Villareal said. The cop and his dog took a seat several booths away. The deputy glanced at them, but then focused on his lunch. Sure that he could not overhear them, she continued.

"Now, did you go by the airbase?" Villareal asked Meany.

"It looks like, well, an airbase. I never served, so I wouldn't know."

"The guards?"

"Some at the gate, but no, like, tanks or anything."

"We can deal with some gate guards. Did the weapons get delivered?"

"Weapons?" asked Meany, confused. "Besides your gun?"

There was supposed to be a weapons delivery; she would have to sort that out in San Antonio herself. She had not fully briefed Meany on the purpose behind the twenty Somalis that the People's Republic had, with considerable effort, smuggled across the border wall into Texas. That was no small thing; the stretch of border protecting the new USA from Mexico was almost as fortified as the border protecting Mexico from the People's Republic.

"Forget you heard that," Villareal said, the sweetness back. "You have done your part by finding the safehouse and meeting me. The People's Republic will not forget the sacrifices of you and your comrades."

"Well, when can I come over? I mean, to the PR? Maybe we could, you know, meet."

"We will tell you when and make arrangements. Until then, be ready to assist in the struggle."

"The sooner this fascist regime is finished, the better. I don't see why you blues don't just invade. The people will be happy to help overthrow this Nazi government."

Villareal smiled as if amused by a child, which, in a way, he was. The allies in the red were useful, but immature and even foolish. The Americans were not going to free themselves until their minds were freed, and they would resist that. Most would never accept change. This Meany character spent too much time with his comrades. He did not understand that these creatures, these Americans, were beyond saving. They would never be won over. They must be broken, and many of them must be eliminated. But that was down the road. The likes of Meany would not have the stomach to do what was necessary.

She put down her food and stretched her right arm. It was hurting again.

"You okay?" Meany asked.

"I'm fine."

"Here, we have to pay for our medical care. It's like genocide. But you get the best care in the PR and for free."

Villareal grunted in the affirmative. She had been wounded in the service of the PR, and she still was not fully healed. No, it was not the fault of socialism; it was the need to defend against red aggression that caused any flaws in the system. She swallowed the last morsel of her cheeseburger.

"I can't believe you eat that crap," he told her. In fact, it was the best meat she had eaten in quite some time, a fact that had already irritated her.

"I'm vegan," Meany explained. Was that an air of superiority? People in the PR would kill for this meal, and here he was talking about his bespoke diet.

"I definitely want to see you come to the People's Republic," she said pleasantly. He beamed and smiled, though he should not have.

Her eyes flicked up and met the deputy's. He was watching them. Then he looked down at his fries.

"I'm going to leave," Villareal told Meany. "You are going to wait a few minutes before you leave."

"Is that it for this assignment? Will I see you again?"

"I think you'll see me again."

The woman Meany knew as Hannah got up and walked out, passing the deputy and Gilligan (she smiled at them) and going out through the parking lot door.

Meany took out his iPhone 22, opened it with his face, and looked at Twitter. What he saw disgusted him – so many fascists. That @FullAutoGalt guy belonged in a camp – someday, these fascists would pay.

After five minutes, he got up. The officer was gone – no, there he was, outside at the wheel of his cruiser with the dog in the backseat. The cop was doing something with his own phone and glanced up, then back to his screen as Meany walked by.

Having parked in the remote northern corner of the lot, as instructed, it took him a bit to walk across the sweltering pavement to his beat-up Camry.

He had his hand on the door handle and was pulling the driver's door open when the police cruiser pulled up beside him.

"Hold on a minute," the deputy said as he stepped out of the SUV.

Meany froze, his breath caught in his throat. He turned to the cop. The deputy was standing there, looking him over. The dog was locked in the back, but was giving him the stink eye through the rear side window.

"Yes, officer?"

"I'm a deputy. Now, I don't see your weapon. Is it concealed?"

"I, I don't carry a gun," Meany said, which made the deputy even more suspicious.

"Just keep your hands where I can see them," the deputy said. His own hand was hovering over the Glock on his hip. "Now, my dog alerted on you when we walked by back in the store, and he's pretty good at smelling marijuana. Do you have any marijuana on you, sir?"

"I...I," Meany said.

"I need a yes or a no, sir."

"Uh, no."

"Okay, I need to search you for weapons for my own protection."

"Look, I haven't done anything wrong."

"I need you to step to the rear of your car."

"You're just hassling me because I look different."

"Sir, step over there *now*." The deputy pulled his handcuffs out of their pouch.

"I'm sick of this fascist oppression!"

"All right, now you need to..."

The deputy stopped in mid-sentence. He stared past Meany, who saw blood trickle from the cop's mouth before he fell in a heap. Gilligan went crazy inside the SUV.

Villareal was there, standing outside her Taurus, her SIG pistol with suppressor in her hand. She lowered it and looked around. No one seemed to have noticed what happened.

"You killed him, Hannah," said Meany, unbelieving. It was only then dawning on him that he was far deeper in this than he was ready for.

Villareal raised the pistol and shot him in the face. Meany dropped to the pavement by his open driver's door.

She turned to the dog. It seemed like it was on the verge of tearing its way out of the police cruiser. She was unsure of how dogs worked – maybe it having smelled her could make it useful for finding her. No sense in taking chances. She pointed the SIG and fired.

Villareal got back on I-35 heading south. They would be looking for her now. With Meany alive, it would have been easy for them – he would have rolled over after a couple of punches. He had only been playacting as a revolutionary operative. She was the real deal, and she was confident she could remain one step ahead of them for the next 48 or so hours, until she pulled off her mission and exfiltrated from the red. After all, she was the one they feared, the one they called Circe.

3.

Three hours of shooting in the Texas sun left his fingers raw from loading mags, as well as a slight ringing in his ears despite ear protection. That summed up Kelly Turnbull's afternoon. It was a good day. That he was out on the range alone, unbothered by the incessant chatter of other humans, had made it even better.

His apartment in Dallas was depressing, but he was saving money for his ranch. Not a lot yet – even a light colonel's salary with no family allowance only left so much – but give it time, he told himself. A place out in the middle of nowhere with just his dog seemed like a worthy life goal.

Of course, the first thing he did after he got home and took out the dog was clean his Wilson Combat .45. It was a few months old – his previous M1911 had to be disposed of, since he had left its ballistic evidence all over Dublin when he was there on a mission a few months before. Luckily, the guys from Task Force Zulu had carte blanche to obtain whatever shooting irons they preferred – one of the few perks of the gig besides the ability to do pretty much whatever needed to be done to accomplish their mission. He had a Kimber 1911 somewhere in his apartment that he used when he was between Wilsons – the manufacturer usually had a backlog of orders.

Satisfied that his duty handgun was good to go, he fed the dog and then himself. There was one Jim Hanson's Man Meat ribeye left, but he could have sworn it was a New York strip and, besides that, he didn't feel like cooking. Fortunately, he had some Popeyes fried chicken left over from the other night, extra spicy. He ate it cold and was happy; he had eaten both much less and much worse, so he did not complain.

Now, he needed to relax. Turnbull flopped back into his favorite leather chair, took a swig off a Shiner, and hit the remote on his Samsung. Fox News was on, something about riots in Lima. Apparently, the pro-Chi-Com faction was trying to pull off a coup. No doubt the PR was involved somehow, the bastards. Though he had worked south of the border, he had never been to Peru; he hoped not to break that streak.

There was something about a shootout at a truck stop with a sheriff's deputy and his dog being killed – that sort of thing did not happen much anymore. The next story demonstrated part of the reason why there was so much less crime in the new United States. The talking head on the tube was reporting on a pervert who hurt kids; he was going to hang live in a few minutes as an object lesson. Turnbull had no objection to this and felt the creep was getting off easy. He would have been smart to have defected, since they loved his kind in the People's Republic and even had a nice, innocent-sounding name for these creeps – "minor attracted persons." But Turnbull had seen enough people die and had no intention of watching the execution. The degenerate was not worth his time.

He changed the channel with the remote. The screen informed him that he was watching season three, episode four of *The Dennis Miller Mysteries*. There was the star wearing a trench coat in what looked like a police station, talking to his captain.

"Damnit, Miller, I need results!" bellowed his boss – Turnbull recognized the actor as Bernie Casey III.

"Hey, throttle back on the shamus shaming, Chief," Miller replied. "You dealt me a hand with a viable suspect roster that's shorter than the track list on *Greatest Hits of the Starland Vocal Band.*"

Turnbull sighed. The dog growled, bullying him for more food. Sometimes, Turnbull wondered why he had ever bothered to bring that puppy out in Indian Country all those years ago. This was an extremely demanding animal.

"Leave me alone," Turnbull said and took another swig.

His cell phone rang. The caller ID was "PAIN IN MY ASS."

"Hello, Clay," he said.

"Kelly, get into the office."

"I just sat down with a Shiner."

"Pour it out, I need you sharp," Clay Deeds replied. Turnbull recognized his boss's tone – serious.

"I'll be there in thirty," Turnbull replied, then added, "How long am I going to be gone? Do I need to do something about the dog?"

"Yeah, have someone watch your mutt."

Turnbull hung up. Great. Better pack a bag. On the screen, Dennis Miller was being introduced to his new partner, a bodacious woman packing a sawed-off shotgun.

"Chief, I don't need a new partner, savvy? I'd rather take a body shot of Bob Crane's New Year's Day morning jacuzzi water off the hairy torso of Ernest Borgnine."

"Mill-*er*!" howled his boss. The frustration reminded Turnbull of Clay, less the pop cultural references.

Turnbull flicked off the Samsung. His pet sat staring at him, knowing something was up.

"I think the real mystery is what the hell Miller's talking about," Turnbull told his dog. "Okay, you're going back to the kids next door for a while." That would cost him a ten-spot a day, but those kids liked the animal, and the animal seemed to like them.

He stood up and slid the pristine .45 into the loop on his belt.

"Look, I'm probably a bear, maybe a daddy, but you're definitely an otter. You're too old to be a twink," Hiram Clanton told Casey Warner, who nodded in agreement. He saw Turnbull walk into the otherwise deserted office suite in downtown Dallas.

"Hey, Kelly," he bellowed.

"What are you two talking about?" Turnbull began, then thought better of it. "I don't want to know."

"Any idea what this secret squirrel huddle is all about?" asked Casey. He was taking the opportunity to clean his Walther PDP Pro SD pistol. It had a suppressor-ready barrel.

"No idea," Turnbull said. "Peru's going to hell, but I don't know what that might have to do with us."

"Which one's Peru?" asked Clanton. He was a big guy, with a full beard, a lot of tatts, and an accent that crawled out of some holler in Tennetucky. He carried a Smith & Wesson Model 500 in S&W .500 – a huge gun that seemed small in his gigantic paws. Casey often mocked him for choosing a revolver with a five-shot capacity instead of a modern semiautomatic, to which Clanton would reply that he only needed one shot per target.

"Peruvian food's incredible. Chicken, french fries. I think they cook guinea pigs," Casey said.

"I've eaten worse." Clanton had. They all had. Clanton was a former Air Force pararescueman; one of their key tasks was retrieving downed pilots, and he could easily toss a flyboy over his shoulder and carry him. He had decades of special ops experience, but Hiram Clanton probably ate worse regularly growing up. He also learned to be one hell of a tracker long before he joined the Air Force – if you didn't track, you didn't eat.

Turnbull collapsed into a generic office chair. There was a jack o' lantern sitting on the desk in an adjacent cubicle. A number of them had spooks and ghosties hanging on the room dividers. He suspected that on the 31st, if he was in the office and not out in the field, Casey would definitely show up in costume.

"Clay says he's inbound," Clanton told him.

"Where's Mundi?" Turnbull asked.

"I think he's over the line," Casey said. He meant that Edmundo "Mundi" Vega was in the blue, on some operation in the People's Republic. Of course, they had no idea what it was; only Clay Deeds did. He was the chess master, and they were, if not pawns, bishops, or maybe rooks.

The door clicked open at the far end of the suite, and Deeds came in, confirming the door was shut behind him. Then he walked past the deserted cubicles until he reached his men.

"Gentlemen, thanks for coming out," he told them.

"I don't recall having a choice," Turnbull grumbled.

"You didn't. But you gentlemen are my 'Break Glass in Case of Emergency' team, and I don't break the glass unless I need to."

"What's up, boss?" Clanton asked.

"Circe."

Turnbull leaned forward. "What?"

"You heard me. Your girlfriend Circe popped up."

"My ribs still hurt from where she shot me," Turnbull said. "Well, let's go get her. Where is she?"

"Here."

"Here?" asked Casey before Turnbull could react. "Like 'in the red' here?"

"Like in Texas here."

"How do you know?" Turnbull asked.

"Well, we don't, not with absolute certainty, but we can make a pretty good guess," Deeds explained. "Yesterday, someone capped a sheriff's deputy and his canine at a truck stop off I-35 near Temple, Texas. Deputy Ronald Coltrane, age 31, a former 11 Bravo in the 4th Infantry Division. And his dog, Gilligan."

"Somebody needs to pay," Turnbull said coldly. Deeds continued.

"Killed a civilian too, an Ellis Meany, age 27. He was a little commie poser out of Austin. Our counter-intel guys were aware of his cell, but they didn't think it was anything more than some malcontent UT dropouts. But right before he got shot – nine mil to the forehead – he met up with a mystery woman in the fast food joint at the truck stop."

"You think it was Circe?" Turnbull asked. "She's already toast if I meet her, but you throw in a cop and a dog, and it's full on grapes of wrath level payback time."

"The dead cop means a full court press, so a lot of folks have been digging, and they dug up a lot," Deeds explained. "Tracked her credit card. She bought gas and a burger. Genevieve Juliet Burnham. Late thirties, single. Came into DFW this morning out of Montreal, flying on a Canadian passport. We reached out to our sources in the Great White North. The identity was professional, good enough for initial scrutiny, but they dug, and it's fake."

"This Meany guy must have brought her the gun," Turnbull said. "No way she'd risk trying to get it through customs."

"The CI guys didn't think Meany's cell was in contact with the blue," Deeds said. "Apparently, the spy hunters underestimated them. That meet-up had to be set up before she flew in. Meany was acting under orders."

"So, why's he dead? Shootout?" Clanton asked.

"Ballistics said the same gun killed Coltrane the cop, Gilligan the dog, and Meany. No one heard a shot, so she was probably running suppressed. One other thing. The officer's cuffs were out."

"He was going to arrest Meany. Meany was a weak link, so she did them both," Turnbull said. "He was expendable and she expended him. Tracks with how she used her team in Dublin as bait."

"Cold-hearted woman," said Clanton.

"Sounds like our Circe," Turnbull said.

"I'm not ashamed to say I'm a little aroused," Casey said. "Except for shooting the dog. Bitch."

"Yeah, that's just wrong," Clanton agreed. He loved animals, and, in fact, spent his free weekends working with the bears, monkeys, and raccoons at the Dallas franchise of the Ruthless Nature Fighting Challenge. This interactive experience was one of the popular brand's many post-Split spin-offs, which included not only the Ruthless Variety Progrum but Ruthless Muffler Shops, Ruthless Chirpractic, the "Ruthless Kidz" cartoon series, and Ruthless Body Spray, which promised that its users would "Smell Smug."

"Do you have fresh photos?" asked Turnbull.

"Yes, from the airport, none at the truck stop. Not great quality. She'll change her appearance."

"I'll know her," Turnbull said. "She shot me. We have a bond."

"That's what I'm counting on," Deeds replied.

"But why's she here?" Casey asked.

"No idea," Deeds told him. "The next big city down I-35 is San Antonio, and we know Meany was there – he bought gas in town yesterday with his parents' credit card. Circe's a terrorist; she has to be planning something. But there are no sports events, rallies, anything like that. No obvious targets."

"I guess we're off to San Antonio," Turnbull said.

"Find her, and find out what she's up to. If it's Circe, it's big. They wouldn't waste her on something minor. But be careful. She's killed operatives before. And she almost killed Kelly."

"Yeah," Turnbull said. "She and I need to have a little discussion about that."

"Just find out what she's doing here before you shoot her, Kelly," Deeds told him.

"You know me, Clay," Turnbull replied, standing up. "I always ask questions first, then shoot later."

4.

"I guess my favorite show is *The Sound of Music*, or maybe *Dirty Harry: The Musical*," Hiram Clanton said from the backseat of the Navigator, talking over the chatter on the radio. He began to sing the chorus of "Feeling Lucky?," the latter's first act showstopper:

And now you got to pick
Did I only shoot five or all six?
There's no way that you can duck me
So, ask yourself... do I feel lucky?

"It was okay, I guess. I saw it with Matthew Marsden at the Wyly Theatre in Dallas, but I really liked *Hunchback!*" Casey said from the driver's seat, turning down the radio volume. Now it was his turn to vocalize:

I've got a hunch
It's looooooooove!

"Stop singing!" Turnbull yelled. He reached forward and shut off the radio completely. This damn showtunes discussion happened every single time they were stuck together in a vehicle listening to *The Larry O'Connor Show*.

"The musical is a great American art form, Kelly," Clanton said defensively.

"Just drive," Turnbull demanded. "Let's sit here in blessed silence."

The Texas landscape was slipping by, mile after endless mile, as they headed south on I-35 toward San Antonio. Outside of Temple, they passed the truck stop where the shootings took place; the forensics teams had scrubbed it, so there was no reason to stop.

Their gear was in the back, go-bags and weapons. For his long gun, Turnbull chose a Heckler & Koch 417 in 7.62mm with all the fixins – optic, designator, and fifteen 20-round mags. That was excessive by anyone's standards, except Kelly Turnbull's. He felt he was running a bit light.

The techs had cracked Meany's cell the old-fashioned way– they used Face ID. It was a bit of a challenge. By the time they got around to trying it with his iPhone, Ellis Meany was not looking his best. In addition to the deterioration caused by the sweltering heat, the nine-millimeter hole in his forehead confused the algorithm. But they had had this problem before and brought make-up and wood putty. The newly refreshed corpse of Ellis Meany soon opened the phone and exposed all the secrets therein.

That, combined with pings from various cell towers, allowed them to put together who he talked to and where he went for most of the previous 72 hours. But Meany had enough fieldcraft savvy to turn off his cell most of the time he was inside the city limits. Where he went while the phone was off was still a mystery for now, but perhaps his friends would know. The counter-intelligence folks had grabbed some of his comrades in Austin, and the prisoners were now waiting in San Antonio.

Turnbull was sifting through the iPad that graphically displayed Meany's movements before he turned off his phone.

"Looks like this Meany guy was driving around in the southwest part of the city and turned on his phone to make a call. The call was to a burner. But what's around there? Either of you guys know San Antonio?"

"I did my basic and pararescue training there at Lackland Air Force Base," Clanton said. "I mean, it was a while ago, but I still remember the town."

"Well, what's there that's interesting?"

"I'd say Lackland itself, but it isn't interesting," Clanton replied.

"What else, anything you can think of?" Turnbull pressed, getting frustrated.

"If I were a terrorist, I don't know what the hell I would target down there," Clanton replied.

"Meany was looking for or at something," Casey said. Turnbull was irritated at their dead end.

"Let's talk to his buddies."

The San Antonio offices of the Internal Security Division were appropriately ominous. The ISD had taken over the Federal Bureau of Investigation's counter-intelligence role after the Split, and that discredited organization was disbanded. The Task Force Zulu guys had worked with ISD before, and there was no love lost between them. The ISD's job was to carefully build cases, while Task Force Zulu's job was to destroy anything in its path.

Inspector Wilcox of the ISD met them, and they showed him generic military IDs – all of them were still serving, even though they had been seconded to Zulu. Wilcox wasn't having any of it.

"Yeah, spooks," he said. "I bet those aren't even your real names."

They weren't, but none of the three operatives bothered to clarify that.

The ISD agent motioned for them to follow and led them down the hall to an elevator. The elevator went down to the underground, where they kept the cells. It wasn't particularly pleasant above ground, and it was actively oppressive below. Lots of fluorescent lights and linoleum. Even the furniture was banged up, probably military surplus from 50 years before.

Turnbull wasn't sure whether the aesthetic was intentionally designed to break the spirits of the traitors brought down there for interrogation, or whether the government was just too cheap to decorate it any better.

"We got three. Picked them up in Austin. No real records for any of them – at least not criminal records – until now. But they'd all been kicked out of UT for agitation." Academia in America no longer tolerated commie nonsense, a big change from before the Split, when academia actively promoted it.

There was a row of 12 cells, each with a full-metal door and smaller internal doors for conversation or passing trays. Wilcox came to a halt at the end of the corridor. He pointed.

"Benji Hartman, 23. He's got a mouth on him, but that bleeding wound in his lip was from a metal stud. No piercings in the cells. He doesn't shut up, but he hasn't said anything useful yet." He pointed to a second door.

"Sheila Jorgensen, 24. Pretty typical daddy-issue radical. Upstanding citizen parents that she wants to scandalize by hanging with blue-loving trash. She's scared. I don't think she ever expected her rebel cosplay to get this real." He pointed to a third cell door.

"Omar Saleh. Immigrant. Parents were Iraqi and brought him here after the war. Not a lot of love for the country that took them in. His best day is when we denaturalize and deport him." Wilcox didn't have to say what the worst day was, but they all understood that America didn't take kindly to terrorists.

"Let's start with Benji," Turnbull said. "Open up."

Wilcox called down to the guard station to have number six unlocked.

"So, what's our strategy, Kelly?" Casey asked.

The door swung open. Benji was sitting on the thin industrial mattress atop his cement bed. There was a clot of blood where the stud had been removed, probably not gently. The prisoner was not in a jumpsuit but in his street clothes – he wore a Bruce

Springsteen concert t-shirt, either as a political statement or ironically. He hopped to his feet and stepped forward.

"I demand my lawyer, you fascist...."

Turnbull punched him in the mouth, and he staggered and fell back on his fourth point of contact. It took him a second to catch his breath because he was inhaling blood from his split lip. He looked up from the floor as Turnbull stepped deeper into the cell.

"Listen, dumbass, I don't have a lot of time, so let me give you the good news, the bad news, and the worse news. The good news is if you answer every question I ask you, I'm not going to hit you again."

Benji seemed confused but also pleased. He wisely stayed silent, awaiting the delivery of the less happy news.

"The bad news is that yeti standing there," Turnbull said, pointing back at Hiram Clanton with his thumb. "He is going to hit you if you don't answer every question I ask you."

Hiram rolled his right fist in his left hand.

"I hate me some blue-loving sons of bitches," the hairy operator growled.

"And the worse news," Turnbull assured the prisoner, as he pointed at Casey, "is that if the yeti doesn't convince you, we're gonna leave you here with this sociopath."

Casey smiled weirdly from behind his black birth control glasses.

Benji looked around towards Wilcox.

"You can't do this!" he protested. "I have rights!"

"I'm gonna give you some rights," Clanton spat, stepping forward.

"Okay, damn it, you want to know about Ellis Meany?"

"Please," Turnbull said politely. You were in dire straits if Turnbull was your least worst option. Turnbull dismissed his partners to talk to the other captives.

"Look, we never wanted it to go this far. We were a collective, and yeah, we think the government sucks. There's no law against thinking the government sucks, right? We just appreciate what they are trying to do in the blue, in the People's Republic. You know, they care about people, they let people be free."

"Have you ever been to the People's Republic, Benji?" Turnbull asked.

"No, of course not. Well, my parents once took me to New York as a little kid before the Split, but no, not since the country broke up."

"I'm not so sure you'd like it, but go on."

"We had a grad student who taught us at UT before they kicked us out. Well, he hooked us up with people up in the blue."

"You were in contact with the People's Republic?"

"Yeah, a woman. She said her name was Hannah. We talked to her over the Internet. It's been going on for like a year. Look, she wasn't, like, a secret agent. She was just a normal person – a college teacher – and we talked about politics and what it was like to live in the blue. We were just talking."

"Until you stopped talking. When's the first time she asked you to do something for her?"

Benji sighed. "Look, we were talking about militarization, how the reds are always trying to make war and everything. Well, she asked us, you know, for some information for a paper she was writing. She wanted us to go out on I-35 and count the number of military convoys. You know, data for her research. We didn't think it was any big deal."

"For her research," Turnbull repeated. Of course, every road movement was tracked by Chinese satellites, just like U.S. satellites tracked PRC troop movements. The Chi-Com data was passed to the People's Republic, which had no space program— too expensive and technically difficult. The blue certainly didn't need to recruit a bunch of LARPing college dropouts to tally up Army trucks going in and out of Fort Hood. The task was designed to acclimate these traitors to their handler.

But Benji knew it was a big deal, at least subconsciously, which is why he was defensive about it. And it was a big deal.

Their handler was starting them off small, but her requests would get bigger, drawing these punks in deeper. Classic source cultivation.

Turnbull continued to press, but gently, since Benji was giving it up without resistance. The prisoner didn't seem evasive; he seemed not just eager to please, but eager to justify himself. That was no doubt out of self-preservation rather than from an ideological shift caused by the realization that he was being exploited by his gal pal across the border.

"Then she asked you to do more things," Turnbull said.

"Yes," Benji confessed. "She would ask us to go get things and then hand them over to someone who met us, or to take things from a courier and deliver them somewhere– things like that. But we never hurt anybody. We never stole, like, secret documents or anything."

"But then something just happened, something unusual," prodded Turnbull.

"Hannah asked us to go find a place in San Antonio. A place for about twenty people to stay temporarily. They got dropped off three days ago by one of those big rigs, you know, a truck. I don't know the details because it was Ellis that Hannah was talking to directly. I just know that one day, a courier came to our collective's apartment and dropped off like $5,000. Ellis took some of it and bought a gun at a gun show. I thought it was a bad idea. I told Ellis we shouldn't do it, but I think he wanted to impress her."

"You would be surprised how often it's about women."

"Well, Ellis was very set against the patriarchy," Benji objected.

"It's almost always about women when it comes to guys who are very set against the patriarchy," Turnbull assured him. "Who were these people, and where are they now?"

"I don't know where they are. Ellis came to San Antonio himself to help them find a place, rent it, and get them settled in. I never went there, but he said they were foreign."

"Foreign?"

"Like, Somalian. He said most of them didn't speak good English, and they were always chewing this drug."

"Were they armed? How were they equipped?"

"I don't know. Ellis didn't say. Look, who are these people? What are they going to do?"

"I think we both know, Benji. I think they're probably going to try to kill a lot of people."

Benji grew pale. He knew what that meant for his short-term future; he wouldn't have a long-term future if that happened.

"Is there anything else you can tell me that might help me find these Somalians?" Turnbull asked.

"He – Ellis – was very excited to meet Hannah," the prisoner said. "Where is Ellis? You can ask him."

"Let's just say it was a bad first date," Turnbull told the captive as he walked out of the cell.

Back inside the Navigator, they compared notes. The stories matched in the essentials. None of them thought their respective prisoners were holding back. The radicals were scared, and properly so. If some sort of terrorist event took place, they were potential accomplices, and the new United States did not play. The lack of playing was one reason there were so few terrorist incidents.

"Twenty Somalis," Casey said. "Like Ireland on steroids."

"The PR uses these guys as cannon fodder," Kelly observed. "They're religious nuts hopped-up on their cud drug, probably all related by clan, and when they get offed, no one really misses them."

After the Split, the PR had thrown open the gate to Somalis, flying them in by the jumbo jet load primarily into what was then called "Minneapolis." Under the guidance of Secretary of Demographic Adjustment Ilhan Omar, they had become the city's overwhelming majority and renamed it "Mogadishu." It was a great day of celebration among the newly arrived citizens, with the ceremony conducted in various Somali dialects. The only dissonant note was the land acknowledgement, which enraged the Somalis who felt they had conquered the city fair and square. Sadly, Secretary Omar was unable to attend the renaming festivities, having been the victim of a crime of passion committed by a jealous brother.

"So, these guys are going to take hostages or go on a shooting spree or something," Clanton said.

"That's gotta be it," Casey opined.

"Everybody's got guns, though," said Turnbull. "This is the most heavily armed society since the Mongols."

"And most polite," piped up Casey.

"That's a good thing," opined Clanton.

"What I mean is if they went on some kind of shooting spree out in public, they would get shot to pieces long before the cops arrive," Turnbull explained.

"Maybe a school?" Casey suggested.

"All the teachers are packing, plus security," Turnbull mused. "Maybe. There *are* a bunch of bad guys. Benji said twenty."

"We're kind of at a dead end," Clanton said.

"Let me call Clay and brief him," Turnbull said.

Clay Deeds listened to Turnbull's report with interest.

"They had to have come over the Mexican border," he said. "As strange as that seems."

"I thought the Border Force had it locked down tight," Turnbull said.

"It does," Deeds replied. "But there's the human factor. I'll get back to you."

The three stopped at a Whataburger for some chow. Clanton ordered three patty melts, extra sauce.

"You know that's going to kill you," Casey told him.

"Then I'll die a happy man."

"You got a point."

For his part, Turnbull was mulling over the situation. Step One was done – identify the target. Step Three would be handled all in good time – wipe them out. The problem was Step Two – find them. He slurped on his sweet tea.

They checked into a Hampton Suites in South San Antonio, each hauling his weapons duffel and go-bag up to his room. The guy at the counter was notable because he was carrying an old German Luger. Clanton pronounced him a hipster as they rode the elevator up.

Turnbull got the call from Deeds just as he settled down for a nap. They had nothing more they could do; after all, they were not detectives. They did the clean-up.

"Kelly, looks like I was right. The Border Force Internal Affairs people had one of their own under suspicion. They just reviewed the data from all his inspections for the last week. Seems he let a big rig in from Ciudad Juárez into El Paso the other day after it scanned hot for bodies. They jammed him up, and he copped to it. Ten thousand bucks."

"The guy's going to swing for ten thousand if they do what we think they're going to."

"Yeah, he says he thought they were Mexicans and got really upset when he found out they might be blue operatives. Turns out he lets in lots of loads; that's how he got his vacation home in Aspen. Guess who turned him?"

"A woman. Online romance?" asked Turnbull.

"A chaste one. They never met, but it sounds like our girl. Anyway, we know the truck and there's a BOLO out for it." Clay used the acronym for "Be On the Look Out." If he were still in the USA, that driver would be found quickly. It's hard to hide a semi.

The drivers exited the two Ford vans and then walked to a Kia driven by the manager of Discount Wheels Rent-A-Kar. It was the only place in town that rented cars for cash; Villareal suspected that if she used the Genevieve Juliet Burnham VISA card again, it would pop up hot, and a SWAT team would be on her before she finished signing the paperwork. Enter the guys at Discount Wheels; they specialized in people with specialized issues who needed vehicles. You paid for it, but you got discretion.

As she took the keys from the manager and handed him four thousand dollars, she smiled, knowing what trouble he might soon be getting into from this iffy transaction.

The warehouse smelled of bodies, khat, and overflowing or otherwise misused toilets. The men differed in origin. Some were born in North America, some were off the boat with varying degrees of freshness. But they all spoke the same Somali dialect and traced their patrilineal lineage to the same region north of the original Mogadishu. Their clan was the Hibirya; they fancied themselves renowned warriors, and each clansman could proudly tell you of the thirty-seven members of the clan who fell battling the Rangers, Delta Force, and 10th Mountain Division during the October 3, 1993, incident Americans referred to as "Black Hawk Down." The men of the Hibirya had allied with forces under General Mohammed Farah Aidid, the warlord targeted by the U.S. forces. Their tribal chief had ordered them to fight, and so they did, even as they died in heaps. The khat had helped.

Then the clan moved to America, the land of their foe. The fortunes of the Hibirya had changed; their once allies had become enemies, and escape was their best course of action. They ended up in Minnesota, a place of cold weather and strange Americans, even by American standards. The natives were infidels, but also fools. They allowed themselves to be taken advantage of, for some reason assuming their new guests would honor their ridiculous customs and rules. The Somalis mastered the system the Americans so earnestly adhered to, finding and exploiting every weakness. They excelled at fraud, welfare exploitation, and political corruption. The Minnesota Democratic–Farmer–Labor Party, the pre-Split Minnesota version of the Democratic Party, was unready for the power of a solid block of new voters who cast their ballots – and many false ones – as directed by their chief, known as the "Ughaz" among the Hibirya. The name of the head of the clan for other clans varied, including such titles as "Sultan," "Imam," and "Garad."

Ughaz Yusuf Ali Abdullahi had decreed that the men smuggled into Texas would go on this journey into the heart of their enemy, and they did.

The leader in San Antonio was Jama, and it was he that Medea Villareal asked for when one of the fighters cracked open the door in response to her three knocks – any other combination of knocks would have been ignored. Further attempts to enter would have been answered with a burst of 7.62x39mm bullets from one of the AK-74s that Villareal had arranged to be delivered earlier that day. The weapons were the easiest part of the whole operation; she just had one of her many internet friends buy and deliver two dozen assault rifles – fully automatic, as assured by the correctly interpreted Second Amendment in red America – as well as a stockpile of ammunition and magazines.

Her buyer was a local weapons aficionado with a grudge against the United States for tossing him and his dreams of citizenship out of boot camp for simply responding to the come-on by that little tease of a female private. He had gotten a discharge and lost his two front teeth to boot when she butt-stroked his face after he attempted to stroke her butt after sneaking into the female troops' barracks shower. A few hours before Villareal knocked on the warehouse door, she had knocked on the buyer's front door – although not until she had completed her counter-surveillance sweep and satisfied herself he was not being watched by the local Gestapo.

The buyer was very excited to meet her – she looked at him and immediately understood the scenario running through his mind. He had picked up the dump he called a house in anticipation. The shabby one-story ranch would have been a mansion for many in the PR; the years since the Split had been hard ones, something that the reds were entirely to blame for.

The weapons buyer presented a handful of paid invoices for the hardware, having fronted the purchase with every spare dollar he had after pawning a significant part of his own arsenal. He had delivered the arms a few hours before, as agreed. He stood there, expecting to be paid back, plus his commission, in cash and, perhaps, even affection. Villareal paid him back in lead.

After the truck stop shootings, the Americans would be going all out to find their mystery woman. If they were at all competent – and she knew they were – they would know she was the one they called "Circe," the one they kept trying and failing to kill. The fascist agent in Dublin had come close; every time a jolt of pain shot down her arm, she was reminded that another inch to the right and his bullet would have killed her. Like the buyer, he was on her list. But personal beefs were secondary to the mission; this job was of the gravest importance. And, as both Meany and the buyer discovered, she was taking no chances.

One of the Somali men by the front door took her upstairs to see Jama. The floors were strewn with prayer rugs and greenish globules where the originators had failed to bother to walk over to the trash cans they were using as spittoons. Villareal reminded herself that they were not undisciplined; rather, they were free of the neurotic constraints imposed by the white supremacy paradigm that still infected even blue society. If they had not been Somali, she would have shot the leader and promoted his deputy with the lesson in discipline bleeding out on the floor. Jama survived today, but only because of the soft bigotry of low expectations.

"You need to clean the weapons," she told him. Jama had already distributed them. Guns were everywhere, leaning on tables, lying on the floor, hanging around necks.

"No, they are already clean."

Was he really that foolish, or was it he did not want to be seen taking orders from a woman? The role of patriarchy in Somali culture was unmentionable in the blue – one could never be sure if the most oppressed of the opposing parties involved was the blacks or the women, so it made sense to avoid the dynamic altogether. But this was her mission, and she needed a solution.

Sometimes the best course of action with a man was just to smile, which Villareal did.

"It happens tomorrow. We must leave at 6:30 to be there at 7:45 for their formation."

"Yes, yes," Jama replied, as if her reminder was a painful nuisance. She responded with more smiling.

"We need beer and food," he told her.

"You should have plenty of food," Villareal responded.

"We ate it. And we need beer."

She looked around at the prayer rugs, but did not raise the question of why Muslims would be drinking. One of the things she was warned not to do during her training was infidel-splain to them about their religion.

"No beer, too dangerous," she said, her smile met with a frown. She lowered her voice. "I spoke with Ughaz Yusuf today to tell him how pleased we are with his warriors. He told me to remind you to have your men clean their weapons."

Jama examined her face carefully. It obviously was a lie, but then it *could* be true. If it were, and he did not do as instructed, he would have to answer to the Ughaz. But only if he lived, which seemed unlikely.

"I will have them clean their weapons," he announced to her.

"Thank you," she said, as if it were his decision. "Now, I will be here in the morning to take you there. The vans are downstairs on the street. I know your men will be ready."

"We will be ready," Jama replied. "But we are still hungry."

She took a chance on infidel-splaining.

"Jama, none of you will never be hungry again when you are all in paradise."

5.

Turnbull was in bed by 11:06 p.m. At 11:13 p.m., his phone rang. It was Clay Deeds.

"Kelly, get down to the police station. I'm texting you the address."

"More dumbass cosplay radicals?" Turnbull asked.

"Drunk Somalis picked up by the local yokels based on the alert we put out. They came up as blue when I ran their fingerprints through my sources." Turnbull assumed that somehow Clay Deeds had illicit access to one or more People's Republic fingerprint databases.

"Rolling!" Turnbull hung up.

Less than thirty minutes later, Turnbull, Casey, and Clanton walked into the precinct. The sergeant at the desk immediately knew what they were.

"You the spooks?" he asked.

"Where do you have them?" Turnbull asked, ignoring the question.

"We've got them together in the interrogation room," the cop replied. He anticipated the next question. "We did it because we were hoping they would talk. The room is wired and videotaped. But all they do is talk in their own language. They both had a lot of beer. They made a stink in a dive on the south side of town. They just wandered in, started ordering beers, then they tried to walk out without paying. They were unarmed. When our cruiser showed up, the bartender had them against the wall with a 12-gauge."

The desk sergeant motioned for the trio to follow him into the back.

"Have they said anything?" Turnbull asked.

"Only about how our mothers are infidel whores."

"Did you beat the crap out of them?" Casey inquired.

"They might've gotten a love tap or two, but we kept them intact because we knew you'd want to talk to them. We saw the national security BOLO for random Somali illegals. They had no ID, and when we asked them where they were from, they told us to kiss their asses. What are these guys? Terrorists?"

"Where is the video monitor?" Turnbull asked, again ignoring the pending question.

The desk sergeant walked him to the control room. The monitor showed two Somalis handcuffed to chairs in the interrogation room, occasionally babbling in a foreign language.

"They know enough English to talk smack to us. We'll get somebody in here to translate these tapes tomorrow and see what they're talking about."

"Why are these guys out drinking and making trouble?" Clanton asked, but the answer was obvious. Neither one was a particle physicist.

"Maybe they wanted one last party before martyrdom," Casey speculated.

"That would make tomorrow the big day," Clayton observed.

"Okay," Turnbull told the desk sergeant. "We got it from here. Whatever you see or hear, you just let us do what we need to do."

"Spook stuff," the cop said, nodding.

"What's the plan there, Kelly?" Clanton asked.

"We don't have a lot of time," Turnbull said, pulling out his earplug box. "I'm going to try the direct approach."

Casey sighed, and he and Clanton both began inserting their own ear protection.

The desk sergeant looked puzzled – Clanton finished stuffing the orange plugs in his ear canals and asked him to go grab the first aid kit.

Turnbull walked into the interrogation room, opened it, and stepped through, his .45 out. One of the men started to talk, so he was the one Turnbull shot in the kneecap. The man screamed, and blood splattered out on the floor.

"Who are you and what are you doing?" Turnbull asked, leveling the gun at the man's intact kneecap.

Outside the room, the desk sergeant stepped forward with the first aid kit and handed it to Clanton. He seemed shocked.

"Thanks," Clanton told him. "We got this."

"Hell, *I'm* ready to talk," the desk sergeant said. "I'll leave you boys to it."

"Look, stupid," Turnbull said to the terrorists collectively. "We know you're here to kill a lot of people, which means I can do anything I want to you."

The wounded one was sobbing, and the intact one started speaking in his own language, very fast and emphatically.

"Stop talking," Turnbull told him. He looked at the injured man. "*You* can talk."

"What?" the wounded Somali asked plaintively.

"He might be deaf from that gunshot," Casey speculated.

"Oh, he can hear me fine," Turnbull said, gesturing with his big, black gun. "Now, I know you are from the People's Republic, and I know you speak English, at least enough to insult our boys in blue. Understand that I am the captain now."

The man just looked up at him, uncomprehending. Maybe it was the pain, or maybe he hadn't seen that movie. Turnbull sighed.

"I'm counting to two. You don't rate three, and I don't have the time to waste. One."

"Okay!" shouted the wounded man. His running buddy began haranguing him again in what was presumably Somali. Turnbull pivoted the gun to point at the uninjured man's face.

"Yeah, tough guy, it's easy for you to say when I'm not aiming at you. But I am now, so stop talking."

Turnbull turned back to the wounded man. The man spoke in fairly good English, broken by the occasional gasp or groan.

"I don't know exactly what we are going to do. We came in a truck. They brought us Kalashnikovs. Our leader made us clean them then. I don't know where we will go. I only know we're going to do it tomorrow morning, 7:45 a.m." He grimaced and moaned. That knee was really bleeding.

His partner started up again, but Turnbull didn't shoot him. He just smashed him in the face with his .45 so that he fell on his back on the floor. Turnbull pivoted back to the wounded Somali.

"So, you're going to go shoot something up at 7:45 tomorrow morning. What then? What's your escape plan?"

The man looked at him strangely. "We don't have one. We will kill infidels until we die. They will not have guns."

"Where the hell in red America will people not have guns?" Turnbull scoffed. Maybe the pain was causing this crazy talk.

"I don't know. They will take us there, and then we will do this thing. Please, my leg!"

Clanton came in with a tourniquet from the first aid kit. As a pararescueman, he was essentially an EMT. The big operative knelt down in front of the chair and began to apply it. The wounded man was breathing heavily and groaning between sentences.

"Where were you staying? Where are your friends?"

The man was more concerned with Clanton's ministrations. Turnbull was not having it.

"Hey, you need to listen to me and answer my questions, or I'm going to pop that other knee, you got me? Now, where the hell are you staying?"

"I don't know. We wanted to go get some beer. We left and went walking until we found a bar."

"What's the address of your hideout?"

The Somali looked uncomprehending.

"I don't know," he said, as if Turnbull was the stupid one. "It was a building. They all look alike."

Turnbull almost asked him how he planned to get back, but he doubted they had thought that far ahead. They wanted beer, so they went to get beer. Whatever happened next would happen next, Inshallah.

"How many of you are there?"

The man hesitated, and Casey took that moment to tighten the tourniquet. He howled.

"You've got a question pending," Turnbull said.

"There are twenty of us, plus the infidel woman," he gasped as Clanton worked to cover the wound.

"Tell me about this woman."

"A white woman, or maybe Latinx." Yeah, definitely from the blue.

"Did you get a name?"

"I did not talk to the whore."

"You're a classy guy. Now, let's hear from your buddy." Turnbull stepped over to where the other Somali lay handcuffed to a chair on his back. He seemed upset.

"What else do you know?" Turnbull asked, punctuating the seriousness of his inquiry by pointing his pistol at the man's face.

"I am Hibirya! We are warriors, not cowards. I will tell you nothing."

"I don't know what a Hibirya is, but I know I'm going to shoot you in the knee if you don't say something interesting in about two seconds."

"Go to hell!"

Turnbull shot him in the knee, and he screamed. The man was now rolling back and forth to the extent he could while bound to the chair. There was a lot of blood. Turnbull felt bad for the janitor.

"Now, what else do you have for me? Do you know what you were going to hit tomorrow? Do you know how to get back to where you're staying?"

90 | PANAMA RED

"They do not tell us these things!" That was all the man was able to get out. Judging from this pair's proven track record of stupidity, Turnbull was inclined to believe that their handlers would supply them with only the absolute minimum of information.

Turnbull continued to ask the men questions, sometimes accompanied by a swift kick to a wounded leg. That got him some shouts and moans, but no useful information. It was pretty clear that they didn't have anything more. After Clanton patched up the second Somali, the three Americans adjourned to another interrogation room, where Turnbull called up Deeds.

"Yeah, Clay, they're exactly what they seem. A couple of dummies who snuck out for a little Budweiser before the big day, and the big day starts tomorrow at 7:45."

"That's very precise. What happens at 7:45 that they would want to shoot it up?" asked their chief.

"Good question," Turnbull admitted. "We are drawing a blank here. You know, we don't have many of these shoot 'em-up episodes anymore now that everybody carries. It just doesn't work too well. Where do you find a large number of people without weapons?"

"I'd say a school, but our schools are very well-defended. Plus, why would they come to San Antonio for a school? There are schools everywhere, and a lot of them would have a much longer response time from the police. No, Kelly, there's a reason behind this. We just don't know what it is."

"They saw Circe, but didn't interact with her," Turnbull informed Deeds. "Infidel whore, I believe they called her."

"The alliance between the communists and the jihadists was always a bit fraught. If they ever finish us off, they're going to turn on each other. In any case, I'm going to make some calls. We need to flood the area around that bar. Their hideout can't be too far away."

"We'll get down there, but the clock is ticking. In about seven hours and forty-five minutes, they're going to hit something somewhere in San Antonio."

"I wonder why," Deeds said. "Any indication of the motive?"

"No, I don't think these guys are individually motivated by much except khat, beer, and maybe the occasional horny goat. But I've been asking myself that too, Clay. Circe is no amateur. She's top-level. She wouldn't just do terrorism for the sake of terrorism. There are going to be second and third-order effects from whatever she's doing."

"If she uses Somalians from Minnesota, she's going to know that we are going to know who was behind this, and the United States is going to react," Deeds said. "We always have when they sponsored terrorism in the past. The Army builds up on the borders, the Air Force is up in the air, and the Navy surges up into the North Atlantic." After the split, all the Pacific naval bases had been taken by the blue, to the delight of the Chinese.

"Do you think she's trying to start a war?" asked Turnbull. The country had barely avoided a major civil war when it split apart years before, following negotiations and the Treaty of St. Louis. Turnbull had enough harsh experience in the People's Republic to dispel any illusions of peaceful reunification. There was going to be a war someday, but why rush it?

"None of this makes any sense," Clay Deeds observed.

"I know it makes sense to Circe," Turnbull replied. "I just wish we knew why."

"Did they come back?" Medea Villareal demanded of Jama. Gone was the smiling indulgence she had shown earlier. When the Somali leader had called her and told her that two of his men had disappeared, she had come right away, though it was in the early morning hours.

"No," Jama answered sullenly. He was ashamed about having to explain to a woman, especially an infidel woman, but he had no choice. He fully understood what the disappearance of his two fighters meant.

For her part, the woman was not interested in rubbing Jama's failure in his face. It was pointless to attempt to correct his leadership deficiencies now. Even alive, he was unimportant, a mere tool to be used, but within a few hours, he was going to be dead, along with all his men. His fecklessness would no longer be her problem.

"Get them ready. We will get in the vans and go now," Villareal told him. Her tone left no room for dispute. The men would wait out their last hours before the operation inside the two cramped Ford Econolines, as opposed to lounging in the relative comfort of their hideout.

Jama knew she was right – the fools who had disappeared, probably in search of drink or women on their last night of their lives could compromise the operation. Of course, they hadn't been told much about it. Jama himself had only a vague inkling of much of the plan, yet perhaps the hateful red secret police could extract enough information to lead them back here if the two were captured. If they were foolish enough to sneak away to find beer, they were foolish enough to run afoul of the authorities.

Jama briskly turned and began issuing commands in his native language. The man moved slowly, and he had to shout to get them on their feet and gather their gear. But he didn't even bother to try to keep them from taking the time to stuff their mouths with khat. That was almost as important as their weapons.

Once in the two vans, with the designated drivers behind the wheel, she led the little convoy in her rental car. As they drove, she noticed first one police car, then another, then another, all heading the way the terrorists had come. She smiled. Once again, Circe had slipped through their nets. And, in a few hours, those same fascist policemen would be walking through a field of bodies, looking for survivors. If her catspaws did their work well, there would be few.

The sun was up, and the operators were drinking coffee. They were sitting at a table in a coffeehouse, trying to look inconspicuous. Around them were normal people going about their normal lives, not knowing what was coming. On the upside, even if they were not all citizens, most of them were armed.

Why not stop for coffee? Driving around San Antonio was essentially pointless. There were dozens of police cars cruising through the area where the bar that the Somalians attempted to drink and dash from was located. One more vehicle with three operatives in it wasn't going to help much.

"There are a lot of things I don't like about the blue, Kelly," Casey said, lifting a cup of joe to his lips and savoring it. "The worst is the responsible coffee. I freaking hate responsible coffee. Reusing grounds is an abomination."

Casey's phone rang. He put down the cup and took the call. Turnbull watched him with interest.

"Okay. Nothing there? Did you canvass the area? Any witnesses see anything?"

He listened some more, then said "Roger," then hung up.

"Our desk sergeant friend," Casey explained. "They think they found the hideout. Don't get excited. They're pretty sure this was where they were, but it looks like they left a few hours ago. The only interesting tidbit they've got is that there were a couple of white vans parked out on the street last night, but they're gone now."

"Circe is driving them around cooped up in vans until zero hour because she figured the dumbasses would get caught and spill," Turnbull said.

"Well, she got that right." Casey observed.

"On the bright side," Hiram Clanton said. "At least *we're* not going to be driving around not knowing what we're looking for anymore."

"Yeah," Turnbull replied, unenthused. "Now, we can drive around looking for white vans. That are probably only 10,000 in San Antonio."

"So, where do we go look? Back to the area around the hideout?" asked Casey, but he didn't sound like he thought that was a great idea.

"The cops have that covered," Turnbull observed. "How about the southwest, where Meany was driving around?"

"Might as well," agreed Clanton. "Maybe he was scouting."

"Or maybe, when this all goes down, we will be an hour away during rush-hour traffic," Casey remarked glumly.

"You got a better idea?" Turnbull asked.

"Nope."

"Then let's go."

"Mustapha needs us to stop," Jama said into the telephone. He was in the lead van, which was following behind Villareal's vehicle.

"Tell him to piss in a bottle," Villareal said, pushing the red button to hang up. Just what she needed, to blow the entire operation because one guy couldn't hold it and attracted the cops by committing public urination. Of course, in less than an hour, having to pee would be the least of his concerns.

Right now, the bladder status of her band of killers was the least of her concerns.

She was already agitated, not just because of Jama's incompetence but because of the effect of it. Two shooters out of twenty were 10% of her force. She figured they could get through five or six magazines of 30 rounds each, between 150 and 180 bullets, which could be expected to kill ten to fifteen targets. Now, 20 to 30 Americans would live because of those fools. But, she reminded herself, it wasn't the numbers. It was what the American government would do in response to them that mattered. She did not understand why this was the objective; all she had been told is what she needed to know.

She looked at the map on her navigation system. They were about twenty minutes away.

"Seven-thirty, Kelly," Casey said.

Turnbull sighed. They weren't going to be able to stop it. They would have to help clean up the mess.

"I really hate this part of San Antonio," Clanton said. "I get triggered just thinking about basic training."

"You're triggered by *Air Force* basic training?" Casey asked from the driver's seat. "Were you unsatisfied by the mint the drill sergeant left on your pillow every night?"

"Hey, it was hard," Clanton protested.

"Yeah, it made *Full Metal Jacket* look like *The Care Bears Movie.*"

"I'm going to have to agree with Casey on this one, Hiram. That's really sad." Turnbull said.

"No, it was *mentally* tough."

"Oh, *mentally* tough," laughed Casey.

"They are nuts on attention to detail. You might not know it, but I'm a very right-brain guy. Detail doesn't come naturally to me. Every morning, you get inspected, your uniform, your haircut, everything, because if you miss one detail, that plane you're working on may crash. That's why I got the shakes when they mentioned 0745. You get out of the chow hall, you go out there for the 0745 inspection, and you are screwed if you have even a dot of eggs or ketchup or whatever on your uniform."

Turnbull pivoted in his seat.

"An oh seven four five formation?" he asked.

"Yeah, every morning," Clanton said, the pieces coming together in his head.

"Recruits don't carry loaded guns, do they?" asked Casey.

"Nope. Drill sergeants do, but there aren't that many. Gate guards do, and the gate's only a couple of hundred meters from the parade field," explained Clanton. "Oh, man."

"The one place in the new United States where almost nobody has guns, and it's on a freaking military base," Turnbull spat, grabbing his cell phone. Casey was working the navigation system.

"We are eleven minutes from the front gate," he said, accelerating.

Turnbull dialed. Clay Deeds picked up. There was no time for formalities.

"They are going to hit the basic training unit at Lackland Air Force Base," Turnbull said. Clay Deeds didn't ask him how he knew.

"On it. Are you there?"

"We're about 10 minutes out. We're cutting it close. I want a block at the front gate. I want that whole damn gate shut down. I want those recruits the hell out of there."

"I'm making the calls. I don't know if we'll get through in time."

Turnbull hung up.

"Drive faster," he told Casey. Then he turned around to Hiram Clanton in the backseat.

"Reach over into the back back," Turnbull ordered. "And pass up the heavy metal."

"Give your men their orders," Villareal directed Jama over the speakerphone in her car. "Tell them to fight through the gate and go to where the soldiers are lined up, then kill everyone they see." She hung up.

Jama made a call to his deputy, who was in the trail van, and passed her instructions. Then he told the men in the van with him in their native language. Mustafa seemed to have difficulty paying attention, and he kept squirming. Well, his suffering would not last much longer.

They each wore their web gear loaded with their magazines, and their weapons were in hand. Several were pulling their bolts as Jama gave them their final instructions.

"Kill all of the infidels," he told them. "Fight until they martyr you. Tonight, I will see you in paradise surrounded by beautiful virgins."

The man shouted their assent, and several began to pray. Mustafa just sat there, suffering.

"There they are," Casey said. "Maybe two hundred meters ahead."

They were behind the little convoy, and a quarter mile from the airbase's front gate.

"Catch up," Turnbull directed. He looked down at his HK417. He did not need to charge it; he did that a ways back. Like the others, he had slipped on his gear, including a ceramic chest plate.

At his feet was Casey's SCAR assault rifle, the stock leaning over the console so the driver could grab it when he needed it.

Behind him came the clack of Hiram Clanton and his SIG Sauer M250 light machine gun, an Israeli variant chambered in 7.62mm instead of the smaller 5.56mm round. It was belt-fed from a pouch attached to the underside of the weapon.

"The gate's still open," Turnbull said – in the distance, he could see guards in uniform with their tactical gear calmly processing civilian vehicles through the gate and onto the base.

Casey was catching up to the vans. The terrorists slipped into the left turn pocket to the base. A Ford sedan ahead of them continued on just a bit, then pulled over. Turnbull noted it but paid it no mind.

"If we can catch them at this red light, we can take them here," he directed.

"That's some hard odds, Kelly," Hiram said.

"Six to one," Casey said, accelerating.

"I'm open to better ideas," Turnbull offered.

"No, this is fine. A shootout on a busy public street is cool."

"We take them in the vans," Turnbull said. "Don't let them out."

They rolled forward toward the waiting convoy.

"It's green. There's the left turn light!" Turnbull shouted. The vans made their left turns into the road leading up to the main gate. "We'll hit them at the gate."

"The lanes aren't clear," Casey said. "They have to stop."

"What about the civilians and gate guards?" asked Clanton, hefting the light machine gun. "This hog's kind of indiscriminate."

"They're unlucky," Turnbull replied. "Get the cleanest shots you can. Try to watch your background."

"Pass that SCAR on over, Kelly," Casey calmly requested. Turnbull lifted it out of the footwell and laid it across Casey's lap, barrel toward the door.

The trail van's red brake lights came on; it was slowing. There were at least five visible Air Force gate guards; the terrorists would have to take them out, or at least suppress them, to get through the base's front gate.

"I see three civilian cars ahead – okay, one just cleared through," Casey reported. "Okay, there are two."

"Close up the distance. I want us right on their asses!" Turnbull shouted. In the distance, a few hundred yards into the base, a class of recruits – several hundred – were falling into formation. If the Somalis got through, they would be slaughtered before the Security Police could organize a large enough counterattack to stop the massacre.

"Another car went through," Casey yelled. He was braking, and the Navigator was now maybe forty yards away from the trail van.

"Get ready," Turnbull said. He unlocked his door.

It happened all at once, the lights and the sirens on the gate going off in a blaze of flashing red and the howl of alarms. The last civilian car had moved through and got six feet into the base before being violently thrust into the air as the buried barrier pillars shot upwards from their silos.

Turnbull pulled the sling over his head and clicked the selector switch to AUTO.

"Casey, front van with me. Hiram, rear van with your LMG." Turnbull was referring to Clanton's light machine gun.

The vans froze, with the red brake lights on the trail vehicle back on.

"Now!" Turnbull yelled as Casey hit the brakes. The Navigator's anti-lock brakes did not let it skid; instead, it came to a stop perhaps 10 yards behind the rear van. Turnbull threw open the front passenger door and rolled out, as did Clanton through his; they had trained on this drill a million times. The Somalis, not so much.

But the terrorists did open fire. Up ahead, two of the security police at the gate were cut down immediately by AK rounds coming from inside the first van. The other security policemen scrambled for cover.

The sliding door on the rear van flew open just as Turnbull raised his rifle.

Two men hopped out, both with Kalashnikovs, and tried to get their bearings. What they got was a hail of lead. Turnbull zeroed in on the guy to the left and shot him down. There was red splatter across the passenger door. The other nearly had his weapon up when Turnbull put a burst into him center mass. He was a slim guy, maybe 130 pounds, and the bullets pummeled him backwards several feet before he fell.

Turnbull charged forward, as did Casey on the other side with his Belgian FN SCAR assault rifle. He was out wide several feet and already putting rounds into the front vehicle.

Clanton focused on the trail van, rushing forward to rest the machine gun on the Navigator's hood before opening fire on full auto into the stationary vehicle. Holes ripped across the rear door and right side, shattering windows and blowing out the back passenger side tire. He was firing long bursts, riddling the vehicle with heavy 7.62mm bullets.

Turnbull got nearly up even with the first van, and he started to fire. Its side windows collapsed in a cascade of glass as Turnbull sprayed into it from the passenger side, while Casey unloaded on it from the driver's side.

An arc of brass flew out of the action with each squeeze of the trigger. Then nothing. Turnbull was dry.

"Reloading!"

Turnbull knelt, dropping the empty mag as he did and reaching instinctively to his web gear for a fresh one. There was movement inside the van, and the passenger door opened. An armed Somali stumbled out, blood on his face, with his weapon in hand. The terrorist saw Turnbull and took aim, then jolted and shuddered under the impact of a barrage from a security policeman who could not have been older than twenty. The Somali dropped, and the airman's eyes went wide. He looked at Turnbull. Turnbull nodded and sent the bolt forward, then blew off the entire new mag into the van, aiming diagonally to avoid hitting Casey, who was doing the same on the other side.

Behind them, Clanton was walking a stream of gunfire at passenger level across the length of the trail van. The noise was overwhelming, the road littered with dancing spent brass.

Turnbull went black on his second mag and let his rifle hang by its sling. He drew his Wilson Combat.

"I'm clearing the van!" Turnbull yelled.

"Let me reload," Casey called back, out of sight on the other side of the two wrecked Fords. You could hear glass breaking and metal groaning. "Okay, do it!"

"Moving up!" Turnbull yelled, pistol ready in a two-handed grip. He got to the open sliding side door. There were bodies on the seats, and the seats were slick with blood, glass, and gore. No targets. He moved to the open passenger door that loomed over Jama's corpse. From behind, he heard Clanton yell: "Rear van clear!"

Turnbull peered inside the front compartment. The driver was bloody, but alive, and he fired his AK as Turnbull reeled back and around the door pillar. One of the bullets struck at an angle and bounced across the surface of his ceramic chest plate. It still felt to Turnbull like a solid punch to the solar plexus.

But there was no time to dwell on it. Turnbull spun about to the open sliding door and opened fire with four shots. The AK fell onto the console, and there was red gore sprayed across the broken glass of the driver's side window.

"No, please!" someone cried from inside the back of the van. Turnbull pivoted. His sight post centered on the terrified face of a young Somali, probably as young as the airman who saved his bacon sixty seconds before.

The man had no weapon – his hands were empty and up, palms showing, which saved his life. He was splattered with blood, but other people's. Turnbull had assumed he was dead.

"Out, now! Slow! Move!"

The young terrorist made his way past the corpses and the shredded seat cushions, shuddering and breathing unsteadily, finally stepping out onto the asphalt.

There were scores of security police reinforcements rolling up. The other airmen were tending to their buddies who the Somalis had shot down. The civilian who had been caught on the barriers was standing there with a .357 magnum. She looked like a grandma otherwise.

Turnbull had his weapon on the prisoner as Clanton walked up.

"Anyone breathing?" Turnbull asked.

"Hell no. Looks like a *Friday the 13th* marathon in there. What you got here?"

"I don't know how he lived, but he did."

"Well, he ain't coming in our vehicle, Kelly. He's pissing himself."

A pair of security police gingerly took charge of Mustapha, who seemed more relieved than scared. Reflexively, Turnbull dropped the empty mag from his HK and let it fall to the brass-strewn pavement, where it clanked and bounced. He slipped a fresh one in – habit – then looked up.

Across the busy main street was that Ford sedan he had seen pull away from the vans. A woman was standing beside the open door. She had black hair.

"Circe," he said, bringing the rifle up to his shoulder as she slipped back behind the wheel. The red dot covered her, and then it went black. Cars and trucks, civilian cars and trucks, were passing between them. He saw the Taurus pull away; there were multiple freeway entrances ahead of her. She was in the wind.

"I'll be seeing you, Circe," he growled. Next time, she wasn't getting away.

As she drove away, Medea Ekaterine Villareal was thinking exactly the same thing about Kelly Turnbull.

6.

Over the years, Clay Deeds had developed a formidable poker face. He was deploying it now for the benefit of the Secretary of War. The cabinet official was always combustible, and now he was burning out of control.

"Damnit, Clay, this could have been a major bloodbath instead of a minor one." Neither man counted the dead Somalis. The Secretary continued.

"Two dead airmen, and no doubt the People's Republic did it. What were they thinking? And what the hell do I tell the President?"

"You tell him my guys waxed them, sir."

"See, there's the problem. There were terrorists inside America for your guys to wax. The country pays you to keep terrorists the hell out!"

"We are not the Border Force."

The Secretary frowned. "Do you have any idea why the hell they would provoke us like this? What was in it for the PR? They didn't even try to hide who they were."

Deeds pondered the question for a moment before speaking.

"There would have been no tactical impact – they planned to kill a bunch of recruits, but that would not affect our overall combat power. All it would do is make the U.S. mad. It makes no sense to get us angry for no reason," Deeds said.

"It's crazy."

"But they had a reason. We just don't know it yet."

"Isn't that your job? To know stuff? You're the wizard of intelligence. You're so spooky I don't even know your real name. So, what do you *think* is their reason?"

"I don't know," Deeds admitted. "Yet."

"I don't need this right now, Clay," the Secretary complained. "This is very stressful. I'm not ripped like Pete Hegseth. I have an Air Force doctor whose whole job is to be on my back about my blood pressure, my A1C, and my big, fat ass. You know, I have to gobble a handful of Viagra just to make it happen. And thanks to Pete, every time I go visit a base, the Marines want me to do push-ups with them. Do I look like a man who does push-ups?"

"Well, sir, we can all do with more exercise," Deed suggested pleasantly.

"I'll take that under advisement. But this is getting ugly. Things are falling apart. We have almost no allies. Most of Europe hates us. We put out a fire, and another one breaks out. Do you know what's up in Peru? The Chi-Coms want a foothold there, and not just for the rare earths and *pollo saltado*. They want to grab a piece of the Western Hemisphere."

"I seem to remember something from high school history called the Monroe Doctrine," Deeds recalled.

"It's only a doctrine if you can back it up. The blues are happy to have the commies on the ground in South America. Frankly, I'm surprised they haven't invited them onto the North American mainland. They already leased Pearl Harbor to the Chinese. I guess they know that would mean war."

"It will come to that someday," Deeds warned his superior.

"Hopefully not on my watch," the Secretary said ruefully. "Well, after this morning's events, now we need to make a show of force. We have to send the Navy ships we have left to float off the New England coast and look threatening, as well as have the Army go on high alert along the border, all because of these terrorists."

Clay furrowed his brow; his poker face was gone because something had just occurred to him.

"Can we do both, a show of force off New England and a show of force off Peru?" he asked.

The Secretary laughed bitterly.

"No. The whole west coast is blue – no red ports, so we have no Pacific fleet. We're stretched thin already, and to get the ships we got in the Split over to the Pacific from the Atlantic, should we have to stop a Chinese force, we would have to sail through Panama, and that's a freaking mess, too. We're subject to the whims of *el Presidente* Bonifacio Alberto Maria Guerrero. The Secretary exaggerated the Spanish pronunciation. He continued.

"The guy's a lunatic, and the PR's diplomats are all over Panama City, along with the Chinese, trying to get control of the canal. So are ours. He's too nuts to deal with. But dealing with Peru is a hypothetical because right now I have to focus on dealing with the PR's latest move."

"Yes, you do," Deeds said, his mind working on the puzzle. "You *have* to respond to this attack. You can't *not* respond."

"Great. You understand my problem."

"I'm beginning to," Deeds said. The likely purpose behind the aborted attack on Lackland was now clear to him. He even admired whoever came up with the scheme a little. Very cynical, and very clever. He sat silently, in his own head, thinking about it.

"Are you going to keep me in suspense?" the Secretary finally demanded.

"They launch an attack to cause enough casualties to make you react, but not to go to full-scale war."

"Yes. If they hit kids at a school or something, we would be DEFCOM 4 right now."

"So, they hit a military target. And they knew our likely response because we've responded that way previously."

"And?" gesturing with his arms open wide.

"They *want* you to send the Navy to New England," Deeds said. The Secretary considered that for a moment.

"Because if we do," the Secretary of War replied, working it out in his head. "Then we can't block a move on Peru."

"I would strongly suggest you get your strategic intelligence assets looking for a Chinese task force getting ready to sail to Peru while the United States Navy is busy waving our big stick at the blues up in the North Atlantic," Deeds advised his boss.

"Yeah, I'll do that," the Secretary promised. "But there's something else we still have to decide. How do we respond to this attack? We can't just let it pass, by which I mean I need to tell President Banks we're doing something about it, and he has to agree."

"Why don't you let me handle the response?" Deeds offered.

"You and your Task Force Zebra?"

"Zulu. Yes, how about I send them in to deal with the people behind this? These were Somalis or Somali immigrants living in Minneapolis, I mean, Mogadishu. They are from a specific clan, the Hibirya. They have a chief, Ughaz Yusuf Ali Abdullahi. The 'Ughaz' part is a title, not a name. And there is a woman, an operative. Her codename is Circe; we don't know her real name. She's been a rock in our shoe for a while. His boys executed it, but she planned it and led it."

"What about them?"

"I'll have my guys go grab Abdullanhi and grab her too, if they can."

"You want to kidnap a clan leader and maybe also a spy who you don't even know, and that's the payback?"

"Sure, we put them on trial, yada yada, justice is done. But the real benefit is that this will take some time, time where you don't have to send our forces to the opposite side of the globe from where we need them."

"It could work," the Secretary conceded. "At least to keep the President satisfied for a while. He's pissed. I had to talk him out of airstrikes. But Clay, this is a snatch mission. What if your boys can't snatch them?"

"Well, then it's Plan B."

"Plan B?"

"Yeah, we kill them."

"Hmmm," grunted the Secretary. "That's a very Clay Deeds answer. You got guys who can pull it off?"

"Sir, I got guys who are chomping at the bit."

The Directorate was in a high-rise in the secure zone in what had been Minneapolis, sealed off from the teeming masses of the city by walls, guards, and guns. Bureaucratic infighting has seen the Directorate exiled there, outside where the real power in the PR lay – New York City, Chicago, and Los Angeles. But being at a distance had its advantages. It was largely away from prying eyes.

It was her first stop when she got back; she did an in-depth debrief with her boss and others, then went home. Just a few hours later, she got a summons back to headquarters.

Medea Villareal was lucky enough to live inside the zone despite a rather mediocre privilege level of 6. Latinx status was no longer as exceptional as it once was, being too Catholic and family-oriented. Her formal sexuality identification was bi–again, not particularly interesting. That was the default preference when self-identifying to the People's Republic government. It placed her rather low on the pyramid of oppression, which was compounded by its inaccuracy. She was not actually bisexual; she was both straight and cis, though not particularly interested in either men or gender roles. Being straight/cis was a problem for those seeking career opportunities; those in the system who did not look on s/c folx, as they were sometimes called, with disgust were actively suspicious of them. S/c coded red.

The thought had occurred to her that perhaps she could juice her PL up to 7 if she formally changed her gender identity to "asexual," a move which would have the benefit of being both useful for her career and relatively accurate. This was less an erotic preference than an aesthetic one. Men in the People's Republic tended to disappoint her.

Take the Somalis she had worked with recently. They were patriarchal religious fanatics as well as perpetually stoned, something she would never consider saying aloud but which was true nonetheless. The other men she encountered in the blue – Villareal would fend off interested women with excuses or outright hostility, whichever seemed most effective – were a constant source of frustration. Some would cry, others would figuratively rend their garments over their complicity in the patriarchy. This performative weakness may have worked with most blue women, many of whom were aestheticized with mass-proscribed SSRIs and mass-produced Chardonnay, but it turned Villareal's stomach.

She attributed her disgust at their softness to implicit bias stemming from her heritage – her father was a good communist, but he was a better Cuban in that he pursued women with more ardor than he pursued the Revolution. This is why her mother had left them when Villareal was young, well before the Split. It was not that he had another woman; he had *women*, an endless parade of them – but no trans-women, ever. He was harshly transphobic in private, and, like most ardent male feminists, he treated women like trash, which the most outspoken leftists among his many paramours (he did not discriminate based on politics) absolutely loved.

Regardless, in recent years, Villareal had chosen voluntary celibacy over the inconvenience of dealing with blue male emotional incontinence and, in the rare cases a relationship seemed poised to move up to the physical level, going through the trouble of negotiating, filling out, and then having notarized a People's Form PR-769 – "Memorandum and Agreement of Consent to Sexual Contact."

Even worse were the potential partners who insisted on also submitting People's Form 769-1-A, the "Kink Annex," and checking off the predilections they were agreeing to indulge in.

Options included various types of "Furry Play," "Cross-Dressing," "Scat," or, most alarmingly, the section titled "Other" that required the parties to write in a detailed narrative of otherwise unknown practices. Of course, when filed, those documents were scanned into the databases of the People's Bureau of Investigation. In her previous life as a PBI agent, before being recruited into the Directorate, she made considerable use of these files in her investigations.

Villareal had no car – perhaps she would get cleared for one as she rose up the ladder – so the Directorate sent one to her apartment to pick her up. It pulled up in front of her building and waited for her.

She lived inside a multi-story apartment complex where University of Minnesota students had once roomed before being forced into collectives. It was located on the edge of the secure zone – she could see the wall from her window, with People's Security Force guards patrolling along the catwalk with AK-47s to keep out the unauthorized masses. Her neighborhood was as downscale as the secure zone got, but it was better than living outside. Living inside the wall had been a reward for her service; she hoped for and expected further rewards in the future for her dangerous service to the People's Republic.

Coming home from a mission outside the PR, especially one into red America, always gave rise to wrongthoughts that she worked hard to suppress. It was stress and lack of sleep that made her think them, she told herself. She was exhausted after escaping from Texas. Under a new identity – this one Colombian – she had flown to Bogotá, then turned around and used a third identity to fly north through the designated commercial airspace corridor over the United States to Walz International Airport outside Mogadishu. The statue of him in the terminal had taken the place of one of Prince; his aggressive heterosexuality triggered too many travelers to allow it to remain, so it was replaced with one of the late Deputy President of the People's

Republic of North America. Tim Walz had served in office for a mere month before passing away in a tragic skipping accident.

The elevator in her building was still out of service when she returned from the mission, and she had to walk up three flights of stairs. Several bulbs in the hallway light fixtures were burned out, but at least the power was on. There was a puddle on the worn-out industrial carpet below a brown spot where water had leaked through the ceiling drywall. She had filed a work order to get it fixed months ago, and one six months before that. After the abolition of rent, things had changed. It had struck her as ironic that now that everyone owned the housing, no one seemed to take care of it.

She dismissed that wrongthought and chalked the leak up to the red economic warfare aimed at economically strangling the People's Republic. When the fascist red regime finally fell once and for all – something she worked tirelessly to achieve – the People's Republic could devote the resources it was forced to spend to defend itself on improving the lives of its people. And if her contribution to that great day helped make it happen, it would not be unreasonable to expect to be rewarded with an upgraded living situation.

Her apartment was spartan, like a 1989 New Mexico motel room in grave need of an update. She forced herself not to compare it to The Lucky Cowpoke Inn on the outskirts of San Antonio, where she had stayed– it took cash and required no credit card, and it looked like the kind of place that took cash and required no credit card. But the rented room was still at least comparable, and perhaps a touch nicer, than her real-life home.

She sat in the back of the Directorate car, a dark Buick that predated the Split. She had ridden in these official cars before, and the looks the working people threw at her offended her. She was not some elitist; she was a warrior in the struggle, and these people should show respect. To the real members of the elite, as opposed to those who queued up at the gates each morning to be checked before entering the secure zone to work at their menial jobs, the Buick was nothing. Many had their own cars; some even had drivers. They lived a whole different lifestyle.

They should, she told herself. They are doing the truly challenging work of leading the People's Republic. That's what she always told herself about the class system ever since that day as a PBI agent – before the Directorate spotted her talents and brought her into the dark world of foreign direct actions – when she helped raid a cell of subversives. There was a poster depicting a smiling, elderly man on the wall. She knew who he was from her anti-terrorist training: Milton Freidman, the capitalist icon whose evil was on par with that of Hitler, or worse, Trump.

One of the cell members, a young man in manacles, was being dragged away to torment and, if he was lucky, a camp. He looked her in the eye and said, "You're complicit in this whole damn system."

"A system where everyone is equal, you capitalist pig?" she shouted back. It was instinctive; she had grown up at protests with her father shouting things like that. Of course, as a child, she was yelling it *at* the cops, not yelling *as* one of the cops.

"Some people are more equal than others," he said, and one of the PBI agents punched him in the gut, then hustled him out.

Some people *were* more equal than others in the PR, and she could not deny it. But she chose to consider it a good thing. Why not? Those who contributed more should receive more– and she had herself in mind. She did not know enough about capitalism to understand that she was accepting its basic moral argument.

As she flashed her identification to the desk guard – a painfully thin man in a PSF uniform with a worn Beretta M9 on his hip – Villareal looked across the lobby at the metal detector. No one was standing there; it was still broken. It had been broken for months. Nor had anyone bothered to update the flag that hung forlornly off its pole set on a stand in the corner; it was from several iterations ago, with the light olive stripe representing, for some reason, Hawai'ian, Pacific Islander, and

Māori Peoples, much nearer the top than on the current version. The stripe had dropped in subsequent revisions in favor of more oppressed demographics.

The broken magnetometer was not a problem. In fact, it was welcome. It would save her the bother of removing her SIG from her canvas handbag and showing the card that authorized her to carry a weapon at all times. That privilege was another perk, a reward for a job well done. The little favors, the tiny advantages, they added up. She knew they were buying her loyalty, and she was eager to accept, but she also knew she would have given it freely.

The elevators were working here– two of the four, at least– which was good. She was going to the twelfth floor; the signage labeled it the "Department of Motor Vehicles" to deter random visitors. No one ever went to the twelfth floor unless they were directed there.

An armed PSF guard was standing in the landing when she stepped off, bored by her sentry duties, and she waved Villareal past after comparing her name to a list on a clipboard. The operative stepped to the internal door, looked at the camera mounted up and to the right on the wall, and waited for the buzz. It came. She walked inside the reception room.

Immediately inside the door and about to exit was Carlos Trent, tall, thin, in a suit. He sized her up, and she returned the favor.

"Medea," he said. "Good to see you back. I hear she was disappointed."

"Really, Carlos," Villareal replied. "I'm surprised she would take you into her confidence."

She suspected "Carlos" was not even his real name. He looked like a "Charles." And his bi act was almost too much to bear – Villareal knew he was married, and to a woman-identifying woman. His solidarity flexes made her cringe; on one Day of Furry Visibility, he had shown up for work dressed as an anime aardvark. He often brought doughnuts into the office, which cost a significant number of ration card credits, to fight Fat Genocide. Trent was a striver, a headquarters dweller who earned their promotions – he was ostentatiously a "they/them" – through figurative bloodletting in home office internal struggles, instead of actual bloodletting in the field.

She held him in contempt, and she knew he returned it.

"Always a delight to see you, comrade," he said, ignoring her insult. "Now, I need to go handle some important matters."

"But nothing as important as my meeting, which I see you were not invited to."

"Careful with your reputation, Medea. You're getting known as the girl who can't quite make it happen."

He walked past her and out of the reception area. Villareal could hardly believe it – he called her a "girl." But making a complaint would likely backfire – Trent was not foolish enough to make that play unless he had something on her. He collected dirt – she had seen him use it to cut the legs out from under rivals before. And, like everyone, there was dirt to be had on her, anywhere from a drunken microaggression to something worse.

She put him out of her head and approached the desk.

A middle-aged transmale in a faded summer dress sat at the reception desk. It was well past noon, and her five o'clock shadow was manifesting. The nameplate facing visitors gave a name and pronouns. Brenda Lucretia Wiggingham's pronouns were "herself/theirs. Herself cocked their head at another door on the wall to the rear.

"She is inside waiting," Brenda stated. "With a very important person."

Villareal sensed an accusation underlying the statement to the effect that she was somehow late, although she was nearly half an hour early for the appointed time. It made no sense to argue or explain. Without a word, the operative opened the door and walked inside.

There was a long conference table beside a window that looked out over Mogadishu. From there, you could see beyond the secure zone wall into Shariatown. That nickname was frowned on but used almost universally; the name of that neighborhood in Somali was nearly unpronounceable, though it also translated approximately as "Shariatown."

On the far left wall were two signs: "HATE HAS NO HOME HERE" and "NO MERCY TO THE ENEMIES OF THE PEOPLE." Hanging on the wall to the right was the dagger-through-the Bible-emblem of the Directorate, with its motto, "Hakuna Adui Aliye Salama Kutokana Na Kisasi Cha Watu." The rough Swahili-to-English translation was, "No Enemy Is Safe from the Vengeance of the People."

There were two individuals in the conference room. That was odd; there were usually at least a couple of minions to take notes or otherwise assist. Her supervisor sat with classified-marked papers strewn on the table before her. She was a woman-identifying woman, Allegra Barnes, who had been in the Directorate since the Split. Rumor was that she had been with the old Central Intelligence Agency and had helped fight right-wing elements inside and outside the government before the United States broke in two. Barnes was cold and cunning – she hated the United States with an icy fury.

Barnes had been Villareal's mentor in the dark arts of direct action. She had been the mentor of Carlos Trent as well. She liked to have a stable of loyal subordinates and cultivated promising up-and-comers; she also ruthlessly culled those who failed to perform. Villareal had seen it several times. Those who failed and were without protection by some senior official were terminated, sent off to some dead-end duty tallying wheat crop forecasts. Those with the protection of another senior Directorate official took more effort to destroy; usually, it was a surprise revelation of some racism, sexism, Islamophobia or similar malignant thoughtcrime that even a guardian in the upper echelons of the Directorate could not make disappear. Trent, the budding collector of weaknesses and transgressions, was learning from the best.

In short, Barnes had reached the exalted status of someone who was generally feared. She was fearsome enough and connected enough that she was unafraid to use the pronouns "she/her."

Across the table from Barnes was someone else who Villareal immediately understood was formidable, even more so than Barnes herself. It was a man in a tailored suit, unusual in that Villareal would have described him as "distinguished" if it was not something of an indictment. Cultivating that kind of male energy was frowned upon, if not forbidden. It combined cis-patriarchal emanations with class supremacy. Whoever he was – this important person – he did not care.

"People's Agent Medea Villareal," Barnes told the man by way of introduction. He looked the agent over, still with that air of superiority that came with self-evidently being her superior. A neuro-typical, Villareal was sensitive to such tells and indicators; if she had been neuro-atypical, she might not have been, but she would have had a higher privilege level.

"Sit," he directed her, his voice cold. She did, across from him, with the view over the city behind him. He did not give his pronouns; she assessed that he considered himself beyond such affectations.

"Medea Ekaterine Villareal," he said. "The Americans call you 'Circe.' They fear you. You've killed several of their operatives. Did you know that the mythological Circe was the aunt of Medea?"

"I know."

"Before Medea killed her own children, she helped Jason steal the Golden Fleece. I suppose she was an operative in a way."

Villareal said nothing. Her father had named her "Medea" in accordance with the feminist principles he adhered to when convenient. The mystery man continued.

"And Circe, of course, was a sorceress."

"I know."

The man changed his tone from pleasant banter to focused aggression.

"Texas was your second failure this year," the man declared. Villareal looked to Barnes.

"Senator Harrison is talking to you, People's Agent Villareal."

Now she recognized him – the Chairman of the Senate Foreign Security Committee. He was important. Villareal had read a fawning, oddly erotic profile of him in *Manháhtaanung Nalaháki* magazine – the new name in the Lenape persons of indigenousness tribal language for *New York* magazine. The article had been written by Olivia Nuzzi.

Harrison oversaw the spies and spooks. But what was he doing here?

The senator continued with her indictment.

"You failed to kill Rory O'Riordan earlier this year. Now, you failed to properly execute the Lackland operation. Your team was eliminated, and they managed to kill only a couple of junior soldiers. Both missions were critical. And you failed."

He looked at her expectantly. Villareal assessed him and his potential motivations, as she was trained to do. A senator would not come here to review an agent's record of successes versus failures, and for each of these failures, to the extent Lackland even was a failure, she had notched several successes. No, he wanted something. He had another mission for her. That's why he came, to look her in the eye to see if she could pull it off.

She formed a strategy, just as she had been trained. Lying or equivocation were potential courses of action, but he would see through those. She decided to try modified performative honesty.

"The Dublin mission was a failure," she conceded. "Lackland was not. Its purpose was never to generate casualties. The purpose was to execute an attack attributable to the People's Republic without igniting a full-scale war with the red. And since we conducted the attack and there is no war, it was a success."

Harrison continued to stare at her, not with interest but with pure calculation.

"Do you have an excuse for Dublin?" he asked.

"No," Villareal answered. "I have an explanation and lessons. But I expect those were of interest to Comrade Barnes when I provided them. I don't expect they would be of interest to you."

"And why not?"

"Your interest is the bigger picture. Mine is the short-range target."

"And Lackland," the senator said. "Are you sure it succeeded?"

"I know I did what I was directed to do. I do not know the bigger picture."

"Would you like to?"

That question stumped her for a moment. Why would it matter what she knew, unless she needed to understand for her next mission? If she were expected to understand, then she was being raised to a new level. That intrigued her.

"If that will serve the interests of the People's Republic."

"A perfect and clichéd answer," Harrison said. "But the smart one under the circumstances. You can't be sure of my intentions. You want to see where this is heading."

No point in pivoting to deception; he was reading her perfectly. Keep going with honesty, she told herself. It might work.

Barnes was scrutinizing her as well, Villareal noted. Her superior had clearly suggested she was ready for something more. Unnecessary talk would be more likely to talk herself out of whatever was coming than brevity, so she was brief.

"Yes," Villareal answered, looking him dead in the eyes.

"Your mission in Texas was not to kill some recruits. Your mission was to cause just enough outrage in the red to get them to do what they always do when tensions rise, which is move their naval forces off the New England coast in a demonstration of power. Do you know why I wanted them to do that?"

He said "I," not "we," Villareal noted. Senators, even powerful ones, do not control foreign policy. This was his operation, off the books and outside the rest of the government.

"I assume so that they are not somewhere else," she answered.

"Exactly."

"Did they?" Villareal asked.

"Did they what?"

"Send their Navy off our coast."

"No," Harrison said. "Not yet. And it does not seem that they will."

"You need a Plan B," she said. Immediately, she wondered if he would think she was referring to the abortion pill guaranteed by the 77th Amendment to the People's Constitution, located between the 76th Amendment ("The right to express physical love shall not be limited by age.") and the 78th ("All persons, peoplex and folx, including but not limited to people of color, people of colors, LGBTQ+12s%&VW@() folx, furries, peoplex of heft, and others occupying a position or positions of concern within the rainbow of intersectional oppression, shall have the right to representation in cultural products, including but not limited to books, movies, videogames, performance art, and mime, but not cispeople of pallor or Jews.")

Barnes smiled. She had trained her subordinate to always have an alternative plan. It pleased her to see Villareal had listened.

"I do have one," Harrison said. "And I mean me. This is my plan. There are factions within this government who are disloyal to the cause, who are seduced by the trinkets and pomps of the fascists. What we are discussing is not an official mission. Do you understand?"

Villareal was tempted to look to Barnes, but clearly Barnes was on board. And that meant she needed to be, too.

"Yes."

"There are risks, not just in the mission itself, but here at home should it be revealed."

"I understand."

"And there will be rewards for those who successfully assist me."

Villareal knew it was Barnes who had suggested that the senator leverage her ambition. And her gut told her to let him leverage it.

"I understand," she told him.

"You are Latinx?"

"Yes."

"You speak Spanish?"

"Yes."

"The issue is Peru. Our Chinese friends, with whom I have a close relationship, will be intervening with a naval force and troops to suppress the local fascist forces and establish a people's government. The reds will seek to block our Chinese friends with their Navy – they still claim that their imperialist Monroe Doctrine is in effect."

Villareal knew about James Monroe from college history. She knew he was an imperialist, as Harrison had observed. She also knew that he owned slaves. That was the extent of her knowledge of him.

She was not surprised that Senator Harrison and the Chinese were working together. The People's Republic of China was not an enemy of the People's Republic of North America – in many ways, the PRC was a role model for the PRNA. She understood that there were traitors everywhere in the blue; her career at the People's Bureau of Investigation had focused on ferreting them out. It was entirely possible that these lackeys of the red racist regime were trying to undermine the People's Republic of China to help their capitalist, imperialist, patriarchal masters. Therefore, helping Senator Harrison would not be treason but, rather, serving her country. She allowed herself to accept this reasoning.

The senator continued.

"What you call 'Plan B' is Panama, or rather, its canal. With American ships not drawn away from their homeports on the Atlantic and Gulf coasts, we need access to the canal to be denied to the Americans. They will seek to send naval forces through into the Pacific when they detect the Chinese People's Liberation Army Navy sailing for Lima. Unfortunately, and unlike the Americans, we do not have the military power projection capability to seize the Panama Canal."

Villareal's face betrayed a hint of a frown. The red imperialists had the power projection capability to invade and conquer her ancestral home. The local fascists had then barbarically hanged many of the Cuban Communist Party cadres from the lamposts. Now, the island was capitalist, its false prosperity hiding the moral rot of its fascist regime.

"Panama's president is Bonifacio Alberto Maria Guerrero. Our press portrays him as a valiant stalwart of the resistance to Yankee imperialism, but that is necessary in order to woo him into our orbit. In reality, he is a drug-addled, alcoholic, sociopathic lunatic with delusions of greatness. Our diplomats are unable to secure his support, nor can the red diplomats. Your mission will be to bring him, with the aid of our Chinese friends, firmly to our side, so that when we need the Panama Canal shut to the American Navy, it stays shut."

"Timeline?"

"You should be on the ground there with your team in no more than, say, three days."

"Is that doable?" asked Barnes.

"I assume our diplomats will support the mission," Villareal said.

"I'll arrange it."

"I need men," Villareal said, her beneath-the-surface excitement such that she neglected to say "people."

"With this schedule, I'll have to use Somalis as muscle," she continued.

"Are you sure, after what happened in Texas?" asked Barnes. Villareal had reported the men's ill-discipline and generally poor performance in San Antonio.

"I don't have time for anything better. I'll need a few dozen for security and in case things need to get kinetic. I'll go to Ughaz Abdullahi and explain that I want his best men. I assume transport to Panama will be arranged."

"Yes," Barnes said. "I'll get Trent to arrange it." That pleased Villareal – Trent supporting her op was a sweet little coup. But now the senator was eying her with what might have been a trace of doubt. That had to be assuaged.

"I can do this job," Villareal told Senator Harrison, making sure to look him in the eye. She had been trained that this was a particularly effective way of conveying seriousness; the habit within the People's Republic was to avoid direct eye contact, something that began among young people during the first COVID epidemic.

"I want to make something abundantly clear," Senator Harrison told her, leaning forward. "This mission, my Plan B, must succeed. It *must* succeed. I do not care if you have to promise Guerrero the moon, promise him a pile of gold bars, or sleep with him. I want it done."

"Can I kill him?" Villareal asked. It was a serious question, and Senator Harrison answered it seriously.

"Not unless you can replace him with someone more pliable."

"I understand."

"And Agent Villareal," the senator said. "I expect *you* to have a Plan B as well."

"I always have a Plan B," she replied. But at that moment, she did not even have a Plan A.

7.

"I prefer to work alone," Turnbull declared.

"You're a hurtful man, Kelly," Casey chimed in.

"Even an ape like you would have a problem bringing out a pair of prisoners," Clay Deeds said. "If it comes to that, which seems unlikely. No, you're taking the yeti and Ron Weasley here."

"Road trip!" announced Hiram Clanton.

"I'm not the Ron Weasley of this group," Casey protested. Turnbull ignored him and spoke directly to Deeds.

"I think the chances of grabbing a tribal chief out from under the nose of his tribe, and maybe also Circe – who we can't even be sure is in Minneapolis..."

"Mogadishu," corrected Casey. Turnbull paused to glare for a moment, then continued.

"Seems like a Hail Mary, Clay. Who the hell thought up this plan?"

"I did," admitted the spymaster. "And I got the Secretary of War to sell it to POTUS."

"Do you hate me, Clay?" Turnbull asked.

"*I* love you, Kelly," Casey interjected.

"Stop talking," Turnbull directed.

"Kelly, I would be delighted to have you gentlemen kidnap the Ughaz Abdullahi and bring him back for an in-depth discussion with our interrogators. The same is true of Circe – she's been a giant pain in our tails for too long. But we don't expect you to snatch them. I expect you'll fall back on Plan B and shoot the Ughaz after you figure out there's no way to grab him. As for Circe, I don't think you'll even cross her path. She's gravy; this Ughaz character is your main target."

"I'm now totally confused," Turnbull said.

"The reason I need you gentlemen to go to Mogadishu and draw some second blood is that the blues drew first blood, and there has to be payback. You three going in means the President won't be pulling the trigger on other responses that have second and third-order effects that don't concern you."

"Well, I'm concerned because it's my butt on the line, as well as these two characters' butts," Turnbull replied.

"I am very concerned with my butt," Casey concurred, nodding. "Am I really Weaselly in this?"

"Hell, I don't care about my butt. Let's go," Clanton added.

"I, too, am concerned with your butts," Deeds assured them. "I don't want you to get killed. I certainly don't want you to get captured. I would love you to bring me this Ughaz gentleman and Circe all wrapped up with a bow, but I'd be satisfied with being able to report that Abdullahi is cavorting with his 72 virgins. Capping Circe would be gravy."

"So, see if we can snatch them, and when we see we can't, bang bang," Turnbull said. Deeds nodded.

"Sounds almost like a vacation," Casey said. "A low-stress little jaunt."

"Casey," Turnbull said. "Do you think there is any chance this is not going to go completely sideways?"

"He's got a point," Clanton agreed. "You know Murphy's law – 'Anything that can go wrong will go wrong?' Turnbull's Law is 'Any mission will turn into World War III.'"

"I'll pack extra ammo," Casey announced.

"You leave tomorrow morning to meet your ride," Clay Deeds told the men of Task Force Zulu. "Better get to the armory and choose your iron."

"We're the Penetrators," the Army Aviator said from behind his Ray-Bans.

"Too much information," Casey replied. The pilot did not find that amusing. Clanton did, and grinned. Obscured by his glasses, the flyer's eyes rolled. He'd heard it before, about a million times.

The four of them were standing outside in the midwestern sun on the tarmac at Mason City Municipal Airport, but the small rural landing field was now mostly occupied by the military. Mason City, Iowa, was about twenty miles south of the old Iowa-Minnesota border; it was now the border between the United States of America and the People's Republic of North America.

"When's the brief?" asked Turnbull. On the runway, the unmarked government Cessna Citation III that had brought them from Dallas was taking off.

"At 2100 in the ops building," the pilot, a Chief Warrant Officer Three, replied. "Is that all your gear?"

The three members of Task Force Zulu each had a pack and a small duffel loaded with weapons sitting at his feet on the asphalt.

"Yeah, weight's not going to be an issue," Turnbull told him.

"There are transient quarters next to the ops building. You can get chow there. The mission goes at 2315 hours. You might as well sleep."

"Okay," Turnbull said. The men hefted their luggage and walked to the quarters. Before they racked out, they inspected and assembled their gear. Turnbull was carrying his Wilson Combat CQB; he sometimes took a 9mm weapon if he thought he might have to source ammo locally. The blues considered .45 caliber racist since it had been developed to kill the wild indigenous Moro tribesmen of the Philippines, making it hard to find in the PR. The others took their usual handguns as well.

As his backup, Turnbull carried a 9mm– his compact SIG Sauer 365, again worked up by Wilson Combat.

For long weapons, they went with standard old-school M4A1s. The carbines were small enough to carry in a bag, particularly broken down, but they were still common enough in the People's Republic that a casual observer would assume they were left over from before the Split. Each carbine had an old Army issue M68 Close Combat Optic; it would do the job, but not necessarily draw attention by being an unusual make or model. Each man had 15 mags for his long gun. They each carried multiple magazines for their pistols, or in Clanton's case, speed loaders for his enormous wheel gun.

In the midst of the blue, their best defense was not being noticed. To that end, each of their packs contained a fitted People's Security Force uniform. They also carried a stack of 100-credit Baracks, some gold coins – everyone took gold – as well as a satphone to call home, a Chi-Com-made XiPhone knock-off of the iPhone for use once inside the blue, a small high frequency radio, some energy bars, a roll of toilet paper, and Imodium, lots of Imodium. You did not want to drink from a waterworks that hired and promoted based on DEI, but if you had to, you wanted plenty of stop-up pills.

The gear came first; once they were satisfied it was squared away, checked, and packed in their shabby backpacks – they would be initially going in dressed as unhoused folx – they racked out. At 1900 hours, they got up and went to the small dining facility, sitting at the rear and eating their last decent meal for the next 72 hours, their estimated time of completion.

At 2100 hours, they were standing tall in the ops building's secure briefing room, which had been shanghaied by the unit that was providing them with their ride.

The old Army had the 160th Special Operations Aviation Regiment (SOAR), known as "the Night Stalkers," and based at Fort Campbell. They still operated there, almost all of the personnel having chosen to stay in the red at the time of the Split. Their job was to provide the best helicopter pilots in the world to support special forces operations; Turnbull, Clanton, and Casey had all worked with them countless times at home and abroad, in training and war.

But after the Split, the Army found it needed a new capability, the ability to secretly and securely enter and operate inside the People's Republic. The 161st SOAR was brought online, with the unfortunate nickname "The Penetrators." While it provided endless amusement to their passengers, these aviators did one thing, and they did it very well. They got in and, just as importantly, got out of PR airspace better than anyone else. They also supported other missions and trained in America and abroad with U.S. forces.

Once alerted for this insertion mission, which was almost routine for them, they had scrambled three aircraft to Mason City Municipal Airport to await their passengers. The flyers had no idea who the three men who looked like jacked hobos were or what they would be doing; all they knew was their own mission.

A major in a flight suit, the mission commander, gave the briefing himself. His pilots sat together, taking notes.

"We depart at 2315 hours. We're flying MH-60Ps supported by an MH-60X electronic warfare platform. One of the 60Ps will be the decoy, making a probe over the border. That will set off their electronic systems, and the 60X will do its thing. While they are focused on that, your 60P aircraft will penetrate and take you to your objective."

The three operators sat back listening; there was no more joking about penetration.

"Mogadishu is about 125 miles north of the border. The terrain is flat, with some forests and some high wires and broadcast towers. Of course, the ten miles on each side of the border were supposedly demilitarized by the Treaty of St. Louis. If we have to land on our side, Border Force or local paramilitaries – mostly farmers – will be your rescue. The other 60P is available for extract if we go down over the line. The 60P has a minigun and an MK 19 grenade launcher, so we have firepower if we need it. If we go down, rescue will home in on the bird, so stay close."

The briefing continued with technical details related to the flight plan, including weather – it was clear and warm, terrain – there was none to speak of, and air defenses in the blue – not many, but they could ruin your day if they had the opportunity.

The briefing concluded, and there was time for another cup of real coffee and to hit the head before they grabbed their gear and made their way to the large hangar where the aircraft were parked outside of the view of prying eyes. The blues were not geniuses, but they were not complete idiots; they knew that if the MH-60s were in Mason City, there was going to be a penetration. Chinese satellites, drone incursions, and even the occasional turncoat passing on information could all convert a routine mission into an ambush, bloodbath, and huge embarrassment.

Out on the plains, you could tell when you crossed from the United States into the People's Republic. American farmers worked their crops right up to the high-tech fence and utility road that marked the border. South of the line, there were houses with lights and vehicles. Even in the dark, the land looked tended and cared for.

Then you crossed over into a different world. The farms in the demilitarized zone were few and far between in the blue. Even in the scant moonlight, you could see the contours of the old farms from before the Split. Most were abandoned. Farming was hard work, and you were not working for yourself. Those not forced into collectives were required to turn over the vast majority of their crop to the government at government-set prices. The PR bitterly resented even the tiny residual the growers were allowed to keep. The farmers left for the cities; before the border had been sealed, they fled to the red.

A few tried to retain their ancestral farms, but that was doomed; the PR's Supreme Court nullified ownership of huge tracts of land, ruling that various Indian tribes were the rightful owners, and subsequent claims by European invaders and their descendants were void. Left unmentioned were the ownership rights of the tribes that the tribes the settlers displaced took the land from.

But most of all, the People's Republic was dark. Every farmhouse in the U.S. practically blazed with light. Vast areas north of the border were black, either unoccupied or blacked out. There were towns, but even from the air they looked dreary. And the roads were largely empty, with only a few vehicles on the roads. Even I-35, which ran north to old Minneapolis, was nearly deserted.

The landing zone was much closer to the city proper than they expected; in fact, reaching it meant flying over the southern suburbs. The Penetrators bluffed their way through, hiding in plain sight by flying along, but below, the flight path into Tim Walz International Airport. They used their electronic warfare suite and aerial maneuvers to confuse air traffic control, many of whose controllers did not speak English because insisting on that was either racism or white supremacy; it varied. When one air traffic controller got angry at how they were in closed airspace, the American pilot fell back on this training. He insisted that the controller was racist for expecting him to obey commands and called him "a punk ass bitch;" the ATC backed down, and the insertion went off as planned.

The black helicopter, marked in People's Republic Air Force livery, including the 17-stripe rainbow on the tail boom, flew in low over the Mississippi River that wrapped around the east and south side of the city. The river narrowed there, just southwest of the Cedar Avenue Bridge. On the north bank was Mound Springs Park, a wooded area with open space only along the banks.

The pilot descended and hovered; the crewmen at the minigun and the MK 19 motioned the passengers to hop out. Turnbull was happy to know he would not be leaping into the water. Instead, they jumped down a few feet into wet, sandy soil, which the rotor wash still kicked up enough to obscure their sight but also the sight of any observers. Once they hit the dirt, they scrambled for the brush. The helicopter moved off down the river; it would do a couple more fake insertions to confuse any observers before peeling off south for home.

Turnbull felt that familiar rush. He was back in the deep blue.

8.

The three operators, in their hobo clothes, took cover among the trees and undergrowth as the muffled sound of the MH-60P faded away. Their carbines were out; disembarkation was a dangerous time, and they needed to be ready if they landed on something or someone unfriendly. They did not carry night-vision gear, so they had only the pale moonlight for illumination. Slowly, their eyes and ears acclimated to the environment. The river stretched before them was empty of traffic and oddly silent. It was after midnight on a weekday, and as expected, there was little traffic noise. Occasionally, they would see a vehicle crossing the Cedar Street Bridge to the northeast.

There were no bird sounds, which did not surprise them. They understood that wildlife in the vicinity of urban centers tended to become a source of protein. Rats and pigeons were still common, but anything else had long ago been roasted on a spit to supplement someone's meager protein ration.

The standard operating procedure when there was no expected threat was to stay in position and acclimate for between fifteen and thirty minutes. After twenty, it started getting a little chilly. It was October, so the weather had not yet turned the region into an ice box. Still, it would feel good to move.

They marched through the brush in line, Casey point, then Turnbull, then Clanton bringing up the rear with about ten meters between them. The shoreline was forested inland from the water for a few hundred meters. They were not alone. The park had more or less permanent inhabitants, people who chose to live out there in the woods for whatever reason. The authorities never bothered them; maybe that made up for the hardships of living rough. The Americans saw some warming fires flickering between the trees, and Casey had to move left or right to avoid lean-tos and tents erected in small clearings. They had their suppressors on if things got dicey, but they preferred things not get dicey. The locals let live, and therefore lived.

After several minutes, the squad came to a chain-link fence surrounding what Turnbull knew from their map recon to be the old Martin Luther Campus, a huge, sparkling assisted-living facility before the Split. Now, it was something else. The chain link fence was no doubt designed to keep the inmates in. The facility had been a place for the elderly, those with dementia, or simply too frail to function on their own. But now it was a dumping ground where the old and forgotten ran out the clock. Once the inmates got there, their clocks did not have that far to run.

The three passed by on a path that wound around the complex outside the fence. Through the wires, they could see several people in white robes staggering about in the overgrown grass under the moonlight. The facility didn't bother to lock the doors, and those who wandered away either found their way back inside before they got too cold or didn't. It was all the same to the unlucky and generally surly employees whom the Department of People's Labor had assigned there as Occupational Specialty 733B workers – "Caregiver, Elderly (Institutional)." Those with that designation often received it as part of their restorative justice therapy following an incident – or incidents – of justice involvement.

Turnbull shivered. The white figures out on the lawn looked like extras from one of George Romero's zombie movies. He hated zombie movies.

There was a shout, female, from one of the top floors. Some of the windows were still open well after midnight – none of the workers bothered to close them, and the inmates either could not close them or did not have the capacity to think to do so. Parked out on an asphalt pad was a windowless van that read "People's Coroner," awaiting the morning passenger load.

The trio pressed on around the fence line, heading north.

They were grateful to leave the Martin Luther campus behind – a sign out front, poorly painted originally and marred with graffiti, identified it by its new name, "The Joe Biden People's Dignified Refuge for Youth-Challenged Folx No. 23." To its north lay a residential neighborhood in what had been the pleasant suburb of Bloomington. The town was now called "Mahali Ambapo Mzungu Alikandamiza Watu Wetu," which, in the language of the Anishinaabe tribe, meant "Place Where the White Man Oppressed Our People."

The neighborhood was mostly single-family houses that had once sheltered middle-class families. It used to be a pleasant, leafy place to raise your kids. Most people had two cars and a well-tended lawn back then. But post-Split, there was no real middle class. You were either part of the *nomenklatura* – the elite – and lived inside the secure zone, or you were a prole at best. The neighborhood was dark – Turnbull and his men knew from the area briefing they had read that power went out at ten at night and came back at seven in the morning, if it came back at all. There were few trees but many stumps. That answered the question of how the residents stayed warm in the harsh Minnesota winters.

No one was on the streets, of course. They walked along the sidewalks, weapons ready, figuring even if they were seen and the homeowner had the inclination, no one would have a telephone to call the People's Security Force about the unhoused-looking gentlemen strolling through their little slice of paradise with M4s in their arms.

Casey slowed, and Turnbull caught up.

"It's October," Casey said. "What don't you see?"

"The point of this conversation."

"No, Kelly. Halloween decorations. There are no Halloween decorations."

"I don't think these folks have anything to celebrate." To his right, rusting away in a driveway, was what had been a 1970s Firebird perched up on blocks. That was it for autos; there were certainly no functioning cars. These people did not rate a vehicle. These people probably had been assigned 2 or 3 privilege levels; the only way to get lower was to be a class traitor, like a convicted capitalist or a libertarian.

"What are you going to be for Halloween, Kelly?"

"Far from you. Now, keep your head on a swivel."

"I might actually take Clay up on it and go as Harry Potter this year," Casey continued.

"Sheesh," Turnbull hissed. He took point in order to escape that conversation.

They were forced to go left a block here and right a block there to avoid dead ends and continue north, but they made good progress. No one engaged them, though a man gave them the stink eye as he sat on his dry-rotting front porch puffing a dying cigarette – even from the sidewalk, Turnbull recognized the brand, "Worker's Pride," made from leaves sourced in Malawi. The smoke was sour and rough; the PR retained most of Virginia and could have grown its own high-quality tobacco, but the growers picked up and left for the red once the nationalization of the companies and collectivization of the farms were announced. Now, the fields lay fallow or were taken over by collective farms that grew weed; people would work those because they could do well skimming from the harvest and selling it on the black market.

Their rendezvous was at 5:00 a.m. Turnbull was unhappy about everything involved in it, but beggars can't be choosers, except in the People's Republic, where being unhoused was good for a one- or two-point privilege level spike. The meet was a couple of miles away, but they were making good time.

They did not see a single car come along in any of the neighborhoods they passed through, including any PSF cruisers. The security forces did not bother patrolling. If there was a crime, it was unlikely the PSF would even respond – unless the crime was political. Street crimes were presumed to be due to some form of oppression. In the past, *if* there was a response, it would often be by social workers. Then the social workers got sick of being beaten, robbed, raped, and murdered, and stopped responding. They blamed their own unconscious bias for their victimization, but still quit going out on calls.

At People's Boulevard – it had once been called "American Boulevard" – they made a right. They needed to do so to go through the underpass beneath Cedar Avenue, which was less like a surface street than a freeway. It had been built that way to handle all the traffic pouring into their destination.

"Ta-da," Casey said as he caught up to Turnbull, who was pausing in the shadows of the underpass to look out over their objective, the Mall of America.

It was once billed as the largest indoor mall in the Western Hemisphere – 129 acres – with hundreds of stores, restaurants, theaters, and even an internal amusement park with rides, including a roller coaster. Built in 1992 at the height of the malling of old America, it had faced the challenges of online buying, COVID, and the general cocooning of Americans, yet survived. It did not survive the Split, at least not in its original form.

Within months of the Split, the Mall of America was seized from its owners without compensation and turned into a workers' collective. They changed the name to "Mall of Indigenous Recognition," which did not mollify the Indian tribe whose corporation had owned a chunk of the operation. Within a year, the Mall was abandoned by its tenants. The PR government paid the 10,000 employees for a few more months, but the

Department of People's Labor then involuntarily reassigned all the workers as needed by the People's Republic. They were all made some form of menial laborer; though many requested it, none received an assignment as a poet, artist, or "dreamer."

"Okay, let's move," Turnbull said. They headed south, along the western edge of the vast spread of brutalist multi-level lots that rose up on either side of the Mall itself, obscuring their view. They could see old billboards on the walls: "DEFEAT CLIMATE INJUSTICE," "SMASH THE PATRIARCHY," and "GET THE HELP YOU NEED: REPORT YOURSELF FOR WRONGTHINK AND THOUGHTCRIMES." The last one featured the only caricature of a conventionally-abled white male with no bizarre piercings, hair, or tattoos that Turnbull had seen in any PR propaganda. The subject was on a telephone, apparently reporting himself for ideological heresy. Turnbull wondered if the blues had read Orwell and took *1984* as a user manual rather than a warning; in fact, after the Split, that is exactly what had happened.

The three Americans pressed on and began to encounter more people. Some had made crude homes along the embankments under Cedar Avenue, often in ruined RVs. A few were awake; these gave the trio of operatives a close inspection. The weapons made most of them think twice about interacting with the strangers. Most of them.

"You the devil?" one man shouted, but they were nothing special. Turnbull had heard the man shouting his question at anyone he saw – including some people only he saw – for the last few hundred yards.

"You the devil?" he bellowed at Hiram Clanton.

"No, friend," Clanton replied. "But I reckon I've met him."

Oddly, that seemed to satisfy the curious gentleman. He stopped yelling, at least for as long as the trio was within earshot.

"Not liking this," Casey said as the three men huddled to pick out their route.

"The parking structure is high ground," Turnbull said. "If they have guns, we're vulnerable."

"More likely they huck chunks of concrete and other junk down on our heads, if they're inclined to do anything," Clanton observed.

"Okay, sweep high and if someone looks uppity, cap him," Turnbull said. They nodded and broke the huddle.

The three moved fast along the north side of the western parking structure, weapons actively scanning the seven levels for potential hostile targets. A head did appear peering over the cement wall on the fifth or sixth level; it might have been a man, a woman, or something else – that was impossible to tell at that distance. The red dot danced on its head, but it pulled back inside. They completed the rapid movement across the north end and turned the corner south onto the surface street running between the parking structure and the mall proper.

On the right was the first level of the parking structure. There were crude shelters of various types – tents, derelict cars, and even wooden slats set diagonally against the walls. But it was late and chilly, so it was quiet. There were shadows in the murky dark of the lot, people watching them. But no one acted the fool and took them on.

To their left was the imposing structure of the Mall itself, a cement hulk that rose up into the sky even above the parking structure. The western entrance was there in the center of the western wall, the glass all smashed out, so it was wide open. The sidewalk was caked in what looked like mud.

There were people there, a band of perhaps a dozen men and women in worn, but still functional, clothes that were once Patagonia or Arc'teryx-branded. Their hair was kempt, and their faces washed; they at least tried to maintain their appearance. Most held spears or clubs, clearly homemade but still sharp and solid. A couple had bows, actual hunting bows that were ungently used but clearly still worked, since the archers had vicious hunting arrows nocked. They were alert and ready, with the ones in the back facing the rear as security.

A tall man, mid-forties, serious and armed with a buck knife in a scabbard and a tomahawk that was in his belt, stood ahead of his troops. He did not smile as he assessed the three red operators. Hanging around his neck – around all their necks – was a crude metal cross on a chain.

Turnbull approached alone; he did not have to tell Casey and Clanton to provide him cover if he needed it. They independently decided they would take out the immediate threat to Turnbull first, then the archers, then the rest. To that effect, both switched their selector to "AUTO."

"I'm looking for Briggs," Turnbull said.

"I'm Joseph Briggs," the man said. "The Reverend Joseph Briggs, leader of the Minnesota Baptist Church Militant."

9.

Lit by torches, fires, a few functioning floodlights, and rays of the rising sun streaming through holes in the roof, the Mall of America still impressed Turnbull despite its ruined majesty. They were walking cautiously through it toward the south end, where the Minnesota Baptist Church Militant congregation apparently resided.

"This is neutral ground," Briggs assured them, but he and his followers seemed to be taking no chances. They gripped their weapons and moved quickly but quietly, heads on swivels. The Mall was a multidimensional environment, in that a threat could come from your floor, one above, or even one below. The Baptists seemed comfortable in the environment, at least as comfortable as one could be. As Turnbull walked with them, he began noting scars and even some healing wounds. Several walked with a limp; one was missing his left hand. What kind of church was this?

The Americans took no chances. They had their M4s ready to engage whatever appeared from whatever direction. Briggs did not seem to like that.

"You should keep the iron out of sight," he told Turnbull.

"Some kind of religious objection?" Turnbull asked.

"Guns attract attention," the minister replied.

"They also resolve problems," Turnbull told him. But they were getting attention. As the Militant Baptists passed, Turnbull could see movement and shadowy faces on the fringes of the open space and in the shadows.

One of the flock approached their shepherd. He had a homemade halberd.

"Reverend, we got M&Ms on the left up high."

Briggs looked up and to the left.

"I see them. Watch them, brother. Watch them close. If they are going to make a move, it will be outside of neutral ground."

"By SpongeBob?"

"Yeah. Keep your eyes open, your weapons ready."

"SpongeBob?" Turnbull asked as the congregant moved back into his place in the rough formation.

"Yes, SpongeBob," Briggs said, gesturing to a large, fading, and peeling portrait of the cartoon character painted onto a multistory wall. He could make out the words "NICKELODEON UNIVERSE" running across the smiling mutant's visage.

It was dark, but Turnbull could see that they had walked into the ruins of an amusement park inside the Mall itself. The skeleton of the rollercoaster was still there, with many metal pieces missing from the track. Metal was valuable. Other rides were in even more advanced stages of disassembly. Here and there, he could see various cartoon characters he didn't recognize, their images still on walls and signage.

"Stay alert, brothers and sisters!" Briggs said just loud enough to be heard. He turned his attention to Turnbull. "The entrance and atrium areas are neutral ground; that's where the food comes."

"The food?"

"The community gruel truck. Every early afternoon, unless they forget, and that sometimes happens. The tanker comes, and everyone loads up on gruel for the day. That's what was on the sidewalk, the spillage, though most of what gets spilled gets scooped up. The PR kindly keeps us fed, sort of. But they will drive past if there's fighting, so everyone agrees – the entrance and atrium are neutral ground. The park is *not* neutral ground."

"You have different groups living in here?"

"Tribes. Pagan, of course. We know most of them by their stores. The Gaps, the Nordstroms, the M&Ms."

"The M&Ms?"

"There is a huge M&M store here. Back before the Split, it was several floors of nothing but candy. That's all gone. The ones who live there now are the M&Ms, and they are probably the most dangerous of the lot. Degenerates, living in squalor. They control the dope trade in here. They live in a cloud of pot smoke and fornicate all day and night when they aren't trying to ambush anyone they can catch alone."

Turnbull scanned at ground level and then checked the high ground. A few faces here and there, watching them, withdrawing into the dark when he met their gaze.

"Kelly, look," Casey said. Turnbull followed his companion's pointing finger to the filthy floor of the Mall. It looked like a bronze baseball plate; obviously, someone had tried to pry it out of the cement without success. He got close enough to read the raised inscription in the dim light.

Metropolitan Stadium

Home Plate

1956-1981

"Before the Mall was here, this was a ball park. I think they played football here, too. My Dad saw games here, but it was gone before my time," Briggs told them. "Come on, we need to move."

They got another five or ten steps before the spear, tossed from above, hit the concrete floor in a shower of sparks. Turnbull acted on instinct; he saw the movement, swung his rifle toward it, and fired three suppressed shots on semi-auto. At least one connected; the back of the head of the thrower disintegrated in a pink puff of smoke.

As this happened, there was a shout from the floor, and at least a dozen wild men, mostly in shorts or ragged jeans, charged out of the darkness howling, waving weapons.

The churchmen reacted fast. Turnbull, Clanton, and Casey reacted faster. They immediately selected targets and opened fire. Several of the charging ambushers staggered and fell; their buddies saw this and turned tail. The men ceased firing, and the bodies of the attackers lay twitching and abandoned.

Briggs muttered a prayer under his breath. He did not seem particularly broken up by the carnage.

"The wrath of the Lord is upon you," he told the dying. Turnbull figured it was an Old Testament verse, but he wasn't sure which one. Briggs looked out over his flock. "Let's move."

The Minnesota Baptist Church Militant occupied the south end of the Mall of America, primarily the old B&B Theater multiplex. There were blockades at each stairwell and each entrance to their domain, plus plenty of guards with their melee weapons.

Briggs had one of his acolytes take the trio to a converted room that had obviously been cleaned for their use. It was probably the theater manager's office at one time. Once alone, Casey sat down, back to the wall, and began to clean his weapon. Turnbull did the same; Clanton did not have to be told not to break down his yet. He sat with a view of the door.

"So, are these like some kind of religious nuts?" Casey asked. "I grew up a Baptist, and I don't remember so many spears."

"They've survived in the blue for this long," Clanton observed. "Maybe the Good Lord is looking out for them."

"They're very connected," Turnbull said. "Clay says they have sources and contacts all over the city."

"Good for them," Clanton said. "These blue sons of bitches could use a little Jesus."

Having been up all night, it was a good opportunity for some rest. They would not be moving until the evening, so Turnbull left Clanton and Casey to get some Z's. He went looking for Briggs.

Turnbull wandered through the Church's domain, weapon slung, and got a lot of looks but little conversation. People were working with a purpose. Some were sewing, others were preparing weapons. Women, many of whom were pregnant (something very unusual in the blue, which had a birth rate far below replacement level), were caring for toddlers. Older kids were being instructed – reading, writing, and the Bible. There were a lot of copies around, something you did not see in the blue very often. In the eyes of the People's Republic, the Good Book was akin to a copy of *Mein Kampf* or *The NAMBLA How-To Manual* in the U.S. No respectable person had one in his bookcase – but then, there were a lot of books no respectable blue had in his bookcase.

He figured there were between 100 and 200 people in the congregation. Apparently, several of the theaters had been converted into dormitories. But one was their church. That is where Turnbull found Briggs, on the stage behind a podium decorated with crosses, an altar, and even some flowers someone must have collected from outside. There must have been some power to the Mall, since a few lights were on, so they were not in total darkness.

The pastor was animated in the best Baptist tradition. There was plenty of fire and brimstone. He was preaching to about forty of his people about how the time would soon come to drive the pagans and unbelievers out of their city, their country, and their world.

Turnbull was good with that.

When Briggs finished the sermon and was talking to his people as they filed out, Turnbull approached him.

"So, you're going to conquer the world?" he asked.

"That's right," Briggs said. "This is where the rebirth begins in this abandoned shopping mall in the middle of a Satan-inspired communist dictatorship. Remember the parable of the mustard seed. The most lowly little seed, planted and tended, becomes a glorious plant."

"Pretty ambitious for a guy leading a bunch of civilian men, women, and children," Turnbull noted.

"Don't count them out just because they aren't soldiers like you. They are soldiers of Christ. And a lot of them have done a lot of fighting since the Split."

"How do you know Clay Deeds?"

"I was an intelligence officer in the Army before the Split. Got out to go to seminary. A bunch of leftists. I was, well, unpopular with the Pharisees. Founded my own church. I guess Deeds saw all this coming. He made contact with me well before the Crisis and the Treaty of St. Louis. He gave me a satphone; we tapped the main electrical circuits outside and ran it into the Mall so we have some lights and the power to keep it charged. I expect he set up networks in a lot of blue cities. Planted his own mustard seeds, so to speak."

"And the blues leave you alone?"

"That's right. They have no real clue about what we have here, how we are growing, what our plans are. If they did, they might come in here and clean us out. They would certainly stop feeding us."

"You said something about gruel?"

"That's what we call it. It's some kind of corn and wheat mush that gives you enough calories to live on. Tastes like paste and dog vomit, but we're thankful for it. The blues are good about one thing: subsidizing degenerates – and us. The Lord provides, and sometimes His means are our enemies. You want to come out and see the festivities? It's almost time."

"Sure, why not?"

"You're dressed for it. You look unhoused. But you need to lose the M4. We keep firearms on the down low to avoid attention."

"What about the guys my boys and I smoked?"

"Well, the M&Ms are going to be mad. They may want a sit-down and demand compensation. But they are not going to run to the People's Security Forces; even if they did, the PSF is happy to stay out of here. At least, until they find we're preparing for a crusade. That's why we have spies on the outside in Minneapolis – I'll never call it 'Mogadishu' – and why we are stockpiling guns. That's the price for us helping you – Deeds will get us a weapons shipment. Someday, probably not for a few years, but eventually, we will convert enough souls and then rise up against this satanic regime."

"Outstanding," Turnbull said.

Briggs motioned him to follow.

Turnbull left his carbine with his companions and covered his .45 with his jacket.

"Can I get a spear or something?" he asked. "I want to fit in."

"No weapons at feeding time," Briggs said. "That's the one thing all the tribes in here can agree on. Nothing interferes with dinner."

Briggs led the way, with Turnbull behind him and dozens of men and women with jerry cans and buckets. As they went through Nickelodeon Universe, more people joined the procession, but they did not wear crosses. He also noted that the bodies of the wild men they had shot down were gone. Only a few red splotches remained behind.

As they approached the western entrance, the small crowd became a massive throng; Turnbull wondered just how many people made the ruins of the Mall of America their home. Nearly everyone carries some manner of container. It was the one thing they had in common. The Militant Baptists tried to look clean and neat to the extent possible. The wild men, like the M&Ms, looked like savages. Others wore long dreads or shaved their heads. Some seemed to have found a stockpile of old woodland camouflage Army uniforms. A small sect was all transvestites.

"We don't judge," Briggs said. "At least not at feeding time."

The masses waited patiently outside the door beneath the portico over the entrance, where the Americans had linked up with the Church, joined by additional bodies from the massive parking structure.

"The truck goes to us first, then to the eastern entrance," Briggs told Turnbull. No one else paid him any mind; they were focused on the calories coming their way.

"The People's Republic would happily let their normal citizen starve to feed these degenerates," Briggs said. "It's not benevolence. It's not charity. It's a statement. We saw that before the Split, when the old Democrats took the side of the criminals, the illegals, the bums every single time over normal people. That's their religion. This is their sacrifice. And the Lord has a sense of humor because that feeds the very people who will be their undoing."

A clamor arose from the crowd, as necks craned north in anticipation.

"It's coming!" someone shouted. Turnbull was tall enough to see it – a tanker truck with a faded rainbow on it lumbering down the road. Printed across it were the fading words "IN THE PEOPLE'S REPUBLIC FOOD IS A HUMAN RIGHT." The vehicle came to a halt before the masses, its brakes squealing. Turnbull could see perhaps a half-dozen black hoses with nozzles on the side of the tank.

The crowd pressed forward – but it was not out of control. Rather, each individual seemed to act with exaggerated calm and politeness. Queues formed in front of each hose, and men from the crowd took them down and began filling containers. There was no discrimination: M&Ms filled the jerrycans of Church members or skinheads or perverts, and vice versa. The truck had a driver and a supervisor who said nothing but scowled at the crowd. It was likely him who decided whether the crowd was behaving properly and who exercised the sanction of driving away if not.

The distribution system worked. The gruel gushed out of the tank at an astonishing volume, but the crowd was well-practiced in the art of filling its containers. What spilled out was, for the most part, scooped up from the sidewalk. Still, the surface was coated by the residue of past spills, and the dried gruel was nearly as hard as the concrete it sat upon.

"They sometimes give us some cinnamon on holidays," Briggs said. "Like on Indigenous People's Day, AOC's Birthday, or at the end of the Pride Months. But during Ramadan, it only comes once every three days because we're supposed to be fasting. The Somalis insisted on that."

The truck was there for precisely fifteen minutes; Turnbull noted the supervisor checking his watch. In that time, the people filled hundreds of containers and carried them away. The crowd was a fraction of its former size when the supervisor checked his watch one last time, then shouted, "That's it."

The crowd obeyed, turning off the valves and carefully hanging the hoses back on the truck's side. It pulled away, revealing a crowd on the other side of the street – the people from the parking lot had likewise been downloading their dinner on the reverse side.

Briggs gathered up his remaining people, and they walked back to the south end of the Mall.

"Looking forward to supper?" Briggs asked.

Turnbull shook his head.

"Deeds did not tell me exactly what he wanted us to do," Briggs said, clearly unhappy, and he sat with the three Americans. "And, frankly, he's not giving us enough guns to make it worth it."

"Guns? Aren't you supposed to turn the other cheek?" asked Casey.

"Son, you misunderstand the Scriptures. Despite what the blues and the Methodists tell you, Christ was not some sandal-wearing pinko sissy. Just ask the moneychangers in the temple.

He told his disciples to sell their cloaks and buy swords. You see any cloaks?"

"See, I could go to your church, pastor," Clanton said. "I was a Methodist as a kid, and if I never hear another guitar in a church service, it will be too soon."

"If I have my way, we may come to you," Briggs said, adding, "*Deus vult.*"

"*Deus vult?*" Turnbull asked.

"God wills it," explained Briggs.

"Look, we need to go into the Somali area," Turnbull began.

"Shariatown? All straight-up jihadi. They don't exactly take to our kind there. You know what they do to Christians."

"I've dealt with Somali jihadis here and overseas," Turnbull said. "I'm not any happier about it than you, but that's the mission. We need to find this Ughaz Yusuf Ali Abdullahi of the Hibirya clan and snatch him. And a Latina woman who works with him, if we can."

"I don't know any Latina woman in Shariatown, but I know the Ughaz. He's bad news. His clan dominates there; it's his town. It will be hard to get close to him. He has a headquarters, and it's guarded. His militia runs everything. He also oversees the Committee for the Promotion of Virtue and the Prevention of Vice – "the Mutawa," which is the Arabic word for religious police. They go around bullying the insufficiently faithful and hunting the infidel. The PR government generally leaves them alone. Word is he pays them back by supplying soldiers."

"That's true," Turnbull said. "How are your contacts inside Shariatown?"

"We have faithful in there just like we do everywhere, but understand what you're asking. You or me – we're infidels and that's bad. They'll hurt us, but probably – not certainly, but probably – not kill us just for being Christian. But an apostate who leaves Islam for Jesus? That's a different story. They get medieval."

"Medieval is an improvement," Casey said. As had Turnbull and Clanton, he had spent a long time in the Somalia area of operation and had no illusions about the barbarity of his enemy.

"We'll need help finding our way around," Turnbull said. His tone indicated this was not a request.

"I do not want to take the chance of exposing my people inside," Briggs said. "I'll do it myself. I worked in there until it got too dangerous and we went underground here at the Mall. I know my way around."

"Okay," Turnbull replied.

"You need to tell your boss I want double the M16s and double the ammo he promised."

"I'll tell him," Turnbull promised.

There was a rap on the door.

"Come in," Briggs instructed. It was one of his male congregants who came inside, knelt by his minister, and whispered in his ear. Briggs listened and then nodded. The man left.

He looked at the three Americans.

"Your friend is here."

"You're the shortest Marine I ever met," Casey told the stocky jarhead who was dressed in civilian clothing from the same derelict collection that his three comrades from Task Force Zulu wore. And he was not that short at 5'6; his comrades just towered over him.

Edmundo Vega dropped his pack and hugged first Casey and then Clanton, but not Turnbull. It was nothing personal, but Kelly Turnbull was always uncomfortable with public displays of affection in any form, and his friends understood this quirk. The old friends did shake hands.

"I heard you were in the blue," Turnbull said.

"Yeah, I finished what I was doing for Clay, and he vectored me over here to Minne-so-cold," Mundi said cheerfully. "Said you're totally 'ed up without me, so I came to square you away."

"You even know our mission, Mundi?" asked Turnbull.

"Nope," he said, shaking his head. "But I figure if Clay picked you *pendejos* to do it, it can't be that hard."

"Watch the language, there, Mundi," Casey said. "That's a priest."

Mundi turned to Briggs.

"You Catholic, father?"

"No," Briggs said firmly.

"Good, because I'd have to confess, and we probably don't have enough time for that. So, what's the op, Kelly?"

"Got to snatch or shoot a Somali warlord in the heart of Shariatown, which he owns. And there's a female blue spy named Circe who is extra credit if we can get her too."

"You know, Kelly, we special operators have a pretty checkered history of going into the heart of Somali towns and snatching their warlords."

"My dad was in Gothic Serpent," Clanton said. "A ranger. He would never watch *Black Hawk Down*."

"It's not going that way, folks," Turnbull insisted. "Reverend Briggs, I need you to take me and Casey in so we can find an OP – observation position – and watch this guy for a day or so. Then we'll go in and grab him and haul ass out before they even know we were there."

"Or shoot him," Casey said. "I could just pop him at a distance suppressed, and out we scoot. Clay said he would be happy with him dead."

"Clay said try to grab them so our boys can find out what he knows," Turnbull corrected, though he much preferred Casey's solution to this tricky problem. He was acutely aware of the challenges of infiltrating a hostile city, pulling off a snatch mission, and then exfiltration without getting shot to ribbons by the enraged local population.

"What do we do while you two are snooping and pooping in Shariaville?" asked Mundi.

"Sharia*town*," Casey corrected.

"Let me sketch out my idea for you," Turnbull said. "Some things will need to get done while we're doing our recce."

He turned to Briggs.

"Can we leave tonight, Reverend?"

"Yeah," Briggs said. "I just need to take care of something before we go."

"What's that?" asked Turnbull, concerned there might be a problem.

"I need to pray."

10.

"So, let me get this straight. *Harry Potter* – satanic, right?" asked Casey.

"I hate when you do this," Turnbull said before Reverend Briggs could answer.

"Do what?" Casey replied.

"Speak."

"Kelly, I'm just killing time while we sit here watching, getting some theological insights."

"All the magic nonsense is definitely contrary to what the Bible teaches," Briggs answered. "Rowling pillaged Christian themes, but avoided Christ. And far too many people substituted Potter fandom for having an actual faith. So, not great. Maybe not satanic, but read C.S. Lewis instead."

The minister was sitting in the corner of the dark, vacant apartment they had taken over on South 6th Street. Turnbull was at the window, sitting on a folding chair, watching the entrance to the three-story office building across the road, where the Ughaz had his headquarters. A Somali flag flew outside it; they did not bother with the banner of their alleged country, the People's Republic.

Casey was bored. They had been there for several hours, and nothing had happened. It was all routine, men and veiled women going in and out.

"Just checking because, you know, you do come off a little like the minister in *Footloose*," Casey said.

"John Lithgow's character was the hero of that movie," Briggs argued. "His son drinks and dances and gets killed in a car wreck. He says, 'No more.' It's not popular. But no one else got killed in a DUI since he banned dancing. He's taking a hard stand to save people from themselves."

"Never really thought of it like that," Casey admitted. "I mean, I just thought it was about how Kevin Bacon had to rock and the church tried to make him not."

"Old Hollywood tried hard, but couldn't change the truth. That's why so many classic villains are actually the good guys."

Casey was about to add something, but Turnbull cut him off.

"I will literally shoot out your tongue if you don't stop talking," Turnbull said. "Your turn at the window, Chatty Boy."

Casey sighed and got up, walking across the open floor to the chair by the window where Turnbull had been watching the Hibirya building. He sat down and started up again.

"You know, pastor, I was once in a Tone Lōc tribute band called 'The Funky Cold Medinas.' I started on the turntables but moved to human beatbox. Didn't work out. Went Army, and the rest is history."

"You definitely need to repent," Briggs said. "We need every righteous Christian man for our crusade." The minister looked over at Turnbull, who slumped down against a wall.

"How about you. You ready to fight the jihadis?"

"I've been fighting them for as long as I can remember. And communists. And traitors, perverts, mutants, whatever. Sure, I'm down. Let's go."

"You think we're religious fanatics," Briggs said. "You think the blues are eventually going to notice us and stamp us out like bugs."

"The thought had occurred to me," Turnbull answered.

"Oh, ye of little faith. If you have faith, you can move a mountain."

"I'm running a severe faith deficit lately, padre. Look at what the country has turned into. And it's not going to get better anytime soon. Like I said, I've been fighting so long I don't know anything else."

"And there are more battles ahead," the minister said. "You, me, and Vanilla Ice here, we might not even be around when the final victory comes. But it will come."

"My pal is not much on having a positive mental attitude," Casey interjected from the folding chair by the window. "And Vanilla Ice was underrated as a musician and now, as a congressman."

"Let's all focus on winning this battle," Turnbull said. "Hell, we should focus on just surviving it."

They had left the Mall of America several hours before in a van with "CITY OF MOGADISHU PLUMBING" painted across the side panels. They were dressed accordingly, in plumber regalia, complete with the smells.

"Guess you don't do much laundry," Casey said upon taking an initial whiff.

"That would break the illusion," Briggs said, pulling on his overalls.

"What's the thought process behind the turd wrangler get-up?" Turnbull asked. Briggs might be a little blinded by the light, but he seemed to have a reason for doing things, and he had survived as the leader of a cell of subversive Christians in the heart of the blue for years.

"No one messes with plumbers. There's the obvious reason, but also, if you mess with plumbers, they stop coming, and soon you're swimming in your own sewage. Just like the community gruel tanker yesterday. Even the thickest thugs understand that if you mess with the tanker, it doesn't come back, and you don't eat. But worse, everyone else who is not eating because you acted the fool is going to take it out on you. Same logic. We've used that van and these outfits to get around town for years and never had a problem."

Briggs was correct. Entering Shariatown meant entering a whole different world. It was armed men keeping order, veiled women scurrying along with their children, no alcohol, and the blaring call to worship from the minarets of the government-funded mosques that seemed to be on every blocks. This part of Mogadishu was hard to distinguish form the original.

Physically entering Shariatown meant passing through a checkpoint where a half-dozen khat-chewing Hibirya gunmen stood guard to keep outsiders from wandering into their domain. PSF cruisers, on the rare occasion they sought to come inside, would be waved past. Same with ambulances – again, rare, since medical evacuation services outside the secure area were minimal at best. They also let through food tankers and official PR vehicles. Shariatown was effectively self-governing, and many of its former denizens held city and state offices (at which point they moved into the secure zone), but the clan was not yet strong enough to fully assert itself. It still pretended to respect the authorities, mostly.

Khat was sold on the street. Men walked with automatic weapons. The hijab was mandatory for all women in Shariatown, though a substantial number wore the more extensive burka at the behest of their male relatives.

They had driven north from the Mall of America toward Mogadishu proper. The downtown area of what had been Minneapolis was divided by the wall that split off the secure zone. The rest was outside, including Shariatown, and that was where they headed. The checkpoint was easy to pass through. A wide-eyed Hibirya militiaman with an AK stepped up and managed to articulate the word "Papers" even as his nose crinkled, presumably from their scent. Briggs merely lifted a pink document – the third page of a triplicate form that resembled a work order – and the guard waved them past.

Turnbull relaxed in the back, lowering the weapon he had ready under a tarp if they had needed to shoot it out.

"Told you," Briggs said. "Really, who the hell would pretend to be a plumber?"

They approached the culmination of a protest of mostly unattractive white women in red robes and white hats. They carried pre-printed, and well-used signs, demanding the end of the patriarchy in red America.

"Handmaids," Briggs said. Turnbull rolled his eyes.

"They look like idiots," Casey said. "I remember them from before the Split. How come they are never hot?"

"I remember they used to protest Trump dressed like that," Briggs observed. "Say what you will about him, but I never saw him as an advocate for women wearing *more* clothing."

The plumbing van passed the women as they took off their handmaid robes and put on their hajibs and burkas to go about their day.

The men drove on unmolested until they got close to their objective. They cruised the block along South 6th, noting the security out front of the Hibirya clan offices. It was about eight in the morning, and there was just one sentry out front.

"I thought there would be more guards," Turnbull said as they passed.

"Some of the fighters work for the clan militia as a full-time job," Briggs explained. "Others are, I guess you could call them, reservists. They take home their Kalashnikovs and will come running if called. But my people say that the word is that some of the full-time fighters have been called away for something."

There was an apartment building down the block from the headquarters. It looked shabby, with some windows broken and boarded. That made it typical– everything looked like it was falling apart. Briggs pulled over to the curb.

"One of you come with me," he instructed. "Grab a toolbox."

Turnbull elected to accompany the minister. In their plumber duds, they walked up to the door and went through. There was trash on the floor; it smelled of mold. Turnbull followed him up the steps to the third floor. There was sound from inside most of the doors: talking, television, and music. Others were vacant, including Number 33. It faced the street. Briggs walked to a door where there was some noise indicating occupation. He pounded on it as Turnbull looked up and down the hall. All he had was the .45 handgun; his M4 was back in the van with Casey.

A woman opened the door, baffled. Several bodies moved in the dim light behind her. She said something in a foreign language. Briggs held a pidgin conversation with her, emphasizing the English word "manager." She kept saying "Number 2, Number 2."

Down they went to Number 2, and Briggs pounded on the door. An angry, bleary-eyed man weighing in at 130 dripping wet answered with a flurry of what had to be curses in his own language. Then he paused as he attempted to figure out who these men were. Briggs launched back into pidgin and even gestured with a wrench. The whole thing took about five minutes and ended up with the manager opening up Number 33. It was empty except for a card table and some chairs; apparently, it was being used as a rec room.

"Two days, two days," Briggs told him, turning the wrench in mid-air. The man nodded and went back downstairs.

"He didn't even ask what was wrong," Briggs said. "Of course, why would people show up pretending to be plumbers? He's not even going to call his boss about it."

"What's he care? It's the magic of socialism," Turnbull said. "Nobody owns nothing, so nobody cares."

They began their surveillance. Most of the people coming to the clan headquarters were clearly locals. The clan was more than just a loose familial group; it functioned much like the old mafia. People showed up with problems they had brought to the municipal government before the Split. The municipal government under the People's Republic found the nuts-and-bolts activities of administration both tiresome and dull. Pothole filling went from rare under the pre-Split Democrats to nonexistent under the PR. But there were still plenty of proclamations and initiatives to be passed and celebrated in the lapdog press. The previous week, one council member had accused another of a "macro microaggression" by noting that the aggrieved pol was late to a meeting. For seven days, the city government had been at a standstill as its employees met in struggle sessions designed to wring out the white supremacy this "obsession with punctuality" demonstrated.

In the absence of a functioning municipal government, it was the clan that stepped in to fill the void. A steady stream of men and women in hijabs, flowed into the Hibirya headquarters seeking favors, employment, or to have someone sent over because their neighbor was drunk and playing loud music.

Booze was the Mutawa's special bugaboo. These religious fanatics enforced sharia law in the clan's jurisdiction with the formal approval of the city government – opposing a special foreign justice system would have demonstrated Islamophobia and was out of the question. They were armed with pistols, and their offices – and cells – were located inside the headquarters building. As Turnbull and Casey watched, they streamed out and then returned, usually with some unfortunate in custody.

After a few minutes, there was a wailing-singsong cry – the call to prayer, broadcast over the whole of Shariatown from strategically-placed loudspeakers. Briggs rolled his eyes. The guard outside the headquarters produced a small rug, dropped it on the sidewalk, and began praying.

After it ended, things went back to business as usual. Sometimes one of the clan's technicals would pull up, a light white pickup with a machine gun mount welded on the back operated by a half-dozen fighters. Otherwise, it was mostly regular with people entering and people leaving.

"Lots of folks," Casey said. "No sign of the Ughaz."

"Probably inside. He lives there on the top floor. His office is on the second floor, but most people never get up there. They only get in front of a deputy."

"You sure we would know him if he did come out?" asked Turnbull.

"I've seen him. He usually has a retinue, some flunkies, and a couple of guards. He needs protection. There are smaller clans that would love to displace the Hibirya. Plus competition in the clan itself. Me and my clan against the world, but me and my brothers against the clan, you know?" said Briggs.

"So, you're an expert on them?"

"I needed to get to know them because I evangelized here, even when it started to get ugly after the Split. We still have faithful here, Somalis who have seen the truth. Like I told you back at the Mall, if they get caught, it would be pretty horrible. That's why I'm here personally and trying to keep them out of it."

"Hey, Kelly, come here," Casey said.

"More of your nonsense? Are you going to talk about *Star Wars* or something?"

"No, I'm a Trekkie, but only for red *Star Trek*; *Star Wars* is girlboss garbage. But you need to see this, quick."

Turnbull got to the window and gazed out. There was a Buick, obviously government, parked out front. The door opened. A female with dark hair stepped onto the sidewalk and brushed past the guard to head inside.

"Circe?" Casey asked.

"Looks like her from here. Mark the time," Turnbull said. Casey did on a notepad.

She was obviously there for a sit-down; the Buick was waiting outside for her. Try the hit now? No, they were down two men, and while Briggs meant well, he and his Glock were probably more trouble than they were worth.

"So, what's our girl doing in there?" Casey asked. He had made the same assessment of her identity, and there was no need to discuss it with Turnbull.

"She likes using Somalis as muscle, probably because they will go on suicide missions without whining," Turnbull said.

"It's an honor thing and a Muslim thing. If the Ughaz tells them it's *jihad*, then if they die they are martyrs, and then they get their virgins," Briggs explained.

"So, it's basically leveraging incel sociopaths," Casey observed.

"Eliminating the excess," Briggs said. "With pagan polygamy, there aren't enough women for all the men. You have to do something with a society's men who can't find a mate before they do it themselves. The rape rate in Minneapolis is atrocious, but totally covered up."

"I bet pointing it out is a macro microaggression," Turnbull said.

"The most macro," said Briggs. "They get told the 72 virgins lie and they die for it."

"So, you guys at the Church Militant don't go for all that sex stuff?" prodded Casey.

"Oh, we intend to be fruitful and multiply," Briggs said. "The Mutawa tries to keep contraceptives out of Shariatown and forbids abortion – you can't bring that up in polite blue society either, because abortion is a sacrament to them in the PR – but the Somali women take advantage of this culture of death. Their birthrate is dropping below replacement; the birthrate in the blue is maybe the lowest in human history, with official anti-natalism and abortion practically mandatory. But we embrace sex, within the confines of holy matrimony. Part of our grand strategy in our crusade is to outbreed them."

"We're doing that in the red, too," Turnbull said. "The propaganda gets annoying." He remembered *The Dennis Miller Mysteries* being interrupted by those ubiquitous "You got a need...to breed!" public service announcements starring Tom Cruise and whatever ingenue he was currently married to. The last great movie star had left for the red as soon as the Split happened and the blue banned Scientology.

"You should find a woman, get married, have kids," Briggs told Turnbull.

Turnbull glared.

"It's not so much that he doesn't like women, padre," Casey said. "It's that he doesn't like others in general."

"Why twenty of my best fighters?" the Ughaz demanded. He sat behind his desk in his second-floor office, his cup of tea untouched. To his side stood his trusted aide, an older man who regarded the infidel woman with a suspicion that the more urbane chieftain chose to disguise.

Medea Villareal sat before the Ughaz's impressive desk in one of the chairs that the clan leader ensured was slightly lower than his. He liked to look down on those he addressed.

Her tea cup was not untouched. She took a sip before responding, but had to adjust her hijab to do it.

"This is a critical operation," she said. "The training is coming along well. We leave tonight."

"I would like ten men back. You do not need twenty."

"I need twenty," Villareal answered. She smiled to disarm him and sipped again.

"To go to Panama?"

Villareal stared for a moment. She was wargaming responses when he continued, smiling at his success at surprising her.

"You did not know that I knew where they are going. Well, I know many things. Many things. I am not some fool you can come to and take his warriors without me knowing what it is for."

"It is for the defense of your country, the People's Republic of North America," she said slowly and deliberately.

"How many of my men, good men, strong men, have died defending the People's Republic in Ireland, in Texas?" the Ughaz asked. "Yes, I know these things. Now, I want to know what you intend to do with my men, if they will become martyrs like all the others. My men are not afraid to die, Ms. Villareal, but they are difficult to replace."

Villareal exhaled slowly, gathering her thoughts. The Ughaz waited, smiling. It was the first time he had had the better of her, and he liked it.

"They will help me seize the Panama Canal," she told him. "This is of paramount importance to the People's Republic.

"This is of paramount importance to whoever you work for, Ms. Villareal," he said. His use of the gendered term "Ms." instead of "Mx." or "comrade" annoyed her, nearly as much as his flaunting her marital status to her face.

"I work in support of the People's Republic," she said carefully.

"You speak like a lawyer, but do not worry. Whoever your master is, he has kept his part of our bargain in the past, and I believe that he will do so in the future. Of course, should he not, I would have to go to the real authorities, and that could be embarrassing for him and for you."

The cunning bastard, she thought. She suppressed her irritation at the use of the term "master," his casual assumption that she had a master, and worse, that it was a man. This chauvinism was no doubt a relic of his culture, she realized before suppressing that wrongthought.

"You asked me to come here to discuss the progress of your men's training, and I have," she said. "You've received the initial payment in arms and gold as well." He had demanded gold; the chieftain was clever enough not to be paid in stacks of depreciating Baracks that could not be easily converted for transfer to the rest of the clan waiting in Somalia to come to North America.

"Yes, I have been paid. But I want more, now that I know how important this operation is. Do you expect me to trade the lives of my men for a few rifles and a little bullion?"

The clan chieftain smiled broadly and chuckled.

"No, Ms. Villareal," he said. "You should expect me to trade the lives of my men for *many* rifles and *a great deal* of bullion."

11.

Circe left the Hibirya clan headquarters on 6th Street 28 minutes after she arrived. There was no glad-handing or hugs; she walked out the front doors, crossed the sidewalk, and slipped into the waiting Buick. It disappeared toward one of the main gates into the secure zone a mile or so down the road. The clansmen did not see her take off her hijab.

Turnbull and his companions kept watching. Nothing. It was closing in on noon.

"When do you think they will close up and call it a day?" Turnbull asked Briggs.

"They are open all night. There's a communications room in there for the militia, but they shut down to the public at probably eight or so. It's not like they have formal hours."

"We need to hit them tonight," Turnbull said. "I want it dark for our exfil and for the chopper. My map recon says Peavy Field Park is as good a place as any for the pick-up. Out of Shariatown and wide open."

"It might work," Briggs said. "But it's not outside of Shariatown anymore. They've expanded into the adjacent neighborhoods, and they hold sway there, but the good thing is the Mutawa will keep it clear of any activities. Wouldn't want anyone doing anything immoral, like dancing or people being happy."

Casey laughed.

"The Ughaz is probably not going anywhere," Turnbull said. "But we can't be sure. You stay here. Call me on your XiPhone if he leaves or Circe comes back."

"Are we writing her off?" Casey asked.

"Yeah, let's pass the final before we start worrying about extra credit. When we're coming back here for the show, I'll call you ten minutes out and you can get changed. Then go out the back door and we'll grab you in the alley."

"What if someone comes in here while you're gone?"

"Look like a plumber. Plumb something. And if that doesn't work, smoke 'em suppressed and hope no one notices."

"Roger," Casey replied. They all hoped it didn't come to that.

"Reverend, you and I are heading back to the Mall. Let's go by the park. I want to learn the route and see if it's a suitable LZ."

"When are we coming back?" Briggs asked.

"*We* aren't. My boys and I will come back tonight with a showtime of 7:55. The sun sets at about 6:00. You've done enough."

"I can help."

"You can't."

"One thing, and it's a bit sensitive," Briggs said.

"Shoot."

"What if one or more of you gets captured? No offense, but they'll be very persuasive, and if they learn about us, that we're a subversive church who helped you, they'll come."

"Don't worry about that," Turnbull said. "We're not leaving any of us alive in their hands, even if the rest of us get smoked trying to rescue him."

Briggs regarded him dubiously.

"That's what the last round in the last mag is for," Casey said, serious for once.

"That would usually be a sin," Briggs said. "But I think in that scenario, He might make an exception."

The unit had conducted a couple days of close-quarter combat training out at an old Minneapolis police facility where officers had trained until the organization was defunded. Carlos Trent, under orders from Allegra Barnes, had provided several male trainers to run her twenty men through their paces; Trent did not elaborate on their backgrounds, but she assumed the trainers were ex-American military who had chosen to stay in the blue. They were very careful with how they explained the status of their trainees; she wished they would dispense with the formalized language that was designed to obscure the truth in an effort to avoid complaints of racism, Islamophobia, and whatever other potential hate crimes that could be inferred from less than glowing reports. There was no time for it, but she realized that this itself was wrongthinking.

There was always time for social justice.

Still, from her own observations, she saw that her troops were barely competent at close-quarter battle and their marksmanship was appalling. But she did not need a special operation team. She needed bodies who could get the job done by showing up, spraying and praying, and not running away because if they caught a bullet, they would get laid in the afterlife.

Her men seemed to resent her presence and would have resented her even more if she had overtly attempted to lead them. To mollify them, she wore a hijab to the training area. It did not seem to help. She was a woman and an infidel, and it was unclear to her which category of inferior made them hate her more.

Once again, she worked through an intermediary. Farah – she did not bother learning his other names – was in his late thirties and therefore at least a decade older than most of the men. He was scarred from battles back in his homeland and in his new land, and he took no guff from the men, slapping them or throwing the butt of his AK into their guts when they displeased him. He also knew English well enough to communicate clearly;

KURT SCHLICHTER | 165

his irritation with having to deal with an American woman – they still called citizens of the PR "American" – was obvious, but he kept it in check. The Ughaz was quite clear about what he expected.

She watched the training continue, iteration after iteration, even as the sun set. Her plan was forming inside her brain.

After her morning meeting with the Ughaz at his office, she has returned to the Directorate to meet with Barnes. They talked in a secure room with Trent taking notes; no one else in the organization could know about their plans. Trent was obviously uncomfortable in his supporting role and trying not to show it, but Villareal saw that her taking the lead was killing him inside.

As for Plan A, she would play that by ear, forming it once she saw the ground truth. But she already knew her Plan B. She researched and planned it using her special, unfettered access as an operative in the Directorate to the red Internet, which functioned exponentially better than the blue Internet. The PR internet was burdened and bedeviled by all manner of electronic scolds and warnings regarding improper searches and disallowed thoughts. Half of one's time was spent dismissing pop-up boxes warning of potential misgendering or other thoughtcrimes. Moreover, AI monitors were always watching, and sufficiently dire online behavior was reported for prosecution. She had arrested such malcontents while in the PBI.

Villareal's work was something of an exception in the Directorate; most of the unmonitored red Internet use in the Directorate was to access forbidden red cis-porn, with themes like cheeky cheerleaders, naughty nurses, and the like. That sort of thing was of no interest to her, which probably disappointed Trent. She had no doubt he was tracking her browser history personally.

When she described her contingency plan, Barnes was taken aback by its audacity, but was reconciled to its logic. Trent's face betrayed nothing, probably concealing his secret hope that she would fail in spectacular fashion.

"You are authorized to execute your Plan B if there is no other way," Barnes said.

"I need to be prepared if it becomes necessary. I need a demolitions expert with appropriate skills. And I need a captain for the vessel."

Barnes looked at Trent.

"You'll have them," Trent promised, though he had no idea how he would make that happen. Villareal would not get the satisfaction of him admitting he could not come through. "They will meet you there."

"It will take several days," Villareal explained. "I will have to act to prepare it before I know if our main effort is successful."

"If *el Presidente* comes around, he's not going to care that some Liberian liquified natural gas tanker had been temporarily … annexed," Barnes said. "Focus on winning Guerrero to our side. Use the satphone. Tell me what you promise him, and I'll get it."

She meant Senator Harrison would get it, Villareal knew. He was calling the shots.

"I also need more to give to the Ughaz. He's changing our deal."

"It's been hard to cover for what we have already committed to him," protested Trent.

"That's a dangerous game he's playing," Barnes said. Her failure to acknowledge Trent's objection indicated she had overruled it. He was to make it happen.

"Some more guns and some more gold is a small price to pay," Villareal assured her. It was not her place to make that judgment, but she did so nonetheless.

"I'll confirm. I expect that will not be an issue. You can tell him tonight."

"There will be a bus here in several hours," Villareal told Farah as she prepared to depart the training site.

"Eat first, and then continue to train the men. When it comes here, load the buses and you will be taken to the airport. I will meet you there."

"I am looking forward to the heat," Farah said. "This Mogadishu is too cold."

Villareal smiled in response. Soon, these gentlemen would learn the wonders of humidity. Somalia was a dry heat. Panama was not.

12.

"Nice rides," Turnbull said, appraising the two People's Security Force Ford Explorer cruisers sitting in a loading bay out of sight on the south end of the Mall of America. "Except the driver's side window on this one is shot out, and it looks like the driver's brains are all over the passenger seat."

Clanton and Mundi both shrugged; Turnbull was happy that Casey was back at the observation post watching the Hibirya clan headquarters building because he undoubtedly would have started riffing on *Pulp Fiction*.

"GPS units out?" he asked, though he knew the answer. The pair had taken the 60 seconds to do that at the crime scene so as not to lead the PSF to the Church Militant's lair.

Both men were wearing PSF uniforms. Clanton's was clean and fit him well despite his size. The tailors back in Dallas had made it special for him. Mundi had to take the one that worked best from the four dead PSF officers from whom they had liberated the vehicles.

"You got a blue's blood on your shirt," Turnbull observed. "Is that the best one?"

"Well, Kelly, two of the others were too big, and the third was a *real* mess."

"I guess we know who stays out front with the cars."

"Lucky you, chico," Clanton said, patting his buddy on the shoulder.

"I called in the Penetrators via satphone," Turnbull said. "We're on a 69-minute clock." He consulted his watch, again thankful that Casey was not around to sound off about the time hack.

The men adjusted their own watch timers as Turnbull continued the briefing.

"Pick up is Peavy Field Park. The main landmark is the George Floyd statue about a quarter mile away. You got maps. Get oriented." He handed over his own map, pointing to the extraction point. He did not elaborate on why he was telling them; if he went down, they needed to Charlie Mike– continue the mission. And none of them marked their maps in case they went down and the enemy recovered one.

Turnbull turned to Briggs.

"Thanks for the help," Turnbull said.

"Tell Deeds not to forget our guns," Briggs said. "We have a crusade to launch."

"Well, good luck."

"We got better than luck," Briggs responded. "We have Him. I'll pray for you guys. But if you get separated, don't come here and drag the whole PSF along with you."

"If we get separated, we jump in the Mississippi and float home," Turnbull said, only half in jest. Then he turned to his men.

"Let's roll."

Turnbull drove, with Clanton beside him in the passenger seat and Mundi driving the trail SUV. He was wearing his own PSF uniform, though the pistol in his holster was non-standard. His M4 was locked and loaded, with a suppressor, and rested next to him.

They headed north and came to the checkpoint into Shariatown. The guards were listless and bored; it was the younger ones who drew the night shift, and they were unhappy.

Turnbull was stopped by a kid of maybe twenty with a slung Kalashnikov. He seemed very officious. The older ones lounged in chairs to the side, amused at making the new guy do the work.

"Papers," he demanded of the PSF officers.

The audience watched this interaction with interest.

"Shove it," Turnbull said. The other guards burst out laughing, and the kid seemed unsure of what to do. He had grown used to people hopping to since joining the militia, but this American was not intimidated.

"We're done here," Turnbull told him as the kid stood staring. Turnbull hit the gas and rolled through, followed by Mundi in his trail vehicle. The other guards thought this was the funniest thing they'd ever seen.

Turnbull watched in his side mirror to see what the kid would do. He had his money on nothing, but if the punk shouldered that AK-74, it was going to get ugly. Turnbull won that bet. The kid just stood there, enduring the jeers of his comrades, as the two-vehicle convoy headed north deeper into Shariatown.

Medea Villareal slid into the back of the Buick assigned to her. The driver had an AK on the front seat, though no one was expecting trouble. She leaned forward.

"Take me back to Shariatown."

They met Casey behind the apartment building he had been using as the OP. The American was in his PSF uniform with his M4. He got in with Turnbull and Clanton and shut the door.

"Nothing new. The Ughaz is still in there, but the traffic into and out of the building is way down."

"Let's do it," Turnbull said, hitting the gas and moving the SUV to the end of the alley with Mundi directly behind, alone.

"Still one guard," Casey said. Turnbull turned right, went down to the end of the block, then made another right onto South 6th. Mundi kept up.

"You hold the lobby," Turnbull told them. "Hiram and I go upstairs. At some point, the shooting is going to start. Put that off as long as possible."

"Roger," Clanton acknowledged.

"Aye, captain," Casey said.

The street was largely deserted, with only a few cars parked at the curbs. The sidewalk directly in front of the headquarters was clear, with room enough for the two Explorers. The streetlamps illuminating the face of the building were the only ones on the block that worked.

"Give me the briefcase," Turnbull instructed Clanton, who complied. Briggs's congregation had scrounged it from the Mall. There was nothing in it.

Turnbull crossed the street against traffic – though there was no traffic – and glided to a stop at the curb in front of the doors. Mundi pulled his vehicle in right behind. The young guard, with a Kalashnikov slung around his neck, took a great interest in the two PSF vehicles, but did nothing overtly hostile. The Somali stood on the sidewalk, staring at them, waiting to see what was happening.

All three exited the lead vehicle, M4s slung but readily available, with Turnbull leaving the keys inside and the engine running. Mundi got out of his idling SUV as well, then stood there watching their vehicles. His locked and loaded M4 was on his driver's seat in easy reach through the blown-out window – he had knocked the remaining pieces of glass out back at the Mall so the window appeared, from a distance, merely open instead of blasted out. If someone got close, then it would be dicey.

"For the Ughaz," Turnbull said to the guard as the three men brushed by. He lifted the briefcase for emphasis. Turnbull surmised that people often brought tributes to the Ughaz and that it would not raise suspicion. In any case, the three of them were past the guard and inside the lobby before the sentry could react.

172 | PANAMA RED

The lobby was fed by two hallways extending to the right and the left, and straight ahead were stairs. There was an elevator too, but that was closed off with tape. The assault team had assumed the lifts were down – a safe bet in the blue.

A trio of Somali men were in the lobby or at the head of the hallways extending off it. Two of the three were armed but made no hostile movements. They seemed more curious than threatening.

Casey planted himself in the lobby with a view down the hallways and up the stairs. He heard the crackle of radio static down the hall to the right; he figured that was their comms room.

Turnbull bounded up the stairs, M4 across his back. So far, no one had seemed concerned that it was not a PSF standard AK; some of their elite blue internal security units did carry the M4. Nor did anyone notice he was not carrying a standard Beretta in his holster; they did not seem to notice Clanton's massive Smith & Wesson Model 500 revolver either.

Move quickly with a purpose and look like you belong – most of the time, that was enough to bluff your way through.

At the landing on the second floor, a pair of guards with their AKs lying against the wall stood up from a couple of folding chairs and looked quizzically at the two large PSF men climbing the stairs. Turnbull lifted the briefcase.

"Ughaz," he said to them. "Ughaz."

He shook the briefcase.

They seemed confused and actually glanced at each other. Behind them was a closed double door, grand enough to be the chieftain's office. The hallway ran perpendicular to the stairs.

Turnbull stopped and gestured at the door again with the briefcase.

"Ughaz," Turnbull said again.

Mundi shivered a bit as he waited by the SUV. The guard was looking at him oddly. He smiled and turned away. The guard seemed perplexed and said something. It sounded like "Shirt."

"We need to see the Ughaz," Turnbull told the more important-looking of the guards, his voice registering the urgency of his errand.

"No, no, no," said the guard, gesturing with his hand.

"I need to see him," Turnbull repeated. He waved the briefcase. "This, for him."

"Not now. Meeting!"

Turnbull looked over to Clanton, who met his eyes.

Turnbull nodded.

"On your shirt," the guard out front said. "Is that blood?"

Mundi shook his head.

The guard walked over, brows furrowed. He stopped a couple of feet away, staring at the broken glass along the rim of the driver's window, and at the remnants of the hastily cleaned-up mess in the front seat.

"What is that?" he demanded.

Mundi smiled and whipped the M4 out of the SUV through the window. The sentry began trying to unlimber his rifle, but there was no chance of beating the operator.

Mundi shot him twice in the chest and once in the face with the suppressed weapon. The sentry's body fell backwards on the sidewalk, and the brass clinked across the concrete.

Mundi walked over to the front doors, noticing a pair of pedestrians a few yards down the street who had seen what happened and scattered. He mounted the stairs and stuck his head into the lobby.

Casey was standing there with a couple of bored Somali guards, the third have wandered back down the hall.

"We're blown," Mundi said.

Casey nodded, lifted his weapon, and shot both guards in succession. It was suppressed but still loud– 140 decibels.

The sound of the shots downstairs distracted the guards facing Turnbull and Clanton. Turnbull slammed the empty briefcase into the side of the leader's head. Clanton drew his revolver and fired two shots into the other guard; one .500 magnum slug was more than enough; two was pounding the rubble.

Ears ringing, Turnbull went through the door into the Ughaz's office. Behind him was a third thunderous gunshot; Clanton finished the guard whose head Turnbull had just gone upside with the briefcase.

Never leave a live enemy to your rear.

A pair of men, elders of some sort armed with pistols in holsters, were sitting in front and beneath the Ughaz before the desk; the chieftain himself was already on his feet.

Turnbull shot the elder on the left twice and then put two rounds into the one on the right. They dropped, and Turnbull fixed the pistol on the chief's face. The warlord froze in place, petrified and utterly confused, as Clanton rushed through the door past Turnbull, who kept a bead on the target's center of mass. When Clanton reached the terrified clan leader, he punched him square in the jaw. The man fell, and Clanton knelt down to get to work.

There was a ruckus at the end of the right hallway. Casey took aim. A man with an AK stepped out into the light tentatively, trying to see what was happening. He saw Casey drawing a bead; a moment later, he dropped with two rounds in him. There was more excitement from his friends out of sight inside the room.

"Okay, guys, where are you?" Casey whispered as he searched for targets down the hall.

Clanton rolled the groggy captive onto his face and pulled his arms behind his back, pinning him with a knee to the spine. He set the thin man's wrists together and bound them with a heavy black zip tie.

Outside the office, Turnbull saw movement down the second-floor hall and fired twice with his pistol. There was a yelp of pain.

"Come on!" he yelled to Clanton. The big guy was moving like pond water.

More movement. Turnbull blew off the last two rounds from the mag and dropped it, replacing it with a fresh one. He slid the pistol into his holster and brought his M4 around.

Clanton drew another zip tie from his pocket and bound the man's legs. He took a black hood from a different pocket and pulled it down over the man's head. The chieftain was struggling now and cursing. Clanton punched him in the kidney, not hard enough to burst anything, but sufficient to make his point.

Someone thrust an AK out of a doorway down the first-floor hall and opened up on automatic. Casey stepped out of the line of fire as the man blew off a whole mag of ammo. His ears were ringing, and the smell of gunpowder was making its way up the hall. When the man went dry, Casey leaned back and drew a bead on the goateed head of a fighter trying to assess the battle damage. That was the last thing the man ever assessed.

Outside, people were starting to appear in windows, looking out to see what all the gunplay at the headquarters was about. Down the street, in both directions, men were coming outside, none of them armed – yet. The gunfire inside was continuing in intermittent bursts. Mundi fervently hoped none of his mates were hit – they didn't need that complication.

A Somali fighter stepped out from a room down the hall holding a handgun; Turnbull shot him twice, and he dropped.

There was shouting; the American pivoted to look down the opposite hallway, but it was dark and silent. That was good.

"What's keeping you, Hiram?" Turnbull shouted as he pivoted back to cover the threat.

"He's heavier than he looks, Kelly!"

Clanton had the chief over his shoulder in a fireman's carry, pausing at the double office doors to confirm that it was clear to pass across the landing to the stairs.

"Go!" Turnbull barked, and Clanton rushed past him to the stairs. Another face appeared out of a doorway down the second-floor hallway. Turnbull blew off several rounds in his direction, then followed Clanton, who was bellowing.

"We're coming down!"

Casey recognized that bellow from the stairwell as the yeti's cry. Per the plan, the diminutive Ughaz was bagged and tagged and slung over the big operator's shoulder. Turnbull was coming down behind him on the stairs, covering up toward the second floor.

"Hold up!" Casey said. He squeezed off about ten rounds down the right hallway, then five or six more down the left, where he had heard some shouting but not taken any fire. Satisfied that the Somalis were suppressed, he summoned Clanton.

"Okay, it's clear!"

Clanton bounded off the stairs and through the hallway danger zone, followed by Turnbull. Casey remained the trail man, covering the withdrawal.

Two men with AKs were coming up the street fast, shouting something in their language. Mundi heard a couple of long bursts inside and hoped the fight was resolving because this was getting hairy.

A third man sped out of a tenement doorway, his weapon in hand – did everyone have a rifle in this town? It was like being in the red. And now they were approaching, cautiously, probably not sure if the PSF man with a rifle outside the front door was friend or foe.

Mundi clarified that with three sets of two shots at the armed men. One was still standing, so Mundi gave him a third, and he spun like a top before falling. They were thin guys, and the 5.56mm rounds worked fine.

Clanton burst outside through the front door and down the two cement steps past the dead guard, heading for the back door of the lead SUV.

"They're right behind me!" he shouted.

Mundi went for his driver's door, but saw another armed man down the way in the opposite direction on 6th Street. The operator paused to shoot him, then slipped in behind the wheel.

Turnbull was next, coming out the front and heading toward the first SUV. Clanton had flung open the back seat door and tossed the bound captive in the back. The man groaned when he landed on the hard prisoner's seat. Clanton slammed the door closed and slid into the driver's seat.

There was now AK fire coming from down the block. Turnbull opened up at a gunman in a third-floor window across the street. The guy had just started blasting away, not very accurately, as his rifle rounds had slammed into the face of the headquarters building. Turnbull's return fire shattered the window pane above his head, and he pulled back out of sight.

Now Casey was out the door, headed to the trail cruiser. Like Turnbull, he ran around the front to get in the passenger seat.

Clanton did not wait to be told to hit the gas; the cruiser was moving even before he slammed the door shut, with Mundi and Casey right behind.

Ding!

A round had hit a side panel, then another. Turnbull dropped the passenger window, and his suppressed muzzle was outside it as he searched for targets along the street and among the windows. He heard more gunfire and saw some impacts on the street.

"Everyone's got a gun here," Clanton complained.

"Just like home," Turnbull replied. He grabbed the mic on the dash– they had set their own frequency for comms.

"You two good?" he asked. There was a pause; in the side mirror, he could see Casey's muzzle leaning out of his window, engaging someone.

"Yeah, we're cool. You guys?"

"Good to go."

"The package?"

"Intact," said Turnbull. He craned his neck around to gaze backwards at the writhing form lying in the back seat and to confirm his assessment.

"Contact front!" Clanton yelled. There were three or four men on the street ahead, all armed.

Turnbull leaned out his window, M4 aiming forward, and fired a burst. It was meant less to kill than to suppress, but he did drop one guy who lay wriggling in the street as his buddies scattered. The PSF cruiser rushed past him, and his buddies rallied and opened fire. One round punched through the rear window of Turnbull's SUV.

The radio came alive with Casey's voice.

"We're taking more fire, Kelly. They're everywhere. It's like we kicked an anthill."

Casey's complaint was punctuated by a round digging into the hood.

From his seat, Turnbull could see more shapes running out into the street, some holding cell phones and directing the action, others doing the shooting.

Turnbull pivoted to Clanton.

"Drive faster."

The Buick pulled up in front of the headquarters, having passed bodies in the street and on the sidewalk. There was a small, agitated crowd out in front of the clan headquarters building, mostly armed. No one was paying any attention to the dead man on the sidewalk. People were tracking his blood across the concrete.

Villareal stepped out and was immediately the center of attention, angry attention. Why were they mad at *her*? Spotting an aide to the Ughaz, she made for him, ignoring the stares of the others.

"Ali, what happened?" she demanded.

"Your people! Just minutes ago!" he shouted, furious. "Why did they come here, kill our men, seize our chief?"

"What the hell do you mean?" she asked.

"Your PSF, they came, started shooting, took the Ughaz!"

"PSF?" Then it hit her– the whole scheme was coming apart. Harrison's plot had been discovered. They were rolling up the participants. She would be next.

No.

Wait.

Think.

If they were internal security forces, they would still be here. They would not just come in and out, and besides, arresting the Ughaz would cause an uprising. No, this was something else.

"*Who* came, exactly?" she asked, trying to project calm. It worked. He settled somewhat.

"People's Security Force. Two vehicles. They came inside, killed guards, killed elders. Then they took the Ughaz away. Carried him out."

"How many men? How many PSF?" she asked him.

"Three or four. They left this," the man said, handing her a stainless-steel magazine. It read "Wilson" and was clearly not a common 9mm magazine. More like a high-end .45 caliber.

She had seen the gun in the hand of the operative who had almost killed her in Dublin. He had an M1911. A .45.

It was *him*. On cue, she felt a twinge of pain from her arm.

"Why would your government do this?" the aide demanded. The crowd was growing more agitated, and she began to feel the threat. But there was a bigger threat.

"It wasn't the PSF. It wasn't our government. It was the reds. It was the Americans. They wanted to take your chieftain alive because of what he knows," she explained. "We have to stop them before they escape."

"We are calling up men to stop them before they can get out of Shariatown," the aide told her. "Everyone has a XiPhone. We are calling them all, telling them to come with their rifle and stop the PSF."

They had better stop them, considering what Ughaz Yusuf Ali Abdullahi knew. And good luck to any real PSF in Shariatown tonight. They would need it.

The glass from the windshield flew into the passenger compartment. It was shatterproof, so it did not disintegrate, but it was looking rough.

Turnbull aimed his weapon at the men lining the streets. They were pouring out of their buildings now, like hornets from a hive, most with rifles, a few with pistols, and the shotcallers with their cell phones. There must be a phone tree or something–clearly, their location was being reported. The clan was coordinating its response.

He pulled the trigger; Turnbull had switched to automatic because there was no real way to aim from the careening PSF cruiser. He hoped to suppress and scatter the defenders, maybe get a lucky hit every once in a while.

The stream of brass arced out of the ejection port, the empty shells collecting on the floor. Clanton was adding to it, trying to fire one-handed as he drove. Turnbull went dry and dropped the empty. It joined at least five others in the footwell. Dull, hollow thuds from impacting 7.63x39mm rounds sounded as he slapped in another mag.

"Damn, Kelly, where the hell are they all coming from?" Casey yelled over the radio. Turnbull grabbed the mic as a round smashed his side mirror.

"Just be glad they suck at shooting," he replied. "Keep moving."

They *were* lousy shots, most choosing the tried-and-true spray-and-pray methodology of their homeland. But there were so many of them firing that, even with a low individual hit probability, the likelihood of a lucky shot was rising.

The rear passenger window caught three shots, and the hooded Ugaz was covered with shards. He was screaming something that sounded profane. At this rate, his rescuers were as likely to off him themselves as rescue him.

"Damn it!" Clanton yelled. Turnbull looked through the pockmarked windshield at an improvised roadblock, a pile of trash cans, junk, and some burning tires emplaced across the road and defended by a horde of fighters.

"Crash through?" asked Clanton.

"No, turn around," Turnbull ordered.

"Turn around?"

"We'll get stopped and then we're screwed," Turnbull said. A round went through the roof between them and buried itself in the console.

Clanton braked, and behind them, Mundi barely braked in time to avoid a rear-end collision.

"Turn around, we need to go back around the block," Turnbull yelled into the mic, then aimed his weapon out the window and hosed down the roadblock while Clanton worked to complete his three-point 180-degree turn.

"Go, go, go!" Casey shouted over the air as Clanton finished the turn and zipped past them. Casey continued to spray the roadblock with automatic fire as Mundi turned his SUV around and followed.

"Go back the way we came a block, go right, then right at the end of the block and keep going," Turnbull said. He knew the roads were laid out on a grid.

Sort of.

The gunfire in their direction thinned out a bit, and they got several blocks before it started up again. A man rushed to the sidewalk as they passed, spraying across the front right quarter panel. There were three pings on sheet metal, then a soft thud.

"I hope these are run-flat tires," Clanton exclaimed, but Turnbull ignored him. He put his red dot on the shooter's chest and pulled the trigger. The man staggered and fell in the gutter.

Clanton accelerated.

There was something happening on the other side of the street at the curb up ahead. Fighters were running about and jumping on what seemed to be a burning car. As the little convoy approached, Turnbull saw it was a wrecked PSF sedan. Clearly, it was a case of mistaken identity. As the two SUVs passed the confused crowd, several of the fighters were waving body parts of the occupants like trophies.

"Sucks for them," Clanton observed. "Where we at, navigator?"

"Wait one," Turnbull replied. He emptied his mag at some scattered fighters, dropped the mag, and replaced it. Then he pulled out his paper map – the XiPhone did not have GPS capability – and looked at a passing street sign.

"I think they changed the street names," he said. "This is now called 'Victory to Our Glorious Martyrs Boulevard.'"

"Do you even know where we're going?" asked Clanton.

"Sort of," Turnbull replied uncertainly. "Go south and go fast."

More rounds hit the SUV, this time on the driver's side.

"Kelly, technical left! It's shadowing us one block over!"

Turnbull looked past Clanton's massive bulk and out the driver's side window as they went through the intersection at the next block. He saw it, a street over, a white technical – some kind of pickup truck packed with bodies and a mounted light machine gun of some type that blazed away at them as they crossed the intersection.

"We should have brought a rocket launcher," Clanton groaned.

Turnbull looked at his watch. Nine minutes to pick up. The satphone sat in the console, covered in glass fragments but undamaged. It was on and waiting for a call.

"Pick up the pace," he told Clanton as two more holes appeared in the hood. He leaned out the window to spray up at the roofs of the buildings lining the road, pausing only to reload.

Turnbull had started with a lot of ammo, but he was beginning to run short. There were four mags left, counting the fresh one he had just inserted.

"They put stuff in the road. I gotta weave around it!" Clanton decelerated, then accelerated after he maneuvered by and between the obstacles, firing out the window with one hand at anything that looked like a target.

"Out!" he yelled. Turnbull pulled the man's gun over to his lap and reloaded it, then handed it back.

They went through the next intersection. Turnbull braced for another burst of machine gun fire. But no technical.

"Where's our friend, Kelly?"

"I doubt he got bored and left," Turnbull said. He grabbed the radio. "You guys have eyes on the technical?"

"Nope. Hold on." There was a pause, and Turnbull heard shooting from the trail SUV. Casey returned to the radio net. "I can't see it, Kelly. Where did it go? Hey, we're running low on ammo. How far?"

Turnbull ignored him. He was looking through the shattered windshield at a large intersection up ahead. In the center was a monolith; standing upon it was the statue of a stocky man with his fist raised in the air. And he saw the white of the technical parking in front of it across the road.

"Damn it, they're going to try to cut us off at George Floyd Square!"

The technical, a Toyota, was parked in the road ahead of them broadside with the machine gunner and the half-dozen shooters in back all opening up.

Turnbull fired through his windshield, blasting out some of the remaining shards, but seven guns to one was not going to end in his favor.

"Get down and hit 'em!" Turnbull commanded. "And make sure you're belted in."

Clanton bent to the side and hit the accelerator as a tsunami of lead hit the onrushing cruiser.

The Ughaz's aide put down his phone and turned to Villareal, who was next to him in the back of the Buick. Up front were her driver and a Somali gunman.

"They are at George Floyd Square. We are going to trap them!"

"I want them alive!" Villareal told the aide, but what he said into the phone in his own language did not sound like an admonition to handle these invaders with kid gloves.

The SUV hit the side of the Toyota pickup truck at about 30 miles per hour. Front airbags deploy, for belted occupants, at around 16 MPH. The sensor, when the deployment criteria occur, initiates a chemical reaction that fills the airbag with nitrogen gas in a fraction of a second. The airbags worked as designed, despite their age and the haphazard maintenance protocols of the PSF motor pool. The forward momentum of Turnbull and Clanton's bodies was absorbed by the cushions even as the metal groaned and the remaining glass in the SUV shattered and fell into the passenger compartment.

In the back, the Ughaz did not fare as well. He slammed into the rear of the front seats, then bounced back. He was moaning piteously when Turnbull beat down the rapidly deflating airbag and turned to check on their captive.

"You okay, Hiram?"

"That rung the hell outta my bell, Kelly," the big man said, shaking it off.

"Get him in Mundi's ride," Turnbull ordered. He forced open his door with some effort and stepped out, gun and satphone in hand.

The Toyota was on its side and back a dozen feet. Their SUV was an old police cruiser with cop suspension and a push bar up front. It was not going anywhere – the entire crumple zone had crumpled exactly as designed, but the Toyota was smashed almost beyond recognition.

The occupants were worse off. The ones in the passenger compartment were messed up, but the six or seven in the back were all ejected. They lay scattered on the ground at the feet of the statute; the subject looked down upon the scene in a suit and tie. The plaque, which was splattered with a goo that likely came from one of the technical's crew, read:

George Floyd
He/Him
Hero, Role Model, and Lover

Improbably, one of the fighters was struggling to his feet and seemed to be looking for a weapon. Turnbull dropped him and ran back to the trail SUV. Clanton was shoving the Ughaz in the back, then joined him in the rear. Turnbull got in on the other side. He would have no problem shooting out of the rear passenger window since it was totally blown out.

"That was awesome," Casey told Clanton as Mundi pulled away.

"I feel like I got hit on the head with a sledgehammer," Clanton complained.

"There's smoke or steam or something coming out of the holes in the hood," Mundi said, looking at the front end of their surviving vehicle.

"We're close," Turnbull replied. "Don't stop for nothing. We got about four minutes."

A couple of men ran out of an alley and began firing wildly. Bullets lanced low through the passenger side door.

"You hit, Casey?"

"No, but he almost blew off my jewels!"

"Oh damn," Clanton said, looking out the broken back window. Turnbull rotated to face the rear.

At least three technicals and some other cars were roaring up the street behind them, perhaps a quarter mile back.

"Mundi, you should speed up," he said.

"That the park?" Mundi asked. Up ahead was a large, open green space. Bums and hobos were living around the perimeter of the park and inside on the old ball field.

Turnbull keyed the satphone and set it on speaker so he could scan for targets. It picked up.

"This is Pericles," Turnbull said.

"This is Leonidas," replied the pilot.

"Maybe not the best code name for someone called 'a penetrator,'" Casey suggested.

"What?" asked the confused pilot.

"Stop talking and shoot things," Turnbull told his comrade. He addressed the flyer.

"We're a minute out. There are tents and shelters in the LZ."

"Not for long."

"We're in what looks like a cop car, except it's shot to bits. Don't shoot us. But there are a bunch of technicals and other cars in pursuit. You can shoot *them.*"

The SUV jolted and groaned as Mundi hopped the curb and tore through a preexisting hole in the fence. They were now on the unkempt, grassy field. He hit the headlights to avoid running anyone over unnecessarily.

"I got you," said the pilot. "You got me?"

"No, it's dark as hell," Turnbull said.

"Okay, stop. We'll come in on you."

"Well, we have company right on our ass."

"Like I said, not for long."

Mundi braked to a stop. The Americans rolled out of the SUV with their weapons.

"I got maybe one more mag," Casey said as the muffled helicopter roared in over them – it had noise-dampening technology. The tents and shelters in the immediate area blew away in the rotor wash.

"We have them, and their helicopter!" the aide shouted triumphantly. "Go, go!"

Their Buick was at the rear of the pack, with the technicals up front and a variety of work trucks and other civilian vehicles packed with eager fighters rushing ahead across the grass of Peavy Field Park.

Villareal saw the police cruiser's headlights and that it had stopped. She could not see the helicopter, but despite its noise-dampening technology, she could hear it.

"Stop!" she ordered.

"No, we have them!" shouted the aide.

"Stop the damn car!" Villareal screamed at the driver. At the end of the day, he worked for her. He hit the brakes, and they rolled to a halt, perhaps 400 yards from their quarry.

"No, no! We have them!" howled the aide.

"We don't have anything," Villareal replied.

Turnbull and the other operators opened fire at the approaching onslaught. He went dry almost immediately and reloaded his last mag, intending to make it count. Then the aircraft's MK 19 grenade launcher began to belch out 40mm shells, and its mounted minigun erupted with fire. With one in nine rounds incendiary, the rate of fire was such that the tracers made it look like a solid finger of fire lancing through the onrushing pursuers.

The vehicles chasing them blew up and rolled over under the fusillade. None of them got closer than 100 meters. The operators watched, fascinated.

Clanton bent back inside the vehicle and grabbed the prisoner. He carried the wriggling sack of humanity around the smoking PSF cruiser and tossed it into the aircraft. Next came Mundi, then Casey, followed by Turnbull.

He climbed into the aircraft, and the sergeant manning the minigun was grinning at him like a madman. Turnbull smiled back.

"I gotta get me one of those."

PART II

13.

The air conditioner was on even as streaks of rain trickled down the glass of the rear window. The streets were deserted because of the weather, but she could feel the tension and was glad she had security. One of her guards sat up front; the other one was with her in back, mercifully silent. The embassy had supplied the SUV and driver.

As they passed through the city streets, she saw two vaguely human shapes hanging from an overpass. There was a crudely painted sign tied to one. It read "TRAIDORES."

She spoke Spanish. It meant "traitors." She smiled. Evidentially the *presidente* understood how to deal with fascist pawns.

It was hot, humid, and mostly rainy in Panama City. Medea Villareal's Cuban blood should have immunized her, at least somewhat, to the October weather in Central America. Perhaps her time in Mogadishu, Minnesota, had impacted her genetic disposition. She found it somewhat uncomfortable, but her Somali troops were suffering greatly. Minnesota was cool and moist, while the original Mogadishu was hot and dry. This city was hot and wet. Her hired men would not stop complaining about it, but she did not understand their language and did not care.

She had too many things going on to focus on transitory discomfort.

One was the event that evening, if you could call it an event. It was more of a presentation – she was being presented to *El Presidente* Bonifacio Alberto Maria Guerrero that evening as the new Deputy Chief of Mission (DCM) of the People's Republic of North America to the Bolívarian Republic of Panama. There were several aspects to consider; it had to go well.

But it very well might not, so she was also thinking of Plan B. In fact, she had gone to see the subject of that exercise with her sea captain, her demolitions experts, and a couple of guards. She saw it bobbing at anchor from the Bridge of the Americas spanning the entrance to the Panama Canal. She was no seaman, but she could see that the tanker was on the downslope of its useful life. She was surprised that the *Greyhawk Paladin* was even floating, but it would not need to do that for much longer *if* Plan B became necessary.

The sea captain was one Conrad Johnson, a drunk who made no attempt to hide it. His license had been pulled after he piled his freighter into a bridge pillar off Boston; he was a straight male whose ancestors came from Germany, so there was no easy way to leverage the hierarchy of oppression to shift the blame. Villareal used him because he needed her; that was the best kind of person to use. Carlos Trent deserved grudging credit for finding him.

The same with her demolitions expert, Frank Devlin, a descendant of a long line of demolitions experts all the way back to the Irish Civil War. He needed her, too; he was in prison for selling explosives. The government official responsible for the explosives he sold was mad mostly because Devlin had not had the courtesy to cut him in. When the explosives went missing, he was an easy scapegoat, though guilty as hell. Like Captain Johnson, he was a man with few options who was offered money and a second chance by this mysterious woman who flew them off to Panama.

"It's not the flame or fireball we care about," Devlin explained. When Villareal had outlined her idea, he was thrilled about it beyond the enticements of freedom and cash – American cash, to be paid to him wherever he chose to live afterward. And he enjoyed talking about it, too.

"You might have heard of fuel-air explosives – basically, you disperse a vapor and detonate that. It generates a massive blast wave. I've been talking to the captain here about how the Panama Canal operates, doing my calculations. If the ship is in the right place, we'll get the effect you want."

"There are two sets of locks," Villareal said, looking to the captain for confirmation.

"Yes, the Gatun Locks on the north and the Agua Clara locks on the south. The Gatun Locks, which are a century old, have two lanes. The Agua Clara are the newer locks, and it is a much bigger single lane. The new locks opened in 2016. The lock mechanisms are in the midst of their first major overhaul that is scheduled to be finished in two months. That leaves all traffic going through the two Gatun Locks lanes. If Agua Clara was open," the sea captain said, "we'd need another tanker."

"But will it work?" Villareal demanded.

"Sure, *if* the ship is where it needs to be," Devlin said. "The only problem is not being aboard when it happens."

Villareal smiled.

"What do we need to do to get in position?" she asked the captain.

"Pay the toll, get the pilot aboard. We can float out there on Gatun Lake until you give the word. I can set everything, and we can get out of there."

"What about the pilot?" asked Bold. "He's Panamanian, right?"

"We won't need him once we get in position," the captain said. "You send the word, then I can set up everything. Your boys here can take care of him."

Villareal continued with her dry smile. She would not be sending word. This had to be done right. If and when the time came, she intended to be there herself to ensure the drunk captain and the mad bomber, as well as her Somali guards, did not screw up her Plan B.

"Pay the money. Get the ship in ready and in position," she told Mx. Viveca Bold, the resident Directorate agent at the embassy. Bold's cover was as the Assistant Deputy Consul for Diversity, Equity, and Inclusion. Bold wore a flowery blouse, a long skirt, and – in Villareal's opinion – too much mascara and too much rouge. It drew attention to her strong jaw.

Agent Bold swallowed, her Adam's apple bobbing, and carefully wrote down Villareal's instructions. This was the biggest operation Bold had ever been involved in, and this woman-identifying woman who had just flown in with a platoon of gunmen did not seem like someone who tolerated failure.

"It will be ready, comrade," Bold said, her voice deeper than she liked.

"Two days," Villareal reiterated, her face displaying zero flexibility. Viveca Bold nodded and wiped her face; her mascara was dripping down her cheeks despite the Chevy's A/C.

"I understand."

And then there was the third issue that was weighing on Villareal's mind. The reds had succeeded in Mogadishu, and now Ughaz Yusuf Ali Abdullahi was in the hands of the Americans. That he would suffer did not bother her; in fact, that was a silver lining to this dark cloud. She had no use for him other than as a source of meat for her grinder, and now that he could not supply her with armed men, he was nothing to her except a vaguely irritating memory.

Her problem was that the chieftain knew at least some of what she was doing here in Panama. Had the Americans already known about her mission and snatched him to find out the details, or was the abduction retaliation for the Lackland Air Force Base attack? It did not matter much; the result would be the same. They would know about her mission soon enough. She had zero confidence that Abdullahi would keep that information to himself.

"Embassy," she commanded. The driver grunted in affirmation. Villareal turned to look into Bold's face.

"You will help me get ready for tonight and accompany me."

Bold nodded and swallowed again, her Adam's apple bobbing once again. But this time, it was not because she was afraid of Villareal.

"I'm surprised Abdullahi wasn't in worse shape when he got here," Clay Deeds said to Turnbull and the other three operators. They had been on the ground in Dallas for just five hours and had barely unpacked when their boss called them back and assembled the team in the SCIF – the secure, compartmentalized information facility.

"Sure, he was banged up," Deeds continued. "Really banged up, but nowhere near as much as I would expect of someone who literally will not shut up. I know how much Kelly hates people who talk."

"I never touched him," Turnbull said. "Okay, he was yelling on the plane back from Iowa, and I did kick him, but it wasn't that hard. And he did stop talking."

"Boss, I really don't think you dragged me away from my *Harry Potter* marathon, and these boys from their Shiners and chili and sleep, to talk about the prisoner's condition," Casey observed.

"I like Japanese beer, like Sapporo," Mundi said. "Or Kirin."

"What's wrong with Shiner?" demanded Clanton. "You some kind of communist?"

"Gentlemen!" Deeds yelled. "The point here is not that Abdullahi is talking but *what* he is talking about."

"Okay, Clay, then what's the point?" asked Turnbull. "I kind of would rather be having chili and sleeping after a Shiner or four."

"See?" said Clanton to Mundi. "Shiner is a man's beer."

Mundi flipped off the yeti.

"We didn't even have to threaten him," Deeds continued, ignoring the Great Brewski Debate. "In fact, all I did was offer him a Pepsi, and he started telling me about how your girlfriend is making martyrs of all his boys."

"My girlfriend?" asked Kelly. "Circe?"

"Medea Ekaterine Villareal. That's her name. We ran it through my sources.

"He's got good sources," Casey affirmed. Deeds ignored him, too.

"Half-Cuban, and she was at the People's Bureau of Investigation for several years, but then she disappeared. The records don't show she was fired – in fact, she's a true believer with a nearly perfect ideology score, though she lost points for thinking outside the box. I'm guessing she got recruited to the Directorate. She's smart and ruthless, as we've seen in the past."

"Is she hot?" asked Casey.

Turnbull gestured "so-so" with his palm.

"She's a normal 6 and a Casey 9," Clanton chuckled. Mundi high-fived him. Casey flipped him the bird.

"There was suspicion she was cis, but they investigated and cleared her as bi. She/them, privilege level 6."

"Would," Mundi declared.

"She had you at cis," Casey said.

"How about you, Kelly?" Clanton laughed.

Turnbull growled.

"Now, if we can get serious here," Deeds said. "Circe was leaving later on the night of your snatch for Panama with about twenty Somali mercs. That's all the guy knew, the where and the when."

"But not the why?" Turnbull asked.

"But not the why," Deeds confirmed. "But I can guess the why. The Panama Canal."

"Twenty of those guys are trouble, but it's not enough to overthrow the whole country," Mundi said. "I've operated there. *El Presidente* has it locked down pretty good. His military is either loyal or scared. He'll kill you and hang your body off an overpass as soon as look at you if he smells disloyalty."

"I think she's down there to help talk *Presidente* Guerrero into shutting down the canal," Deeds said.

"Panama is the cartel crossroads, but if he closes the canal, the money dries up and the country revolts," Mundi countered.

"I mean shut it down to us, the U.S. Navy."

"That's a good way to get invaded again," Turnbull observed.

"It wouldn't need to be closed for long, just a few days. We couldn't mount an invasion that fast."

"Maybe I'm slow, but why would shutting it down for a few days be important, boss?" asked Clanton.

"Because our satellites have detected a Chinese People's Liberation Army Navy task force heading to Peru. It's light on warships, but heavy on ro-ro transports like they used on Taiwan." He was referring to the "roll on/roll off" vessels that carried military vehicles for rapid deployment.

"An invasion force," Casey said.

"Enough force to help the Peruvian communists win," Deeds said. "If we get between them and Lima, they either turn their ships around or get sunk."

"So, the People's Republic convinces Panama's homicidal dictator to close the canal, and then there's no way we can get ships into the Pacific in time to block them," Turnbull said. "The Chinese get Peru and People's Republic gets the eternal gratitude of the PRC."

"Bingo," Deeds replied. "Gentlemen, the backfield is already in motion. The U.S. is going to stop that Chinese fleet the easy way or the hard way, which means we need the canal open."

"There goes my movie marathon," Casey said. Clay Deeds checked his watch.

"Seventy-four hours from now, the United States is sending two new *Halsey*-class cruisers, the U.S.S. *Andrew Breitbart* and the U.S.S. *Charlie Kirk*, through the Panama Canal. These are mini-battleships with thick armor designed to survive whatever the PLAN throws at them, from drones to hypersonics, and to hit back twice as hard. A bunch of *Zumwalt* and *Burke* destroyers will follow on within 48 hours, while the *Enterprise* carrier group will be steaming offshore in the Atlantic – it can't get through the canal because it exceeds the Panamax dimensions."

"What do you want us to do?" Turnbull asked.

"Convince *El Presidente* Bonifacio Alberto Maria Guerrero that he needs to let our ships through his canal despite what your girl Circe has to say about it."

"Why aren't we using our diplomats?" asked Casey. "Make their useless asses earn their pay for once."

"We tried that. *El Presidente* was unwilling to be reasonable. The diplomats think they can get him to come around, but we don't have time for that. We need a different approach."

"How do we do it?" Turnbull asked.

"Use your powers of persuasion, Kelly," Deeds ordered. "You got whatever you need. Be unreasonable. But do it."

The embassy of the People's Republic of North America was in a whitewashed office building just outside the diplomatic zone. The United States had kept the original American embassy; after the Split, the PR had to find its own digs and rented a former bank office where billions of cartel drug dollars had been laundered back in the day.

There was a patch of creeping mold, or perhaps moss, along the sides and near the seams in the stucco. It gave off a vibe of decay and rot, as if the building were disintegrating from the heat and humidity. But then, most of the other buildings in Panama City were the same. It was once a vibrant city; now, a pall of fear hung over it, permeating all its nooks and crannies.

A few unkempt Presidential Guard soldiers lounged outside the embassy gate on the street in a pair of old Hummers, the machine guns mounted outside the turrets showing, if one got close enough to inspect them, streaks of rust. Out front, a flag flew from a pole covered in peeling white paint. It was not at half-staff, but the top of the banner was several feet below the peak. Someone did not care enough to raise it to its full height; in fact, no one had bothered to take it down the previous evening and then run it back up the flagpole in the morning. If one had inspected the PR flag, not only would they notice its wear and tear, but that it was several iterations old.

Villareal's SUV was through the gate by the guards – not Marines, as the PR had no Marine Corps. The idea of elite naval infantry was simply too inherently patriarchal. Instead, the PR Air Force got the embassy security gig. Inside their guard shack, they carried aging M16 rifles and wore blue slacks and white shirts as their uniforms, with a rainbow sash around their midriffs. One of the guards had a bushy beard; the other's face was obscured by a leather mask. He was channeling a sexy beagle.

The driver took Villareal up to the entrance and idled under the awning, a blessing since the rain was still coming down. She ordered her guards to wait outside for her and followed Viveca Bold inside.

The embassy's foyer was devoted to elaborate displays and signage that apologized to the people of Panama for America's myriad transgressions. In the center was a sculpture of an indigenous woman, hands raised to the sky in agony, distraught because – as the plaque helpfully explained – "The racist imperialists of the Old United States committed the unspeakable earthcrime of separating the body of The Great Spirit with the so-called 'Canal.'"

Villareal ignored the displays and followed Bold up the steps to the second floor. There were rooms for visitors, and word had come down ahead of Villareal that she was to be provided every courtesy and assistance. She ended up with one of the two suites reserved for very distinguished visitors. It was awkward when she was initially led to Suite A, only to have Bold open the door to reveal what was very obviously the scene of some sort of orgy the night before. Those partaking had failed to clean up; Bold quickly ushered the visitor to Suite B, which had not been defiled or littered with the wreckage of the prior evening.

"The ambassador believes it is important to transgress patriarchal and fascist sexual mores," Bold had muttered by way of excuse. Villareal did not care.

Now, ensconced in her suite, Villareal removed her SIG P229 from her handbag and left it on the coffee table between the couches.

"I'm going to need clothes," she told her subordinate. Appraising Bold, she discarded any notion of borrowing something from the trans woman's wardrobe.

"I've sent people out to get you some clothing options," Bold replied.

"You'll have to help me prepare," Villareal announced. "I will use make-up, even though that caters to patriarchal conventions of female beauty. "

"We must make sacrifices," Bold concurred sadly, but she was thrilled by the opportunity.

"Tell me more about *Presidente* Guerrero," Villareal continued.

Bold sucked air in over her teeth, which were somewhat askew. Most dentists had fled to the red upon the nationalization of all medical providers and the incorporation of all medical professionals, including dentists, into what the PR called the National Caring Corps.

"He's clearly one who acts out, but that's to be expected considering the racism, patriarchy, and anti-indigeneity imposed upon the Panamanian people by the United States," Bold told her.

"You've met him?"

"I have. He is...," Bold looked for the right way to convey the information without falling into the trap of ethnocentrism, racism, or anything of the kind. "He is a product of the society that America broke. He displays sexism, but it's not his fault. He is a proud Latinx man."

Villareal knew something of proud Latinx men, but she took a tiny measure of enjoyment in watching her assistant squirm.

"He can be transphobic," Bold conceded. "He asked me if I was...."

"Yes?" Villareal demanded impatiently.

"He asked me if I was 'a chick with a ....'" Bold did not finish *el Presidente's* quote and did not need to. Villareal quelled a smile at the assistant's discomfort.

"Again, he is suffering from the false consciousness imposed by the colonialists upon his people."

Villareal, who remembered the contempt her father, the communist, had for "trannies and homos" in the movement, let the agent sweat for a moment before speaking.

"His preferences? Women?"

"No, not all women. He does not accept trans women as women, though we believe he has experimented. He is fluid when it comes to experimentation, especially when he is drinking or taking drugs."

"And when does he do that?" asked Villareal. Bold looked at her, surprised.

"All the time," she said. "The National Assembly chamber is a continuing party. He holds court in there and has since he dismissed the Assembly a few years ago. It is enormous. There is a platform where he sits with the VIPs, and down below are tables and benches for his men and his guests. It's usually full of drunken soldiers, eating, grabbing women – he does not believe in women soldiers. All the women are for ... entertainment."

Villareal grunted. She looked over Bold's face. Too much blush, too much mascara. She looked like a man desperately trying to be some red American version of a woman. It was odd how those most transgressive always seemed to be most fixated on the traditional. But the problem was still there to be solved – the most effective way to present to *el Presidente*.

"How do you think I should be dressed when I go?" Villareal inquired. Again, the implications made Bold nervous.

"If you look conventionally attractive, he might seek to gain your consent to further erotic activity," Bold answered. "Or maybe not seek your consent, though he tends to be careful with diplomats. He is unstable but cunning. He smells weakness and takes advantage of it."

"Then I'd better be strong," Villareal said. "Now, you will help me with my hair while I clean my pistol."

14.

This was the moment when things got real for Kelly Turnbull, when the crew popped open the airplane's cabin door and he first breathed in the air from wherever in the world he was.

The wet, hot atmosphere of Panama flooded into the jet, and he immediately took it up through his nostrils. In the Middle East, the air is dry and grating, plus it stinks. You know when you land there – no place else smells like it. But these tropical locations were different. Instead of searing you, it surrounded you and cooked you. The scent reminded him of rot and decay.

"I'm already sweating," complained Casey Warner. He had his travel pack in his hand.

"Grab your stuff," Turnbull instructed. He looked down to the tarmac. A ladder truck was pulling up, and not too far away sat a black Blazer idling in the heat. Just one? Was the embassy that 'ed up?

"They're gonna stuff all four of us in that?" Hiram wondered aloud.

"Government efficiency," Mundi Vega noted.

The flight had taken several hours. All of them were experienced military vets, so they all were able to crash out and sleep not long after takeoff. All except Casey; he stayed up using the plane's Starlink as @FullAutoGalt to argue on X – it was X again that week – about dope legalization in the red with a libertarian bearing the *nom de Twitter* @RandPaulyShore69.

Casey blocked him after the guy dropped the "OK, boomer" bomb.

"I'm not a damn boomer!" Casey insisted out loud.

After Clay had briefed them – and it was brief – Turnbull went down to the arms room with his men to get their iron. They had just turned in their M4s a few hours before, and the armorer's assistants had already inspected and cleaned them. After a huddle, the four operatives agreed to draw them again. They also decided on several Benelli M4 tactical shotguns, just in case. Casey got himself an M14 accurized for long-range use.

"I'd like some hand grenades, too," Casey said.

"You guys starting a war?" the armorer asked as he sent one of his minions scurrying to pick up the grenades from the endless weapons racks behind him.

"We want to finish one," Turnbull said. He pulled out his Wilson Combat .45. "I need some hollow points and some more mags. Give me some ten-rounds."

After his assistants gathered the items, the armorer passed over a bag of magazines and many boxes of ammunition for their drawn weapons and their unique handguns. The operatives, helped by the assistants, began loading them there on the counter. Yet, Turnbull was distracted.

"Hey," he said to the armorer, pointing. "When did *that* come in?"

The armorer turned around theatrically, then looked back at Turnbull, smiling.

"Oh, *that?* Well, *that* just came in a few weeks ago."

"It's beautiful."

"It's not for you, Turnbull."

"I want it," Turnbull said.

"You can't have it, not *that.*"

"Oh, I can have anything I want," Turnbull assured him.

The armorer made a call upstairs. He got his answer.

"I guess you *can* have anything you want," he conceded.

"Pack it up," Turnbull instructed him. "And give me a big pile of ammo with it."

Casey and Clanton waited out on the tarmac in the sun for the embassy to get its stuff together and send over a second SUV as well as a small truck to carry their gear. Mundi and Turnbull went ahead to the embassy.

The streets of Panama City were tense. There were lots of members of the Presidential Guard on duty, which usually meant sitting on or about their vehicles, hassling passersby, and generally appearing menacing. Regular folks were in short supply, and not only because it seemed to start raining every few minutes. If the soldiers didn't harass them, gangs of surly-looking punks would.

"This used to be an okay town," Mundi said as he manspread in the backseat of the Blazer, his M4 on his lap. "It's gone to hell."

"President Guerrero's priorities are not the general welfare nor domestic tranquility," explained Katie Armand. Armand was in her thirties and served as an agricultural advisor at the embassy. This meant she was actually undercover for the FIS – the American Foreign Intelligence Service, which had replaced the disgraced CIA after the Split. She did not have to tell the operatives; they had assumed it when they saw her in the Blazer, wearing a Duke University ballcap to appear inconspicuous. The FIS liked to pluck rich kids with big brains, but bigger egos, out of the New Ivies.

"Have you met him?" asked Turnbull.

"Yeah," Armand replied. "Unfortunately. The first time, he propositioned me. And the second. He also propositioned my assistant, who is a man. Guerrero is not picky. I've never seen him not under the influence of something or not on the make. He's basically living an old school rock star lifestyle except he has an army and happens to control the most strategic waterway in the entire world."

"How's his hold on the Panamanian Army?"

"Tight. I mean, he created it. After the 1989 invasion, Panama eliminated its military and turned it into the Panamanian Public Forces. It was really a police/paramilitary thing. Well, Guerrero still managed to use it to stage a coup. With the Split underway, the U.S. was in no position to react. Guerrero said that a country without an army has no dignity."

"He has a point," Turnbull said.

"Well, he built a national army with him as the commander-in-chief, and he dismissed the civilian government."

"Just to be clear, he's the bad guy?" asked Casey.

"Ignore him," Turnbull told Armand. "You said he had a tight hold on the military?"

"Tight, but there are cracks. Every officer in these kind of regimes at least wonders if maybe he could be the next guy in charge. So, Guerrero is paranoid, and he is always looking for traitors. A few weeks ago, Guerrero decided a couple of his majors were plotting against him in cahoots with us."

"Were they?" asked Mundi. "Plotting against him in cahoots with us?"

"Oh, definitely. The plotters came to us and asked if we could help, and we told them they were on their own, but we would back them if they got control. Colonel Manuel Ruiz – that's his bloodhound, his head of security – got wind of it, and they hauled the two to his party palace at the National Assembly. Guerrero had his adjutant, a real nutcase named Captain Saramago, gut one of the plotters with his Bowie knife. The other got off relatively easy. They just shot him. Of course, Ruiz also sent out his thugs to do their families."

"Charming," Turnbull said. "So, he's always high?"

"And usually drunk, too," added Armand. "But don't let that fool you. He's smart. He knows he's in power because we have not chosen to focus on him and come down and kick him out like we did Noriega in 1989. He plays the PR and the PRC off against us, and vice versa. Sometimes they back him against us, other times we back him against them. The guy has an uncanny survival instinct."

"There's a woman who is on the ground, a PR operative, along with a couple of dozen Somali fighters. You know about that?" Turnbull asked.

"We heard. The Somalis are in a cheap hotel downtown. She's in the embassy. There are also a couple of non-Somalis. They're in the same hotel, but in suites. They are not freaks that we can see – half their embassy is she-males, furries, or worse. We're not sure who they are. Their passports are fake. Just like yours."

"You sound like you have good sources," Mundi observed.

"We do more here than sip gin and tonics and play Spy vs. Spy," she replied. "Look, I'm not sure exactly what you are doing, but it sounds like you are going to try to negotiate with Guerrero about something."

"Who told you that?" asked Turnbull.

"I figured it out because the State Department folks are really pissed off. Typical State bitching. They say you'll screw up all their hard work and ruin the U.S./Panama relationship."

"Kelly here is hell on relationships," Mundi said.

"We don't have time to play diplomatic footsies," Turnbull said. "I need to go see this Guerrero guy tonight."

"Kelly's going to charm him. Or bribe him," Mundi told her.

"Since you have good sources," Turnbull said. "I need your people to keep eyes on the Somalis – what they do, where they go. And on these two mystery men. Find out what they are up to."

"There's another thing, and if this wasn't so important – even I can see that whatever you guys are doing is way above my pay grade – I wouldn't bring it up."

"What?" Turnbull asked.

"There's another guy, a lieutenant colonel. Pretty clean, for a Panamanian officer, as far as we can tell. Popular with the troops, trained in the PR, and he apparently hates the blues. He's Catholic and thinks they are demons."

"That would explain a lot," Mundi said.

"He might be able to help you. And down the road, he even might be the right guy to finally coup this sociopath out of power."

"I want to meet him before I go see Guerrero," Turnbull said. The driver pulled into the embassy gate and was waved through by the Marine guards.

"I'll make that happen," Armand said. "Anything else you gentlemen need?"

"Luck," Turnbull replied.

The old National Assembly building was deeply unimpressive from the outside. It looked like it was at the cutting edge of design in 1972 – a massive, boxy, and uninspiring structure of white and blue, with a large office tower where every other window had an air conditioner jutting out. The paint was peeling, and the roof seemed ready to cave in. The Panamanian regime was living off of older, better times. Villareal forced herself to ignore the uncomfortable, and likely illegal, parallels to her own country that her mind presented.

There were palm trees planted around the building, likewise unmaintained. Dead branches mixed with live ones. Fronds littered the ground. There was a pot-holed parking lot surrounding the complex. It was half-filled with both civilian and military vehicles. This was fenced off with concertina and secured by a contingent of perhaps a hundred Presidential Guards who lay about in various states of indolence.

Near the building – too near for any sensible pilot – was an old Huey helicopter in Panamanian Army livery.

"That's *el Presidente's* personal aircraft," Bold told Villareal, unnecessarily since this was painted on the tail boom. "It's always warmed up and there is always a crew. He takes it between here and the National Army's headquarters across town.

The sentries watched as the SUV from the PR embassy pulled up, and as she stepped out, accompanied by Viveca Bold and two of her Somali bodyguards. They did not do anything more than watch; she noted their eyes were red, and the area stank of pot and even more noxious odors. The threadbare bushes up against the building obviously doubled as a latrine for lazy soldiers with bulging bladders, or worse.

"This way," Bold told her superior, heading toward a double door leading to a lobby. They were unmolested by the guards as they walked through; the doors apparently were kept open. From across the lobby, immediately inside, came music – some sort of electronic dance noise.

"It's open to any soldiers and friends of *el Presidente* who want to come in. They can get food and some drinks and join the party. It never ends."

"Is Guerrero here all the time?" asked Villareal as they walked into the lobby. The floor was littered with trash, old bottles, food wrappers, and the occasional used condom. It smelled like dope, urine, and mold – very much like her last mission to San Francisco.

"Seems like it," Bold said. "This is where he does his business, whether with local civilians, his military, foreign governments, and indigenous entrepreneurial pharmaceutical organizations."

The word "cartel" was forbidden as racist, Western supremacist, and colonialist.

The lobby once held displays highlighting the history of the isthmus nation; those displays were abandoned, the glass in the display cases was shattered, and the artifacts were missing. Besides the trash, several people were staggering about. There was an officer in uniform with his arms around a pair of laughing women; he was urging them to go upstairs. Another man in civilian clothes fell to the floor in a puddle of his own sick.

"The chamber is there," Bold said, a hint of dread undergirding her voice as she pointed across the open space to a pair of elaborate wooden doors that were ajar. The music was coming from inside.

Villareal strode forward, taking the lead. At the doors, the music was almost unbearable. She opened them and looked inside.

The chamber formerly housed the 71-member unicameral National Assembly, back before the coup Guerrero had launched "to protect the people of Panama from the rich who plunder them, the cartels that poison them, and the thieves who steal them blind." This was true. His coup was intended to remove the currently governing coalition of plutocrats and criminals; what he did not announce was that he would be replacing the old thugs with an entirely new governing coalition of plutocrats and criminals with whom he was in league. That was five years ago; the Americans, busy with other concerns, such as their blue neighbors to their north and west, chose to ignore it. After all, Latin American thugs were generally interchangeable.

Within a month, the National Assembly had tested the waters by denying him approval of a bill about water fluoridation. Guerrero was not displeased with the substance of the gesture but with the fact that they dared defy him. He dismissed the National Assembly, consolidated rule in himself, and announced that the National Assembly building would be opened to the people of Panama so he could demonstrate his largesse and generosity.

What began as a glorified soup kitchen had, five years later, morphed into something out of one of Bosch's most intense fever dreams.

Villareal took in what was laid out before her. The floor of the chamber where the assembly members had once sat was covered with long, crude wooden tables. They and the benches were stained and filthy. There were dirty plates piled high, white powder residue, and the guests' guns. Weapons were allowed in the chamber, and the pockmarks on the walls, along with the occasional dark reddish-brown spots on the hideously foul carpeting, indicated that occasionally they got used.

The air was thick with smoke, both tobacco and pot. The floor was thick with debris, including broken plates, chicken bones, and cigarette butts. The carpet was moist both from humidity and a thousand tipped Atlas beer bottles – the dictator had nationalized the brewery early on. The beer bottles were everywhere, along with empties of cheap whiskey and occasional wines. People were carousing, drinking, yelling, gambling, and grabbing food off trays that workers circulated with – much of it was whole chicken and fish.

To the front of the chamber, there was a massive wall. Underneath a banner with a smiling portrait of *el Presidente* hung the seal of Panama, as if it were still a country and not the private domain of one man.

At the foot of the front wall, the vast platform where the speakers had once been was now the VIP area. There were real tables there, large wooden ones that looked like they had been pilfered from the homes of rich people, and they had. Wooden benches provided seating for the guests. In the center of the tableau was a large chair, like a throne. It was empty at the moment, but that was clearly where the dictator held court.

A thin man in a military uniform with red, narrow eyes, a revolver in a holster and a comically large Bowie knife in a scabbard at his waist, had been sitting alone milking a bottle of Atlas when the blues entered the room. He got to his feet unsteadily and brushed himself off. A torrent of crumbs fell to the floor. He walked over, less unsteadily than Villareal would have predicted.

"This is Captain Saramago, the president's adjutant," Bold said.

"Who does the tranny bring us now?" Saramago asked in accented English, looking directly at Villareal. Bold gasped. Villareal did not allow her eyes to move from his.

"I am Comrade Villareal of the People's Republic of North America," she said. "And I have come on urgent business to speak to the president about a matter of great importance."

Saramago considered this for a moment.

"Do you have an appointment?" he said with deadly sincerity, then exploded in laughter. Villareal could smell the liquor.

"No, no, you can come down to the front, up on stage. It's a place of honor, and you are obviously an honorable lady." Saramago paused, thinking. He turned to Bold.

"She is a lady, right?"

Villareal had chosen to wear slacks and a blouse, not too feminine but feminine enough. But she also wore her SIG pistol in a holster belted around her waist.

"I identify as a woman," Villareal responded coldly.

"Okay, I've got to check for the President because he does not want to be surprised, you know what I mean? Like him." Saramago gestured at Bold "He's got a *pincha* in that dress. He's tricky."

Villareal suppressed her instinct to react to this severe misgendering; out of the corner of her eye, she saw Bold was on the verge of blubbering.

"Take me to the president," she commanded.

"I'll take you to the stage, but the President comes out when he wants to come out and not until then."

"Do you want our weapons?" Villareal asked.

"Oh, no. You keep your guns. The President is not afraid. Just remember, though, if you use your gun, it better be for a good reason or he will be very angry."

There was some attention from the people in the cheap seats who were close enough to hear the exchange over the driving dance music that was coming from a stack of amps off to the side of the stage, where a DJ stood holding one headphone up to his ear and fiddling with the dials on his board. The rest of the hundred or so people in the room were engaged in their own activities, all to the background music of what sounded like remixed and autotuned Fleetwood Mac cover.

"I could be killed for talking to you," Lieutenant Colonel Julio Jesus Rosas said to Kelly Turnbull. Katie Armand was with them, as was Mundi Vega, who Turnbull brought along to translate. It was not necessary. Colonel Rosas spoke perfect English.

"You'll probably get killed at some point. From what I hear, your *presidente* is insane and sees enemies everywhere," Turnbull said.

"He has enemies everywhere. His skill is playing one off against the other. You reds against the blues and the Chinese, this cartel against that one. He's a survivor, like a cockroach."

"What would it take for you to boot him out and take over?" Turnbull asked. He was not one for beating around the bush. Rosas turned to Amrand, concerned.

"He's asking me to launch a coup?" he asked.

"I'm asking you what it would take to launch a coup," Turnbull said. "That's different."

"You really do want me to get killed."

"Armand here tells me you have the loyalty of the honest Catholic officers, and that's substantial."

"Colonel Ruiz watches us all the time. His spies are everywhere."

"But these rebels think of you as their leader even if you aren't rebelling yet."

"Are you saying the United States would support a move on the President? With force? Another invasion?"

"No, I'm not saying that. You would be on your own. Maybe with a little help."

"What little help?"

"There may be a moment when you have an opportunity to act. I just want to know if an opportunity presents itself that you might seize it."

"And you will provide this opportunity from the goodness of your heart, because you Americans love Panama and want to save its people?"

"No," Turnbull said. "I don't give a damn about Panama or Panamanians. Your problems are your problems. My problem is the blues, and things may go down where the blues are your problem, too. You know them. You lived in the blue. The blues will make a play for influence here, and along with the Chinese, take your lunatic *presidente* out of the picture. That's the only way it gets worse than living under the generalissimo. With Guerrero, you can keep your head down and still live like human beings. If the PR starts calling the shots, they will take everything. Your money. Your kids. Your faith."

"Authoritarian versus totalitarian," Rosas said.

"You know it's true. Guerrero wants your obedience, but the communists want your soul. So, let me ask again. If an opportunity presents itself, will you take it?"

Villareal and her three companions sat on the stage at a table for nearly an hour, waiting, turning down beers and platters of sickly-looking chicken. The two Somali bodyguards desperately wanted to partake of both the beer and the entrée, but the last thing Villareal needed was them drugged up or vomiting up their guts from food poisoning. They sat there glowering at her. That it was desperately hot and humid did not help.

Viveca Bold was inconsolable, but Villareal was in no mood to be consoling.

"Did you hear what he said to me!" the transwoman demanded.

"Shut up," Villareal replied. "Get a hold of yourself."

Bold was even more dumbfounded, and Villareal realized she might have made a mistake. Those microaggressions were a tool in Bold's hands; but if, say, Carlos Trent were to obtain word of them by promising Bold advancement or other favors, they would be ammunition. That is assuming Bold was not part of

Trent's web already; the more Villareal thought about it, the more she thought that Trent would absolutely seek to saddle her with one of his catspaws as an assistant.

She began to consider how Bold might be taken out of the picture somehow. It would be better to do that than go through some struggle session down the road and risk being terminated from the Directorate or worse for wrongthink. It was inevitable that this minion would decide to make a complaint, amplified by Trent, that Villareal was insensitive to her lived experience of oppression as a woman of penis possession.

Captain Saramago had disappeared into the back area through a door behind the stage. He was gone for ten minutes; in that time, there was the sound of a helicopter outside. After a few more minutes, he emerged again and stumbled over to their table on the VIP platform.

"*El Presidente* is coming," he announced. Then he turned to the crowd. "*El Presidente!*"

The DJ killed the song, a remix of Young MC's "Bust A Move." The crowd shakily got to its collective feet and began to wildly applaud.

The DJ dropped the needle – electronically – on the theme from *Rocky*.

Hands held high in the air, *Presidente* Bonifacio Alberto Maria Guerrero stepped out of the door and onto the stage to thunderous applause.

15.

The *Presidente* held his pose for almost a minute, savoring the ovation. He was perhaps 5' 7" tall, with thick but longish black hair that had not recently seen shampoo. His rough skin was bronze and bore a sheen of sweat – not surprising or uncommon among the attendees, since the chamber was stiflingly hot. His tan uniform was filthy and rumpled, with stains memorializing his most recent meals and several buttons undone. It was also too small; Guerrero was packing something of a gut. Cinched around him was a leather belt with a flap holster holding a pistol.

His eyes were red and moist, but intelligent and shrewd. There was something undeniable about him, something that made it hard to look away.

Villareal stared, taking it in. He glanced at her, and she met his dark, probing eyes. The dictator was sizing her up even as he was accepting the accolades of his followers.

Behind the President stood Colonel Ruiz. He looked put together – not pristine, but at least not as if he had slept in his clothes for two weeks. He was busy scanning the crowd, looking for treason.

Next to him was a Chinese People's Liberation Army colonel, his uniform pressed, his hat perfectly set upon his head, also carrying a pistol. Colonel Wang's face was blank, his eyes missing nothing. His job as an advisor to *el presidente* was less about counsel than surveillance.

Captain Saramago was gone, having run off the stage toward the main entrance at the back of the chamber.

The music began to fade away.

"Silencio!" the dictator bellowed jovially at the throng. The volume dropped, did not go absolutely silent. He shouted it again, this time not jovially. This time, the crowd went dead quiet.

"*¡Una cerveza!*" he shouted, and the crowd once again cheered as a young woman, maybe in her late teens, ran to him with a bottle of Atlas. He leered at her; she was terrified.

"I will talk with you later, my pretty," he said in a Spanish stage whisper as he grinned. Villareal heard it from 20' away. The frightened serving girl fled off stage, leaving the dictator with a bottle in his hand and the crowd amused.

Guerrero backed up to his throne and settled into the seat, studiously ignoring the four PR representatives. Colonel Ruiz did not ignore them; he was looking them over with considerable interest. Villareal recognized him as Guerrero's enforcer and noted he had several armed men who looked serious as opposed to bedraggled just off stage.

Captain Saramago returned, leading a pack of civilians and some military men with him. One of the civilians was a child leading an extremely mixed-breed dog on a leash. The adjutant stopped the group at the front of the stage, where Guerrero towered over them. Then he trotted back up on the platform.

"Mr. President," he shouted in Spanish. "Your people have come to you for judgment and justice!"

Guerrero nodded sagely.

"First, one of the children who is blessed with your benevolence has a gift to present you," shouted Captain Saramago. There was more cheering. Saramago descended the steps to the floor and brought the child with the dog up to the stage.

The child stood there, petrified, while the puppy seemed baffled. Saramago gently prodded the kid.

"You are the father of our nation," the kid said, straining not to misremember her text. "On behalf of the children of Panama, we present this animal to you so you can rescue it from poverty and hunger like you have rescued us." She thrust out the leash.

Guerrero slowly and a bit unsteadily dismounted from the throne, walking over with his chest thrust out. He paused to pat the child on the head and took the leash. Then he turned to the crowd.

"How we treat lowly animals reflects our souls," he said. "I thank you for this gift and promise that I will not only take care of Panama's children but also our stray and wild animals!" There was cheering anew. Saramago guided the kid to the stairs so she could exit and rushed back to take the leash from his master. The captain then tied the dog to the center table: it promptly lay down.

Next, Saramago called up two soldiers. Their hands were zip-tied.

"These two soldiers fought on duty," Saramago said. "They ask for your judgment and mercy."

"What were you fighting about?" the President asked the trembling men. "A woman? Yes, no doubt a woman! A good thing to fight over, but not on duty. Well, we must know who is right and who is wrong. Captain?"

Saramago nodded, then drew his Bowie knife. To the momentary relief of the men, the adjutant sliced off their bonds.

"You wish to fight? Then fight!" commanded the dictator.

The men stood, blinking.

"I said fight!" shouted Guerrero. "Fight until one of you cannot stand!"

The men stood there, unbelieving. Saramago drew his pistol. Then they fought. After five minutes, one man lay on the stage quivering. The other, missing several teeth, remained on his feet.

"You won," Guerrero said to him. "Congratulations."

Captain Saramago snapped his fingers, and several members of the Presidential Guard, lounging below at a table on the chamber floor, helped the winner off while others dragged away the loser.

This audience went on for an hour, as Guerrero entertained tributes, adjudicated disputes, and dispensed guidance to his supplicants. Each ruling earned vigorous cheers. And, finally, it ended with the President calling for more beer for his people.

Saramago stepped over to Villareal.

"He will see you now," the captain said. She followed him back to the throne as the DJ pumped up the volume.

"It is an honor, *Señor Presidente*," she said to him in Spanish.

"Speak English so prying ears cannot hear us," Guerrero directed. "So many ears." He looked over at the Chinese officer. The Chi Com seemed irritated.

"The Chinese are a close ally of the People's Republic," Villareal said.

"And of Panama! Everyone is friends with Panama. The Americans, too! The Chinese were kind enough to give him to us to teach us how to be soldiers. Maybe I'll give him that mutt as a reward. He does not like my other food!"

Captain Saramago laughed a bit too hard. Villareal looked down. There was a reddish-brown stain on the floor. Guerrero saw where she was looking.

"I had to deal with a traitor in my midst," he said, shrugging. "No one can escape being sniffed out by my bloodhound, Colonel Ruiz. Except now I have another doggie. I wonder if he can smell traitors, too?"

Villareal smiled her disarming smile. Guerrero continued.

"So, you are here, dressed very pretty, but with a gun. I think you are a very dangerous lady. What do you want?"

"My country has a request."

"A favor?"

"It is something very important."

"And since it is important, what does your country intend to do for the people of Panama if I grant this favor?" he took a swig of Atlas. Villareal could see there were white grains caught in the uncut hair of his nostrils.

"Of course, there would be a commensurate favor in return."

"Are you part of the favor?" he asked, leery. "You are a little pretty, but I always say that every woman looks the same in the dark!"

Saramago erupted in laughter again. Villareal maintained her composure.

"I mean," he continued. "That she-male over there almost convinced me to give him a chance. I know it is important for you blue Americans to have diversity, and I do not want to offend you for turning down the advances of a woman simply because she has a *pincha*."

Saramago's chuckling continued.

"You can have whatever you want," Villareal said. "But the real prize is the friendship of the People's Republic."

"Oh, we Panamanians know very well about the friendship of Americans. And you are all still Americans to us, blue, red, or green. You see, you are imperialists. We know this. But what is this favor? It must be a big favor if they sent you instead of your ambassador."

"The People's Republic of North America would respectfully ask that the Bolívarian Republic of Panama close the canal to the American Navy for five days, beginning the day after tomorrow."

Guerrero stared at her for a long moment before chuckling.

"You have drunk too much or snorted too much while you were waiting for me," he replied, wagging his index finger in her face. "That is impossible."

"Not if you order it," Villareal said.

"So, your People's Republic and your Chinese friends will send an army here to protect me from the red Americans when they come to drag me off to prison like they did to Noriega?" he shouted, loud enough that some of the people on the floor looked up from their table. Colonel Ruiz met their gaze, and their eyes dropped back to their food.

"We can make it worth your while," Villareal said. "And we can protect you."

"It must be very worthy to be worth our while. And no one can protect us. Only Panama might protect itself, but, of course, we are deprived of the means to do so. No, you are asking us to commit suicide. And why? What is so important about keeping the U.S. Navy out of the canal?"

"That's our concern."

"No, it's my ass, so it is my concern."

"What will it take to make you say you will do this for us, *Señor Presidente*?" she asked, trying to keep the edge of impatience out of her voice.

"Let me think," replied the dictator. He turned to Saramago, but Saramago was staring across the chamber at the entrance. Guerrero's eyes followed his subordinate's.

In the doorway across the chamber stood Kelly Turnbull.

"You're big," *el Presidente* told Turnbull on the stage as he swayed on his feet and slurred his heavily accented English. He pivoted to consider Hiram Clanton. "You are ... bigger."

Then he looked at Katie Armand.

"You are pretty. I don't think you have a secret like that one does." He pointed at Viveca Bold.

The whole team was there, armed only with sidearms. That bothered Turnbull because there were multiple threats – the President and his guards, the crowd of drug and booze-fueled reprobates out on the chamber floor, and the blue delegation – the Somali bodyguards, a Chinese officer, some transexual from the PR embassy (probably a spook), and a woman he had seen before.

Turnbull had already had one eye on Medea Villareal since he entered the chamber and was called down to the stage with his clique. He pegged her immediately as Circe, and it was all he could do to keep from drawing his .45 and removing her from the situation permanently.

Circe felt the same way; her fingers itched to grab the grip of her SIG P229 and finish what she had started in Dublin. But this was neither the time nor the place; even if their host was not offended, the American had four more shooters with him, if you counted the female – and Villareal instinctively counted her. In fact, she might be the most deadly of the bunch, if you believe every movie and television show made in the PR since the Split.

She bided her time.

And Turnbull bided his time as well. There would be plenty of time to deal with Circe later.

"This is a very important representative of my government," Armand told the dictator.

"More important than your ambassador?" asked the dictator. "Your friends, the blues, sent us someone more important than their ambassador, too." He took a swig of Atlas Lager, then continued.

"Welcome to Panama. Meet my new dog. I think I will call him 'George Bush.' You like that?"

"You need to be more specific about the George Bush," Turnbull said. "He seems like a nice dog, but you seem more of a lion or tiger guy."

"No, I'm just a little doggie. You big countries, you are the lions and tigers. But I still have teeth."

"That's why we respect you," Turnbull lied, smiling.

"So, why do you big countries seem so interested in our little one?"

"We want to make sure that we're all in agreement that the Panama Canal remains open to traffic without discrimination," Turnbull said. "And, if that happens, my country would be favorably inclined toward Panama," Turnbull said, adding: "And to its leader."

"Well, that woman over there – not the she-male, the one without a *pincha* – she wants me to close it to your Navy."

"Oh, then we would not be favorably inclined toward Panama. And especially not toward its leader."

"Is that a threat?" Guerrero exclaimed. "Are you insulting the dignity of the Panamanian people?"

Turnbull bent closer.

"Yes," he said.

The dictator looked into his eyes for a moment, and Turnbull wondered if he saw at least a kindred spirit, however remotely related. Then Guerrero burst into laughter, pointing a filthy index finger at Turnbull.

"I like you. You're tough. I like her, too, that blue woman. She's tough, for a woman."

"Well, we men need to stick together," Turnbull said.

"But not with that tranny woman," the President said. "He or she is not what she appears. Ask Saramago – he knows!"

There was a smattering of laughter from the crowd, most of whom were busy eating, drinking, and groping. Saramago laughed too, uneasily.

"It's only right that we honor you with a present, Mr. President," Armand interjected. Turnbull looked at Clanton and Mundi and gestured toward the chamber door. They nodded and went out.

"What is it, this present? That blue woman offered me nothing but the friendship of her people, and that's not worth the paper I use to wipe my butt."

There was another smattering of laughter at the leader's witticism. For her part, Medea Villareal was staring daggers at Turnbull. He wondered if she was calculating the odds with two of his shooters out of the chamber. He decided on a kill plan– if trouble went down, she was first to die.

"I think you'll like it," Turnbull said. "We're both soldiers, right?"

"I am just a lowly colonel," said Guerrero. "I could have promoted myself to general. But then, I thought of Libya's Colonel Gadhafi. He was a humble man. Always a colonel."

"I remember. He died after he was overthrown, and the rebels used a bayonet on him as a suppository," Turnbull said, smiling pleasantly.

The room went quiet; Guerrero stared him in the face again, then burst into laughter. So did the crowd.

"But what a way to go, am I right?" he crowed. More laughter.

There was a rumble at the rear of the chamber. Clanton and Mundi were coming in, along with a cart pushed by a couple of Presidential Guards they had shanghaied.

"Oh," said the President, admiring the gift.

"Bring it up here," Turnbull said. The men did so, assembling it on the stage.

Villareal was fuming.

"It's beautiful," Guerrero said.

"Behold, the High Ground Defense M134HG Minigun. It's a battery-powered 7.62mm Gatling gun with a 1200-meter max effective range. It fires 3,000 rounds a minute," Turnbull recited.

The fearsome black weapon was mounted on a tripod and was linked by cables to a battery case. There were two grips at the rear of the mechanism, and six 18-inch-long rotating barrels. It was about 60 pounds, just barely man-portable – if you were a huge man.

Clanton was, and he had a box of ammunition in his hand. He looked to Turnbull. Turnbull nodded.

"Set it up and load it."

Clanton bent down to connect the cords and attach one of the ammo cans to the flexible feeding mechanism.

"You going to let him shoot that in here?" Armand whispered.

"It's his gun and his crash pad," Turnbull replied.

Clanton stood back up and nodded.

"It's all ready," Turnbull said.

Guerrero looked at him, suspicious. To the side, Colonel Ruiz, whom Turnbull had recognized as the secret policeman for the regime, was not pleased, but he was wise enough to remain silent.

224 | PANAMA RED

Turnbull gestured to the rear of the weapon. The President stepped over and tentatively put his hands on the grips. He lifted the barrels.

Turnbull and his crew placed their fingers over their ear canals.

The roar was tremendous. Guerrero blew off a three-second burst over the heads of his audience and into the wall and the ceiling at the back of the chamber. Orange streaks from the rapidly rotating barrels seemed to coalesce into a single orange beam. One in nine rounds was a tracer.

It shredded the wall up about twenty feet from the floor, seeming to saw a line straight through it and up to the acoustical tile on the drop ceiling. The holes smoked from the pyro rounds; bits of plaster and ash fell down onto the partiers below.

Guerrero laughed explosively, then fired again. The sound was like a jackhammer; their fingers barely deadened it. The poor dog, tied to the table, withdrew beneath it.

More holes appeared, more debris rained down. The President stepped back and let go of the grips, his grin wide across his shiny, pocked face. He threw his hands up above his head as if celebrating a great victory. The crowd cheered him.

"This is a good present, amigo," he told Turnbull. He looked at Armand. "You never brought me such a present before."

"This is a very important man," Armand replied. Ruiz stared at her; Turnbull could see his contempt. Ruiz was definitely dangerous and bore watching. But then everyone in this madhouse was dangerous and bore watching.

"You brought me nothing like this, either," the President said to Villareal. "You blues are very disrespectful to a Latinx man like myself." He put his hand on his heart over his soiled tunic.

Villareal smiled her deadly smile and got up from her seat. She barely heard the slurred ramblings of her host over the ringing in her ears, but she would never show it. She stood and walked across the stage to join them next to the smoking weapon.

"My country will offer you more than a popgun, *Señor Presidente*," she said. "Thinking they can buy your country's pride with a toy is insulting."

"I think she is trying to stir up trouble," the President said to Turnbull. He put his hand on the weapon mount to hold himself up.

"Mx. Medea Villareal," Turnbull said, extending his hand. She smiled again, then shook his hand. It was rough.

"So, you know my name. I thought you called me 'Circe.'"

"We did. Now, we know the correct witch's name."

"I am at a disadvantage," she said. "What's your name?"

"Call me 'Bob.'"

"Bob the diplomat," said Guerrero.

"I'll find out your real name within a few days," she told Turnbull.

"If you're around that long," he replied.

"There's another edge to that sword. I don't miss twice."

"I don't miss once."

"You did in Dublin." That stung Turnbull's pride because it was true.

"Now you two are bickering like women, which can be very confusing when the People's Republic is involved. I think it is time for Mx. Villareal to make her counteroffer."

She smiled.

"What you and your people deserve is above my authority. I will tell you tomorrow."

"Yes, yes, tomorrow," Guerrero said. "You will come here for dinner, both of you and your friends. You too, Mx. Armand, I mean *Miss* Armand. Then we eat and talk, maybe shoot my present some more. And then we come to an arrangement. So, both of you, bring your presents!"

Captain Saramago was coming around the nearest table to examine the minigun, but the dog was crawling out from under the table, and the adjutant tripped. Guerrero laughed, and then so did the crowd, as Saramago spilled on the floor. The captain struggled to his feet and walked to the dog, pulling back his leg.

"Hey!" Turnbull told him. "If you kick that dog, we'll have a problem."

Saramago stopped, flushed with anger and far too much tequila.

"The dog got in his way. It has to be trained," Guerrero said.

"You heard me," Turnbull said, ignoring the President.

Saramago stood there, leg drawn back, weighing his options. Turnbull was doing the same.

Saramago kicked the animal in the haunch, and it yelped.

Turnbull was on Saramago as the adjutant tried to pull his handgun. With his right hand, Turnbull grabbed Saramago's arm and slammed it to the table. With his left, Turnbull drew the captain's Bowie knife from its scabbard and plunged it through the officer's forearm, right between the radius and the ulna, the point digging deeply into the wooden table.

Saramago howled and collapsed as his legs gave way beneath him. He knelt against the table, moaning, holding his arm, afraid to even try to pull out the blade.

Turnbull looked back to face Guerrero, but said nothing. The President was thinking, too. In the background, several Presidential Guards, as well as Ruiz's men, stood there, armed but awaiting guidance. While Turnbull was perfectly still, his men were each prepared to act if it went south.

Every eye was on the President. He chose to laugh.

And not just a guffaw or a giggle. He howled with laughter, granting permission for his men to join in. All of them did, even Captain Saramago, still pinned to the table, who stuttered a bit as he forced a chuckle through his tears.

"Our guest is John Wick!" he shouted in Spanish. The crowd continued to laugh. He helpfully repeated it in English for his guests' benefit.

"You know, Keanu Reeves is Panamanian," he added.

"That's United States Secretary of Culture Keanu Reeves," Armand said.

"I'm taking the dog," Turnbull told the President. "He's your present to me."

"Take it," the President said grandly. "My present to you. I think it has mange. But maybe Saramago can give it a bath first." There was more laughter, including by the impaled captain.

Turnbull bent down and untied the dog. It limped along with him.

"You don't get a present," Guerrero told Villareal. "Unless, maybe, you go stab Colonel Ruiz." There was more general mirth, but Ruiz was not smiling.

"I will see you, Bob," she told Turnbull.

"Looking forward to it," Turnbull said.

"Tomorrow is going to be a very memorable dinner!" Guerrero bellowed. "I can't wait!"

16.

"Well, that was interesting," Katie Armand said to the four operatives back in a secure embassy conference room. "I don't usually end negotiations by ramming a knife through one of the other side's arms."

"Nobody got shot," Casey countered. "I don't think you appreciate how unusual that is for Kelly here."

Turnbull shrugged and pet George, who was sitting quietly by his seat at the conference table.

The door opened. A sweaty, chubby man with a pink face and glasses entered. Like all the embassy staff, he was a citizen and wore the pin, but he did not seem ex-military.

"Probably Air Force," Clanton whispered to Mundi, who nodded.

"JAG," he added. "Air Force JAG."

"What the hell is going on here in my country?" the ambassador demanded after his aide shut the door. A stream of sweat rolled down his cheek.

"I thought your country was America," Turnbull said. Panama's humidity must be hell for him, Turnbull thought. Good.

"Mr. Ambassador, how good of you to join us," Armand said diplomatically, as appropriate to her diplomatic cover.

"I am the senior American official in Panama," the ambassador told him. "I am at the top of the chain of command. You types are big on the chain of command, aren't you?"

"Yeah, I know about my chain of command," Turnbull replied. "And you aren't in it."

"I don't know exactly what you are cooking up here with Miss Armand, our 'Agricultural Attache,'" he said, actually doing air quotes. "But I'm not going to have you wrecking all the work we have done to keep President Guerrero supporting our foreign policy interests."

"I think I did more for American-Panamanian relations by giving him a machine gun than you have in however long you've been down here pounding gin and tonics," Turnbull said.

"Who are you?" the ambassador demanded.

"You don't need to know. You just need to keep out of our way."

"And if I don't, will you stab me, too?" demanded the diplomat.

"Technically, he usually shoots people in the face," Casey offered.

Turnbull shrugged and pet George again.

"Who the hell do you think you are?"

"I think I'm the guy who got sent here because it's important, meaning no one trusts you to get it done," Turnbull replied. "So, get out of our faces and we'll be out of here before you vapor lock."

"Miss Armand," the ambassador snarled. "Remember, *you* have to stay here after these cavemen depart."

"I'll do my best to lower their profile," Armand said.

"The sooner you thugs are gone, the better. And get that mangy animal out of my building!"

"He's a service animal," Turnbull said. "Emotional support."

"I thought he was talking to you," Casey said to Clanton as the ambassador departed and slammed the door behind him.

"We don't want to make your life difficult," Turnbull said to Armand. "But this mission is important."

"You want to keep the Panama Canal open. I'm not sure why beyond general principles," she said.

"We should probably read her in," Casey said. "She's working with us. She needs to know."

Armand looked to Turnbull and raised an eyebrow – only one. He found it disconcerting.

"Okay, I'll read you in. The U.S. is making a move to stop a Chi Com intervention in Peru to establish a commie government."

"And we need to send ships through the canal."

"Right," Turnbull said, impressed by her pick-up. "In less than 48 hours, the first two Navy cruisers are going to show up to transit the canal, followed by a whole bunch more. We need it open. The blues are trying to close it."

"And you think you can buy Guerrero with a machine gun?" asked Armand.

"No, we'll need to offer him more. I'm not sure what yet. But they are going to make him an offer, too, and who knows what that lunatic Guerrero will do. So, we need a Plan B, which is where you come in."

"That's why you wanted to meet Colonel Rosas. No time to launch an invasion from CONUS," she reasoned, using the acronym for "Continental United States." "Your Plan B is a coup."

"Bingo," said Turnbull.

"But there's not going to be a coup while Guerrero is still breathing."

"Nope," Turnbull said. "There won't be."

"Sheesh," Armand said. "So, you're just using Rosas." It was hard for her to get her head around it all.

"Welcome to the world of black ops," Casey said.

"We're going to his little dinner party tomorrow night," Turnbull said. "We make our best offer, and if that doesn't work, we go with Plan B. He seems to like you, so you back me up when we start bargaining. These three gangsters are our security in case it gets ugly."

"I need to go see Rosas," Armand said. "I won't tell him what's up, but I need to impress upon him to be ready if we call."

"Okay, but be careful. That Colonel Ruiz was giving you the stink eye."

"I think he knows I'm FIS. But I don't think they would touch an American."

"He best not," Turnbull said. "One more thing."

"Yes?" she replied.

"Do you want a dog?"

Armand shook her head.

"I can't even take care of the plants in my apartment, much less a dog. But I do have an idea of who can. And it's within walking distance."

Turnbull looked down at George the dog.

"You want a walk?"

"But I *have* to be there," pleaded Viveca Bold. "It's an all-persons meeting."

Villareal stood to the side of the hallway as the diplomats and other embassy workers filed through the halls like lemmings, heading downstairs to the lobby.

"You think a session about someone using the term 'blackout' is more important than our mission?"

"Of course," Bold said, her face displaying a lot of rouge and heavy mascara, but no sense of doubt or irony. "Stamping out racism is our most important mission."

Villareal calmed herself externally, but internally she wondered if this was some kind of trap Carlos Trent was setting for her all the way from the Minnesota Mogadishu.

"Of course it is. Stamping out racism *is* our greatest priority. And I will certainly note in my report your sterling performance today despite the hideous onslaught of microaggressions you faced at the hands of Guerrero."

"Please don't," requested Bold. "I mean, his transphobia was devastating and I was literally shaking, but he is, well, Latinx."

"I understand," Villareal assured her. Bold did not want to end up on the wrong side of the oppression hierarchy if Latinx status should rise above the ranking of transexuals at some point in the future. Still, this favor could be ammunition for Bold down the road. Villareal had not forgotten their earlier issue; at some point, Bold might make an accusation that her superior had minimized the emotional devastation Guerrero's constant transphobia inflicted upon the young operative because of her own biases as a member of the Latinx community.

"You go to this session," Villareal told her subordinate. Bold smiled, highlighting her five o'clock shadow.

"I feel naked without my long gun," Turnbull admitted as they walked along the deserted Panama City street. The sun was down, and the relentless heat had faded a bit, but it was still so humid he felt almost like he was swimming through the air. George was not bothered. He seemed very happy on his walk, stopping to smell and mark nearly everything along the way. Fortunately, Captain Saramago's vicious kick did not seem to have caused any permanent damage.

"This is mostly safe around here," Armand assured him as they lingered by a bush to allow George to sniff. "Mostly."

And then she drew a Glock 19 and pointed it past Turnbull. His eyes followed her barrel, and his own weapon along with it.

A very disconcerted young man stood there with a machete, his eyes about the size of softballs. He had clearly planned to step out in front of the foreigners. What was unclear was whether he would have merely demanded their money or started chopping and then pilfered their pockets.

What was also clear was that the young man would need to go home and change his pants.

"*No bueno,*" she told the assailant.

"Drop it," Turnbull said. He said it in English, certain the youth had seen enough American cop shows to get the universal message, "Put down your weapon or I'll blast you in the face."

The rusty blade clanged on the sidewalk.

"Get the hell out of here," Armand told him. He understood that, and he ran off the way he came. She bent down, took the machete, and walked over to drop it in a storm drain.

"Nice work." Turnbull said. "Thanks."

"You were distracted by the dog," she assured him. "I get it."

"Now, where are we going?"

"We're almost there."

Brother Miguel greeted them after Armand knocked on his door. He was a Franciscan and even wore a brown robe. His little kennel held about fifty dogs of all types and sizes – mutts, mostly. Several children were busy cleaning, feeding, or playing with them.

"Always room for one more," he said. "Not always not enough money, though." Like many Panamanians, he had a working knowledge of English, a remnant of the old Canal Zone culture before Jimmy Carter gave it up.

"So, you take care of stray animals?" Turnbull asked.

"Yes, but really this is about helping people. Most of these children are orphans, street kids. Helping here gives them a job and money, but they also learn to be kind and think of others. And, of course, St. Francis is the patron of animals. How we treat the least and lowest is the true measure of a person."

"Are you getting donations?" asked Armand. The place seemed a bit more worn down since her last visit.

"Times are hard," The cleric told her. "People are afraid. They stay home. They are reluctant to give charity when there is no certainty in our society."

"What do the people think of their President?" Turnbull asked.

It was not the kind of question one typically asked in Guerrero's Panama, but he was not afraid.

"They think he is both evil and insane," Brother Miguel said. "They are praying for deliverance. But Panama is caught between so many different forces. They lose hope."

Turnbull handed over George's leash, then knelt to say good-bye to him. He stood up and reached into his pocket, withdrawing a wad of bills.

"A little something. I hope you take American."

"It's one of their official currencies," Armand said.

"Thank you," said the brother.

They walked back to the embassy, with Turnbull now fully engaged in looking for threats. It was not often someone beat him to it; Armand was not an operative, but she was doing all right.

At the gate, they stopped out of earshot of the Marine guards.

"I'm going to go meet Rosas and make sure he's ready to be Plan B if we call him," she told Turnbull. "Let me give you his number so you know it to pick up if he has to call you direct."

Turnbull loaded it in his iPhone under "Arered" – as in "Rosas are red – in case someone somehow breached his contacts list.

"Also, can you put a tail on Circe and her she-male minion?" Turnbull asked. "I know you're on her people already."

"Oh, that's already done," Armand said. "They are in their embassy now."

He was impressed. Good initiative. They walked over to the entrance and were met by a young Marine who had apparently had any emotions surgically removed at Parris Island.

Turnbull flashed his fake ID – "Robert Julius Eastwood" – to the guards and went into the embassy. Armand flashed hers, then walked to the parking lot and got into her Ford.

As she pulled out of the gate, a sedan down the street pulled out from the curb and followed behind her.

17.

"What am I looking at?" Kelly Turnbull asked. The sun had been up for a few hours. He was on his second coffee.

"That," Katie Armand explained, pointing out across the water. They were standing on the north end of the Bridge of the Americas, at *la Mirador de las Americas*, a scenic overlook. Looking east, there was the graceful, looping steel bridge carrying the Pan-American Highway across the Pacific Ocean's entrance to the Panama Canal.

"Very pretty," Turnbull said. "Are we seeing?"

"In the water, there," Armand said.

"The ship? That rust bucket?" It had clearly seen better days, and now bobbed in the water at anchor toward the south side of the channel.

"That's the one. That's where Villareal's guys go every morning, and spend all day aboard."

"It's some kind of tanker," Turnbull said. He was really guessing. He knew nothing of ships. He had given Casey his slot to go train on commercial vessel boarding and close quarter combat with the SEALs out of Tampa – their old San Diego haunts on Coronado had been lost in the Split. The old Naval Special Warfare facility was now a resort for furries who preferred sea mammal fursonas. Turnbull was himself a land animal.

"Good guess," said Armand. "That's the *Greyhawk Paladin*. It's an LNG tanker, liquified natural gas. Very old and nowhere near as efficient as the new ones."

"So, you're a tanker expert?"

"I am now, since my guys told me that was where these clowns are going."

"I hear "natural gas" and I think 'bomb.'"

"That's what I thought. Now, in its liquid state, the natural gas won't blow up. What you want to avoid is a vapor cloud explosion. See, it's the gas vapor that goes 'boom,' and in a big way. You have the fire, but also a blast wave and overpressure."

"So, I am thinking a *big* bomb," Turnbull said.

"But, you know, the marine architects have thought of that. There are a bunch of safety precautions built in."

"Not as many as in an older boat," I bet.

"It's a ship. The sailors are very sensitive about that. Anyway, yes, the older ones like the *Greyhawk Paladin* are less safe than the newer ones, but you don't see any of them just blowing up, so that must be pretty safe."

"What if someone doesn't want them to be safe?" asked Turnbull.

"You mean what if they went in and made it unsafe on purpose? Then I suppose it would be unsafe."

"And how big would the boom be?"

"I don't know," Armand admitted. "I assume it would be a pretty big boom."

"Well, I assume the crew would have some idea. Maybe we grab one out of some saloon and have a little chat about what's going on below decks," suggested Turnbull.

"Except no one is going ashore, just those pals of Villareal's. The crew is largely Filipino and from other countries. The captain is Russian."

"That's not exactly reassuring," Turnbull told her. "Who owns it?"

"Something called Bright Star Maritime, LTD. Liberian."

"Ugh. Liberia. Hope I never go there. Okay, then who owns Bright Star?"

"A bunch of other shell companies. Someone took some care to hide the ownership, and it all happened in the last few days."

"Okay, the blues bought themselves a floating bomb. But what do you do with it?"

"Blow up next to a destroyer," Armand said.

"That's not going to happen," Turnbull said. "Because I'm feeding this info back to headquarters tonight, and it's going to the captains of the *Andrew Breitbart* and the *Charlie Kirk*, and they will blow that tub out of the water before it gets within 20 miles of them."

"So, that was her Plan B," Armand said. "A pretty bad one."

"Might have worked if you and your people hadn't figured it out."

"Thanks."

"I didn't ask – how is our Colonel Rosas?"

"Concerned, but not afraid. He's worried we may leave him hanging."

"If we need him, we need him. If we don't, we don't. That's the deal. I hope you told him not to do anything that can't be undone before we tell him the coup has a green light."

"I told him. I don't think he'll stick his neck out unless he knows we're behind him.

"He's *our* Plan B. I just hope ours is better than theirs," Turnbull said.

"Maybe Plan A will work. Maybe you can make a deal with Guerrero."

"I talked to HQ and now I have some more incentives in my pocket," Turnbull said. "Better buy-buy than war-war."

"Of course, the blues are thinking the same thing."

"Yeah, I wonder what they are going to offer. I'm not sure they have anything Guerrero would want," Turnbull said. "Okay, let's get back to the embassy. We have a dinner to attend."

238 | PANAMA RED

Colonel Wang stood up and looked out the window of the People's Republic of North America's embassy conference room. There were devices attached to the windowpanes that made them shake when activated; otherwise, someone outside could use a laser to read the vibrations from the conversations inside and decipher them.

He surveyed the city, and was disgusted with it.

"This place is wet with rot and decay," he announced in clear and precise English, honed by countless hours of drill, repetition, and practice as a young man. "And corruption."

He was right, but his point was irrelevant. Villareal assessed the Chinese People's Liberation Army colonel and his immaculately pressed uniform. She understood his contempt for everyone – Guerrero, his troops, the Panamanians, her minions, and herself. He was a regular officer, a soldier, given a mission to which he was utterly unsuited – advising a lunatic on military matters. And she was a covert operative for whom rules, order, and predictability were to be disregarded rather than embraced.

"Who did he piss off to get assigned here?" she wondered to herself. Viveca Bold was next to her, touching up her blush with a compact. It never occurred to Villareal to share such thoughts with her subordinate.

And it did not help that Colonel Wang refused to hide his contempt for the very things that distinguished the People's Republic, like its eager embrace of diverse identities and preferences. He looked at Viveca Bold as if she were some alien creature, and on the one occasion he used a pronoun to refer to her, Wang used "he."

Villareal had been to China, and she knew that China was utterly transphobic, as well as sexist and racist. It was also aggressively imperialist. But none of these things could be spoken. That itself would be racist, as well as detrimental to the unequal relationship between the two nations. Though some in her government were loathe to admit it for their own selfish reasons, the PR needed the PRC desperately. The United States was growing more powerful – she knew this because she could read between the lines in the intelligence reports that had come across her desk – while the People's Republic was growing weaker. That was another forbidden topic; no one wanted to raise the question of why the vaunted Democratic Socialism that the Democrats of the old United States had built in the blue following the Split was being massively outpaced, economically and otherwise, by the cruel, Dickensian capitalism of the Republicans who took power in the red.

China propped up the PR, economically, diplomatically, and – if it became necessary – would hopefully do so militarily as well. So, when China called for help resolving a problem with the PR's neighbor to the south, Panama, Senator Harrison agreed to help unofficially. Villareal suspected others in the PR government had objected – it was too risky, it conflicted with their own agendas, or perhaps it was just anti-Asian racism.

Her orders were very clear – pleasing the PRC by accomplishing this mission was her objective, and she was to achieve it no matter what the cost. Of course, that did not mean that the PR was the only country that must bear that cost.

"Will your government go along with my plan?" Villareal asked, getting to the point and avoiding a digression into the many moral and intellectual failings of this Third World dictatorship.

"No," he said. "The idea is ridiculous."

Was he being intentionally obtuse, or did he really possess so little imagination? Villareal tried again.

"China does not need to actually give him what we promise tonight," Villareal explained, as if to a child. "We just need his cooperation over the next, say, week."

"If we lie to him, if we do not perform, what stops him from closing the canal to *our* ships? Or the Americans from invading to make sure it never happens again?"

"Those are possibilities," Villareal conceded. "But Chinese shipping is nearly half of the canal's traffic. You have worked with him for some months now. Do you think his ego is larger than his greed?"

"He is controlled by his emotions, and that is compounded by drugs and liquor," Wang sneered. "He is not a soldier or even a politician. He is a madman. I have seen him shoot his own men for barely any reason."

"Are you afraid for your own safety?" Villareal asked, knowing it would poke him.

"I do not fear that petty thug," Wang retorted. But it seemed improbable that the risks of making promises with no intention of keeping them and Guerrero's hostile reaction had not occurred to him.

"I don't think he would dare murder a Chinese officer," Villareal said.

"You don't know Guerrero," Wang answered. "But my life is unimportant. Your lives are even less so. What matters is the strategic situation. What happens if his shutting the canal to U.S. Navy traffic encourages the reds to invade Panama yet again? Then the Americans would hold it and have a stranglehold on the world's most vital shipping chokepoint."

"It could happen," Villareal conceded. "But that is weeks away. We have to deal with those American warships your satellites caught steaming toward the Atlantic entrance of the canal. They come through the canal tomorrow at 4:00 p.m., twenty-four hours from now. The door must be shut to them."

And it would be, one way or the other. Wang was unimaginative, a cog – she had seen enough of them in her own government. To her dismay, socialism seemed to attract them. She found it ironic that for Marxists, parasitical bureaucrats were the cost of doing business, as a capitalist might say. She had long resolved to be something else. She had no real advantages – she was of an undistinguished ethnicity, her gender was suspect, and her preferences questionable. She had nothing truly going for her in the hierarchy of the People's Republic. But she knew she had cunning. She thought out every move, analyzed every potential course of action, and prepared for every contingency. In fact, she had assessed that Wang might be an obstacle – her Plan A was that audacious – that she hedged against him undermining her.

Villareal had ordered the next step of Plan B. As she spoke, most of her Somalis were aboard the *Grayhawk Paladin*, securing it and the crew. Captain Johnson and her explosives expert Devlin were aboard, too, putting the finishing touches on the ship. The vessel was currently underway east through the canal – the toll was enormous, but that expense would be forgotten if she succeeded. It had passed the Miraflores Locks, which raised the ship up to the level for transit through the canal. Now, it would probably be heading through the Culebra Cut, the dug-out waterway that connected Gatun Lake with the Pacific Ocean. Gatun Lake was about 85' above sea level – it varied a few feet. On the other side of the lake to the east, through the two sets of parallel locks, was the Atlantic Ocean. Once through the Cut and across the lake under the control of a Panamanian pilot brought aboard for the task of navigating the canal, the *Grayhawk Paladin* would wait in the lake among a dozen or so other ships – ostensibly, to transit the Gatun Locks. But it was really waiting for Villareal's instructions. If they came, she intended to deliver them personally. There would be no screw-ups.

Wang's self-pity brought Villareal back to the present.

"I was once in line to be a general and command a division," Wang said bitterly. "Now, I am here dealing with savages, amateurs, and whatever that is." He meant Viveca Bold. Bold gasped and looked to her boss for support, staring expectantly. Villareal ignored the macroaggression.

"If the canal is closed, the task force reaches Lima and the forces of revanchist fascism will be defeated with the help of the People's Liberation Army," Villareal said. "And that victory over imperialism will be yours. You will have achieved it. You were not sent to the fringes; you were sent to the decision point. All you have to do is back my play."

He looked at her, considering. She wondered if he understood the idiom – an old pre-Split term she was fairly certain should be unacceptable and possibly illegal for some reason she could not quite put her finger on. It was probably patriarchal; most hard-to-categorize examples of wrongthink were wrong because they were patriarchal. It was the default micro/macroaggression category.

"I will, but you must consider what the other Americans will do," he said.

"You mean the reds?" Bold interjected.

"I don't understand your colors," snapped the Chinese colonel. "Red is the color of revolution, and blue of fascism, yet your fascists are red and your socialists are blue!"

"It came from old America," Bold explained.

"You Americans were weak and foolish then as now," Colonel Wang declared.

"Can I count on your support tonight?" Villareal asked, ignoring the jibe.

"Yes," the colonel said. "I will go to my own embassy and communicate my plan to my principals, then meet you there."

His plan. Villareal smiled her disarming smile.

If it went to hell, she would be certain to ensure that it was his plan. And that her Plan B would save the day.

18.

"I think we're overdressed," Casey observed as they drove by the slovenly guards at the National Assembly parking lot. The Americans wore polo shirts and 5.11 tactical khakis, accessorized with their pistols.

"Those boys look like they've had a hard weekend, and it's only Thursday," Clanton said.

"Stay mellow in there," Turnbull said. He checked that there was a round in the chamber of his .45 and slid it back into his holster.

Katie Armand hung up her Android phone. The Americans in the back of the embassy SUV looked to her expectantly for the news.

"Rosas is getting ready," she announced. "He still wants to know what kind of support he'll get."

"If it has to happen, I'm going to deliver him what he needs most," Turnbull replied.

"If Rosas and his Catholic officers make a move and fail, they all die, and so do their families."

"If we give him the go, it's not going to fail," Turnbull said. He was mostly confident of that.

Mostly.

"I see the Big Cheese is on scene," Clanton said, looking over at the Presidential Huey on the landing pad. He identified it by the subtle words "EL PRESIDENTE" that were painted on the sides of the tail boom.

"He'll make a grand entrance," Mundi said. "It's like a cult."

"If they offer you Kool-Aid, hard pass," cautioned Casey.

"Could you make a shot from those high-rises over there on someone climbing into that chopper?" Turnbull asked, pointing at some apartment buildings a few hundred yards away that overlooked the landing field.

"With my M14? Yeah, probably," Casey said.

"Good," Turnbull replied. He turned to Armand.

"You need to get one of your minions to get me a room on this side of that building," Turnbull told her. "Like, tonight. I bet there are plenty of vacancies with the National Assembly being history and all."

Armand nodded, dialed her Android and put it to her ear.

The SUV pulled up to the door, and everyone got out. It was hot and humid, especially compared to the Chevy's air-conditioned interior. Katie Armand from the embassy wore a citizenship pin on the lapel of her blue blazer. You could see the grip of her Glock underneath it when the jacket swung open as she walked. She was talking into her phone. They gave her a minute to give instructions to her subordinate on the other end.

It smelled like mold and soldier pee.

There was no one there to greet them out in front of the National Assembly building. There was no organization, no order, just the same collection of people staggering through the lobby, and the noise of the DJ banging through the open doors to the main chamber.

"This is less a White House than a frat house," Clanton observed.

"I'm thinking this would be like the White House if Hunter Biden had ever been president," Casey added.

"The hookers would've probably been more Ukrainian and Lithuanian, though," Mundi said. "I don't think he could handle the Latin heat." The ladies on scene seemed to be part of the local color.

"Can you guys not talk once we get inside?" Turnbull asked as they went through the outside doors into the trashed and reeking lobby. He sidestepped a puddle of something hideous. "And can you start practicing for that right now?"

They crossed through the lobby without incident, except for a couple of drunken soldiers who nearly stumbled into Armand. She moved out of the way just before they could crash into her, and they thought the near collision was hysterical. They had AK-47s slung over their backs. Everybody seemed to be packing, except for some of the ladies of the evening. Most of them weren't wearing enough to conceal a weapon, let alone much else.

The five walked into the main chamber, which looked like a combination of the world's lowest-rent Oktoberfest and a Cinco de Mayo celebration at a discount Vegas off-Strip hotel.

"Keep alert," Turnbull advised.

"We will be the only ones who are," Armand said. She walked through a cloud of dope smoke from a trio of giggling soldiers passing an enormous joint between them.

"Remember that band Cypress Hill?" Clanton asked aloud.

"This is like that sweaty rave scene from one of the *Matrix* sequels," Casey said as they started walking towards the platform at the front. "Except everybody here is ugly."

"Didn't the guys who made that go to the blue after the country broke up and start winning Oscars?" asked Mundi.

"Yeah," Casey replied. "But they aren't guys anymore. At least we got Keanu in the Split. I hear they made *Matrix VII: Virgin Summer* last year, and the guy playing Neo was Michael Cera. You know, there's a big argument in the sci-fi/fantasy community about whether movies made in the blue count as canon or not."

"See what I have to deal with?" Turnbull muttered to Armand as they reached the steps up to the VIP platform. The M134 minigun was still there on its tripod, with ammunition boxes piled next to it. There was additional brass all over the stage – apparently somebody had been trying it out again.

Captain Saramago was up there. So was Medea Villareal, who sat next to Guerrero's Chinese advisor, Colonel Wang, as well as Viveca Bold, and a couple of Somali guards who looked absolutely baffled by what was happening. They were all on one side of a long, wooden table. Somebody had taken a little time not only to clear the table but to wipe it down. Of course, there was still a reddish stain where Saramago's arm had leaked out after he had made the mistake of kicking a dog in front of Kelly Turnbull.

"At least we're on time," Armand said.

There was no sign of the President or his enforcer, Colonel Ruiz. No doubt those two would be joining the festivities once all the guests were in place. Making the guests wait reaffirmed their status as supplicants. The guy might be a drunken, drug-addicted sociopath, Turnbull reasoned to himself, but he understood the trappings of power. That was probably why he was still alive.

Saramago came across the platform to the top of the steps. Turnbull noted that the captain's forearm was bandaged, and his hand looked swollen. He was clearly unhappy to see the American.

"How's the arm, Captain?" asked Turnbull. Saramago had a handgun in his holster, but it was going to take him a little effort to get it out. That's why Turnbull's plan to take out the officer, which he made after seeing the Panamanian adjutant when he walked into the chamber, was not to shoot him in the face. He would grab the man's good arm and break it. This would leave the unfortunate officer with a matched pair of bandages and probably give President Guerrero a good laugh. It would also, as impaling the man's arm against the table top the prior evening had, send a not-so-subtle message that it was a bad idea to screw with these Americans.

Actions, Turnbull understood, spoke exponentially louder than words.

Saramago did not answer, and he did nothing to hide his burning hatred, except he kept his mouth shut. The president's toady pointed the Americans to the opposite side of the table, where the blue representatives sat. They would be facing each other at a distance of just a couple of feet.

"There's no way this could go terribly wrong," Armand whispered.

The Americans walked over to their seats, even as Saramago disappeared into the back. Turnbull settled onto the bench at the far end, directly across from Medea Villareal.

"Good evening, Bob," the blue agent said. Turnbull was a little surprised. She hadn't had her people figure out his real name since yesterday, and he was grateful. Someday, he'd be back in the blue undercover, and he preferred that they did not know he existed, at least under his real name.

"Hello, Circe," he answered. She was dressed not provocatively but femininely, though less so than Viveca Bold, who wore a black cocktail dress.

"You know my name," Villareal said. "But you're still using my code name."

"You'll always be Circe to me," he said. She smiled mirthlessly.

"I still don't know your real name." Villareal had passed the request to research this American back to Carlos Trent; obviously, he was slow-walking it if he was pursuing it at all.

"Let's stick with 'Bob,'" Turnbull suggested.

"I just missed getting you in Minnesota, Bob," she said.

"Not for lack of trying," Turnbull replied. "You might teach your boys some marksmanship. But I missed you in Dublin, so I guess we're even."

"We are not even close to even," hissed Villareal.

"You seem angry," Turnbull said. "You shouldn't let your emotions get involved. This is business, not personal."

"It's personal for me," she said.

"Well, maybe you're right. You've hurt a lot of people, so maybe be it's a *little* personal," conceded Turnbull.

Down the table, Casey stifled a laugh at their exchange. He turned back and met Viveca Bold's glare.

"Not interested, dude," Casey said.

"I'm looking for a *real* man," Bold replied. Casey turned toward Clanton.

"I think he's talking about you," he said.

"She!" hissed Bold.

"Nah," Casey said. "We don't do that."

Villareal composed herself. She smiled her dark smile and aimed it at Kelly Turnbull.

"Do you expect President Guerrero to accept whatever offer you're going to make?" she asked.

"I think that would be in his long-term interest," Turnbull said. "So, what will you be offering?"

"It's very hard to shop for the man who has everything," said Villareal. "Power, women. He already has those things."

"Money?" Turnbull offered.

"Oh, they never have enough of that," Villareal assured him.

"We'll see how it goes," Turnbull said. "But you'd better hope he goes your way, because if he doesn't, your Chinese friend here is going to be very upset." Turnbull figured they knew about the two U.S. Navy cruisers that would be entering the canal the next day, if everything went his way.

"I don't think you've been formally introduced to Colonel Wang," she said. "Colonel Wang, this is Bob. I don't think that that's his real name."

The Chinese officer grunted and nodded once, his officer's cap staying perfectly in place. He radiated the fact that he would rather be at any other place in the universe than there speaking with them.

"Say it, Kelly," Casey whispered to Clanton, who was sitting down from Turnbull at the table. "Please say it!"

"Colonel Wang," Turnbull said. "No offense."

"Yes!" Casey whispered, and Clanton smiled and nodded. Apparently, the colonel was not a fan of *Caddyshack* or much else; he just sat there coldly glaring at Turnbull.

Turnbull suppressed the desire to ask the Chi Com colonel if his hat came with a free bowl of soup.

"*¡Atención atención!*" cried Captain Saramago, who had come back to the stage from out of the door to the backstage area and was now addressing the crowd. It took a minute for most of the attendees to look up from their beer or booze or pot or cocaine or hookers, and offer their blurry attention.

"Stand for our leader, our magnificent father, a warrior, a statesman, a lover, the modern incarnation of Simón Bolívar, the President of the Bolívarian Republic of Panama!"

"The ayatollah of rock 'n' rolla," Casey whispered. Turnbull shushed him.

"*¡Presidente* Bonifacio Alberto Maria Guerrero!" shouted the emcee, with Saramago theatrically waving his arm to introduce their hero.

Now, the crowd was on its feet, to the extent it could stand, many of them swaying, bracing themselves on their tables and using their rifles to hold themselves upright. But they were cheering, clapping, and hooting and hollering, some toasting with their Atlas beers, others stepping up on the tables to shout the praises of their dictator.

Guerrero walked out of the back area, his uniform buttoned to the neck this time, mercifully keeping the tufts of chest hair from spilling out. He may have shaved, but not well, and it seems he may have patted his longish black hair into place. He still looked tousled and moist. Guerrero was smiling broadly, his hands fists lifted high above his head as his guests welcomed him to the stage.

He was a mess and a lunatic, Turnbull saw, but the President was undoubtedly charismatic. He had most of these people in the palm of his hand. And for those not in his hand, there was Colonel Ruiz, who stepped quietly out of the door behind his boss and sat there watching everything and everyone.

"This is a very important night for the Bolívarian Republic of Panama!" he shouted to the crowd in Spanish. "Tonight, the Americans, both kinds, the red kind and the blue kind, come to us on their knees, begging for our friendship. And of course, we have the Chinese here, too, and they likewise know to respect us. For our Canal, which we built, and which we maintain, and which we control, makes us the center of the globe, and everyone around the globe must acknowledge our greatness and our independence!"

Armand translated for Turnbull.

"*They* built the canal?" he whispered back when she finished.

"Maybe we don't argue that detail here tonight," Armand suggested.

"Forget it, he's rolling," Casey added.

"Our greatness is assured, it cannot be denied. The Panamanian people will receive the respect and glory that they are due under my leadership. You are my people, and I will never fail you!"

That brought down the house, with 100 or so people hooting and cheering on their *caudillo*. And he was drinking it in, just as he had been in back, drinking in everything else he could get his grimy hands on.

"Now, I will have dinner with our guests and I will talk to them, so be very quiet! These negotiations are very sensitive, very delicate. But, people of Panama, I will bring you back to greatness!"

There was more cheering and howling even as he walked over to the table. Saramago brought a chair and placed it at the end of the table, between Turnbull and Villareal. The dictator sat down in it with a thud.

"Good evening, my *amigos*! Welcome to my table, where we shall eat and negotiate before all my people."

Turnbull could have disputed whether they were actually *amigos*, but chose not to.

"It is an honor to be the guest of such a respected leader," Villareal said, looking at Turnbull. "And such a staunch foe of the imperialists."

Guerrero nodded self-consciously as he accepted her praise.

"I like imperialists," Turnbull said. "If it weren't for imperialists, people around her would still be sacrificing each other to their winged snake demon-gods. And nobody would be sailing through the isthmus because there wouldn't be a canal."

Guerrero found this amusing. Villareal did not.

"Mr. President, we do not mock and laugh at the victims of the European genocide that this envoy from his racist regime celebrates. We show solidarity with the victims of colonialism."

"And you can believe that when the People's Republic gives back all its land to whichever Indian tribe last conquered it," Turnbull said. "But they haven't, and they never will. You know, President Guerrero, you and I are men of action. We say what we mean and do what we say."

Guerrero liked the offhand compliment and nodded as Turnbull continued.

"These are just words. The People's Republic will come here with their Chinese friends, who laugh at you behind your back, and pretend to be friends of you and your country. I've been there. All they care about is their weird perversions and pretending to be better than other people. But they never do anything. It's all talk. That's what they are, all talk. But when I talk on behalf of the United States, that means something."

"Mr. President," Villareal said. "My country, and our Chinese friends, have always shown solidarity with the struggle of colonized people."

"They want to colonize *you*, Mr. President," Turnbull said. "Not with soldiers and ships and planes, but with all the weirdness and sickness that infects them. Look at that."

He pointed to Viveca Bold in her cocktail dress, her beard-stumbled cheek trembling.

"*That* is what they want for your country. Do you have a son, Mr. President?"

"I think I have many, too many," he answered. "I am a powerful, potent man. I do not know them all!" There was generalized laughter at the clever dictator's answer.

"Would you like to come home and have your son tell you he's now your daughter? Because that's their colonization. It's not by soldiers. It's by perversions."

"Well, one man's perversion is another man's entertainment, am I not right?" There was more laughter. Then he became more serious. He continued.

"You two are enemies. It must be hard to sit at this table together, but it is not unprecedented. Not many know it, but I am a student of history. Yes, I read many books. There's much to learn from history. Do you know about Hannibal of Carthage? And Scipio of Rome, who finally defeated Hannibal and forced Carthage to make peace? Hannibal was driven out of Carthage by very jealous civilian politicians. This is why I do not allow civilian politicians. You cannot trust them. But after that, Hannibal was at the court of an eastern king, and Scipio came to visit, and he and Scipio sat down to dinner together. No, really – this is a true story. It is in the history books. At this dinner, Scipio asked Hannibal who the greatest generals in history were, and Hannibal thought about it. Then he said Alexander the Great was the first, and Pyrrhus of Greece the second. Do you know who he said was the third? Hannibal himself! And he said he would have been the first if he had defeated Scipio!"

Guerrero roared with laughter.

"You like my story?" he asked.

"I have always been a big fan of Hannibal," Turnbull said. "The double envelopment at Cannae was genius." Guerrero considered this and nodded, then looked at Villareal.

"Dead white men have nothing to teach us," she told Guerrero. "They are the cause of injustice, not the solution."

"Hannibal was from North Africa, so not exactly a person of pallor," Turnbull observed. Villareal fumed – despite having a history degree from Yale, she had never heard of Hannibal. Or Scipio. Or Carthage. And all she knew of Rome was that it was a racist patriarchy that was unworthy of study. But she did have an extensive understanding of LGBTQA+#2s¥% issues as they were related to serfdom in medieval Lichtenstein.

"They say every man thinks of Rome three or four times a day," Guerrero said, looking at Villareal. "So, you are excused." Then he looked at Viveca Bold.

"I don't know how it would work with you, though."

"I never think of Rome," Bold lied. In fact, try as she might, she found herself thinking of Rome every day. And it was tearing her apart.

Several serving girls arrived with platters. It was some kind of fish dish. There was also a bottle of Atlas beer for everyone. The servers laid down their trays and departed.

"Eat," the President commanded. They did, silently. Villareal briefly considered taking the knife she was using to gut her entrée and using it to gut Kelly Turnbull. For his part, Turnbull had gamed out how he would, if necessary, draw his .45 and fire it into her guts under the table, not unlike Han Solo in the original cut of *Star Wars*. By law, as part of the campaign to stamp out cultural Marxism, this was the only version allowed in red America.

But it was unnecessary to execute his contingency plan. Instead, there was détente through dessert, which was some sort of banana flan confection. After the diners had finished, the serving girls took away the food but brought more beer. Villareal made it a point to match Turnbull's consumption.

Guerrero watched them both carefully. Turnbull desperately wanted to get to the point, but he had sat through enough endless meetings in enough foreign hellholes to know that you can't rush things. They're going to happen on their own time, and in the Third World, time is entirely different than it is back in Dallas. They were on President Guerrero's clock, and he was enjoying himself. He was perfectly content to let time tick away. Turnbull was the one on a deadline, not the Panamanian strongman.

Finally, after what seemed like an eternity, Guerrero announced that he was finally prepared to hear their offers.

"Since we have a long relationship with the United States of America, I will let the U.S. go first," he said.

"What you say is true," Turnbull began. "Our nations have a long history together. You don't have that with these two, the People's Republic of North America and the People's Republic of China. What we're offering you is security. A renewed alliance. A promise to defend you and your country from all threats, foreign and domestic."

Armand didn't like this part, nor did Kelly Turnbull, but this was *realpolitik.* The Panamanian patriots had their interests, but the United States had its own. To the extent they matched, that was fine. To the extent they didn't, Turnbull's country's interests trumped anything else. He continued with America's proposal.

"America is offering you an ironclad promise to make sure that you aren't overthrown the minute these two decide they're done with you. You know we have the forces to do it. If you continue to allow our ships through the canal, you get a signed alliance with the United States of America. That means something. Most importantly, it means you don't have to watch your back."

"Interesting," Guerrero said, except he didn't sound particularly interested. Turnbull had expected that, but he had also expected the dictator to understand the flip side of the coin. America could preserve him in power yet, if necessary, throw him out with another invasion. But that couldn't happen before the deadline to get those cruisers through the canal. Villareal was right about one thing – it's hard to figure out something to give a man who already has a country.

Out of the corner of his eye, Turnbull saw a junior officer come and whisper in Colonel Ruiz's ear. Ruiz stared at him harshly, but after a moment, he realized he was staring at Armand. Did he know? That would have to wait. Turnbull hoped Rosas had taken Armand's advice to disappear for the time being.

Villareal's reaction was to laugh, a laugh without joy.

"Mr. President, you should be insulted by this, but not surprised. These Americans have nothing but contempt for you. All they offer you is your own country. You already have it. What we offer is much more. My Chinese friend, Colonel Wang, will tell you himself that his country agrees. It is time for another Bolívar and for revolution in Latin America. I know that Simón Bolívar is one of your heroes – a great leader who freed much of this region from imperialists. In just a few days, China and the People's Republic will help the freedom fighters in Peru liberate themselves from the fascists. It won't end there. Next will come Ecuador, and then Colombia, which is right on your doorstep. But we cannot lead the masses of Latin America. Only a Latin American can. A leader who is proven, who is respected, who is strong. That leader is you. If you join us now, you will be the leader of northern Latin America when it is liberated in a second Bolívarian revolution. That is what we have to offer. Not just the country you already have, but more countries to come."

Guerrero seemed impressed, and he looked at Colonel Wang.

"Is this true, my Asian friend?"

"My nation is of the opinion that you are the obvious choice of a native leader to lead the newly freed peoples of Latin America," he recited without enthusiasm.

"Also," Villareal said, as she lifted a brown leather valise to the table and plopped it down. "Here is $100,000 as a token of our appreciation for your courtesy tonight."

"Is that American money or your ridiculous Baracks?"

"American," she replied, resenting it.

"I knew we should've brought some money," Armand whispered.

Saramago relieved his master of the valise. Now, Guerrero looked at Turnbull.

"You offer me nothing that I don't have already, American. And you don't even offer me the courtesy of a small gratuity for taking you into my home here for dinner. I am very disappointed. But this minigun here, I do appreciate that."

Turnbull leaned in towards the President.

"If you actually believe they're going to install you as the dictator of some imaginary Latin American empire, and that you'd be anything but a puppet and a figurehead waiting for them to pull the trigger on the gun that'll always be up against your head the second you fail to do exactly what they tell you, then you're the drunkest, highest man in this whole building. Which is saying something."

"You might be correct about drunkest and highest, but you are not a very respectful man, American. That can be dangerous."

"Mr. President, you know what we do to people who lay their hands on Americans. It's not like the old days. It's not like before the Split. We don't give a damn who you are. That's a line foreigners don't cross."

"You are brave, American, not smart, but brave. I will give you that. And since you are my guests, I will not do to you what I would do to anyone else who spoke to me like that – leave you hanging headless by your feet from an overpass. Now, you and your friends get the hell out of my palace. I need to work out the details of this alliance between the peoples of the People's Republic of North America and the People's Republic of China, and the Bolívarian Republic of Panama."

Turnbull stood, and so did the rest of his people. No one put their hands on their weapons, but they were all thinking about it.

"Wait," said President Guerrero. "I think it is time for a change. The Bolívarian People's Republic of Panama. Yes, I like the sound of that."

The audience cheered raucously.

"You should rethink this, Guerrero," Turnbull growled.

"You Americans go before you've worn out my welcome," the President snarled. "You will leave this country tomorrow, or we *will* lay our hands on you. Tell your Navy ships not to bother knocking on our Atlantic door, because they will not be coming in."

Villareal sat beaming. Even Colonel Wang's mouth betrayed the hint of a smile at one corner that turned slightly upwards.

Turnbull paused, weighing his options. Armand took hold of his upper arm.

"Let's go," she said. Guerrero pointed at her.

"And you, Miss Agricultural Attache, make sure you stick to farms and livestock. Anything else could be dangerous."

"*Now*," she reiterated to Turnbull.

He turned, and the Americans followed him down off the platform. The partygoers could not hear the details, but they knew who had won the negotiation and who had lost, and they were cheering wildly. Someone threw a cigarette, and it bounced off Turnbull's chest.

It took everything he had to keep from walking over and breaking the greasy man's neck. But he consoled himself with the absolute certainty that, one way or another, this guy and most of his comrades were going to die as a result of Guerrero's bad choice. The United States might not be able to strike before the deadline to save Peru, but there was no way it was going to allow a creeping Bolívarian cancer to metastasize northward from Peru through Ecuador through Colombia, and then through Panama and beyond through Central America to Mexico, landing right on the doorstep of the United States. The U.S. was never going to take the chance of millions of refugees heading north; America had already experienced tens of millions of people at its southern wall and was not about to let that happen again.

As they climbed back into the SUV, Turnbull looked around at all the Panamanian troops lounging about without a care in the world. They were going to care eventually. It was just a matter of when.

19.

"There is zero chance that the Chi Coms and the PR are going to let that nutcase be the dictator of Latin America," Clay Deeds said on the secure video screen inside the U.S. embassy's SCIF.

"Thank you," Turnbull responded. "I tried to tell him, but I think he heard just what he wanted to hear."

"In his defense, he's a drunken drug addict who's pretty much insane," Casey added. "I guess that's not much of a defense."

"There's no way we can launch an actual invasion in time to hold the canal open for the *Breitbart* and the *Kirk*," Deeds said. "We have a couple of 161st helicopters and a special forces team in country up north doing some joint training with the Panamanian Army. That's it." The Panamanians were happy to accept training from almost anyone – there was currently a Chinese special forces unit training them at a base in the south. But the Panamanians did not like training missions with the PR because the blue soldiers stopped training for emergency reeducation and self-criticism every time one of the Panamanian troops laughed at a blue soldier's piercing, fur suit, or drag uniform.

"I think we need to go with my Plan B," Turnbull said.

"That's echelons above even my pay grade," Deeds said.

"I didn't know you had a pay grade, Clay," Turnbull replied.

"We all have a pay grade, Kelly."

"Not Sydney Sweeney," Casey said. "Especially when she's first lady once Baron gets elected."

"Focus," Deeds ordered. "Kelly, I will be running it up the flagpole. Don't do anything until I get the okay."

"The clock is ticking, Clay. If we're not out of town by sundown, Guerrero is sending out the posse."

"We're moving at the speed of politicians now," Deeds told them. "Hold fast until I get an answer on your coup play."

The video screen clicked off.

"I can't believe we're doing this," Armand said. "Or maybe not doing it."

"We should just do it," Clanton said.

"This *cuadillo* has got to go," Mundi said. "Of course, I'm biased. I hate communists."

That was certainly true, Turnbull reflected. No one hated a commie like a Cuban. He and Mundi had fed communists to crocodiles. Literally.

"It's going to be morning at the earliest before the politicians get it together and make a decision," Turnbull said. "I say we get some sleep."

"Rosas is going to want to know as soon as possible," Armand said. "These guys are risking their lives just talking to us about it."

"They are big boys, and this is a big boys game," Turnbull said. "My motto is 'Trust no one.'"

"That hurts, Kelly," Casey said.

"I trust you to never stop talking," he replied. "Look, we have our interests and they have theirs. If they align, fine. If not, America first."

"This is getting dark," Armand said. "A lot of moral ambiguity."

"Just assume that morality has nothing to do with it and you'll be a lot less uptight," Turnbull said. "Now, is Rosas secure?"

"He took leave. Told the generals he was going to be with his sick mother-in-law out in the countryside, but he's hiding out somewhere in town. I don't know where. He won't say on an open line."

"I don't blame him," Turnbull said. "That Colonel Ruiz is a snake. Anyway, I'm crashing. You should all do the same." He did not have to tell them to get their gear ready, just in case.

"I'm headed home," Armand said. "You have my cell number. We'll meet here in the morning, 0900."

The group broke, and Turnbull went up to his quarters. On the way, he passed the ambassador in the hall.

"I don't know what you did," he told Turnbull. "But my people told me you have driven the President into the arms of the People's Republic and the Chinese. I *knew* you would lead us to disaster."

"What floor are we on?" Turnbull asked.

"What?"

"The floor. What floor are we on?"

"The sixth, if it matters."

"I thought it was the fifth. Oh well, you can confirm it when you count them on the way down after I throw you out that window if you say one more damn word."

The ambassador was sputtering as Turnbull passed by him and continued down the hall.

"You were a genius," Viveca Bold told Medea Villareal in the conference room at the embassy. Villareal had allowed the junior agent to mix up a drink called a "cosmopolitan," a "cosmo" for short. She had never had one, but Bold swore by then.

"Me and the other hens love to have a few on Saturday nights!" Bold told her. "This is so amazing. You go, girl!"

Villareal was not used to this kind of informal celebration. She kept her own counsel, and that had served her well. Nor did she trust the exuberance of Agent Bold. It seemed too much, and those incriminating items that Bold had on her were still there, waiting to be exposed and pursued. Clearly, Viveca Bold understood this was a terrific victory, and equally clearly, Viveca Bold was interested in latching onto Villareal for as long as it was profitable. But Villareal also understood that Bold had contributed nothing except for completing some simple errands and, now, mixing this drink.

She sipped.

"It's good," she said, and you would have thought Villareal had just presented Bold with a bouquet of roses.

"Thank *you*, comrade sister," Bold replied, a little too huskily.

Villareal took another sip of her drink and mentally reviewed the situation. Plan A was a success, so far at least – she believed nothing until it happened. But even Colonel Wang had been complimentary, in his own way.

"You did not fail," he had allowed.

But she now focused on Plan B, even though it was unlikely to be necessary. The *Greyhawk Paladin* should be entering Gatun Lake by now. When President Guerrero actually rejected the Americans' radioed demand to allow the cruisers approaching its coast to get through, then there would be no need for Plan B. Until then, they must be ready.

Most of her twenty Somalis were on board the ship. Just five were left with her. They would have tasks beyond guarding her person, whether or not things fell through, but things would not fall through. She had beaten the American, this Bob. And if she could, she would assassinate him and his fellow operators when they got to the airport to depart.

That would truly make her happy, she decided. As Bold scrutinized her, Villareal took another sip of the concoction and smiled her smile. Bold returned one of her own. This was emotionally moving for her – Villareal could see her Adam's apple quivering.

"When you get to your room, you can relax and watch some television. We have People's Republic shows here, and no local television except in the media section for operational purposes only," Bold told Villareal. "Their local television is awful. It's all patriarchal and cis *telenovelas*. The Latinx part is good, but everything else is so totally problematic. If we showed it, besides it being a crime, it would trigger everyone on the embassy staff.

So, you can settle into bed and watch *Christian Hunters* or *Follow That Furry*. It's so funny, and Mark Ruffalo really does look like a fox. Or you can watch Julie Kimmel– his bottom surgery is so inspiring." While Jimmy had become Julie and undergone his procedure, he still kept his "he/him" pronouns.

"He's given me the courage to apply for it," Bold gushed. "My appointment is in just eight months!"

"It's a tragedy that the reds have made it take so long to get gender affirming care in the PR," Villareal said.

"Luckily, we're civilized and gender affirming care is prioritized. If it were a rotator cuff or a heart stent, it would be three years," Bold said, adding: "But that's totally because of red America and capitalism."

"I hate them so much," Villareal affirmed.

"So do I. You know, I may go down to the ladies' steam room instead and relax. Maybe you would like to join me?"

Was this another trap, Villareal wondered as Bold looked at her expectantly.

"Perhaps tomorrow. I am tired tonight, and I am frankly triggered by the racism, sexism, and transphobia I experienced today."

"How could you not be? Oh, and the Islamophobia. Appalling."

Another trap? Villareal nodded.

"So much Islamophobia." She recalled arresting a young white male while a People's Bureau of Investigation officer for trafficking in unlawful memes, this one of some comedian named Norm something who suggested that the worst part of an ISIS attack would be the resulting Islamophobia – except he was saying it sarcastically.

She shivered at the thought that such people still existed in the blue, but how could they not do so with red America to the south, reveling in such hate speech?

With her subordinate watching, Villareal finished her drink and stood up.

264 | PANAMA RED

"You have been an essential part of today's success, Agent Bold," she declared formally. Bold beamed as Villareal went on. "You are a credit to women everywhere, and I guarantee that I will see that you receive what you deserve."

Villareal walked out smiling, but for an entirely different reason than why Bold was smiling.

The phone rang twice before Colonel Rosas picked it up. The call was on speaker in Armand's embassy car as she drove to her house. He was using a burner she had given him.

"*Si?*"

"It's me," Armand said, careful since it was an open line. "We are waiting for word."

"Every second you wait, Colonel Ruiz gets closer to finding us out," Rosas said. She could feel the tension in his voice, and she could not deny his right to be tense. It was his life, and that of his family and co-conspirators, on the line.

"I understand. These things are complicated. We will have an answer in the morning."

"If we live that long."

"Are you ready if we call?" Armand said.

"Yes, but you will have to do your part."

"If we get our green light, we will do it."

"I don't trust the blues, but I am not sure I should trust the reds either."

Armand thought about Turnbull's motto. When you trusted no one, that included the red Americans. Maybe Turnbull knew his own side better than she did. But then, he had been doing it longer.

"You can trust us," she said to the Panamanian officer, not knowing if that was true.

"I hope so," he replied. "If this goes badly, you must get my family out."

"It won't go badly," she promised. "But if it does, I'll take care of it."

She hoped she could at least keep that promise.

Turnbull lay back in bed, shoes off but clothes on. His M4 carbine was leaning against the wall next to the Benelli M4 shotgun. His M1911 .45 was on his bedside table. He considered cleaning them, but he had not shot anyone since he arrived in Panama. That struck him as odd.

He would likely get some shooting in tomorrow when the coup went off. Well, *if* the coup went off. Regardless, he inspected and wiped down all his weapons and mags.

Task Force Zulu would surgically remove *el Presidente*, then let the Panamanians sort it out for themselves. One shot from Casey's M14 rifle as *el Presidente* sprinted for his chopper would be enough, and Rosas could deal with the other, lesser heads of the hydra himself.

He flipped on the TV. It was all red American programing, though you could get the steamy local soaps if that floated your boat. The screen came up on *NCIS: Dallas*. Turnbull wondered why the Navy would have a detachment of its criminal investigative service in landlocked Dallas but, apparently, it had one everywhere else. He flipped through the channels and briefly considered watching Kevin Sorbo as Agent Ace Galahad in the series *Commie Hunters*. The scene involved a scuffle in a helicopter between Ace and some pinko, whom he tossed from the chopper.

"That's what I like to see – a communist in his natural habitat!" said the hero to his conventionally sexy female partner. Then there was a public service announcement encouraging women not to be old maids and to get married (and start having kids) before they hit "the big two-five." It was followed by another "service means citizenship" ad, this one for the Navy.

"Ahoy," Turnbull said aloud.

He changed the channel again, settling on *The Dennis Miller Mysteries*, and eventually falling asleep as Inspector Miller was explaining to his flabbergasted chief that his case "makes less sense than the Professor leap-frogging Ginger and Mary Ann to make a play to get Mrs. Howell buck-naked and down for some tropical lovin' among the palm fronds."

Armand pulled up at her house and got out of the vehicle. She walked up the pavement to her door, pulling out her keys. It came fast – there were men in the bushes and they rushed her, grabbing her arm before she could draw her Glock and pushing the agent against her front door.

At the same time, several sedans and Hummers pulled up, with soldiers getting out as she struggled.

"I'm an American diplomat!" she shouted. Several lights went on along her street. The people looked, saw it was the Panamanian Army, and their lights went out.

Colonel Manuel Ruiz stepped onto the porch where the men held her. There were now ten or twelve of them, and she stopped struggling – it made no sense, and she might need her strength.

"I'm an American diplomat," Colonel Ruiz!" she shouted. "I have diplomatic immunity!"

He slapped her hard across the face; she tasted copper and was momentarily stunned. Ruiz showed no emotion; he was just watching her face, especially the left side where he struck her. He decided that it was changing to a lovely shade of scarlet.

"You can't do this!" she said. He hit her again, this time with his left hand on the other side of her face. Being left-handed, this time he hit her harder, and her lip began bleeding.

"You are an insurrectionist plotting the overthrow of the lawful government of *El Presidente* Bonifacio Alberto Maria Guerrero," he said calmly, still watching the red on her face. It occurred to him how much he loved his work, especially when his victims were pretty.

"Bring her," he ordered, then turned and walked to his waiting sedan.

20.

"It worked," Villareal said into the video link. Senator Harrison was in the secure communications room at the Directorate; her superior, Allegra Barnes, was on-screen with him. "The Panama Canal will be closed to the American Navy, at least for long enough for our Chinese allies to assist their fraternal brothers, sisters, and siblings of other genders in fighting fascism in Peru."

"I received the same message from our Chinese friends," Harrison told her. "In their telling, a certain Colonel Wang did the heavy lifting."

Villareal seethed. She needed to choose her words carefully, so as not to project any anti-Asian hate.

"We have a different perspective," she said.

"You promised Guerrero that he could be the dictator of the soon-to-be-decolonized Latin America," Harrison said, but not angrily or even shocked by her audacity. He sounded, if anything, amused.

"I did," Villareal said. No point in spinning it. If it was a mistake, there was no salvaging it with clever phrasing; if it was not, she gained nothing by undermining it.

She would own it, but she would never say those words in that way. To "own it" evoked memories of the oppression of enslaved peoples.

"And he believed it," scoffed Harrison. Barnes seemed equally tickled at the idea. "You were right – we intend to subvert all the fascist regimes in Latin America, starting in Peru, and replace them with socialist ones. But allow them to lead themselves? These people are such children."

Villareal marveled at the term "these people." It was another phrase she would never utter publicly. It hinted at the inferiority of persons of Third Worldness. And yet these two did not bother to hide or shade their thoughts.

Villareal envied their freedom from such concerns. Might she, too, climb so high in the hierarchy that such considerations, so vital and potentially deadly among those in her rungs of society, no longer mattered? Her mind reeled at the idea of what she might accomplish without having to watch every word, like a person crossing a minefield must watch each step lest he/she/they be blown to bits?

"Continue to lead him on. There's no reason to do otherwise, at least for now," Harrison told her. "This ridiculous General Guerrero remaining firmly in control of Panama is to our advantage for now."

She felt no urge to correct the senator as to Guerrero's rank. She simply nodded in acknowledgement and waited for him to continue. He did.

"Colonel Wang reported to his principals, and they transmitted to me, that last night they picked up a coup plotter. Did you hear of that?"

"Not yet, Senator," Villareal said stiffly. Had Viveca Bold known of it and withheld the information, or worse, not known? She would get to the bottom of that later.

"I see," Senator Harrison said. Was that disappointment in his voice that she failed to know something significant in her own area of operations? He went on.

"I am informed that they who they took into custody was an American diplomat. A woman."

"I think I know who that would be," Villareal said. "Obviously, a Foreign Intelligence Service operative who was assisting the American operatives who negotiated for the United States. They were the ones behind the kidnapping of Ughaz Abdullahi in Minnesota. Guerrero ordered them out of the country. They must fly out today. I plan to have my men ambush them at the airport and kill them all."

Harrison considered this for a moment.

"Excellent initiative. After closing the Panama Canal and arresting a diplomat with diplomatic immunity, it would be hard to get the Americans more angry. They will do whatever they do. If they do nothing but fume, they appear weak. If they invade, that will drive more Latin American states into our camp and make our Bolívarian campaign that much easier. These hot-blooded Latinxes hate the Yankees so much that they will eagerly leap into China's embrace. So, feel free to poke the bear."

For a moment, Villareal thought he had misspoken and instructed her to molest a hairy gay man, the context in which she had most often heard the word "bear." Recently, bear rights had become an important new civil liberties movement in the blue and a much-needed antidote to the near exclusively twink-centric paradigm that currently dominated society. But she realized he meant a literal bear, at least figuratively.

"I will," she said. "Poke the bear."

"I am very impressed by your work, Agent Villareal," Harrison said. "I've told Comrade Barnes here that I believe bigger and better things are ahead in your future. Don't fail me."

"I won't," she said.

"Oh, and your Plan B," he said. "Is that still a viable operation?"

She stiffened in her seat.

"It is."

"Good," the senator said. "Because there was a male-identifying person, a dead white male-identifying person, but, surprisingly, he still said something of value. He wisely observed that the one thing you cannot account for is events. You need to be ready. You still need your Plan B."

"It's ready," Villareal said. "One way or another, we will succeed."

Colonel Ruiz smashed Armand in the face again. She was cuffed to a chair; it was unclear where, since they had hooded her for the ride in the sedan. She suspected it was the back area of the National Assembly building; she thought she could hear a dance remix of a Bruce Springsteen song she remembered from before the Split. They never played his music in the red, not because it was banned as subversive or perverted, but because it sucked.

"I asked you a question," Ruiz said amiably, though his eyes betrayed how much he enjoyed hurting her.

She shook off the blow.

"I don't know anything about a coup."

Ruiz hit her again.

"Manuel, be kind to her, she is our guest!" It was Guerero; he held a liter bottle of some dreadful-looking local liquor. He stumbled into the office from the hallway and steadied himself on the desk even as the two other thugs came to a rather sloppy position of attention. "She has diplomatic immunity!"

He found that funny, so Ruiz found it funny, too.

"The American government is not going to sit still for this," she managed to say.

"Oh, I think you are very wrong, Miss Armand. Very wrong. I think the American government will not go to war over the canal now that I am such a good friend of China and the People's Republic. So, that means they will definitely *not* go to war over you. So, you might as well talk. You are pretty now, but after Manuel finishes...I don't think you will still be so pretty."

"I don't know about any coup!"

"I am on the side of Colonel Ruiz. I think you are lying. Maybe have a drink."

He staggered over to her. Ruiz grabbed her face and held open her mouth as Guerrero poured the evil contents of the bottle in.

She gagged, spitting up, while the excess fanned down the front of her blouse."

Ruiz let her go. Guerrero shook his head and she coughed and spit out what she could.

"I don't think she wants to have a drink with me," he said sadly. "You think she wants to kiss me?"

Ruiz smiled.

"I think so," he said.

"Go to hell," Armand managed to say before coughing again.

Guerrero's aspect changed from bemused drunk to vicious psycho as he grabbed her hair and lowered himself to face her, so close she could smell the foulness of his breath.

"You think you matter because you are American? You'll do what I say. You'll be my whore!"

"I'll kill you," Armand promised. Guerreo slapped her hard, sending a spray of blood and spit from her mouth.

"Leave us alone," Guerrero ordered Ruiz and his men. "And shut the door."

"Not answering," Casey said, putting down his phone.

"Where the hell is she?" asked Turnbull rhetorically. Katie Armand had been expected at the embassy that morning at ten. That was nearly two hours ago.

"This ain't good," Clanton said.

"Nothing is good this morning," Turnbull replied. He kicked over a chair.

An hour ago, Clay Deeds had called. Turnbull took it in the secure comms facility.

"You're a no-go on your coup," Deeds said.

"Are you kidding me?" Turnbull demanded.

"Kelly, this comes from the top. The very top."

"Does the top not understand the situation?"

"I explained it. Apparently, they reached out for a different perspective and got one."

"The freaking ambassador."

"That's my read. Anyway, the United States is going to pursue diplomatic avenues."

"Diplomatic avenues?"

"Yes, the ambassador is going to try to talk Guerrero into aligning with us instead of cozying up to the blues and the Chi Coms."

"That guy couldn't talk me into buying a new gun."

"Kelly, I get it. But we're constrained by the chain of command. And you're still a soldier, even if you wear civvies when you fight."

"So, we just let this happen?"

"Like I said, the ambassador will handle it from here. Go to the airport, come home. That's an order."

Turnbull growled.

"I'm getting tired of orders. But, if by some miracle, this ambassador guy talks Guerrero into letting those cruisers through, that *Grayhawk Paladin* is still out there waiting to blow up next to them."

"They know, Kelly. The moment it looks like it will be a threat, they will blast it out of the water. You did good spotting that."

"Yeah, I'm feeling great right about it right now," Turnbull snapped. "What do you think of this, Clay?"

"I think that I tell my boss what I think before I get my orders, then when I get them, I carry them out. And you need to do the same."

"I've seen you not follow orders when you thought they sucked, Clay. And these suck."

"True, and vice versa, Kelly. Not this time. Everyone is watching. And I mean everyone."

"We're leaving some good guys in the Panamanian Army hanging out to dry here. There's a decent chance Guerrero's thugs figure out that some of their own were going to help us topple his little thugocracy, and then they and their families are dead."

"We'll do what we can for them," Clay said. "But you guys are out of there today, no discussion, no debate. Get your boys on a plane, and leave Panama to the State Department."

Turnbull hung up. He then stepped out of the SCIF to call Katie Armand.

Nothing. And when ten o'clock came around, she still had not responded, much less shown up.

"What do we do, boss?" asked Casey. "Besides pack."

"I don't want to be the one to call Rosas and let him down," Turnbull said. "She needs to do it and try to do some damage control on that relationship. So, since she's not answering her phone, let's go find her."

"There's a call from Colonel Wang," Viveca Bold said. "He wants you at the National Assembly building at one. There are some details to discuss with the President."

"Is Wang giving us orders now?" Villareal asked. "Our fraternal Chinese allies need to check their own patriarchal assumptions."

"I know, right?" exclaimed Bold. "Men are the worst."

Villareal went to the hotel room where the five remaining Somalis were residing. They were lounging on their bunks, chewing khat and drinking bottles of Atlas. It smelled of stale beer and socks. She noted some rust on their rifles, probably from the combined effects of humidity and neglect.

Farah, the leader, was away with the contingent on the *Grayhawk Paladin*. She did not know the names of these men, nor had Farah nominated one to be in charge. When she walked in, they all looked at her with a mix of boredom and contempt – it did not help that she was not wearing a hijab. But this was not either of the Mogadishus.

She designated two to come with her – they looked like the two that came with her previously. Of the other three, one spoke passable English. She told him to get an embassy driver to take them to the airport at 4:30 p.m. The Americans would likely be checking-in for the 6:05 p.m. United flight to Dallas, and without their weapons available.

"They will have to cross the terminal to get to security," she said. While one could fly with a weapon in the red, one could not do so internationally. "Just kill them, then come back."

They nodded. She fully expected that the police at the airport would finish them off. Their fate was literally the least of her concerns. That evening, the American ships would appear off the Atlantic entrance to the Panama Canal and demand priority transit. Despite the assurances and promises from the President the previous evening, he still had to come through.

She would be there to make sure he did.

"That's her Ford," Clanton said, pointing at Armand's vehicle at the curb. Casey knocked on her front door again.

Nothing.

Turnbull spotted a face in a window across the street. It disappeared behind a curtain.

"Mundi, go see if they know anything about where she might be." Mundi nodded and walked across the street.

"What do you think, Kelly?" asked Clanton.

"I think something's wrong. They may have figured out what she was up to with Rosas."

Across the street, Mundi was at the door talking to the occupant in Spanish. After a minute or so, the operative turned and walked back as the door shut behind him.

"They didn't want to talk," he said when he got back to the team. "They're afraid."

"Probably should be," Turnbull said.

"Guerrero's *chicos* grabbed her, all right," Mundi said. "Put her in a Ford g-ride and took off with a bunch of soldiers."

"She had immunity," Casey said, incredulous. "She's a U.S. diplomat."

"I don't think she's coming back," Mundi said. "The neighbor used the word '*desaparecido*.' That means 'the disappeared.'

When you go off in one of their security service Fords, no one sees you again except in pieces."

"I think Guerrero's committed fully to his new friends," Turnbull said. "There's no going back."

"Does Guerrero want to start a war with the U.S.?" asked Casey.

"He's drunk, high, and a jerk already," Turnbull said. "Now he's got China and the PR backing his play. Plus, how much madder can America get after he blocks the canal?"

"He's a hell of a gambler," Casey said.

"Kelly, she knows everything about Rosas and the coup plotters," Clanton said. "And that Ruiz guy looks like the kind who enjoys his work."

"These are bad hombres, Kelly," Mundi said. "I know their kind."

"Back to the embassy," Turnbull told them.

21.

"Give them their airline tickets," the ambassador said to his minion. The diplomat was dressed in khaki slacks and a white embassy polo. He looked like he was on the way to a round of golf with a foursome of term life insurance salesmen.

Turnbull and his operatives had encountered the ambassador and his gaggle in the lobby after returning to the embassy. None of them was happy to see the others.

The young State Department officer at the ambassador's side dutifully handed over four printed boarding passes for the 6:05 p.m. United flight to Dallas. Turnbull ignored the documents; Casey took them.

"Guerrero's thugs grabbed Katie Armand last night," Turnbull declared. "They're going to kill her, after they torture her and find out everything she knows."

"What, about your idiotic coup plan? Oh, I know all about *that.* You come here with your guns and attitude, and in a couple of days, you destroy years of careful diplomatic work."

"One of your people is going to be murdered," Turnbull told him. "And you're going to sit here in your embassy behind your Marines and give me crap?"

"Well, she's not really one of mine, is she? They send these spooks with their non-official covers, and real diplomats like me have to clean up their messes. But, in fact, I'm going to go fix this one personally."

"To the party palace? I wouldn't suggest it."

"Unlike you, I know how to reason with people. President Guerrero is a reasonable man, open to negotiation."

"Maybe you and her can hang together headless upside down off the same overpass," Turnbull said. "Except I couldn't care less what happens to you."

The ambassador seethed. There was sweat on his puffy face all the way up to his hairline.

"He wouldn't dare lay a finger on me, but you animals wouldn't understand that. Now, here is what you will do. You will turn your weapons into the Marine arms room, then go sit in your quarters until 4:30 p.m., when we will drive you to the airport. Then you will get on an airliner and get the hell out of my country."

"And you'll let those people who trusted us die? And Armand as well."

"I'll take care of her, but she knew the risks of interfering in Panamanian affairs. No, get out of my sight."

The ambassador and his retinue brushed past the operatives. Turnbull thought he got a whiff of Axe Body Spray from the male minion.

"You need to have me there by one," the ambassador told his minion as they went out the front door.

"SCIF," Turnbull said to his men.

Inside the secure facility, Clay Deeds was on the monitor that hung on the wall.

"We're out of it, Kelly," Deeds said. "We're to leave it to State."

"In a few minutes, they are going to have our ambassador, too," Turnbull said. "He's going to their orgy and trying to reason with that malignant lunatic."

"My hands are tied."

"They are going to torture and kill the girl, assuming she's still alive. Then they will kill all the coup plotters and Panama will be locked into the PR-PRC alliance forever."

Deeds bit his lip. Turnbull knew that look.

"You know what your orders are," Deeds said, slowly and deliberately. "And you know the situation. I trust you to do your duty."

"Our duty?" Turnbull asked. What was Deeds saying?

"Your duty. Good luck," Deeds said. The screen went dark.

The four men were quiet, contemplating. After a moment, Turnbull spoke up.

"She's one of us," Turnbull said.

"Yep," said Clanton.

"We can't just leave her to them," Mundi said. "We wouldn't leave each other."

"Kelly might leave Casey," Clanton said, earning some soft chuckles.

"What did Clay say? 'Do our duty?'" asked Casey.

"I think I know what Clay thinks we're going to do," Mundi said. "But are we gonna do it?"

"I'm not telling anyone to do anything," Turnbull said. "But I know what *I'm* doing."

"So, we're going to let you do it alone?" Mundi scoffed. "You think that's in the cards?"

Turnbull looked at Casey.

"Kinda had my heart set on seeing the new *Star Trek* movie, *Kirk's Revenge*, even though William Shatner is like a hundred, but sure."

Turnbull next looked at Clanton, who shrugged.

"What the hell?" the yeti said. "Why not?"

They all laughed mirthlessly.

"There's no good way in," Casey said. "No way to be subtle or stealthy. No high-speed hostage rescue stuff. We don't know exactly where she is. She might not even be at the National Assembly party palace."

"Guerrero will be there," Turnbull said. "We can be...diplomatic."

"Just walk in and ask for her?" said Clanton.

"Yeah," Turnbull said.

"And what happens when he says, 'No,' Kelly?" asked Mundi.

"Then we do our kind of diplomacy."

Turnbull removed his .45 mag and subbed in a ten-round stainless-steel magazine. He checked the chamber, and there was already one in the pipe. It went into his holster with the hammer back and safety on – M1911 Condition One.

Clanton was sliding buckshot shells into one of the Benelli shotguns, then racked it and added one last red Winchester shell. That made eight – seven in the tube, one in the pipe. He confirmed the safety was on.

"Here you go," he said, tossing it to Mundi and picking up another one to load.

Turnbull slid into his harness. There were front and back ceramic chest plates and M4 30-round magazines in the pouches. There were a lot of pouches.

"Here, Kelly," Clanton said, handing over another loaded Benelli. Turnbull slung it behind his back. His M4 carbine was his primary, but he appreciated the kind of room-clearing firepower a semiautomatic combat shotgun provided.

Casey racked his Walther pistol, holstered it, and then put on his gear. Mundi already had his Benelli and was grabbing a handful of buckshot shells for his cargo pockets. They clinked when he walked.

After the men finished gearing up, Clanton said, "Okay, let's take a minute." They bowed their heads.

"Father, we're in your hands now. Watch over us and those we protect. Amen."

"Very succinct, Hiram," Casey said appreciatively. "I grew up Baptist, and they just go on and on."

"Anything else we have to say, I figure we'll be telling Him soon enough," Clanton said quietly.

Silently, Turnbull added his own addendum, the same thing he always prayed when he knew he was leading men into trouble.

"Lord, please don't let me screw up and get someone killed who I don't want dead."

He opened his eyes and lifted his head.

"Wish it hadn't come to this," Turnbull told his troops.

"But it did," Mundi said.

"It always does," Casey said.

"You know, we forgot to eat lunch," Clanton added.

"That reminds me, we forgot the grenades," Casey announced, looking for the box.

There was a knock at the door. Turnbull opened it, and the ambassador's minion was there, reeking of that awful scent. His eyes widened like frisbees as he took them in in all their geared-up glory, and he barely got the words out.

"The ambassador called to ask if you had turned in your weapons like he ordered you to," babbled the young man.

"No," Turnbull said.

"Do you want me to tell him you didn't follow his orders?" the incredulous young diplomat replied. It had never occurred to him that someone might defy the ambassador.

"No," Turnbull said. "I'll tell him myself."

Presidente Guerrero swayed and leaned against his minigun's tripod.

"You Americans talk too much," he told the ambassador, wagging a sooty finger. "That's why I like the Chinese one here. He doesn't talk all of the time."

At the table on the platform were Colonel Wang, along with Medea Villareal, Viveca Bold, and their two Somali bodyguards, who sat nearby. Out in the crowd on the floor, those few who were watching instead of eating, drinking, smoking, and/or wenching laughed at the insult.

The ambassador ignored the jibe as he used his handkerchief to wipe some of the sweat off his cheeks. The National Assembly chamber was like a sauna.

Patience, he had been taught, was key.

"The American people and the Panamanian people have over a century of friendship," he said gently but urgently. "There's no need to spoil that over a temporary dispute."

"Oh, so now you Americans will help me to achieve my destiny as the new Simón Bolívar?" he asked. "That's very nice of you!" There were some titters of laughter.

"We can do so much for the Panamanian people," the ambassador implored him. "Just use your great wisdom to rethink your decision, and your people will prosper."

"My great wisdom?" he howled. "Captain Saramago, he sounds like you!"

The captain, his forearm still wrapped in a filthy bandage, was taking a swig of Atlas Beer when his boss mocked him. He joined in the laughter as foam dripped from the corners of his mouth.

"You know, ambassador, you are fat and pink, like a pig," Guerrero told him. "And you come from a country of pigs. You devour everything. You steal from our people, but with my new friends, I will resist you imperialists."

Saramago jumped to his feet.

"The President will fight the imperialists!" Captain Saramago shouted to the hundred or so people at the tables on the floor of the chamber. Most cheered; some simply swayed in their seats.

"But I am a good host," Guerrero said, again wagging his filthy index finger at the diplomat. "You sit on your fat ass here at my table. You can dine with me and my new friends, and share my hospitality, but I will not be hospitable to your ships. Your Navy ships will never come through the Panama Canal as long as I am *el presidente*!"

Saramago, acting as his leader's hype man, roused a chorus of cheers from the inebriated audience.

"I think I will leave," the ambassador said stiffly, trying to salvage a fragment of dignity. "I must report this to my government."

"You will sit your ass down!" shouted Guerrero, any residual trace of humor totally absent. "Or I will have Colonel Ruiz here take you like he took that spy of yours who was working with the traitors in my own house!"

Captain Saramago positioned himself to block the ambassador's egress. The diplomat swallowed, patted some of the sweat off his face with his handkerchief, and sat down on the wooden bench seat across from Villareal.

"It's good to see Third World peoples throwing off the yoke of oppression," Villareal told him. She worked hard to contain her glee. The ambassador said nothing.

"Viveca Bold, from the People's Republic embassy, she/her," the junior diplomat said, extending her enormous hand across the table to the frightened ambassador. "What are your pronouns?"

Clanton was shaking his head at several curious Presidential Guards out in the parking lot of the old National Assembly building. None had made a move on the four heavily armed Americans; one had a beer in his hand and another a comically massive joint. They just watched, and Clanton made sure they knew he was watching right back.

Turnbull, iPhone to his ear, was concluding his call to Rosas.

"We will be moving in minutes," the Panamanian colonel told him. "But you have to keep your part of the bargain or we fail."

"If we fail, it's because we're all dead," Turnbull replied. He hung up.

"You should have told him you'll see him in Valhalla," Casey said. "Which is the title of a Matt Betley movie I would have liked to live to see."

"Let's do it," Turnbull said.

"Hey diddle diddle," Clanton said. "Right up the middle."

They began walking abreast toward the entrance to the decaying building. Their weapons hung off them. Clumps of soldiers, civilians, and women were straggling outside. They would look at the Americans and quickly move aside.

The Americans were trouble.

Turnbull took out his earplugs and inserted them – habit.

"You think you're going to live long enough for that to matter?" Mundi said.

"I don't want tinnitus," Turnbull answered, as if it were obvious. The rest looked at each other and shoved theirs into their own ears.

It couldn't hurt.

The men crossed the threshold of the National Assembly building and began walking across the wrecked lobby. People slumped against the walls in varying states of intoxication got sight of them and, even in their impaired states, some instinct urged them to stand up and move away.

The DJ inside the double doors that led to the chamber was playing a remix of Pat Benatar's "Love Is A Battlefield."

They pulled open the doors and stepped inside.

Of all the hundred or so people in the chamber, from those on the floor being feted by their ruler to those honored guests and VIPs on the platform at the front, the first person to see the four Americans was President Guerrero. He was just finishing a tremendous snort of cocaine off one of the platform's tables when he looked up; his moustache appeared to have been dipped in snow.

"You," he growled, incredulous.

Captain Saramago saw that his leader's attention was on the back of the chamber, and now he looked, standing there with his mouth agape. Ruiz saw the Americans, too, and whispered to the half-dozen men he had with him.

Villareal saw Turnbull's crew, and her mind raced. This scenario had never entered her mind. It was not going to go well. She looked around and made her plan; she also slipped out her SIG pistol and held it in her lap.

"The American transphobes are back," Viveca Bold whispered unnecessarily. The ambassador turned in his seat to see what all the fuss was about.

"What the hell?" he exclaimed.

More and more of the audience stopped what they were doing and watched with fascination as the American quartet descended into the chamber toward the VIP platform. Turnbull and his men were about halfway down the aisle when the DJ cut the music just after Benatar sang the word "battlefield."

Turnbull and company kept walking down the aisle past the tables of partygoers, weapons swinging on their slings just like those of his three comrades. His eyes were fixed on Guerero; his men were scanning the audience on the floor, almost daring someone to act.

No one did. *El Presidente* would be the one to decide how this went, and no one else. For his part, the dictator got to his feet and again braced himself on the tripod of the minigun to keep from falling over.

Turnbull reached the bottom of the chamber floor and then mounted the steps up to the platform, followed by Clanton. Mundi and Casey stayed on the floor, planting themselves in front of the first rows of tables and turning to look out over the fascinated audience. Most of them had stopped their activities to watch what would happen, though several still puffed on joints or took a quick swig off a bottle.

"I did not invite you to my party!" Guerrero shouted, the mockery back in his voice. "But now that you are here, why don't you join in the celebration of our new friendship with the People's Republic and China? Captain Saramago, get them a drink!"

"We didn't come to drink with you," Turnbull said, stepping out onto the platform. He was about twenty feet from the President. Clanton's eyes were on the blues and the Chinese advisor at the table.

"What did you come here for then?" asked the dictator.

"We want the girl."

"The girl? What girl?"

"Ask your Colonel Ruiz."

"Oh, *that* girl," Guerreo said, earning a smattering of chuckles from the peanut gallery. "The one who was working with traitors to kill me and turn our country over to the imperialists?"

"You need to leave right now! This is a diplomatic matter!" demanded the ambassador.

"Stop talking," Turnbull growled as he glared at the diplomat, and the ambassador wisely took the hint. Turnbull looked back at Guerrero.

"Where is she?"

"Oh, she is in back, but she is not feeling well. Colonel Ruiz tells me she is very willful and sometimes he can be a little rough on the willful ones."

"Get the girl," Turnbull told him. "Do it now."

"Oh, yes, of course," Guerrero said. "Captain Saramago, bring her out here for her American friends!"

Saramago looked at his master quizzically, only to be met with a scowl indicating the boss was serious. He disappeared into the back through the door on the platform.

The wait was awkward. Turnbull never took his eyes off Guerrero except to glance at Circe. She was careful to make no sudden movements.

The President seemed impatient as the wait passed a minute.

"You sure you and your friends do not want a beer?" he asked Turnbull. "Or maybe some cocaine? It's very good." He wiped his nose and snorted.

Turnbull said nothing.

Captain Saramago pushed Katie Armand out the door ahead of him. Her face was battered, and her hair stringy. One eye was blackened. Her blouse was torn and filthy, with blood and other stains soiling it. Saramago held her up as he pushed her forward. She was handcuffed.

"See, Colonel Ruiz is not gentle. I told you this," said Guerrero with feigned sorrow. "I was not gentle either. Sometimes my temper gets the best of me."

Turnbull remained still as Saramago took Armand to the front of the platform. Her intact eye met his, and she mouthed something; he could not decipher what, but it was certainly not good.

Saramago stopped, holding her up before him with his injured arm.

"Take off the cuffs," Turnbull growled.

Saramago looked to Guerrero, who shrugged. The captain used his good arm to remove a key from his pocket and unlock the cuffs. They fell to the floor of the VIP platform. He held her upright in front of him.

"Let her go," Turnbull said.

"Yes, let that bitch go," Guerrero said, his voice venomous.

Saramago smiled from behind his captive. His good hand went for the Bowie knife at his side, drawing it from the scabbard and raising it just as Armand's hands went for the bandaged forearm holding her in place. Her fingers dug into the wound.

"Ahhhh!" he screamed, turning as she twisted to the side even as he lifted the blade to strike.

Kelly Turnbull switched off the safety as he drew his Wilson Combat CQB and fired from the hip before lifting the weapon up and firing twice more. The first hollow-point slug slammed into Saramago's pelvis and twisted him back to face Turnbull. The second went into his sternum, and the third went between his eyes.

Saramago flopped back onto the platform, splashing blood from the exit wound where his skull was missing a chunk. He flopped and twitched for a moment.

Armand collapsed beside him on the floor.

Turnbull held the .45 in front of him, swinging it back and forth, covering the people on the VIP platform. Clanton pulled his shotgun up, as did Casey on the floor. Mundi had brought up his M4.

Guerrero stared at his adjutant, jerking on his back, and looked at Turnbull, astonished.

El Presidente didn't move, so nobody moved.

The chamber was silent and still, except for the ringing in their ears.

22.

The freeze lasted maybe ten seconds. It seemed like an hour.

Turnbull shifted his weapon from Guerrero to Ruiz, then to the blues, and back. It was when he turned back to the President that Ruiz acted, reaching for the holster at his side to defend his leader. He got his pistol just clear of his holster when Turnbull spotted his movement and cocked his head as if to ask, "Did you really think you were faster than me?"

Turnbull shot him twice in the chest, splattering his mostly clean uniform with two eruptions of scarlet. He fell backward into the arms of his stunned men.

Colonel Wang stood up, going for his own gun – some Chi Com automatic he had never used in combat. Clanton assured that the record remained unblemished; he unloaded a blast of double-00 buckshot into the advisor's chest. One moment, Wang was standing up beside Villareal, going for his pistol, and the next, he was blown over the bench, a spray of red goo splattering those around him.

The ambassador screamed and dove to the floor. Villareal did the same, only without the screaming. Viveca Bold stayed where she was. She too screamed, more deeply and loudly than even the ambassador.

The Somalis went for their rifles; Clanton went for them with two blasts of buckshot. They did not weigh much, and the close-range impact of the swarm of lead pellets blew them both off their bench and back against the wall.

The audience was stunned seeing what was playing out on the platform, at least for the most part. A sergeant who was drunk, but not as drunk as his comrades, thought to grab his AK instead of either diving for the moist, sticky floor or simply sitting in place watching the tableau. Casey was looking for anyone reacting and saw him raise his weapon. Casey spun the Benelli the soldier's way and fired two blasts at about forty feet. The first killed the guy next to the would-be shooter, shattering the beer bottle he had in his hand. The second got the would-be shooter in the shoulder, and he went down.

Mundi took a look at the five gentlemen at the front-most table, clearly officers, granted this place of honor located not on the VIP platform but near it. One's hand flinched in the general direction of his sidearm, and that was enough. Mundi emptied a mag into the quintet in the front row; they died sprawling and shrieking as bottles, dishes, and the table itself were blown apart.

Guerrero had the presence of mind to turn and run around the minigun in the opposite direction from Turnbull. Turnbull saw him making his move and fired at the moving target. The slug entered the right presidential cheek and shattered the dictator's hip. Guerrero fell forward, sprawling, as Turnbull went for a follow-up shot. It was not to be. Ruiz's security men had pushed their leader's bloody body off of them and were taking up their weapons. They were now the emerging primary threat.

Turnbull began to fire his .45 at them, going dry after six shots and several hits. He dropped the .45 and swung the Benelli behind his back up, firing the semiautomatic 12-gauge fast into the mass of guards, joined by Clanton, who was busy emptying his shotgun as well into the six soldiers Ruiz had come with. The blasts painted the walls with their blood; one got off a shot with his AK in their general direction, but the next blast took off his forearm, and the one after that, most of the unlucky soldier's face.

As Bob the American and his huge buddy were engaging the security men, Villareal saw her chance. She bolted forward toward the back door on the platform, keeping low while drawing her SIG pistol.

By some miracle, the Americans did not shoot her as he ran. She considered trying to shoot Bob, but that would draw fire, and she had a higher priority task than dying trying to take out one American operator. As she approached the rear door leading into the back from the platform, she heard a man's voice behind her.

"Wait for me!" boomed Viveca Bold. The transwoman was right behind her, having ditched her heels to increase her mobility.

The thunder of the shotguns ended – they were dry. Villareal sensed an opportunity. She turned and shot Bold in the chest.

Bold staggered and fell on her face; she weighed in at 190 pounds. Embarrassingly, her skirt rode up and revealed her lace panties.

The shotgun went dry, and a whiff of cordite from the eight shots Turnbull had just unloaded hit him in the face. There was movement right – Circe was making for the door. He tossed the twelve-gauge and went to his knee, scooping up the .45 and reloading. As he slipped the fresh 10-round mag into the well, he watched as Circe stopped, pivoted, and shot her own assistant. He had not seen that move coming.

The slide went forward and Turnbull brought the weapon up, blasting off five rounds as Circe dived into the rear doorway and vanished from sight. Following her was out of the question. He had a firefight to win.

Nearby, the ambassador was screaming, and the noise from his hollering was loud enough to be heard over the gunshots and the mild ringing in Turnbull's ears.

Those earplugs had helped.

More of the partygoers were coming out of their stunned stupor. Most were dropping down beneath the wooden tables to regroup. Some of the women of leisure were trying to get out. Casey tried to avoid hitting them as he blasted away with his shotgun at their soldier beaus, some of his shots keeping heads down, others taking parts of heads off.

Mundi dropped his mag, put in a new one, then sent the bolt on his M4 forward. He began engaging targets at the various tables. But now, the soldiers were engaging back.

The crack of a round broke over his head, then there were two more nearby, alerting Turnbull to the new threat. The platform was cleared of uninjured enemies, but there were dozens of intact soldiers out there in the mix of bodies down on the floor of the chamber. Some were starting to shoot back, not well, but they were shooting nonetheless. Turnbull emptied his pistol at various targets out among the tables, then holstered it, bringing up his slung M4 and opening fire on anyone among the Panamanian troops who was moving or trying to organize the others.

Rounds slammed into the wall behind them and into the table over the prone ambassador. He was still shrieking like a castrated banshee.

"Damn!" yelled Clanton. He fell to one knee, putting his left paw on a bloody wound.

"You good?" Turnbull yelled without losing focus. A Panamanian soldier was moving with his AK to a better position; Turnbull put a burst in him, and he dropped.

"Yeah, I'm good!" Clanton yelled. "Just a mosquito bite." He blazed away with his M4, the shells adding to the dozens already littering the platform.

Mundi went dry again. A Kalashnikov barrel poked out from under a table about ten meters behind him, erupted in flame, and he felt a punch in his back under his plate, driving him forward into the filthy carpet and losing his M4. Another pair of rounds went high over him as he twisted his Benelli shotgun around to open fire at his concealed assailant. After four blasts, the shooter was silenced.

He felt nauseous and checked the front of his body. No exit wound – the bullet was still in him. He took a deep breath and started reloading shells into the shotgun.

Casey ran over and knelt, pausing to fire off a burst at a pair of targets running down the aisle. They sprawled as a shower of brass landed on the wounded Cuban.

"Can you fight?" Casey yelled to his wounded buddy.

"*Si*, I can fight!" Mundi said through his grimace, and Casey pulled him to his feet. Mundi immediately engaged a trio of shooters with his shotgun.

The round that slammed into his ceramic plate felt like it broke a couple of ribs, something Turnbull was very familiar with. He had just gone black on an M4 mag, engaging some troops from outside running into the room from the back entrance to the chamber, and was kneeling to change it when the slug hit him. It knocked him on his ass, and his rifle went flying. He had zero idea where the bullet came from. There was a whole host of shooters out there on the floor of the National Assembly chamber now, each one trying to get in the game. It was like whack-a-mole. Turnbull would shoot one gunman, and two more would pop up to replace him.

Clanton was on his good knee firing when he took another hit, this one to the side, and sprawled on the platform floor. More rounds were incoming, and they were flying everywhere. When the bad guys hit, it was pure luck as opposed to skill – but with so many bullets in the air, they really didn't need much skill. The Panamanians could make up for it in volume.

Turnbull realized he had no long gun. His M4 rifle was to his right, a few feet away, and his M4 shotgun was on the ground by the quivering ambassador.

"Throw me that twelve gauge!" Turnbull shouted to the diplomat. The ambassador looked at him as if he were insane, and at the gun as if it were a live cobra. It wasn't happening.

"The hell with this," Turnbull said aloud as he painfully got to his feet, AK rounds whizzing by like furious wasps.

He reached into his vest, not far from where the 7.62mm Kalashnikov round had impacted the ceramic plate, and grabbed an M67 fragmentation grenade. It was olive green, smooth, and weighed about a pound. Inside it was 6.5 ounces of explosives; the metal skin was designed to twist into razor-sharp shrapnel.

He pulled the pin, and the spoon fell away as he threw it into the chamber.

"Frag out!" he yelled from force of habit, knowing that no one was going to hear him over the din.

The hand grenade arced into the mass of tables and benches. Turnbull had aimed at a group of shooters who were mostly spraying and praying over the turned-over table they were using as cover. The bomb landed nearby, and the explosion sent wood, metal shards, and a couple of soldiers flying. Turnbull grabbed another hand grenade and tossed it at another clump of troops, even as he saw more of the enemy entering the chamber from the back.

Time to change the equation, he decided.

Casey leaned out into the aisle down from the rear chamber door. Several Presidential Guards were entering, but were slowed down by having to navigate around the bodies of their friends. Casey took one down with a burst, then another. The third opened fire on him, and pieces of wood showered him from where the bullets smashed into the table he was using as concealment.

He shot the third one and then checked himself for wounds. Not a scratch.

Turnbull knelt by his buddy. Clanton was down, hit again – but he was huge, and it was hard to miss him. The big man's front was covered with blood, and it looked like a round had shaved past his temple, sending a sheet of red down his cheek.

"I'm good!" the yeti insisted. He was reloading his M4.

Turnbull got up and ran forward, dodging past Armand, who was staying prone even as rounds whizzed by overhead. Further away was Guerrero, his ass a bloody mess, trying to pull himself forward. If Turnbull had a loaded weapon, he would have finished the dictator there and then, but he didn't.

Instead, he bolted to behind the minigun and its tripod.

The round smashed into Mundi's upper chest, and he fell back. This time, Casey saw the shooter and shot both him and the Panamanian to his side. His bolt locked back, and Casey reached for a fresh mag – it took a moment to find one, meaning he was running out.

Mundi was on his back, groaning. He drew his pistol and began to engage any target he saw, but he was not seeing much. He was losing blood, and everything was getting fuzzy.

Turnbull stood erect behind the minigun, two hands on the grips. There was a shooting pain in his right calf; he looked down, and it was bloody, but he could put weight on it. That meant it was just meat.

There would be plenty of time to inventory injuries later, assuming they had a later.

Before him was a tableau of destruction across the width of the old National Assembly chamber floor. There were bodies everywhere among the tables and benches, some on top of them, some below, some twisted up in-between. Corpses littered the aisles; there were black craters where grenades had gone off, especially after Casey started throwing them, too.

But there were still live enemies, a lot of them, taking cover and taking aim. Even as he stood there taking it in, a shot sparked off the tripod. It wobbled a bit.

Turnbull did not have time to care.

Clanton was shooting his M4 carbine when his left arm was shattered by one of the swarm of bullets launched in his direction. He held the M4 one-handed and emptied it on full auto in the general direction of the shooters out on the floor. Then a round connected with his ceramic plate, dead on, and drove him hard onto his back.

He could not get up. He drew his Smith & Wesson 500. He resolved that he would kill the first four bastards that came for him. The fifth round was for himself.

Mundi's handgun went dry. He felt over his vest for another mag, but it was warm and sticky. A wave of dizziness washed over him, and he dropped the pistol. All he could do was stare at the ceiling. There were, he noticed, a lot of holes in it.

Turnbull spotted five soldiers and their sergeant together. Organization and leadership – that absolutely could not happen. The rotary barrels roared to life, and Turnbull aimed them at his target, hitting the red trigger.

Zzzzzzzzziiiiiippppppp.

It was like the orange lance he had seen for the helicopter in Mogadishu, Minnesota. The sergeant was torn apart, red goo and scraps from his uniform flying apart even as smoke from the tracer rounds puffed into the air. Turnbull moved the weapon imperceptibly, and the orange lance shredded the other four, tossing them about like they were in a blender.

"That'll work," Turnbull said aloud.

Nearby the recently deceased were several more soldiers with rifles moving into position. Turnbull opened up again, blowing apart the table they had decided to take cover behind along with the soldiers themselves. He tried to avoid the civilian women among them – most were fleeing, while others were in a fetal position, screaming. One woman picked up the pistol of her dead beau and was shouting something as she popped off shots at him.

She missed. Turnbull's minigun didn't.

The rest of the shooters who were still alive in the chamber made the correct tactical decision that the most immediate threat to their continued respiration was the guy behind the minigun. They began firing on him with renewed intensity.

Turnbull attempted to shift the minigun to engage targets to the stage right, but the tripod was damaged by the round that struck it.

"Crap," he shouted. He reached under the mechanism and detached the gun with a flick of the locking mechanism. With effort, made more painful because of his ribs, he hefted it into his arms. The gun weighed 62 pounds, but the weight actually made it somewhat more stable when he began firing from his hip.

Kelly Turnbull was no longer about short, controlled bursts. He hosed down anything that moved; they fired three shots at him, and he replied with thirty.

Long lines of wood chips erupted in rows across the table tops as he sprayed down the chamber floor. The tracers left smoldering craters; smoke began to rise. Bodies flew left and right. A squad of five tried to enter through the back entrance.

They vanished in the onslaught of 7.62mm rounds, tossed into the air and then dropping to the floor as red chunks flecked the walls.

Turnbull looked over to the DJ booth. The music monger was gone, but Turnbull put a burst into the setup anyway.

"Hang the bloody DJ," he muttered. Then he went back to suppressing the shooters on the floor with extreme prejudice.

The return fire slackened as Turnbull took aim at anyone who dared to shoot his way. He sprayed countless rounds and a fountain of empty shell casings flew up and out across the platform. It was now carpeted with brass. And then the shooting stopped. The minigun's barrels kept spinning, but the ammo was dry.

Turnbull looked out over the chamber, searching for his guys. There was Mundi on his back, with Casey kneeling next to him, M4 rifle in hand. But out among the tables, there was nothing, just smashed wood and dead Panamanians.

He dropped the empty minigun to the floor of the platform.

His ears were ringing pretty good. He figured if not for the plugs, he'd be deaf. But his chest hurt bad. And so did his calf. And his side, too – someone had winged him there as he was manning the minigun.

He looked down and over at Clanton, who was on his back. Armand was right by him, putting pressure on his multiple gunshot wounds.

With his instincts in control, he drew his .45, reloaded it, then slipped it back into his holster.

"We need to go," he said to Armand. "There will be more of them coming."

"He's hurt bad," she said. She looked hurt bad herself. She was now covered in Clanton's blood.

"We need to take him," Turnbull said.

"You psychos! You could have killed us all!" the ambassador shrieked. He had struggled to his feet, red-faced, with a dark spot on his Dockers where what had been his morning coffee had leaked out during the firefight.

"I'll see you in Leavenworth!" he promised.

Turnbull slugged the diplomat hard in the face. The man flew back on the table top, his mouth a red mass of blood and drool. Turnbull came over and grabbed the lapels of his cheesy "U.S. Embassy – Panama" polo shirt.

"If you ever, and I mean *ever*, get in my way again, here, in the U.S., on the moon, I will hunt you down and end you. Look around. You think I won't? Your report is going to be about how my guys and this lady were freaking heroes. And the bigwigs in Dallas better buy it, because if they don't, I'm coming for you."

He threw the man down.

"Yes, yes," squealed the ambassador.

A few feet away, Clanton was still groaning, but Armand was no longer next to him.

She was walking to the other side of the platform, and she had Clanton's enormous .500 caliber revolver in her right hand.

Guerrero was crawling, though it was not clear where he was trying to get to. He had left a ten-foot blood trail from his shattered hip. Oddly, he had not even drawn his own pistol.

"Hey, *Presidente*," Armand said. The dictator stopped and turned onto his back, moaning as Armand lifted the massive gun and aimed it at his face.

"Remember last night when you called me your whore and I told you I would kill you?" she asked.

"No, no, I will work with the Americans! The ships can come through, they can come through! The hell with the damn PR and China!"

"You don't have much say in it anymore," Turnbull said as he approached, stopping by Armand's side. "There's a coup going on and, well, most of your Presidential Guard is dead."

"We can come to an arrangement," he begged.

"I'm going to blow your head off," Armand said calmly.

"No," Turnbull told her emphatically, putting his hand on the revolver and slowly pushing it down. "You can't."

"I can't shoot him?" Armand shouted incredulously. "After what this sick bastard did to me?"

Guerrero allowed himself a smile and nodded eagerly to indicate his compliance.

"Of course you can shoot him," Turnbull said, slowly as if to a kid. "Just not in the face. The people need to see he's dead."

"No!" Guerrero yelled, throwing up his hands as if that would stop a half-inch bullet from slamming into his chest.

It didn't.

23.

Medea Villareal sprinted through the door at the rear of the VIP platform into the administrative area to the rear of the National Assembly chamber, even as Turnbull's bullets splintered the door jamb and nearly nicked her again. The chamber behind her was erupting in gunfire; she was confident the Americans would be too busy fighting for their lives against the dozens of soldiers who had been carousing in there to follow her. She was right, for the moment.

Wang was dead; there was a garish splash of his blood across her blouse. The KIA advisor would require some explaining to the Chinese, but that was hardly a concern at present. Viveca Bold was dead too; the look on his face was priceless as Villareal ensured whatever he planned to do to undermine her was for naught.

"She" Villareal mentally corrected herself. It was wrong to misgender the dead. Even ones who were probably conspiring with your enemies in the Directorate.

Now, everything depended on Plan B. Guerrero was only wounded when she left, but there was no way the Americans did not finish him off before the Panamanian troops finished them. Whoever they installed as dictator would welcome the U.S. Navy cruisers with flowers and cheering crowds.

That simply could not happen.

She had to get to the *Greyhawk Paladin*, but first, she had to find her way to her transportation.

Villareal had a general idea of where she was going and followed the main hallway, hoping it led to an exit. A soldier, an officer by the look of his fancy tunic, leaned out of a doorway ahead of her, a tousled-haired woman in his arms. Was he a threat?

Villareal could not say, so she lifted her SIG P229 and shot them both. They fell to the hallway floor, bloody, and she leapt over their corpses.

The gunfire behind her in the old Assembly chamber was getting louder, and occasionally a round passed through the walls as she ran. There was a roar that shook the building. Sounded like someone was at the minigun.

Ahead, she spotted a "SALIDA" mounted over a metal door with a push bar. Villareal made for the exit.

The transition from inside to outside was not that stark; it was hot and humid inside the building as well. She burst through the exit into the parking lot, almost exactly where she hoped to – at the edge of the landing pad.

With a quick scan of the area, she detected no threats. There was still a tremendous cacophony from the firefight inside, audible even outside on the other end of the building, and that had the attention of the soldiers on guard. They were running toward the sound of the guns, and they paid no attention to what was just another woman running from the building. There were already scores of those fleeing Guerrero's permanent party after it had gone so incredibly wrong.

Villareal bolted for the UH-1 Huey helicopter that sat there on the pad, its Spanish livery identifying it as part of the Panamanian Army. The words "EL PRESIDENTE" were painted in white on the sides of the tail assembly.

The sliding side door on the side of the chopper was open, and two pilots sat inside, each with his fist wrapped around a bottle of Atlas. There was no enlisted crew chief in sight; the officers had sent him to find them more beer, confident that their sole passenger would be busy drinking and drugging himself into a stupor inside his party palace all day and, likely, all night.

She hopped inside the cabin and made for the cockpit. The two pilots were wearing their helmets visors down, with some kind of dance music coming from an iPhone playing over their intercoms. Astonishingly, they had not heard the gun battle. They were more concerned with their beer and relaxing to notice the soldiers suddenly activating and running to and fro in the parking lot through their windscreen.

But the co-pilot on the left – co-pilots in helicopters always sit on the left – noticed her and looked back aghast, yelling, in Spanish, "Get the hell out of here!"

She shot him through the visor of his helmet and pivoted the barrel to the pilot, who dropped his beer to the deck. His dying buddy shook and jittered in his seat.

"¡*Vuela*!" she commanded.

"Fly!"

Turnbull fell to his knee. The wound in his calf was bloody, and it was starting to throb, but it was not impacting his mobility much.

"You hurt bad?" Armand said. She was still holding the S&W .500. Guerrero's legs were still twitching like *una cucharacha*.

"I'll live," he began. He continued, but only got as far as "I...."

It was then that Kelly Turnbull knew beyond a doubt that he was dead. This was it. It was over. Adios.

A dozen soldiers in camo with helmets were rushing into the chamber, M4s up, seeking targets. That was what Turnbull caught first, the weapons, and that changed his mind about his imminent death. The Panamanians carried Kalashnikovs. These were U.S. Army issue, and with all sorts of bells and whistles besides.

Americans. Probably some brand of special ops.

And the newcomers did their special ops thing. They fired a few suppressed rounds into the jumble of tables, benches, and bodies, taking out some surviving Panamanian soldiers, as they secured the room.

Turnbull stood, careful not to make any sudden, scary movements. A trio of soldiers ran down the aisle toward the platform; one wiped out and tumbled, slipping on blood.

The other two, their M4s aimed at the people on the platform, slowed as they approached closer.

"I assume Clay Deeds sent you," Turnbull said loudly.

"I don't know who that is," the leader replied. He had a red dot fixed on Turnbull's chest. "I'm looking for some operators in trouble. The head honcho is Kelly Trumbo."

"Close enough," Turnbull replied. "That's me."

"Your *real* name is Kelly?" Armand asked.

"I'm Captain Chamberlain, 7th Group." The officer lowered his weapon, as did his men with theirs.

"I got wounded men, Captain Chamberlain. You got medics?"

"Sergeant Verdi, Sergeant Sibilia, down here! Wounded!"

The Special Forces medics rushed over to Mundi and toward Turnbull, but he waved the man off to tend to Clanton.

"We were training up north when we got the call," Chamberlain said after removing his helmet. He had a reddish beard. "So we flew down here pronto. Seems like we missed most of the firefight. Holy crap, look at this mess. This was just you four?"

"With little help from that minigun."

"What are you guys? Tier One?" the SF captain asked, impressed by the carnage.

"Tier None," Turnbull said. "We don't exist."

"Too bad the President got away," Chamberlain said.

"Got away?" interjected Katie Armand. "What's left of him is right there." She gestured with Clanton's hand-cannon.

"We saw the President's Huey heading northeast," Chamberlain said. "*Somebody* got out of here."

"I think I know who," Turnbull replied bitterly. "Well, she's in the wind. Again."

"Help me," squeaked a voice from the other side of the table on the platform. Armand took aim, and Chamberlain ran up the steps to the platform with his weapon up. Turnbull bent down, looking underneath the bullet-riddled table.

"Is that a...man?" Chamberlain asked.

"I'm a woman!" insisted Viveca Bold.

"Don't shoot him," Turnbull said. "Yet."

He and Armand moved around the table cautiously, but Bold did not appear to be armed. He was clutching his chest, specifically one of her almost comically large breasts. Between his grasping fingers, they could see a hole in the cloth of his blouse.

"Help me," he repeated, his voice deeper this time.

Turnbull knelt down and examined the wound.

"I think the padding in his fake breast stopped Circe's pistol bullet," he announced, a bit incredulous.

"Drag saved his life?" Armand said.

"Her!" Bold said.

"Probably broke a rib, but there's no entry hole," Turnbull announced. "You're one lucky transvestite."

"Trans-woman!"

"Don't start," Turnbull cautioned the injured she-male. "So, why did your friend Medea shoot you?"

"I don't know, but she's a basic bitch," Bold said.

"Is 'basic' a special kind of bitch?" Turnbull asked Armand.

"It's a girl thing," she assured him.

Turnbull turned back to the blue. Bold sat up, clutching his sore torso.

"Okay, time for payback. Where's your basic bitch going?"

Bold swallowed.

"I can't tell you that."

"She just shot you in your fake breast. You don't owe her anything."

"I'm not going to tell you anything. My name is Viveca Bold, my Privilege Level is 7. I am the Assistant Deputy Consul for

Diversity, Equity, and Inclusion for the embassy of the People's Republic of North America, and I have diplomatic immunity."

"Diplomatic immunity is not a thing in Panama," Armand said bitterly.

"Yeah, we're not doing that immunity stuff," Turnbull told the blue agent. "One more chance. Where's the girl?"

"I won't tell you."

"Great," Turnbull said. "Katie, gimme that Smith & Wesson."

Armand shrugged and handed it over. Turnbull pulled back the hammer. Bold's mouth fell open.

"Okay, from the fact that you didn't have actual woman breasts, I'm thinking you are still just a transvestite."

"I'm a transsexual!"

"Tomato, to-mah-to," Turnbull said. "My point is that you probably aren't getting the work done downstairs until you renovate the upstairs, right?"

Bold looked at him as if he were insane.

Casey had joined them and added, "He means the whole sausage factory is still going on south of the border, right?"

Bold said nothing.

"I'll take that as a 'yes,'" Turnbull said. "Okay, this here is a Smith & Wesson Model 500 in .500 caliber. That's big, if you're not a gun guy, or gun girl, whatever. Now, some people say the .454 Casull is tops, or maybe the .460 Magnum. The old Model 29 Dirty Harry .44 Magnum is not even in the running anymore."

"The who?" Bold stammered.

"You blues are so culturally illiterate," sighed Casey. Turnbull continued.

"Anyway, my point is that the Model 500 is one of the most powerful handguns in the world, and it will blow your junk clean off. So, you gotta ask yourself. Do I feel like some field expedient bottom surgery?"

Turnbull pressed the barrel of the massive handgun against Bold's skirt.

"Because I will do it," Turnbull said.

306 | PANAMA RED

"You should listen to him," Armand advised.

"He'll totally do it," Casey said. "Gimme a sec to put my ear pro back in."

Bold swallowed.

"The ship," he whispered.

"The tanker, the *Greyhawk Paladin*? What about it?" asked Turnbull.

"That's where she's going," Bold said.

Turnbull chuckled and lifted up the barrel. He carefully lowered the hammer on the revolver.

"Well, then, Circe's done. As soon as the *Breitbart* and *Kirk* see her on their scopes, they're blowing her to kingdom come. Good riddance."

"I don't understand," Bold replied.

"Your gal pal is not going to get that rust bucket anywhere near our ships to blow them up," Turnbull said.

"But she's not blowing up the ships," Bold explained. "She's blowing up the locks. The Gatun Locks. She's running the ship into them and setting it off. That's her Plan B."

Turnbull was silent for a moment.

"Oh, crap, Kelly," Casey said.

Turnbull stood up.

"Captain Chamberlain, I'm taking one of your choppers. Casey, grab mags and shotgun shells."

"I'm coming," Armand said.

"And so are me and my guys," Chamberlain said.

"No, you'll just slow us down," Turnbull said. "We've never trained together. Me and Harry Potter here have. Plus, this is probably a one-way trip."

"It's actually Ron Weasley," Casey said.

Turnbull finished wrapping his leg wound as he sat on the MH-60's bench seat. The bullet had clipped a chunk of meat out, but he was functional.

"Cool, back among the Penetrators!" Casey said as the helicopter raced northeast. They were on a vector for the tanker. According to an open-source internet shipping app Armand had brought up on a borrowed smartphone, the *Grayhawk Paladin* was steaming toward the gateway to the Atlantic, the two-lane Gatun Locks. With the newer, larger-capacity Agua Clara Locks closed while being disassembled for periodic maintenance, those parallel channels were the only way through the Panama Canal.

They were moving fast, with the doors open and warm air rushing by. On one side, a mellow crewman sat at a minigun. On the other, the gunner had a mounted MK19 grenade launcher. Not enough to sink the *Grayhawk Paladin*, but enough to provide it some incentive.

Turnbull tested out the Motorola he had borrowed from Chamberlain. The 161st pilot acknowledged, and Turnbull slipped the hand-held radio into one of his M4 pouches.

Casey tried his out, too.

"You read me, Penetrators?" he asked. The pilot was less than amused, but Casey was highly entertained. He slipped his into his own gear, then began to double-check his M4 carbine. Both operators had borrowed fresh mags from the Special Forces guys. Their medics were working on Mundi Vega and Hiram Clanton when Turnbull and Casey left, and the other helicopter would be evacuating them to a hospital. As for Armand, she was going through the site for intel and other items of interest. In fact, she had already found something very interesting, and Turnbull had suggested a good way to dispose of it.

At least he would have one good deed in the ledger if this went bad, and it was likely to go very bad.

He adjusted the Bowie knife in his vest. He had picked up from near Captain Saramago's body not so much to cut anything because he figured that he might have to pry a bulkhead, porthole, or the like on the ship. He was not nautically inclined – ships were long metal coffins, in his estimation, full of places to be trapped in, and if he never set sail on one again, it would be too soon.

Across the chopper, Casey was checking his weapons – carbine, shotgun, handgun. He looked up, and Turnbull was looking at the handcuffs and key he had scooped up off the floor of the platform back in the National Assembly chamber. It was the pair they had used to bind Armand.

"You getting kinky, Kelly?"

"Might be taking a prisoner," Turnbull responded.

"You?"

"Good point," Turnbull acknowledged, shoving the cuffs into his cargo pocket; it was already bulging with buckshot shells.

Medea Villareal had the pilot set down on the bow of the tanker. A pair of Somalis came out with their AK-47s, baffled about why the contraption was there. She ordered the pilot to turn off the engine and waved the gunmen to come over as the rotors slowed and finally stopped.

"Don't you move until I get back," she directed the pilot in Spanish. He nodded enthusiastically. To the curious Somalis, she said, "Get in here and make sure he doesn't take off," she told them. They understood enough English to climb aboard.

"If he starts this helicopter and tries to leave, shoot him," she added. Both nodded.

She climbed down to the deck and started walking back toward the rear of the ship. There was no one on the weather deck, and she needed to ask how to get up to the bridge. But Captain Johnson, accompanied by Farah, came down out of a doorway; he had seen her through the window wandering about.

"Status," Villareal demanded.

"The ship is secure," Farah said. He had experience taking over commercial shipping; back home, it was a family business.

"The crew?"

"Except for a few that we need to sail it in the engine room and mess hall, the crew is locked up below, along with the canal pilot we took aboard. My men are guarding them."

She turned to the captain.

"We're doing this," she told him.

"I figured," he said. "I've gotten the process started. We should begin moving soon. Once we do, it is under ten minutes to the locks."

"Where's Devlin?" she asked.

"Somewhere with his explosives. That's not my job. I have no clue what he's doing."

"Get back on the bridge and get us moving," Villareal ordered.

"One thing," said the captain. "How do we get off it?"

Farah seemed curious too. Villareal turned and pointed to the Huey resting on the deck near the bow.

"We take the helicopter," she said.

"And my men?" asked Farah.

"Lifeboats," Villareal said. There were a number hanging off the side, bright orange and enclosed – far from the open rowboats of the *Titanic* era.

Farah looked at her dubiously.

"Of course," she said. "You will be on the helicopter."

That seemed to satisfy his qualms, at least for the moment.

"What about the crew?" asked Captain Johnson.

"What about them?" asked Villareal. She generally seemed curious about why he would bother asking.

"We got eyes on it," the pilot reported over the intercom. "About two minutes out."

Turnbull strained to see. Lake Gatun was massive. Floating on its surface were a dozen or so ships of every conceivable shape and size, as long as the size was Panamax or less. Before the new locks, like the Agua Clara Locks that were undergoing an overhaul, "Panamax" was the largest size vessel that could transit the Panama Canal's original route. That measured out to about 965 feet in length, 106 feet in width, and 39.5 feet in draft. The vessels were simply bobbing there, waiting for the canal's traffic control to call them forward into the Gatun Locks to begin the process of dropping to sea level and sailing out into the Atlantic.

But one ship was underway. Turnbull recognized it as the *Greyhawk Paladin*. And there was a Huey parked near the bow.

The locks were there, several miles ahead. Villareal could feel the ship slowly accelerating as the engine roared to life. The radio was squawking– traffic control, in English – was very upset.

"Turn that off," she ordered. Captain Johnson stepped away from the wheel and flipped several switches. The outraged demands from the shore went silent.

"I'll set the automatic pilot," he said.

"Are there automatic features that would keep the ship from hitting an object?" she asked. Johnson smiled.

"Disabled. It will go where I point it until it stops," he replied.

"And then ... boom!" Frank Devlin said. He had joined Villareal, Farah, and the captain on the bridge. "Once we hit 15 knots, the detonator sends it up when it falls under 10 knots. It explodes when it hits the lock gates, but the beauty is that nobody can stop it. It's like that *Speed* movie from before the Split."

"Keanu Reeves," said Captain Johnson.

"He's a fascist," Villareal said, irritated at the digression.

"No," Devlin said. "There was another one on a ship instead of a bus and not with Keanu."

"Enough!" shouted Villareal.

They fell quiet.

"How long until we abandon ship?" she asked the explosives expert, composed again.

"About ten minutes," Devlin replied. "We want to be away from the blast."

"What about the lifeboats?" demanded Farah.

"Well, they're closed up tight, so the guys inside might bounce around from the shock wave, but they should be okay. Maybe shook up a little."

"Tell your men to gather on at the stern to load up," Johnson said. "You'll want to use the aft rafts."

Farah relaxed. He did not want to have to explain to the Ughaz how he had lost 14 of his clansmen.

Villareal faced Devlin, who was nervous. She had that effect.

"Tell me this will work," she said.

"Oh, it'll work if we hit the locks. The mass of the ship will do pretty significant damage, but the blast wave from the vapor will blow them off their tracks and wreck all the supporting gear and mechanisms on land for a couple of hundred yards. We just have to hit the locks so they experience the max shockwave. Otherwise, it will just make a big, loud mess."

"We won't miss," Johnson promised. "This ship will hit the locks at 15 knots."

Villareal smiled her enigmatic grin. Plan B was coming together. Pretty soon, she would be in the Huey heading away, and both Johnson and Devlin would be falling into the lake from a great height.

No loose ends.

"What's that?" asked Devlin, looking out the bridge's side window. "You expecting another chopper?"

The MH-60 Blackhawk was speeding across the surface of the lake, directly on an intercept course with the accelerating tanker. There were lush, green jungle islands dotting the surface of the lake.

"We need you to drop us on the deck," Turnbull said to the pilot via his mic. "But do an orbit, have your boys clear any targets first." He turned to Casey.

"I'll find the bridge and convince them to stop the ship," Turnbull said. He did not explain how; he really didn't have to. He continued.

"You go below decks, find the engine room, make sure that no one overrides what we do from an auxiliary control center."

"It's called the ECR, engine control room," Casey replied. "And why again am I going into the ship?"

"Because you trained with the SEALs before and you know things like how it's called an 'ECR,'" Turnbull explained. "Also, I hate being inside ships."

"Fair," Casey said. "I was just thinking how *Grayhawk Paladin* is a total D&D name. You know, *Dungeons & Dragons.*"

Turnbull sighed and shook his head.

"You're like a tenth-level half-orc fighter," he opined. "I'm more of a mage."

"The third reason that you go into the ship is that you'll be far away from me," Turnbull told him.

"You know," Casey said seriously. "I haven't got shot yet. I've been in two big gunfights this week and not a scratch. Mundi and Hiram are all messed up, and you got hit, but not me. That's weird. I'm due."

"What can I say?" Turnbull replied. "Not getting shot beats getting shot, so stop whining."

"You just don't forget about me if I catch a slug down there in the bowels of that ship," Casey said.

"I'll do what Captain Kirk would do," Turnbull said. Casey looked at his partner and furrowed his brow.

"What the hell does that even mean, Kelly?"

"I don't know. It just sounded like something that would make you stop talking."

Farah had begun yelling something Somali and urgent into his Motorola radio, and then he unshouldered his rifle and rushed from the bridge.

"Who are they?" Devlin said, looking at the approaching Blackhawk.

"Americans. Let the Somalis fight them. Keep this ship on course!"

Captain Johnson stepped to the controls near the wheel, making his final adjustments.

"What if they stop the ship? We're at speed, and if we slow down, we blow," Devlin said.

"They can't," Johnson replied without looking up. "There's no way to stop something of this ship's mass with a helicopter. We hit the locks in seven minutes. The question is whether they can blow us up first."

"No, there are safety features to prevent an accidental detonation. That's why we need my explosive setup to make the LNG blow. It's not like the Americans can accidentally set it off, even if they open fire."

Villareal turned from watching the oncoming chopper.

"If they get on the ship, can they disarm your bomb, Devlin?"

"No, not in seven minutes, even if they could find all the components."

Villareal stared at him, screening for deception. No, he seemed sincere. But he was still spooked, and he wanted to make sure she understood.

"When this ship drops to under 10 knots, it's blowing up like a MOAB on steroids," he said, referring to the biggest non-nuclear weapon in the American arsenal, the 22,000-pound GBU-43/B "Massive Ordnance Air Blast," but better known as "Mother of All Bombs."

Villareal kept staring, expressionless, so he added:

"And there is nothing in the world that can stop it."

The Blackhawk pulled up and roared over the deck of the *Grayhawk Paladin*, so low that the rotor wash knocked a pair of the Somali gunmen who had responded to Farah's all-hands call off their feet.

More of their compatriots were appearing, popping out of doorways and bulkheads up and down the length of the ship and blazing away with their AK-47s.

"Take them out!" Turnbull yelled into the intercom.

The door gunner opened up with his minigun. A pair of Somalis disappeared in a pink mist. Another vanished in a shower of sparks and smoke as he tried to run across the open deck.

"What about that Huey sitting there?" the pilot asked.

"Make it not be there," Turnbull said to the pilot. He lifted his M4 to his shoulder and began firing suppressed shots at the Somalis appearing on the deck. Casey added his own rifle fire to the mix. One of the Somalis dropped and skidded across the deck on his face.

The pilot brought the Blackhawk around to bring the Mk19 grenade launcher to bear, and the crewman manning it had an evil grin as he began to engage the Huey that rested on deck. Thud, thud, thud, and on it went – it was automatic fire, but the rate of fire for the 40mm grenades was much lower than a typical machine gun. Yet it was sufficient – the first round fell short and the gunner began to walk them up, blasting craters in the deck until the grenades began impacting the helicopter directly. With nearly a half-full tank of gas, the explosion on the bow was rather impressive.

"Our helicopter!" shouted Devlin. "How the hell do we get out of here?"

"Lifeboats," Villareal said.

"We need to go soon, then," he said. "It's going to be a big explosion."

"Is it ready?" Villareal demanded of Johnson.

"Soon," he answered. "There are islands we have to miss – it has to be perfect!"

She drew her pistol as she watched the Blackhawk hover over the deck at perhaps five feet and drop off two men.

An arc of agony shot up his calf when Turnbull hit the deck with both feet. The rotor wash passed over him and Casey, who followed him out and was crouching beside him, as the MH-60 pulled away to resume providing air cover with the minigun and grenade launcher. He was glad he had ear protection in.

To the front of the ship, there was a huge fire where the Huey had been blasted apart. On the deck itself, it was quiet. The Somalis had learned that to expose themselves in the open was to call down from above a hail of fiery lead, and so they had stopped doing so.

Casey pointed to an open bulkhead, and Turnbull acknowledged it with a nod, covering his partner until Casey had dashed over and through the portal into the ship.

The bridge was above him, but how to get to it was the question. There was no obvious way to do so without slipping inside the superstructure. Luckily, someone had helpfully painted the word "BRIDGE" in block letters on the outside wall by a doorway with an arrow pointing up. He went through after glancing toward the bow. He could make out the locks in the distance, dead ahead.

Now he knew how the guy on watch on the *Titanic* felt.

24.

Johnson stopped working and exhaled.

"It's ready. We're set on course."

Villareal ignored him.

"Farah," Villareal called into her radio. "There are two Americans on the ship. Find them. Kill them. And send me two or three men."

She did not wait for an answer.

"We need to go," Devlin pleaded.

"Not until the ship is secure."

"They can't disarm the explosives in time," Devlin said, even more urgently.

Villareal pointed her SIG P229 semiautomatic at his face.

"We're staying."

The ship was throbbing as the engines settled into a steady rhythm. Turnbull moved fast down the hallway, pausing to skim each room he passed for targets, but not to enter and clear them. That might leave enemy fighters behind him, but speed was of the essence. The locks were coming fast.

He turned a corner, and there was a man – unarmed. He looked Filipino; his apron and the tray of sandwiches in his hands marked him as a cook. The man was terrified.

"Get the hell out of here, get off the ship!" Turnbull hissed, but his red dot was still on the man's chest. The cook nodded and glanced back into the bulkhead he had just emerged from, then dropped the food and bolted away.

There was shouting from behind him in a foreign language, and an enraged Somali fighter stepped out in pursuit. Turnbull shot him twice, and he fell down on the floor.

The American pressed on up a set of stairs to the next deck, which Turnbull figured was one below the bridge. He climbed, slowly but steadily, rifle up. At the top of the stairs, he took the left. That seemed the most likely direction to reach the bridge. He could now hear voices, shouting in Somali, from below him.

Carefully, Turnbull moved forward. Ahead was another set of stairs. Feet appeared coming down, and an AK-47. Turnbull engaged with a burst. The Somali collapsed and slid down the railing to the deck, his AK-47 falling and clattering on the metal floor.

"Damn," Turnbull swore at the noise. He barreled ahead.

Villareal heard the clatter and the thud outside the bridge from down the passage toward the stairs she had come up.

"Wait here," she growled at Devlin and Johnson. "Don't leave the bridge."

"Kelly!" Casey's voice cracked over the Motorola. Turnbull stopped in the middle of the passage and used his left hand to take out the radio.

"Yeah?"

"I shot some guys who were guarding the crew. They were locked in a rec room. I told them to get the hell off the ship, so if you see some civilians, don't shoot them!"

"Roger. I'm heading to the bridge."

"I'm headed to the ERC. Out."

Turnbull slipped the radio back in his pouch and stepped forward. The Somali on the ground wore a very surprised look on his face. The best kind of enemy was the one you surprised when you took him out.

The noise above him up the steps on the next deck was so soft that if he had not been wearing ear protection, the ringing would have drowned it out, yet he did hear it – a clink of metal on metal from Villareal accidentally tapping her SIG pistol against a metal rail.

She still got the first shot, but Turnbull was moving, and the impact of the round sparked where his head had been a millisecond before. Another shot missed before he managed to bring his M4 to bear up toward the top of the stairs and flip the selector switch to "AUTO."

He sprayed a long burst of suppressed 5.56mm rounds upward, the empty brass clattering off the wall of the passage. She dodged left, and when the fire slacked, reached her handgun around the edge of the wall and squeezed the rest of her magazine. Turnbull returned fire. The rounds impacted all over the walls and ceiling.

Villareal pulled back, but was sprinkled with paint chips. Instinctively, she reloaded, inserting her spare magazine. She was now on the wrong side of the stairwell. Returning to the bridge would require her to cross it and expose herself to fire from Bob and his M4. She was outgunned, and there were only a few minutes to get off the vessel. She made her decision and ran down the hallway toward the rear of the ship and the life rafts waiting there.

Turnbull got his foot on the first step of the steep stairway to the bridge just as he heard them coming from behind. He turned and fired a quick burst at three Somalis, winging one of them as his rifle went dry.

The gunmen managed to push their wounded compatriot out of the way so they could attack their quarry, but Turnbull had swung the Benelli semiautomatic twelve gauge around and brought it to bear.

He fired all eight shells – the seven in the tube and the one in the pipe – of 00 buckshot down the passageway. It acted almost like a funnel. He couldn't miss, and didn't.

The three dead men shuddered at the end of the hallway, their nervous systems not yet having got the bad news. No time to reload. Turnbull turned, abandoned his carbine and shotgun, and went up the stairs with his .45 in hand.

At the top of the stairs, he swung out with the barrel seeking targets down the passage where Villareal had retreated. Nothing. Careful not to slip on loose shells, he turned back toward where he thought the bridge might be and started down the hallway.

He was right. It was there.

Johnson saw Turnbull through the open bridge door and went to shut it. It was thick and designed to keep out intruders. There would be no shooting through it. Turnbull threw his body against it to hold it open, then drew the Bowie knife from his gear and slid it into the breach.

It could not close. Johnson briefly relaxed the pressure, and Turnbull took advantage of the pause by throwing his full body weight against the door.

It gave, and he pushed inside, waving the hand cannon in Johnson's face. The captain put up his hands, as did Devlin.

"Who are you?" Turnbull demanded, sliding his Bowie knife back into his gear.

"Captain Conrad Johnson," stammered the sailor.

"Why are you here?"

"To pilot the boat."

Turnbull shifted the gun to Devlin's face. He did not need to be asked.

"Frank Devlin, demolitions."

Turnbull grunted.

"Disarm this bomb," Turnbull ordered.

"I can't, not in a few minutes. It's too complex."

Turnbull accepted that. It made sense. Out the window, the locks were dead ahead and coming fast. He shot Devlin in the forehead and turned his gun on the captain.

"Stop the boat."

"I can't!" Johnson cried, literally. His eyes were moistening as he correctly deduced that he was being forced to give exactly the wrong response.

Turnbull cocked his head, as if to ask if Johnson was sure that was his final answer.

"He set the bomb to detonate if the ship slows down to under 10 knots," Johnson explained. "We're at 15 knots. When it stops after it hits the locks, it goes off."

Turnbull stood there, silent. The barrel looming in Johnson's face. The captain felt compelled to elaborate.

"I've set the automatic pilot to continue forward on this course," he said, gesturing at the wheel.

Turnbull thought about it for a moment.

"Change course," he said.

"What?"

Turnbull pointed.

"Turn the ship between those islands. Put it into that deserted shore to the left."

Johnson looked where Turnbull was referencing, then back at him.

"Use the steering wheel," Turnbull said. "Fast."

Johnson nodded. He cranked the wheel as Casey came over the radio.

"Kelly, the ERC is clear. Several Somalis are DOA. I've told the civvies that they are on a floating bomb and to get the hell outside and abandon ship."

"I'm on the bridge. Get up to the weather deck. I'm having our captain aim away from the locks, but this tub is still going to blow in maybe five minutes."

"Four," said the Captain.

"Circe *didi mau'd* to the back of the boat," Turnbull continued into the Motorola.

"The stern," said the captain.

KURT SCHLICHTER | 321

"You'd best focus on turning this boat, Popeye," Turnbull told him. He put the radio back to his face. Johnson complied and began pushing the buttons on the control panel.

"Call for pick up from the stern in about three."

"Roger, out," said Casey.

"Are we turned?" Turnbull asked the pilot. The captain pointed out the bridge window. The ship had changed course. It was now slowly shifting left – port – toward a patch of deserted shore. It would have to thread the needle between several islands.

"I've set the course in the autopilot," Johnson said. "Don't shoot me!"

"Can someone change it back?" asked Turnbull.

"Theoretically."

Turnbull pointed the pistol at the autopilot panel and blasted off his entire mag. Johnson drew back and threw up his hands as it sparked and smoked.

"How about now?" Turnbull inquired, dropping the empty mag, replacing it, and releasing the slide.

"No," said the captain, surveying the wreckage.

"Now, what's happening in the back of the ship that made Circe – that woman – go there?"

"That's where the crew would gather, if possible, to load life rafts."

"Congratulations," Turnbull said. "You just became more useful to me alive than dead. Take me to the stern."

The rear end of the boat was crowded with civilian crewmen whom Casey had liberated below decks. They were focused on one thing, and one thing only – getting the life rafts ready to load and drop before it was too late.

They paid no heed to the woman with her hand inside her blouse, clutching the compact SIG. The Americans had certainly freed them, she reasoned. That meant the Somalis were likely dead, but that was immaterial to her.

The crewmen had not seen her before, and did not know her as one of the pirates who had seized their vessel. They would probably guess, though, once they could relax after getting to safety. She would have to invent a cover story for inside the life raft, but her gun would make it persuasive. It looked like they were loading five or six crewmen to a raft – if a story didn't work, she had enough remaining bullets to shoot her shipmates.

She stood nearby, watching them load and drop the orange craft into the water. It did not appear so complex. Most of the crew was gone. The remaining crewmen were preparing the last few escape craft. She figured she would slip into the last one.

Looking around, she saw something was wrong.

"No!" she wailed aloud and rushed to the starboard deck railing and looked forward along the line of the ship.

There were the Gatun Locks, but the *Grayhawk Paladin* was no longer heading toward them. Instead, it was sailing directly at a patch of barren coast.

She pulled back, horrified, and as she turned, there was Captain Johnson coming at her, terrified.

He should have been. The hell with subtlety, she thought. She pulled out her SIG P229 and shot him three times in the gut.

The dead captain sagged, but Kelly Turnbull pushed his falling corpse into her. The weight knocked her back hard, and her gun clattered along the deck.

Turnbull pushed the dead man out of the way, and Villareal took a vicious swing at Turnbull's jaw. It connected and made no impact. Turnbull swung at her, and that did. She sprawled on the deck.

"You should stop watching stupid movies where 130-pound women beat up 210-pound men," he said as he walked to where she lay.

Around them, the last remaining civilians had devoted a few precious seconds to watching what was happening. Then they went right back to abandoning the doomed ship.

Grabbing her left forearm, Turnbull pulled her ungently to her feet.

"I thought you reds didn't hit women," she snapped.

"I didn't want to risk misgendering you," Turnbull hissed. "Besides, it's technically ladies we don't hit."

He pulled her over to the starboard rail as the remaining crew dropped one more life raft into the lake. They had taken almost all of them.

Out of the corner of his eye, Turnbull saw Casey waving at something in the sky. He could hear the rotors of the approaching Blackhawk.

"Taking me to the red?" Villareal asked smugly. "I won't talk."

"I don't want you to talk," Turnbull said, a bit confused that she misunderstood. He pulled the handcuffs from his cargo pocket and latched one end around her left wrist. The other he snapped closed around the railing.

"I want you to ride this train to the end of the line."

He stepped back. Casey was now waving the helicopter in toward the stern deck.

"*No!*" she screamed, futilely pulling on the cuffs. "*No!*"

"That's for a lot of folks," he said. "Especially Deputy Coltrane and Gilligan."

"Gilligan?" she shouted. She had heard that name in her red culture acclimation training at the Directorate, but it made no sense to her. "Who the hell is Gilligan?"

"The dog."

"It's not fair!" she screamed, her face red, flecks of spit on her lips.

The chopper descended. The wind buffeted them. Casey climbed up into the cabin, shouting, "Come on, Kelly!" as loud as he could.

Turnbull paused and considered the situation. Then he pulled out the Bowie knife and tossed it over to her feet.

"Now, you have a fair chance," Turnbull said. "Adios, Circe,"

Smiling, he turned away and got on the Blackhawk. He did not look back until the helicopter was a couple of minutes away. In the distance, the *Grayhawk Paladin* shuddered as it smashed into the shore and detonated in a gigantic orange fireball.

Turnbull thought it was actually kind of beautiful.

25.

"Kelly, are you descending into moral relativism?" Clay Deeds asked.

"I'm pretty sure I know what that means, and the answer is 'No,'" Turnbull replied. "The blues are evil communist monsters. But some of the reds are jerks."

On the television in the conference room at the Task Force Zulu headquarters, a dubious Will Cain was on Fox News interviewing the sweaty ambassador about his heroic actions while helping the forces of freedom, led by former colonel and current President Julio Rosas, overthrow the dread late dictator, *Presidente* Bonifacio Alberto Maria Guerrero.

"You know the ambassador wanted to sell Rosas out. And let one of his own get tortured and murdered," Casey said to Clay.

"He knows," Turnbull interjected. "Why do you think he subtly invited us to take care of business?"

"Deniability," Casey said.

"Bingo," Turnbull replied.

"All human institutions are imperfect," Deeds told them. "Because human beings are imperfect. We reds didn't become angels when we split the country."

"I don't know how long I will be doing this," Turnbull said. "I'm thinking maybe I start to do things on my own terms."

"Private contracting is the bomb," Casey said. "You pick your missions, you pick your boss – though we all love ya, Clay – and more money."

"Speaking of money," Deeds said. "There's a question about $100,000 in blue bribe money that got paid to Guerrero. You mentioned it in your debrief. Seems Rosas's men did an audit, and Guerrero never deposited it. And it wasn't at his little palace. Any ideas where it went?"

"Great question," Turnbull said. "Of course, I have no idea, but if I were to, hypothetically, have come across it, I'd have probably given it to the Franciscan brother who takes care of Panama City's dogs."

"Hypothetically," Deeds said.

"Yeah, purely hypothetically."

"Well, you guys don't work for the money," Deeds said.

"I'm thinking I should, if I ever want to retire to a ranch and forget all of this," Turnbull said.

On the TV, the American president was shaking the ambassador's hand.

"Nor glory," Casey said. "Definitely not glory."

Turnbull got up.

"I'm going to stop off, look in on Mundi and Hiram," he said.

"What about after?" Casey asked as he stood up.

"Probably a Whataburger, a Shiner, and an evening of *The Dennis Miller Mysteries*," Turnbull said. "If I can ever figure out just what the hell he's talking about."

"Why don't you come by my place with that Shiner. Three words: Harry Potter marathon. What do you say, Kelly?"

"I say 'stop talking.'"

Kelly Turnbull will return in

the graphic novel

BLUE FLAME

in

2026

ABOUT THE AUTHOR

Kurt Schlichter is a senior columnist for *Townhall*. He is also a Los Angeles trial lawyer admitted to practice in California, Texas, and Washington, DC, as well as a retired Army Infantry colonel.

A Twitter activist (@KurtSchlichter) with over 600,000 followers, Kurt was personally recruited by his friend Andrew Breitbart to write for the Breitbart sites. His writings on political and cultural issues have also been published in *The Federalist*, the *New York Post*, the *Washington Examiner*, the *Los Angeles Times*, the *Washington Times*, the *Army Times*, and the *San Francisco Examiner*, among other outlets.

Kurt serves as a news source, an on-screen commentator, and a guest host on TV and on nationally syndicated radio programs regarding political, military, and legal issues at outlets including Fox News, Fox Business News, CNN, NewsMax, and on shows hosted by Hugh Hewitt, Larry O'Connor, Chris Stigall, Seb Gorka, Jesse Kelly, Tony Katz, Dana Loesch, Dan Bongino, Vince Coglianese, Joe Piscopo, and Derek Hunter, among others.

Kurt was a stand-up comic for several years, which led him to write three e-books that each reached number one on the Amazon Kindle "Political Humor" bestsellers list: *I Am a Conservative: Uncensored, Undiluted, and Absolutely Un-PC*, *I Am a Liberal: A Conservative's Guide to Dealing with Nature's Most Irritating Mistake*, and *Fetch My Latte: Sharing Feelings with Stupid People*.

In 2014, his book *Conservative Insurgency: The Struggle to Take America Back 2013-2041* was published by Post Hill Press.

His 2016 novel *People's Republic* and its 2017 prequel *Indian Country* reached No. 1 and No. 2 on the Amazon Kindle "Political Thriller" bestsellers list. *Wildfire*, the third book in the series, hit No. 1 on the Amazon "Thrillers – Espionage" bestsellers list and No. 122 in all Amazon Kindle books. *Collapse*, the fourth book, hit 121, while *Crisis* hit 29. His previous novel, *The Split*, hit at least 43. *Inferno* hit 59 overall and No. 1 on "Political Thrillers."

His nonfiction book, *Militant Normals: How Regular Americans Are Rebelling Against the Elite to Reclaim Our Democracy,* was published by Center Street Books in October 2018. It made the USA Today Bestsellers List.

His Regnery book *The 21 Biggest Lies About Donald Trump (and You)* was released in 2020 and hit Number 1 on an Amazon list.

His Regnery book *We'll Be Back: The Fall and Rise of America* was released in July 2022 and hit Number 1 on an Amazon list.

His novel *The Attack* was released in January 2024 and hit Number 1 on an Amazon list.

Kurt and Irina Moises wrote and released *Lost Angeles: Silver Bullets on the Sunset Strip* in 2025.

Kurt's 2025 novel *American Apocalypse: The Second American Civil War* was a #1 Military Thriller on Amazon.

Kurt was a successful trial lawyer and name partner in a Los Angeles law firm representing Fortune 500 companies and individuals in matters ranging from routine business cases to confidential Hollywood disputes and political controversies. A member of the Million Dollar Advocates Forum, which recognizes attorneys who have won trial verdicts exceeding $1 million, his litigation strategy and legal analysis articles have been published in prominent legal publications, including the *Los Angeles Daily Journal* and *California Lawyer.*

He was and is frequently engaged by noted conservatives in need of legal representation. He served as counsel for political

330 | PANAMA RED

commentator and author Ben Shapiro in the widely publicized "Clock Boy" defamation lawsuit, which resulted in the case being dismissed and the victory being upheld on appeal.

Kurt is a 1994 graduate of Loyola Law School, where he was a law review editor. He majored in communications and political science as an undergraduate at the University of California, San Diego, where he co-edited the conservative student paper, *California Review*, and wrote a regular column in the student humor paper, *The Koala*.

Kurt served as a US Army infantry officer on active duty and in the California Army National Guard, retiring at the rank of full colonel. He wears the silver "jump wings" of a paratrooper and commanded the 1st Squadron, 18th Cavalry Regiment (Reconnaissance-Surveillance-Target Acquisition). A veteran of the Persian Gulf War, the Los Angeles Riots, and Operation Enduring Freedom (Kosovo), he is a graduate of the Army's Combined Arms and Services Staff School, the Command and General Staff College, and the United States Army War College, where he received a master's degree in strategic studies.

He lives with his wife, Irina, and their two monstrous dogs, Bitey and Barkey, in the Los Angeles area, and he enjoys sarcasm and red meat.

His favorite caliber is .45.

The Kelly Turnbull Novels

People's Republic (2016)

Indian Country (2017)

Wildfire (2018)

Collapse (2019)

Crisis (2020)

The Split (2021)

Inferno (2022)

Overlord (2023)

Panama Red (2025)

Also By Kurt Schlichter

Conservative Insurgency: The Struggle to Take America Back 2013-2041 (Post Hill Press, 2014)

Militant Normals: How Regular Americans Are Rebelling Against the Elite to Reclaim Our Democracy (Center Street Books, 2018)

The 21 Biggest Lies About Donald Trump (and You) (Regnery, 2020)

We'll Be Back: The Fall and Rise of America (Regnery, 2022)

The Attack (Kindle, 2024)

American Apocalypse: The Second American Civil War (Kindle, 2025)

By Kurt Schlichter

and Irina Moises

Lost Angeles: Silver Bullets on the Sunset Strip (Kindle 2025)